His Seventh Stop

HAMMOND FAMILY FARM ROMANCE

IVORY PEAKS ROMANCE
BOOK SEVEN

LIZ ISAACSON

ISBN-13: 978-1638762782

CHAPTER
One

KEITH WHETTSTEIN SQUINTED into the whiteness in front of him, his anxiety shooting off the charts, even for him. He'd lived for the first decade of his life in Montana, which saw more sub-zero temperatures than almost anywhere else in the United States, and currently held the record for the coldest day in history.

Then his daddy had moved the family to the Rocky Mountains in Colorado, and he'd lived through two more decades of long, cold, dark winters.

This one seemed to be starting early, and he still had one more delivery to get through before he could be done for the next several days. For his sister's wedding. For the Christmas holidays.

"In two hundred feet, turn right," his GPS told him, and Keith glanced at the screen on his phone before he tried to find the road again. His windshield wipers worked at double speed to clear the snow landing on the glass, and by some miracle he spotted the turn-off he needed to take.

No one had been out to clear this dirt road, obviously, and Keith wondered if he should even turn down it. Thankfully, he wasn't driving his small truck, but one of the big super duty vehicles owned by Blackhorse Bay.

He loved his job at the boarding stable and riding facility, but as the agricultural manager, he didn't have a ton to do in the winter. Therefore, he helped take care of the horses, and this year's semi-annual sale had resulted in over two dozen equines going to new homes for the holidays.

This was his seventh and final stop of the season, and then all the horses would be home—and he could go home too. He currently lived in a cabin that was twice as big as the one he'd shared with his sister on the Hammond Family Farm. He did live with three other men, but they all had their own bedroom and shared three bathrooms. The kitchen had just been updated, and they enjoyed a six-seat dining room table.

He liked all of the men he lived with, and he'd immediately clicked with the man who lived right across the hall from him— Derrick Hollowell. They'd gone out on blind dates together, showed each other the dating app swipes they made, and played board games and cards on the weekends.

In all, Keith had settled into his new life pretty easily in the past six months. He'd been out with three new women, and while none of them had been an instant love connection, he'd enjoyed himself and already achieved one of his goals: meeting new people.

He'd felt stale at the farm where he'd grown up. He hadn't been meeting anyone new; certainly no one he could date and fall in love with. He hadn't minded his single status until he'd seen Britt with her boyfriend, Lars. They shared so much, and Keith didn't have that closeness with anyone.

He made the turn onto the snowy road, the horse trailer behind him bumping though he drove at the speed of a snail. "How long do I drive down this?" he asked himself. "And will I be able to get out?"

Darkness wasn't for another hour, but with the storm, it felt like nighttime already. As a company rule, his pin had been shared with his boss, the owner of the ranch, and the foreman at Blackhorse Bay, who happened to be one of his roommates. So even if he got stuck out here, they'd know where he was.

He'd filled up the truck before he'd left the facility, so he could probably hunker down in his vehicle for the night. Desperation clogged his lungs, because he didn't want to do that. "Lord," he whispered. "Help me get out of here tonight."

His sister's wedding was in three days, and Keith would absolutely not miss it. He'd strap snowshoes to his feet and hike off this hobby farm to get to Britt's wedding. They were getting married in the big red barn on the Hammond Family Farm, and she'd been over to his cabin multiple times in the past few months of her engagement to show him every detail of the event.

The wind gusted across the road in front of him, but Keith continued on. No matter what, he had to get this horse out of the trailer, and he'd have to turn her loose if he got stuck. "There's a farm up here," he told himself. "No matter what, no one is spending the night in a truck or trailer."

He'd deliver the horse to the farm, and then he'd beg to spend the night here if he had to. He glanced at the clipboard on the passenger seat, which showed him the receipt for the beautiful gray horse in the trailer behind him. "Lindsay Lewis," he muttered. "I hope you're home, Lindsay Lewis."

He kept on, inching slowly down the snow-covered road, but he felt like he wasn't getting any closer to anything. Just more forest. More snow. More wind. Keith only knew he was still on the road, because he didn't run into any trees. Poles had been put up on the borders of the lane too, probably because they got a lot of snow and needed to know where to plow.

Another glance at the clipboard told him this farm had a name, and it was Twilight Fields. He sort of smiled at it, because it felt whimsical. It also felt like something a woman would name a few acres of alfalfa and a handful of horses. He couldn't make too harsh of a judgment, because he didn't even have those things.

He had a twenty-five-hundred square-foot cabin he shared with three other men. They did have a twenty-by-twenty-foot garden behind their house, and when he wasn't out in the fields taking soil samples, working on the watering ratios, or dealing with pests, he worked with dozens of horses.

It's a good life, he thought, and he wondered if that was his voice reassuring himself or God, telling him to be grateful for the blessings he had. Either way, Keith apparently needed the reminder.

Several minutes later, Keith exhaled heavily, trying to get his frustration to go with the air. It didn't, because he still wasn't to this silly hobby farm. His headlights only served to show him just how much snow was falling, and his hopes of getting home tonight plummeted the same way the flakes did.

Finally, the twinkle of a light met his eye, and he drew in a deep breath. "Okay," he said. Some civilization existed out here, even if it was only one house. As his truck continued to pad through the snow, more lights came to life on the house until the whole thing was illuminated in the snow.

He went past it but had to stop at a fork in the road. He couldn't really see left or right, and he didn't know which way to take this horse. He twisted to look back toward the house, and it took a moment for his brain to process that a person stood right at his side window.

Keith yelped and dove away from the obvious serial killer, and to his horror, they opened his door. He had visions of himself being pulled from his truck and dragged into an arctic barn, never to be heard from again.

His first instinct was to kick out, go down swinging. His heart pounded as the chilly air swept into his heated cab, and his leg twitched. "What's—what?"

The person standing there couldn't be more than five feet tall, and they said nothing. They'd wrapped themselves in a hat and scarf that covered everything but their eyes, and Keith turned, keeping his legs toward them in case he needed to kick out.

"I have your horse," he said, his brain misfiring at the name he'd seen on the clipboard. Some of the equines had been Christmas presents for kids, and he really had no idea what this gray was for. He hoped he wasn't ruining a surprise, but at the same time, he didn't want to meet his demise here either.

You watch too many crime dramas, he chastised himself, but the person standing there still hadn't spoken.

"I need to know where the barn or stable is," he said. "Is that where you want the horse?" As he studied the person's eyes, he got the feeling that he wasn't talking to an adult. Suddenly, he remembered the name on the receipt had been female. "Is your momma here?"

"She said to go to the barn," the person said, and Keith would bet good money it was a girl. Maybe a teenager.

"Right or left?" he asked.

She pointed to his left, and Keith nodded. "Okay, thanks." He reached for the door. "I'm just gonna...close...this." He did, and the girl backed up into the swirling snow. Keith wasn't sure about leaving her there and driving away, but he really had no choice.

He went left, his thigh and the door panel completely wet now from the melted snow. He passed a couple of outbuildings until he reached the obvious barn, and in normal light, it would probably be a handsome red with white trim. Classic hobby farm barn material, and Keith almost wanted to scoff.

After pulling the trailer as close to the door as he could get it in these conditions, he dropped from the truck and flipped up the hood on his jacket. He pulled the gloves from his pockets and shoved his fingers into them before he dared to touch the metal horse trailer.

"All right, Shadow," he said to the horse. "We're here. Your new home." He grinned at the gray that had been tethered in the first stall at the very front of the trailer. She'd had to wait as, one-by-one, six of her horsey friends had been dropped off at their new farms or ranches.

He got her out without an issue, part of him wanting to stay in the trailer, because he wasn't getting wet inside. The moment he stepped out of the back of the trailer, his foot slipped on the runner he'd laid out—and which had been getting snowed on.

He yelled for the second time that evening as he lost his footing. He fell backward on the hard, ribbed metal, pain smarting up into his hips and back as he landed hard. "Hockey sticks," he said as a form of swearing, and he looked up into the sky, seeing the snow as it fell in a whole new way.

The flakes landed coldly on his face, and he couldn't get a full breath. He couldn't move for some reason, and then he heard the snuffling of a horse. The clang of hooves against metal. A nicker.

A woman said, "Shadow, no!"

Keith managed to twist and look up toward the voice, but then the icy surface beneath him vibrated and moved as the horse stampeded over it. He curled into himself in an instinctive move—just like wanting to kick out at the person who'd opened his door—but he still got a hoof to the leg.

He yelled out again, unable to stop himself. A prayer started in his gut that he'd survive the next few seconds, because that was all it usually took to get a spooked horse to calm the heck down.

Something heavy pounded him into the ramp, which broke, and he and the horse fell the foot to the snow-covered ground. Keith groaned as Shadow scrambled to her four feet, alleviating the pressure from his body.

"No, no, no," the woman said, and she skidded on her knees in front of Keith, actually spraying him with more powdery snow. "Are you okay? Talk to me."

She didn't wear a scarf and hat covering her whole face. In fact, she didn't have a hat or a hood on at all, and her gorgeous red hair spilled over the collar of her coat. She ripped her gloves off and held them to Keith's face.

"You're awake. You're okay. Tell me your name."

"Keith," he managed to say, but he still couldn't move. Couldn't breathe.

Everything started to turn white, despite the woman saying, "Stay with me. You're okay. She only landed partially on you."

He saw her look away, and when she looked back, pure panic covered her face. "She's gone, and I don't know where she went."

Keith wanted to get up and help this beautiful woman find her horse, but when he moved his leg even a tiny bit, a streak of pain sliced through his torso. He groaned and rolled onto his back, letting the bright spots of hurt prick him all over.

"It's Lindsay Lewis out at Twilight Fields," the woman said. "I've got a guy here who got trampled by a horse, and he's not moving."

Not moving, Keith thought as he let his eyes drift closed. He felt the chill start to settle into his muscles and bones, and he had the strangest thought—*where are my car keys?*—before he let everything go black.

CHAPTER
Two

LINDSAY LEWIS STOOD in the shower, the hot water streaming over her stiff and frozen back, limbs, and fingers. She took a deep breath, trying to tame her emotions. She failed, and the sob she'd been choking on since watching Shadow flop onto that cowboy rose through her body and soul.

She made a noise like a short howl before she could clamp her mouth closed. Lindsay turned her face up toward the shower head and let the water steal her tears. Thankfully, she'd grown up in Texas, with a daddy made of steel and nails, and there were no tears on a cattle ranch.

Her slower-paced life on the outskirts of Denver her comfort and peace, and she'd really enjoyed getting to know her aunt and uncle here. She loved horses, and she'd bought Shadow from Uncle Jack for Sabrina, the twelve-year-old she mentored through the Ranch Sisters program that she'd been participating in for the past five years.

"Can't stay in the shower for long," she told herself. She

didn't really need to bathe anyway; she'd just wanted to get warm. It had taken four of them to get Cowboy Keith into the house, stripped out of his wet, slushy clothes, and into her guest bedroom.

One of them, at least. Sabrina was going to spend the night in the other one, and as Lindsay stepped out of the shower, she thanked her obsessive need to make too much food for dinner. Tonight, she might not have leftovers—if Keith was awake.

He'd passed out, but he'd started to rouse when she'd walked away from her neighbors, shivering. The couple who lived a mile down the road had come on their snowmobile through the forest, and they'd helped her get Keith inside.

The emergency services had been called off, but Lindsay would take the cowboy to the ER tomorrow. He could have broken ribs or a concussion. She hadn't seen much blood from where Shadow had stomped on his calf, and none anywhere else. Not even his head.

His cowboy hat had been knocked off, but Lindsay had retrieved it. She'd turned off his truck and slid the ramp back into the trailer. She'd cleaned everything up, and after she'd dressed in soft pajama pants and an oversized sweatshirt, she ventured out of her bedroom.

She didn't see her neighbors anywhere, but out in the kitchen, Sabrina sat at the table, her phone in front of her. Her mother, Alicia, talked on the video call, and Lindsay went to sit by the girl.

"Are you sure she's okay there tonight?" Alicia asked, pure concern in her tone and sitting on her face.

Lindsay nodded. "Of course. I've got plenty of food, and if the power goes out, we've got loads of wood." She looked over to Sabrina and swiped her dark hair off her forehead. "She helped me carry it all in, and I've had a marinara sauce bubbling away for hours. We just need to boil the pasta, and then we'll eat like Italian queens."

She smiled at Sabrina and then her mother. "Okay," Alicia said. "We'll come as soon as the roads are clear."

"Don't risk anything," Lindsay said. "She's fine here until you can come safely."

"Thank you, Lindsay." The video call ended, and Lindsay let several moments of silence go by. Sabrina didn't like moving from topic to topic too quickly, but she learned quickly and she worked hard.

"Did the cowboy wake up?" she finally asked.

Sabrina shook her head. She didn't speak much, but she listened, and Lindsay had been successful in getting her to open up a little bit.

"I'm assuming Missy and Max went home?"

"Their daughter called," Sabrina said.

"How long ago did they leave?" Lindsay got to her feet and faced the hallway. Her living room sat to her left, the kitchen to the right. The dark-haired, bearded, handsome cowboy down the hall.

"Ten minutes," Sabrina said.

"Do you want to make the spaghetti?" Lindsay asked. "I'll go check on him." She was no nurse, but she could at least make sure he was still breathing. She could take him some painkillers until she could get him to the hospital to assess his injuries for real.

"Okay." Sabrina got up, and Lindsay stayed in the kitchen and helped her light the gas stove so she could boil the water. She'd made this dish with the tween before, so she wasn't too worried about Sabrina burning the house down.

She'd just slip into the bedroom for a minute anyway. As she neared the slightly ajar door of the bedroom where they'd laid Keith, her phone rang. She quickly detoured to the left and into her master suite to answer it.

Derrick. Her brother. Someone safe. She quickly swiped as the phone rang for the fourth time.

"Hey," she said almost breathlessly, hoping she'd caught the call before it went to voicemail.

"Hey," he said. "Did you get your horse tonight?"

"Yeah." Lindsay sighed as she sank onto her bed. "It was…eventful."

"Was it?" he asked. "Because we haven't heard from Keith, and he's not back, and his pin shows he's still at your place."

Lindsay pressed her eyes closed. Of course. Derrick worked at Blackhorse Bay—with Keith. She knew all the men and women there shared their location with their bosses and supervisors. It was a big facility, with animals who could spook and run—the way Shadow had.

"Linds?" Derrick sounded concerned, with a touch of impatience tossed in there.

"He's here," she said. "There was an…accident."

"An accident?"

"The snow made the ramp slippery," she said. "He fell down, and then Shadow spooked, and she fell down—right on top of him. The trailer broke; Shadow ran; Keith passed out."

"He passed out?" Derrick sputtered for a moment, his words all jumbled as he said, "Shadow went where? She fell? Keith's —what?"

Lindsay remembered the way her mind had splintered outside. She'd wanted to chase after the gray she'd bought to add to her hobby farm. She'd wanted to get an ambulance for

Keith. She'd needed to get Sabrina back inside the house before she turned into a snowman.

"I called the Grangers," she said. "They came and helped me get Keith inside. He's in the room next door." She whispered the last sentence for some reason. "We've got dinner cooking. Sabrina is staying here tonight too, because the weather is just too bad to get back to town."

Derrick sighed, but Lindsay couldn't tell if it held relief or irritation. "Can I talk to Keith?"

"I was just about to check on him," she said. "Should I have him call you, or do you want me to try to wake him up and talk right now?"

"I don't know, Linds. How is he?"

"I don't know, Derrick," she said. "I was frozen to the bone, so I got in the shower. He was passed out the last time I saw him." She stood and turned toward the door, shrieked at the tall man-silhouette standing in her doorway, and dropped her phone.

The light in the hallway was on, but her bedroom light wasn't, so she couldn't see his face. Couldn't see much of anything as she looked into the light.

Keith held up both hands and took a step back into the hallway. "Sorry," he mumbled. "I…just woke up." He wore a look of complete confusion—and only a pair of boxer shorts. Lindsay could only stare at the man's muscles that ran from head to toe, ab to ab, and across that broad chest.

He looked at her again. "Where am I?"

Lindsay heard Derrick's tinny voice coming through her phone, and she stooped to pick it up. "I'll call you back," she barked into the device before she hung up. She tossed the phone onto her bed and strode toward the door. With a simple push, she turned on the light so she could see Keith better.

"What's your name?" she asked.

His thick eyebrows puckered downward, but he said, "Keith Whettstein."

Relief flooded her. "Good. You know who you are." She sagged into the doorframe. "I'm Lindsay Lewis. You fell while delivering my horse. You passed out, and I called my neighbors to help me get you inside."

He put one hand on his ribcage and grimaced. "Shadow fell on top of me."

"That she did," Lindsay said with a nod.

"Did you get her back?" he asked. "She ran off."

She reached up and gathered her thick hair into a ponytail at the base of her neck. Without an elastic, she simply let it go again. "Yeah, we got her back," she said. "She's safe and sound in the barn. You're safe and sound here." She nodded past him, down the hall. "I've got spaghetti almost ready for dinner."

"Dinner," he repeated. His eyes widened in less time than it took to breathe. "I've got to call in," he said. "I should've been back by now, I bet." He turned away from her, and Lindsay couldn't help noticing the rippling muscles in his back. This man either worked out incessantly, or he worked hard on the ranch.

Since he worked for her uncle and with her brother, she figured all those hard lines came from his work at Blackhorse Bay.

"Where's my phone?" he asked as he went back into the guest room. "My clothes?"

"Derrick called," she said, following him. "I was on the phone with him when I saw you."

"I'll call him," he said. She now stood in his doorway, and he turned to face her. He stared at her, and a fire started in Lindsay's stomach, burning through her legs to her toes, and then licking up into her chest, her throat, her face.

Keith was a gorgeous specimen of a man, and just because Lindsay wasn't looking for a boyfriend didn't mean she couldn't have one.

"I can just text him that you're okay, and you'll call him later," Lindsay said. "Dinner is almost ready." To her great relief, her voice stayed even, none of the trembling she felt moving through her knees and stomach.

He ran his hands through his hair, which only rumpled it more, making him more attractive. "I, uh, need something to wear."

"Right." Lindsay blinked out of the staring trance she'd fallen into. "Let me check on your stuff. I had Sabrina put it in the dryer." She turned around and marched away from the bedroom, wondering why she'd had such a strong reaction to Keith.

She groaned when she opened the dryer and found his leather jacket there. His still sopping wet, now-ruined, leather jacket. She pulled it out, praying, "Lord, let these be at least a little bit dry."

None of the clothes Sabrina had shoved into the dryer—which included hers and all of Lindsay's too—were dry enough to wear. They didn't seem to be any drier than they'd been when Lindsay had stepped out of them, probably forty-five minutes ago now.

She lived alone, and certainly wouldn't have anything for a man Keith's size could wear. Thinking quickly, she moved over to the closet where she kept her winter gear. She pushed aside windbreakers and her wool coat she wore to church. She bypassed the hoodies and winter coats.

There. A triumphant noise burst from her mouth when she spotted the poncho. "One size fits all," she said as she yanked it from the hanger. She hurried back toward Keith's bedroom and held it up. "I have this."

He turned from where he stood near the head of the bed, and he'd found his phone, because he held it to his ear. "Yeah, all right," he said. "I'll be back when I'm back, I guess." He ended the call and set his phone on the nightstand.

Keith approached, and every step made Lindsay's heart beat faster, and faster, and faster. He eyed the poncho like it might be made of poison ivy, and he'd wake up with all those glorious muscles covered in a rash.

"Your clothes aren't anywhere near dry," she managed to say through her sandy throat. "But you can wear this until they are. Sorry, I don't have anything else."

"It's okay," he said, and his voice came out kindly. "I talked to Derrick." He took the poncho. "He says he's your brother?" Those eyebrows quirked now, and Lindsay wanted to learn all the expressions this cowboy could make.

"Yeah," she said. "And my uncle is Jack Hollowell. He owns Blackhorse."

Keith's jaw jumped as he pressed his teeth together. "Mm, yes, he does." He pulled the poncho over his head, and it barely hung low enough to cover the boxer shorts. His long, lean legs stuck out the bottom of it, and they both looked at them.

Keith raised his eyes first, and he grinned as his stomach growled. "You said something about spaghetti?"

Her own smile emerged, because his was just so delicious,

and she wanted to match it. "Yes," Lindsay said just as Sabrina yelled, "Help!" from the direction of the kitchen.

Lindsay spun, her smile dropping from her face, and ran toward the kitchen, a poncho-wearing-Keith hot on her heels. She couldn't take in the emergency in the kitchen before the lights flickered and went out.

Darkness covered her vision on all sides, and Lindsay took a deep breath and as she exhaled, she said, "Really, Lord? Why can't one thing go right?"

Then Keith's hand slid into hers, and his deep voice rumbled as he said, "It's okay. I've got flashlights in the truck."

CHAPTER
Three

KEITH WASN'T EVEN sure where his truck sat right now, so his promise of providing light sounded really lame inside his own ears. Sparks and pops flew up his arm, almost lighting his blood on fire, and he actually looked down at where his fingers twined with Lindsay's.

Faint firelight flickered somewhere, and he kept Lindsay's hand in his as he took a step further into the kitchen. "Oh, your stove is gas."

"Yes." Lindsay breathed out the word, and Keith's eyes continued to adjust to the darkness. He wasn't thrilled about the power being out, but he wasn't surprised either. During the big storms around Denver, the snow weighed a lot and pulled down power lines. "I've got a fireplace too," she said. "And food. And we'll be fine."

He hoped she had plenty of blankets too, because he wore a poncho and no pants. Keith couldn't remember if he'd ever worn a poncho before. A *poncho*.

He tried to push his current attire out of his mind, but all he could think was, *If the power is out, the dryer isn't running.*

And that meant his clothes wouldn't be dry any time soon. Which meant he'd be wearing this poncho indefinitely.

Embarrassment rose through him, though surely there were plenty of people around the city who'd been stranded tonight. Who'd been stranded somewhere without the greatest options for clothes before.

"Sabrina," Lindsay said, her hand slipping out of his. "Did you burn yourself?"

"The water boiled over," the girl said, and Keith switched his gaze to her as Lindsay approached her. "It splashed."

Lindsay tapped and swiped on her phone, and a flashlight blazed into the darkness. The windows sat in a lighter shade of black, the snow still falling beyond the glass. Keith moved toward the girls, switching on his flashlight too.

"I've got this," he said while Lindsay helped Sabrina. The water in the sink still worked, and she ran it over the younger girl's hand, and then got out a few ice cubes in a baggie for her. As she moved Sabrina over to the table with her bag of ice, Keith managed to pinch out a piece of spaghetti and taste it.

"Definitely done," he murmured to himself, and he twisted the knob and put out the fire beneath the pot. He'd set his phone on the counter with the flashlight shining up to the ceiling, so he could see well enough to get the pasta drained.

He started opening cupboards as Lindsay and Sabrina talked in low voices, and as Keith had reached the age of thirty-two and lived on his own, he could put together a meal. The marinara bubbling on the stove wasn't hard to find, and Keith put the spaghetti back in the pot and poured the sauce over it until it was well-dressed.

He took that over to the table and set it on a potholder in the middle and returned to get the plates, forks, and his flashlight-phone. Lindsay tracked him on the way back to the table, and he sat across from her and reached for the tongs.

"Should we pray?" he asked, pausing to look at the two people across from him. "I mean, we don't—do you…." He let his voice trail off, and he sort of threw his arm across the table and took Lindsay's hand in his. Sabrina reached for him and Lindsay at the same time.

"I'll say it," he murmured, his eyes drifting closed. He sometimes did this at night, in his bedroom, when he was finally all alone. His mind slowed, and he allowed the enormity of the day to melt away as he breathed out. Relaxed.

"Dear Lord," he finally said into the deathly still silence. "We gather before Thee in gratitude for our safety tonight. Please bless any who are out in this storm that they will find shelter and refuge. Bless the three of us to be safe through the night, that we'll stay warm, and that we'll be well-fed. I'm grateful for Lindsay and those who helped get me inside, and bless our families wherever they are that they won't be worried about us, and that they'll be safe, dry, and warm this evening as well."

He paused, because he was so used to praying for health and safety. Growing up, his daddy had always reminded him to remember his blessings during his prayers, and Keith's eyelids fluttered as he tried to find those blessings that he could say out loud with these two near strangers—one of whom he found incredibly attractive.

"We're grateful for each other, and that we don't have to be alone tonight. Amen." He pulled his hands back quickly, suddenly feeling like the one holding Lindsay's hand was coated in a thick layer of sweat.

He looked across the table to Lindsay, and she reached up and tucked her auburn hair behind her ear. In the harsh light of the flashlight-phone, her features were stark and bathed in shadows and bright whites all at the same time.

She still made his breath catch, and Keith's face grew hot. "Spaghetti," he blurted out, as if telling himself to get dinner dished up. He did that, and he gave the first plate to Sabrina, who looked at Lindsay. She nodded, and Sabrina reached for the forks. She passed those out while Keith tonged some pasta onto a plate for Lindsay.

He passed it to her, their eyes meeting. A strong zing pulled through him, and surely she had to feel that too. It felt like someone had caught him with a giant fishhook, the sharpness piercing him through the back and out his belly button, pulling him toward the table, toward Lindsay.

He dished himself some spaghetti and looked across the space to Lindsay. "You made marinara sauce today?"

"Sabrina came over, and it's one of my granny's recipes." Lindsay flashed him a smile and twirled a bite of noodles and sauce around her fork.

"Do you cook a lot?" he asked.

"I do like it," she said. "What about you?"

"I can cook, sure," he said. "I grew up with a single dad, and he made sure my sister and I knew how to take care of ourselves." He flashed a smile at Lindsay. "My sister is getting married in a few days. Her fiancé can't even boil water." He chuckled a little then. "Super great guy, though." He swallowed and decided to stop talking, so he stuffed his mouth full of the spaghetti and homemade marinara.

A groan came from his throat before he could stop himself. The sauce held so much flavor, from the deep herbs in there, cooked well enough that he didn't taste every single one indi-vidually, but all of them together. "Wow," he said around his mouthful of food. Was he ever going to stop embarrassing himself?

He swallowed his food. "That sauce is *amazing*."

Lindsay ducked her head and smiled. "Thank you." She glanced over to Sabrina. "It's good?"

Sabrina nodded, her mouth full of food. But she didn't talk the way Keith had. He smiled at the girl, because while she'd scared him out in the snowstorm, she actually possessed a very gentle spirit. She reminded him of some of the calm therapy horses at Pony Power, the equine therapy unit he'd worked at for years and years before he'd made the move to Blackhorse Bay. The owner, Molly Hammond, gave off that same calm, gentle spirit, and the therapy dogs on the Hammond Family Farm did the same.

"How old are you, Sabrina?" he asked.

Lindsay looked over to her and said, "His name is Keith Whettstein. You can talk to him."

Sabrina took another bite of spaghetti instead, and Keith looked over to Lindsay. She gave him a tiny smile, and some-thing in her eyes told him to wait. Just wait. So Keith also took another bite of his dinner, and a moment later, he was rewarded with Sabrina saying, "I'm twelve. How old are you?"

He smiled at her and said, "Thirty-two."

"Lindsay is thirty," Sabrina said. "That's close to thirty-two."

"Yes." Keith switched his grin to Lindsay. "It sure is."

The power didn't come back on while they ate, and Keith didn't completely bomb with his small-talk skills. He definitely noticed the air around them growing chillier and chillier, but he didn't say anything until Lindsay took Sabrina's plate and piled it on top of hers.

"I'll get a fire going," he said as he rose with her.

She eased over to him and took his plate too. "We brought in wood already," she said. "Thank you, Keith." She turned away and took the dishes toward the sink. "Sabrina, you can go help Keith with the fire."

"Can I have a water?" Sabrina asked.

"Of course," Lindsay said. "Take some for everyone, okay?"

The girl moved over to the fridge and opened the door, and Keith expected a light to burst to life. It was amazing how much he expected power to be there, and how alarming it was when it wasn't.

He left Lindsay in the kitchen, and he moved out of the dining room and into the living room. This was an older house, with two separate rooms, with a big, wide arched doorway leading between them. The fireplace stood in the wall there, dark with cold stones. Lindsay had a TV in the corner, and a couch and love seat facing that.

The room felt really big to Keith, but he wasn't sure why. Maybe because of the vaulted ceiling—that would take a lot of heat to fill, and Keith looked at the stack of wood Lindsay and Sabrina had brought in.

Keith hadn't spent too many nights without power, but he didn't think a dozen logs were going to sustain them. Not in this room, which connected to the kitchen, and then the hallway that led to the bedrooms behind it.

"I learned to build a fire in Girl Scouts," Sabrina said, and Keith dang near jumped out of his skin for a second time that evening. Wow, Sabrina could move silently.

"Yeah?" he asked, his adrenaline pumping through him. "Do you want to show me?"

"Okay." The girl with dark hair got down on her knees, set her bottled water aside, and picked up a couple of smaller pieces of wood. She started building a tent out of them, and she expertly moved over to the kindling bucket. She put that in, and she made long ropes out of newspaper there and put them in too.

She sat back on her haunches and looked at him. "I don't get to do the fire part."

"You don't?" He knelt beside her and picked up the lighter. It was one of those ones that all he had to do was pull a switch, and it would click and ignite the flame. "I think you can do this one. You just hold it like this."

He held it over the light of his phone. "And pull this button here, and it starts." He turned the handle toward her and held it closer to her. She looked at him, anxiety in her eyes. Keith tried to smile calmly at her, and all at once, he knew who he was dealing with.

Britt.

His sister had looked at him like this, and he'd walked her through plenty of hard, new, and scary things for her. "You can do it," he said gently. "I'm right here if something goes wrong, but it won't."

She still wouldn't take the lighter, and he looked at the fire she'd built masterfully. "Where would you light it?" he asked.

Sabrina pointed to a long tail of a newspaper rope she'd left out. "It'll start there and burn into the kindling."

"Then light it right there," he said. Keith told himself to wait again, and he had a lifetime of experience in waiting for his sister. He moved slightly away from her and set the lighter on the stone hearth and waited.

Sabrina looked at the lighter, and then him, and then the logs, kindling, and newspaper she'd constructed. She moved back through the items again, her eyes landing on the lighter and staying there.

"Okay," she finally said and picked up the lighter. She curled her finger around the trigger and pulled it, the lighter clicking and the flame bursting from the end of it. Sabrina startled, and Keith put his hand on her back quickly.

"It's okay," he said. "That's what it does. It's supposed to do that. You did it right." He wondered how Sabrina and Lindsay had come to be together, and he suddenly had a lot more questions for the beautiful redhead who'd found him just before he'd passed out.

Sabrina pulled the trigger again, and when the flame came to life, she moved it easily to the newspaper edge she'd left out. It started to smoke and burn, and Keith did like the way fire moved and consumed. He watched the newspaper blacken, and Sabrina lit the lighter again and started another end of another newspaper rope on fire.

She did it again and again, and with four trails of fire moving toward the kindling, it started crackling and snapping and popping. The wood caught the flame and came to life, and Sabrina pulled the lighter back and handed it to Keith.

"Good job, Sabrina," he said.

"My mom calls me Bri," she said, seemingly out of nowhere.

"Okay." He watched the fire, as did Sabrina, the two of them side-by-side and silent. It reminded him so much of his sister, and his heartbeat leapfrogged for a moment. "My sister is getting married soon. Her fiancé's name is Lars."

"There's a boy in my English class named Lars."

"Yeah? Is he nice?" Keith did love Lars Hansen, and more importantly, Lars loved Britt. Lars would take care of Britt, something Keith had been doing for his whole life. His father's words that he'd done his best with Britt, and he'd made his dad proud over and over rushed through his head.

"Yeah, he's nice," Sabrina said.

In three days, Britt would be married. Off on her honeymoon, and when she and Lars returned, she wouldn't live out on the Hammond Family Farm anymore. Of course, Keith would still have a place in her life, but it wouldn't be the same.

"I'm walking her down the aisle," he said. "Along with my daddy. She wanted us both to do it."

"Does she have a white dress?"

"The whitest," Keith said. "And this shawl made of white fur." He smiled, because Britt loved frilly and lacy things. And apparently, furry things. "Because it's winter, and she doesn't want to freeze during pictures."

"I don't know what a shawl is," Sabrina said.

Keith glanced toward the kitchen, thinking Lindsay should've come out by now. He didn't see her, and he didn't hear her cleaning up in the kitchen. Perhaps she'd gone into the recesses of the house to find blankets and pillows, or sleeping bags and air mattresses. His aching body, which had served him well today by delivering horses to several ranches and farms, wanted somewhere soft to lay and sleep tonight.

"A shawl is like a coat," Keith said. "But it only goes around your shoulders. It doesn't have sleeves like, a back or a front." So it wasn't really like a coat at all. "It'll keep Britt— that's my sister—warm while she's outside for the wedding photos."

"My brother got a new coat for his birthday, but he never wears it."

Keith grinned and asked, "How old is he?"

"Fifteen."

"Sounds about right." Keith chuckled and groaned as he got to his feet. "Come on. Let's go find Lindsay and see if she needs help." He extended his hand to Sabrina to help her stand, and to his surprise, she didn't hesitate as she slipped her hand into Keith's and let him pull her to her feet.

"I like you, Keith," she said.

"Thank you," he said, not sure why. "I like you too, Sabrina." He looked up and spied Lindsay leaning against the wall of the arch, her arms folded and a soft, warm smile on her face that reminded him of the fire, for it crackled too.

It snapped, it popped, and it sent heat straight down to his toes.

Tonight was going to be very interesting, as the power still hadn't come back on, and he'd definitely need a blanket to cover up his bare legs in this ridiculous poncho if he had any chance of impressing Lindsay at all.

CHAPTER

Four

LINDSAY GAZED at the handsome cowboy—sans hat—in that too-short poncho. She'd never seen anyone interact with Sabrina as well as he had, not right out of the gate anyway. Lindsay had worked with a lot of horses, and a lot of men, in her life, and he possessed one of the stronger, yet gentle, personas she'd ever encountered.

He'd dished them all dinner. He'd moved onto the next task of starting the fire without being asked. He probably felt self-conscious and ridiculous in that poncho, but he gazed back at her with something bright and delightful glinting in his eyes.

Or maybe the firelight could throw itself that far. Lindsay wanted to believe the foaming, heated chemistry she felt warmed Keith's blood too, but she'd been wrong about such things before.

"Can we help you get blankets and bedding?" Keith finally asked, and Lindsay straightened away from the wall where she'd been leaning. He glanced over to the bigger couch in the room. "I definitely think we should sleep out here. I don't think they're going to be getting the power back on tonight."

Lindsay held up her phone, where she'd been texting with her brother, her uncle, and her daddy, all while frowning in the kitchen while Sabrina and Keith had gotten this crackling fire going. She stepped into the living room, the heat starting to emanate from the hearth.

"I checked the power company website," she said. "They're saying ten a.m. tomorrow as of right now."

"Yikes." Keith reached up with the hand not holding Sabrina's and ran his fingers through his hair. Since he'd gotten wet, and he had a ton of hair, it sort of stuck out in odd angles, and Lindsay fought the urge to smooth it all back down.

"Okay." He blew out his breath as he surveyed the room, his eyes coming back to hers. "I think we need to try to make this room as small as possible then." He looked up to her century-old high ceilings. "Because it's been below zero for hours, and we've got a long way to go to ten a.m."

The gravity of the situation descended on Lindsay, and she shoved her phone in her back pocket. "Okay," she said. "You're right."

"I can help with the horses in the morning," he said. "We can bring in wood. We can eat everything out of your fridge. But we've got to stay warm."

Lindsay had heard of people freezing to death inside their homes during storms like this, when the power went out for extended periods of time. That would *not* be her, Keith, or Sabrina.

"Yes," she said. "I have sleeping bags meant for winter camping. Plenty of blankets and coats and clothes." She glanced over to the pile of wood, which looked so meager now. "I've got two cords of wood, but we will have to go outside to get it."

Her eyes traveled back to Keith. "Wait. I have a generator for my barn. I put all my chickens and horses in it, but we could—" She stopped as Keith started to shake his head.

"You want your animals to freeze?" He cocked his head and looked at her.

"No," she said simply. "I left my dog out there too. We should bring him in. He'll help keep us warm."

"Sure," Keith said. "You've got how many horses?"

"Seven now," she said. "Three dozen chickens. A big momma pig who has babies in the summer. I raised some turkeys last year, but…." She trailed off again, this time noticing a playful smile tugging at the corners of Keith's mouth.

"I totally want to hear about your animals," Keith said, taking a step closer to her. He dropped Sabrina's hand, and for a horribly wonderful moment, it looked like he'd reach for Lindsay's. "But can we do it when we have the room situated, and beds ready, and more than half my body is being warmed by the fire?"

Lindsay swallowed, unable to look away from him. With his strong jaw, and plenty of that day's growth coming into his beard, those full lips now smiling fully at her, and those deep, delicious eyes, she almost felt mesmerized by him.

She'd never met anyone as handsome as Keith Whettstein, that was for dang sure. And she'd lived and dated cowboys in Texas for decades. None of them held a candle to Keith, and her stomach felt like it had shredded into the spaghetti she'd eaten for dinner.

"I'll help," Sabrina said, breaking the trance Lindsay had

fallen into with Keith. He blinked too, and they both looked at the girl.

"Yes," Lindsay said, taking on the authoritative mantle. "You come with me, sweetie, and we'll start getting bedding, sleeping bags, and coats." She looked at Keith. "I have some old sheets of plywood in the basement that we could probably use to block the hallway and doorways and stuff, to try to make this room smaller."

"I'll see what I can do," he said, already looking around again.

"The fireplace has a fan too," Lindsay said, suddenly remembering it. She moved over to the wall and pushed the switch. "Once it reaches a certain temperature, it'll blow the air back out."

"Does that switch work if the power is out?"

Lindsay looked at it blankly. It had done nothing, but she hadn't expected it to. Number one, the doors on the fireplace weren't closed, and they had to be for the fan to kick on. Number two, it usually took several minutes for the fireplace to warm up to the temperature needed to blow the air back into the room.

"I don't know," she admitted.

Keith pressed in beside her, the scratchy fabric of the poncho brushing her elbow. "It's fine," he murmured. "Go get the blankets and coats and stuff. I'll work on making the room smaller, and then I'll go get your dog and check on the animals, and we'll be fine."

A certain measure of exhaustion pulled through her, despite the spiraling shower of attraction raining down on her from Keith's height. "I feel overwhelmed," she whispered before she could censor herself.

"Hey, it's okay." Keith turned her into his arms and wrapped her in his embrace. "It just feels like a lot, but you've got help." He pulled back almost as quickly as he'd taken her into his hug. She'd barely had time to hold him back, and a keen sense of longing accompanied the sigh as it left her mouth.

"Okay?" He smiled down at her softly, and oh, she wondered what it would be like to be looked at like that only a moment before he kissed her. Her eyes dropped to his mouth, then quickly rebounded away.

"Okay." She took a deep breath and dropped her arms away from his body. "Okay. Yes. Blankets. Pillows. Coats."

"I'm going to get my pants and put them by the fire," he said. "I've got to have something to wear, and the dryer's not going."

"Okay," she said. "I'm sorry, Keith."

"Hey, none of this is your fault," he said. "It is what it is, and we'll make the best of it. We'll survive this, because we're not alone."

Lindsay didn't want to think about what she'd do if she was alone. She'd have eaten, and she could build a fire herself just fine. She'd likely have boiled water on her gas stove to make hot chocolate—which she could still do—and she'd have pulled the loveseat as close to the fireplace as she could get.

That was what she'd have done if she was here alone.

"Let's go, sweetie," she said to Sabrina. As they left the living room, the air brushing her face grew colder and colder, and Lindsay shivered.

"Lindsay?" Keith asked, and she turned back to him. "What's your dog's name?"

"Hamlet," she said. "He's a sweet thing. You shouldn't have any trouble with him."

Keith nodded. "I'll meet you back here."

"Thank you." She smiled and then turned to face the dark recesses of her house. She'd loved this house and farm the moment she'd stepped foot on it. Yes, she was quite a drive outside of town, but she hadn't minded that. She only had a few neighbors, but they'd become good friends. They helped one another in times like this, and they relied on each other. They came together for celebrations as simple as the leaves changing color, and Lindsay had planned to spend Christmas Eve with Max and Missy Granger, and then Christmas Day with her brother and uncle at Blackhorse Bay.

She wondered how long Keith had been there. *Less than a year*, she thought as she went into the first guest bedroom, where she'd been planning to house Sabrina that evening. If Keith had been at Blackhorse for longer than that, she'd have met him last Christmas, as Uncle Jack did a big thing for his employees at the farm.

"Get the pillows," she said to Sabrina. "I'll get blankets and sheets." As they started working, Lindsay started praying. Losing power really was a concern, and she thought of her friends and neighbors. She should check their community social media page to make sure everyone had what they needed.

She prayed for them as she took the quilt and sheets into the living room and dumped them unceremoniously on the couch. Sabrina did the same thing, and they returned to the next bedroom to get more.

Lindsay worried over the power company workers, and if they were out in the storm or not. Surely they were, and she prayed they'd be safe and be able to be reunited with their families soon.

She found herself praying for herself, and her brother, and

Uncle Jack, and then finally…her daddy. So much water had gone under that bridge, but the structure still stood.

Because of me, Lindsay thought, and she felt and heard the bitterness in her internal voice.

It was true that she'd done all of the reaching out for the past five years. She'd done all of the coordination between Daddy and her and Derrick. She managed Uncle Jack and Daddy. She played the buffer between everyone, and she was the one constantly down on her hands and knees, hammering in nails that had come loose, replacing planks in the bridge, and making sure everyone could walk across it.

She had to, because while she'd left Texas, she couldn't just leave her father in the dust.

"Let's get coats," she said as she took Sabrina into the utility room behind the kitchen. The dryer sat there, silent of course, but the door had been opened. So Keith had been moving about her house too, and Lindsay once again shivered at the thought of him.

Or maybe that was because the utility room had always been one of the colder rooms in the house, as it had been added on in an addition, and the temperature here could cause a chill. She moved to the closet and opened it, her prayers starting up again, this time for his pants to dry quickly, for her animals to stay warm through the storm, and for him to be able to check on them quickly and return to the house without incident.

CHAPTER

Five

KEITH SMOOTHED his jeans over the front of the hearth, the heat coming from it made of magic and bliss and everything good. He still had to go outside, a task he'd put off while he'd shivered through the half-done basement, his flashlight not cutting very far into the dense darkness down there.

But he'd managed to haul up three pretty substantial pieces of plywood, and while the one only several feet behind him didn't quite reach all the way to the ceiling, he thought it radiated enough heat back into the living room to be worthwhile.

"Coats," Lindsay said, and Keith turned away from the flickering flames.

"Do you have towels or something we can put around the door and windows?" he asked. "My daddy usually made us do that when we lost power for an extended period of time." Keith should probably call his parents, just so they knew where he was and that he was okay.

"Sure," Lindsay said.

He also nodded to the door around the corner, which neither of them could actually see. "I saw a potbellied stove downstairs. It might be more advantageous to sleep and live down there." The room closed off, for one. He'd seen several doors, but they'd all been closed, creating a much smaller space to heat. And the ceiling was only half as high for another.

"It doesn't work," she said, shaking her head. "I'm, uh, working on the basement very slowly."

It had looked like a war zone of construction materials, if Keith were being honest. He didn't judge, though, because Lindsay clearly normally lived here alone, and she didn't need more than the bedrooms and bathrooms she had on this level.

"Oh, okay," he said. "I found the plywood." He indicated needlessly the piece behind him. "I'll put one up blocking the hallway when you're done, and one going into the kitchen. If we need to use the bathroom or go get something to eat, wash up, whatever, they won't be hard to move."

Lindsay looked over to the wood, the firelight dancing merrily on it. Keith loved that about fire. It never seemed to realize that it only came to life when things were starting to get dangerous. Of course, a summer campfire could be lit just for fun, and Keith had spent plenty of time in the Rocky Mountains after he'd moved here with his family.

Before that, he'd enjoyed the Montana wilderness with campfires, backyard bonfires, and more.

But fire was used to ward off darkness, keep the cold at bay, and warn back animals. It could cause major destruction if left unchecked, and yet it flickered and danced and cast beautiful shadows across Lindsay's face.

Or maybe that was just because she was so incredibly beautiful.

Keith schooled his thoughts and cleared his throat at the same time. "I'm going to head out and check on the animals and get Hamlet."

"Sabrina and I are going to make hot chocolate," Lindsay said, twisting to look at the girl on the couch behind her. "Then we can all pile into blankets and whatnot." She faced Keith again and smiled. "Oh, and I remembered where my battery-operated lanterns are, so I'm going to grab those. Then we don't have to use our phones for everything."

"I'll get my flashlights from the truck on the way back in," he said. "I do want to pull the couches closer to the fire before we actually go to bed." He'd thought about setting shifts for sleeping too, but he didn't bring it up right now. He honestly doubted he'd sleep much tonight anyway.

Stress kept him awake, and the nearness of Lindsay wouldn't help his nerves either.

He lifted his phone. "I'm going to put on these jeans and head outside. If I'm not back in fifteen minutes, you should come get me." He swallowed. "I mean, I don't need us both out there, but...." He glanced at Sabrina, not wanting to say too much. It would've scared Britt, and in fact, this storm probably had her pacing and on-edge. He definitely needed to text her and make sure she was okay.

She'd likely gone down the lane to Uncle Boone's, or she'd made arrangements to sleep at their parents' house tonight. Britt did not like the big snowstorms, and she watched the weather religiously in the winter.

"Oh." Lindsay snapped her fingers. "I found a pair of snow pants in the closet." She fished through the clothing she'd brought in. "They might be too short, but then you won't have to pull on wet denim." She lifted up a pair of black, puffy pants, and Keith blinked at them.

"They're for women," he said.

"Yeah, but I bought them for Derrick's girlfriend a couple of years ago, and she was bigger. They should fit you." She beamed at them like she'd done him a huge favor, but Keith wasn't sure which was worse: the poncho with his legs poking out the bottom or wearing women's snow pants.

Since he didn't want to die tonight, and he did have to traipse through the snow to the barn and back, he took the snow pants while trying to force himself to say thank you. The gratitude got stuck, but he pushed past it and said, "Thank you, Lindsay."

She giggled, her expression turning playful and bright. Her laughter grew and grew, and she waved both hands in front of her as Keith frowned. "It's fine," she said. "It's nothing."

"You're making fun of my legs," he said, moving straight into flirtation mode. It only felt odd for a moment, what with the current situation and all, and then he grinned too.

"I'm not." She laughed some more, and Keith started to chuckle too.

"Or you're calling me fat, then."

"No." Lindsay grinned and grinned.

"Then Derrick's girlfriend," he said.

She radiated pure joy as she shook her head. "No, not at all." She took a micro-step closer to him, but it felt like she'd just crossed continents to be in his personal space. She sobered, though her grin remained. "I can just tell you don't want to wear the pants."

"Of course I don't," he said, looking at them in his hands.

"But you're right. Pulling on wet denim and going outside is even worse." He met her gaze again. "In fact, it's suicidal."

"I can go check on the animals," she said.

He shook his head instantly. "No," he said quickly. "You need to stay here with Sabrina. I'll be in and out."

"I've had this farm for five years," she said, those eyes that he truly didn't know the color of sharpened. With her red hair, they had to be brown or hazel or green. Didn't they? He couldn't wait for the proper light to see them clearly. "I've been out in storms before."

"I'm sure you have," he said. "But I can do it." He leaned closer, wanting to take a deep breath of her skin, her hair, her very soul. "Sometimes you don't have to do things you normally do when you're not alone."

He stepped back, getting into dangerous waters now, the soft, feminine scent of her skin now lodged in his nose. He remembered she'd showered while he'd been passed out, and her shampoo or body wash definitely held hints of orange and cream.

"Okay," she said, her voice somewhat monotone now. "Thank you, Keith."

"Thanks for the women's pants." He stepped into them right there in front of her, and sure enough, they didn't have the required length for his legs. But he pulled them on as far as he could, feeling way too much tightness along his thighs and higher, but he only had to wear them for a few minutes. His jeans would be dry by morning, he was sure.

He'd turn them and rotate them like pancakes to dry all the fabric, and then he wouldn't have to feel so foolish in front of Lindsay.

"Sabrina," he said as he stepped past Lindsay and over to the twelve-year-old. "I'm going to go outside and check on the animals. Will you make me some hot chocolate?"

She looked up from her phone and nodded, "Yes, sir," she said.

He grinned at her. "Thanks." He tossed a look over his shoulder to Lindsay, his smile still stuck in place. An hour ago, when he'd first woke up, he'd been desperate to get home. Get out of here. He'd been grumpy, and Keith usually had to pull himself back from the edge of irritation and find a better path down the mountain.

"Fifteen minutes," he said.

"I'm starting a timer on my phone." Lindsay swiped as if she might actually do that, and Keith rifled through the pile of coats on the couch and managed to find one that would mostly go around his shoulders. The cuffs sat too high on his wrists, but he reminded himself he had a pair of gloves in the truck.

Armed with the best tools he could possibly have, he left the house through the back door. The eaves hung over the deck for a few feet, and Keith quickly closed the door behind him and moved down the couple of steps to the deck to survey his options.

The snow fell in steady, fat flakes, and he found it beautiful. Peaceful and mesmerizing all at the same time. And so, so quiet, he almost didn't dare to breathe, lest he disturb it.

"Dear God," he prayed out loud, the words barely coming out of his throat. "Bless me to get this done and return quickly." His daddy had taught him to rely on the Lord at all times, but Keith was far better at it when things weren't going the way he wanted than when they were.

His dad had told him and Britt repeatedly that God had led him from Montana to the Hammond Family Farm here in Ivory

Peaks, and that He'd lead them in their lives too. If ever there was a time when Keith needed to be led somewhere, it felt like now.

So he took the first step, the path out to his truck clear in his mind and his eyes, now that they'd adjusted to all this country darkness. He moved quickly, his breathing and footsteps in the soft snow breaking the silence.

He made it to the truck, his breath steaming in front of him, and pulled his gloves from the console compartment between the driver's seat and the passenger seat. He seated those on his hands and leaned across the seats to the glove compartment, where he found two flashlights.

With those stashed in his pockets, he left his truck and faced the barn. This was an unfamiliar farm for him, but he'd been inside dozens and dozens of barns. Again, he took the first step, counting on God to guide him, direct him, and keep him safe.

The barn seemed to put off a little heat, and Keith got slapped with it as he slid open the door. He darted inside and closed the door again, all while every horse, dog, chicken, and the big momma pig looked his way.

"Hey, guys," he said easily, beyond glad Lindsay wasn't here to hear him talk to her hobby farm friends like they could answer him back. "Hamlet, buddy, you're coming inside with me."

The blue heeler got to his feet and trotted toward Keith, his docked tail in a downward position. Keith crouched and scrubbed the dog along his jowls and behind his ears. "Unless you want to stay out here." He wouldn't leave the dog out here, because while he probably spent a lot of time outside with Lindsay, he also had a clean coat that suggested he slept at the foot of her bed at night.

What a lucky dog.

"You guys okay out here?" Keith rose to his full height and surveyed the crowd in the barn. The chickens obviously had temporary lodging in here, and it sat closest to the heating lamps. He saw a couple of cats over there too, and they both looked at him almost lazily.

Keith went over to the pig's pen to make sure she had food and water. She did, as Lindsay had been in winter storms before. He walked down the aisle where the horse stalls stood, and they all seemed prepped and ready for this storm. With nothing to do but get back, Keith returned to the larger main area of the barn.

"All right," he said. "We'll come check on you in the morning." He had no idea how long the generator would run, or if Lindsay had replacement fuel. "Come on, Hamlet."

He opened the door for the dog, and the blue heeler left without hesitation. Keith followed him, pulled and secured the barn door closed behind him, and dropped his head to keep the snow off his face.

"Let's hurry up now," he said to the dog, and they made their way back to the house without incident. With every step he took, he realized how prepared Lindsay was. How she cared for her animals—heck, they had a generator to keep the barn warm for them when she didn't even enjoy that same luxury in her home. And maybe, just maybe, how good she could be for him.

Thinking such things felt dangerous, almost forbidden, but Keith couldn't stop the thoughts as they marched through his mind. They didn't stop once he'd entered the house, and they reminded him of how relentlessly the snowflakes fell outside.

"You're back in only eleven minutes," Lindsay said from the doorway on the opposite side of the utility room. She held two mugs, and Keith hurried to shrug out of the wet coat and hang it on the doorknob of the closet.

"Everything is great out there." He kicked off his boots and approached her.

Her soft smile beckoned to him, and he took the mug she offered him, the scent of chocolate and warmth now seeping into him. "Come on," she said. "Sabrina found some cards, and she has a game she wants to teach us."

He followed her into the living room and found that she and Sabrina had indeed moved both couches closer to the fireplace. They barely had room to walk there, and Keith set his mug on the end table that had been positioned between the love seat and the couch, which then curved to close the oval made with the fireplace.

She'd indeed found two lanterns which shone with bright white light, and Keith wondered how long the batteries in those would last. Knowing Lindsay the little that he now did, he suspected she'd have replacement batteries hidden away in one of her cupboards.

"I'll pull those boards over now." He glanced over to her as she sank onto the end of the longer couch.

"Okay," Lindsay said. "Then we can tell you our plan for the sleeping arrangements tonight."

That sounded both ominous and interesting, and Keith hurried to pull the plywood into place, both because it was colder the further from the fire he went, but also, he couldn't wait to find out where he'd be sleeping.

CHAPTER
Six

LINDSAY GLANCED over her shoulder to where Keith paced along the wall from the front door to the piece of plywood he'd put up to block the entrance to the kitchen. He held his phone to his ear, and his expression seemed to change every time he turned to go back the way he'd already come.

He grinned, he laughed, he sobered. Lindsay liked watching him move through a range of emotions, and then he lowered his phone, kept his head bent over it for a few more minutes, and then tucked his phone into the pocket of the women's snow pants he still wore.

He came around to the other end of the couch from where she sat, and he grinned at her too. To have that smile trained right on her brought an electric zip to her pulse. "Sorry about that," he said. "I called my sister, and she had a lot to say."

"What's her name?"

"Britt," he said as he sagged back into the couch. "She's

getting married soon, and storms really scare her. She's at my parents' house tonight—and probably through the wedding."

"Where does she normally live?"

"The Hammond Family Farm." He turned his head toward her instead of watching the fire flicker in the hearth. "Do you know where that is?"

"No idea," Lindsay said, as it hadn't tickled anything in her memory. Then the name Hammond came roaring at her. "Wait. Hammond? Like the family who owns that big company and all those buildings downtown?"

"Yeah," Keith said. "My dad is the farm foreman for Gray Hammond. I grew up there. Well." He rolled his shoulders as if shrugging each one individually but at separate times. "We moved here when I was thirteen. Permanently. My dad ran the farm in the summers while Gray and his family went up to this little town in Wyoming. We came for, oh." He exhaled heavily. "Ten years maybe before Daddy decided to move us here permanently. I've been working there since. Well—"

Lindsay grinned at him. "You say 'well' a lot."

"It's hard to give a whole life story in only a few sentences." He pulled a blanket up off the floor and wrapped it around his shoulders like a shawl. "I went to college for a few years. Got an agricultural studies degree. That's how I got the job at Black-horse Bay. I'm the agricultural manager."

"You haven't been there long," Lindsay said, enjoying the sound of his voice against the crackling flames. "I go out there for the Christmas party and the Memorial Day celebration every year."

"I started in the summertime," he said. "I've only been there for about six months."

Lindsay wanted him to ask her out, but she wanted to see

Keith again once the storms drifted by and the snow got cleared. She tucked her hair behind her ear and asked, "Were you planning on going to the Blackhorse Christmas party?"

"Yeah, sure," he said. "My sister will be married in a couple of days. My folks are sending them to Cancun for a tropical honeymoon and holiday, and I'm going out to the Hammonds for Christmas Eve. And I'll be back at Blackhorse for Christmas Day, later, for their dinner. Are you going to be there?"

"Uncle Jack insists I come," Lindsay said. "I mean, I want to. He and my aunt Lenora and Derrick are my only family here."

"What do you do on Christmas Eve?" He hunkered down into his blanket and smiled over to her. "Make amazing marinara sauce and eat pasta?"

"Tonight, we were supposed to have green salad and garlic bread too," Lindsay said, the foolishness she'd felt when she'd seen those items sitting on the counter, unserved and therefore uneaten, rushing back through her. "So if I was going to do that on Christmas Eve, it would be a better meal than tonight."

"I don't think there can be a better meal than what we had tonight."

Warmth moved through Lindsay. "Well, thank you," she said. She hesitated, trying to decide if she should say what lingered in her head. "I actually bake this *amazing* candied ham for Christmas Day dinner out at Blackhorse."

"Of course you do." Keith grinned again, his chest rising and falling evenly.

"My uncle brings in other things too," she said. "One year, he did this whole buried, smoked pig. The cowboys loved that."

"Sounds delicious," Keith said.

"Aunt Lenora does a big beef roast. Uncle Jack caters the side dishes from this great place in a little town called Ivory Peaks."

"Oh, the Hammond Family Farm is in Ivory Peaks."

"Then you must know The Burger Babe."

Keith started to chuckle as he nodded. "Uh, yeah. The Hammonds own it."

"Sounds like you know everyone," she teased. "I do have dreams about the mac and cheese from The Burger Babe."

Keith laughed outright then, and the sound of it brought cheer to Lindsay's heart. "And I don't know anyone. That's why I ended up leaving the Hammond's farm."

"Yeah?" Lindsay's interest piqued. "What does that mean?"

"It means I couldn't...." Keith cleared his throat as he sat up and scooted back on the couch, so now he sat up straighter. "I wasn't meeting anyone. Like, women." He coughed a couple of times and reached for the mug of hot chocolate he'd set there a half-hour ago. He guzzled the had-to-be-cold-by-now hot chocolate and plunked the mug back onto the end table.

Lindsay's eyebrows went up, and then she burst out laughing. On the other couch, Sabrina kept shuffling the deck of cards she'd found, and Lindsay should probably include her. At the same time, Sabrina didn't seem to mind being in her own world sometimes.

Feeling braver now that the room had warmed considerably and she and Keith had been talking easily, she grinned over to him. "So you left one farm to work at Blackhorse so you could meet more women." She didn't phrase it as a question, and something tingled through each individual cell as she teased him.

"You know what?" Keith picked up his mug and then set it back down. "Yeah. Yeah, I left a small family farm where I wasn't meeting anyone to date, and I moved to Blackhorse Bay."

"And did you?" Lindsay asked. "Meet more women to date?"

"I did," he said. "I've been out with a few women in the past few months."

"And?"

"And what?"

Was he really going to make her say it? The way his brow furrowed in that adorable way told her yes. She better ask. "Do you have a girlfriend?"

Keith swallowed, the firelight highlighting the movement in his throat perfectly. "No," he said. "What about you?"

"No, I don't have a girlfriend," she teased.

He looked at her then, pure vulnerability in his gaze. Enough to make Lindsay settle down and sober up a little bit. "I don't have a boyfriend either," she said.

Keith reached across the middle couch cushion and took Lindsay's hand in his. She had absolutely no complaints, and in fact, she ducked her head and smiled over to him. He stroked his thumb along the outside of hers, and nothing had ever felt so good.

"Is this going to be a problem for you?" he asked, his chin down and his eyes somewhere on the floor.

"No," she whispered.

He looked over to her, something bright and eager in his expression now. Of course, he had his back to the lanterns, so Lindsay couldn't be entirely sure. "What about for your brother?"

Lindsay's mind blanked, and her shy yet giddy smile slipped right from her face.

Keith slipped his hand away and tucked it back into his blankets. "So maybe a problem for Derrick," he said. "You know he's my cabinmate?"

"I didn't know that, no." Lindsay refrained from clearing her throat. She did swallow a couple of times, but she too had drunk all of her hot chocolate and had nowhere to turn for a distraction.

"What about your uncle?" Keith asked. "He's my boss." He looked at her again, his eyes deep and searching.

Lindsay wished she had an answer for him. "I've never dated anyone who worked for him, so I don't know."

"He has a lot of cowboys out there. You've never been out with a single one?"

Lindsay didn't know how to tell him about everything that had happened in Texas. She wouldn't do that on the first date with someone, but she wasn't sure how many hours counted as a date. She couldn't necessarily get away from Keith, and spending time with him constantly, working together to stay warm and stay fed and stay safe—that counted as multiple dates, didn't it?

"No," Lindsay said, swallowing the story that had been partly responsible for driving her from Texas. "I haven't dated much since I moved here."

"Five years ago, right?"

She nodded and looked at her hand and how empty it was without Keith's in it. "Yeah, five years."

"Lindsay?" Sabrina asked, interrupting them. "Can we play cards now?"

"Of course, sweetie." Lindsay pushed herself to the front of the couch cushion and started to stand. She wasn't sure if it was the sudden rush of heat hitting her in the face from the fireplace, or standing up too quickly, or all that pasta and then hot chocolate in her belly, or the way the lantern light and firelight seemed to make the shadows dance and move, but the room spun.

Lindsay groaned, and her head felt too heavy and too light at the same time. Then Keith stood right beside her, the tall length of his body pressing against hers. "Hey, hey, hey," he said, and she could just imagine him talking to a horse like that.

Hamlet perked up, a whine sounding in his throat, but Lindsay closed her eyes against the kaleidoscope of shadows and lights. She gripped Keith's forearm, glad he had both arms around her so she wouldn't fall.

It felt like a minute, but had to be only a few seconds, before she regained her equilibrium. She opened her eyes and looked up at Keith, who watched her with sharp concentration and concern.

Concern.

Only Derrick and her aunt and uncle had looked at her like that lately. Okay, some of her neighbors too—the very ones who'd come to help with Keith this evening. For some reason, Keith's concern carried more weight. It meant more to her.

"I'm okay," she said as she stepped back. Keith did the same, his hands and arms falling away from her body. "I just stood up too fast."

"She takes pills," Sabrina said, and Lindsay whipped her attention to the girl.

"Pills?" Keith asked. "For what?" His hooked gaze came right back to hers, and Lindsay didn't like this concern so much.

"It's nothing," she said. "I think we're sitting really close to the fire, and I just got up too fast." She dropped to the floor, where they'd made a nest of sleeping bags, pillows, and blankets. Beneath that, on the carpet, sat a camping pad, and this was Keith's bed.

"Can we play cards in your sleeping spot?" Lindsay looked up at him, half expecting the cowboy to turn back into the barky, grumpy, demanding man he'd been when he'd first awakened.

He did frown in such a way as to convince her that he could go that route. At the same time, she'd heard him laugh, and she'd seen him loosen up, and she wanted to spend many more hours talking to him and getting to know him.

She wanted to tell him about Porter, and why she'd married him, and why she'd left Texas the following week. Surely Keith would have questions about why her last name and Derrick's—and Uncle Jack's—weren't the same. He didn't seem like the type to simply let things go, and Lindsay found herself wanting to tell him things she'd never told anyone before.

"Keith," Sabrina said, and they both looked up to where he still sat on the couch. "Are you going to play?"

"Yeah, all right." His face softened, and he too scooted to the edge of the couch. Then he dropped right off of it, his long legs taking up the whole span of space between the front of the couch and the hearth.

He crossed them and smiled first at Sabrina in the friendliest of ways. When he swung his attention to Lindsay, pure male energy filled his gaze, and dang if it didn't drive right into her lungs and make her gasp.

She knew in that moment that she wanted to walk a long road with Keith Whettstein. Perhaps her slower-paced hobby farm would be good for him too. Perhaps they could build a life together that she hadn't been able to do with anyone else, despite her best efforts.

Perhaps he could be her Cowboy Charming, swooping in to save her from buying another horse simply to feel like she had control of her life.

Lindsay reached over and slipped her fingers between his. "We'll have to figure out how Derrick and Uncle Jack will react to this," she murmured. "Okay?"

Keith nodded slowly while Sabrina said, "All right, so I learned this game from my brother, and his games don't always work out." She spoke in an even, chill tone, and Lindsay loved her so much.

No, she hadn't expected to have the girl with her overnight. But she hadn't expected Keith to show up so late in the day, then slip, fall, and pass out either.

Lord, if You orchestrated this.... Lindsay thought. *Thank You.*

Now, she just had to see where this road would lead.

CHAPTER
Seven

KEITH FINISHED STOKING the fire and adding more wood to it. The card games had ended an hour ago, and Sabrina had crawled onto the love seat, snuggled down into the pillows she'd been given, and Lindsay had tucked her tightly with a big, fluffy blanket.

The girl had promptly gone to sleep, and he'd moved back to the couch. Sitting on the floor wasn't ideal for his long legs, as he couldn't even stretch them out all the way. He and Lindsay had been talking in muted whispers for the past hour, and she'd just gone to the bathroom.

He glanced over to the makeshift door, didn't see her, and quickly stripped out of the snow pants. He laid them against the hearth, in a tiny space between his bed of blankets and bags, and then slid under the covers.

He'd just turned his jeans, and he'd hopefully have his dignity back in the morning. For tonight, he could sleep in his boxers and all these blankets.

"Should I turn off this last lantern?" Lindsay asked, and the sound of her sweet voice made his blood pump a little harder.

"Yeah," he said. "I think we're done, and the fire's putting off plenty of light if someone needs to get up and use the bathroom."

In the next moment, a click sounded, and the white light from the last lantern extinguished. Only the cheery yellow-orange light from the fire played through the room now, and Keith closed his eyes as Lindsay went around the end of the couch and then climbed onto it. She sighed and groaned, shuffled and moved and played with her blankets to get them in the exact right spot for what felt like a long time.

He smiled to himself but said nothing. She finally settled down, and with the warmth, and the softness beneath him, and the silence only being punctuated by a few crackles and pops, Keith should've been able to fall asleep pretty quickly.

He'd put in a full day of work before coming here, and it had been a busy and eventful evening. It wasn't too terribly late yet, though, because the storm and winter combined only made it seem like midnight when it was really only nine p.m.

Keith wasn't sure how long he laid there, his mind lazily moving through topics—most of which revolve around how to ask Lindsay to be his date to Britt's wedding, and if it would throw Gloria's plans off, and who he'd be kicking off the family table if he did—before Lindsay said, "Are you still awake?"

"Mm, yes," he said, his voice deeper than usual.

"What are you thinking about?"

"How to talk to my step-mom about having a plus-one at Britt's wedding." He might as well be truthful. Things had never gone super well for Keith when he wasn't honest, and he didn't want to try to think of something else he could've been thinking about.

"For me?"

"Yeah," Keith murmured. "If you want. Would you want to go to Britt's wedding with me?"

"You hadn't asked anyone else?"

"No, ma'am."

"It's in three days."

"Yeah, so I don't know if it'll work out." He turned toward the couch and opened his eyes, but all he could see was brown leather. Lindsay obviously lay up there somewhere, but he hadn't seen if she'd laid her head down on this end of the couch the way he had, or if her feet were above him. "I'm going to ask her in the morning. Just to see. If you want to go with me."

"I do," she whispered, and that only made Keith's smile widen. He felt like a jack-o-lantern, all toothy smiles and wide eyes and flickering firelight.

"Will you be my date for the Christmas dinner at Blackhorse?"

"You haven't asked anyone?" he asked her this time, feeling more flirty than he had in a long, long time.

"Obviously," she said with a light whisper-giggle.

"If you still want to go with me when Christmas gets here, then sure," he said.

"Why wouldn't I want to?"

"I don't know," he said. "But one thing I learned from my daddy and my uncle and some of the other cowboys I've known for ages is that things might be going really well between us, and then they might not be. You might not like me outside of your house, when the snow isn't forcing us to talk and play cards."

"I'm pretty sure I will."

"So I'll go with you," he said. "If we're still getting along next week."

"Okay," she said. "Do you normally not get along with the women you go out with?"

"I wouldn't say that," he said. "It's more like...there's no click. If that makes sense."

"It does." She took a breath loud enough for him to hear, and then she asked, "Have you ever been married, Keith?"

"No, ma'am," he whispered. "You?"

"Yes," she said. "For less than a month. We got it annulled, because I left Texas, and he didn't want to come with me."

Wow, streamed through his mind. She'd just left her husband behind? And a husband of less than a month. "Why'd you leave, then?" He tried to ask as gently as he could, but all traces of sleepiness had fled.

"I had to get away from my daddy," she whispered. "There was this whole thing with another man my mom and dad had arranged for me to marry, and I couldn't do that either. So I married Porter—he was the first guy I met when I left my daddy's house for the last time."

"Wow," Keith said out loud. "That's...." He didn't know what to say it was. He didn't want to judge Lindsay, as he'd had no idea people still did arranged marriages. "You said you're from Texas?"

"This little town," she said. "It's called Center. As you can imagine, it's right in the center of Texas. My daddy wanted this ranch, and he'd negotiated my marriage with the Freemans when I was six years old. The only way out was by marrying someone else. So that's what I did." She sounded so sad, and

Keith couldn't even imagine what she might've been through in the past five years.

Keith's thoughts blitzed and then blanked. Since he didn't know what to say, he simply pulled one arm out of the blankets and reached for the couch. He put his hand there, and only a moment later, Lindsay's fingers snaked through his.

"I'm sorry," he whispered.

"I don't want to talk about it anymore tonight," she said.

"No problem." They fell into silence again, and Keith's mind slowed and slowed and slowed, and he fell asleep with the gorgeous Lindsay Lewis's hand secured in his, happier and more at peace than he'd been in a long time.

———

KEITH WOKE and sat straight up in the same moment. His brain moved, and he'd definitely heard something loud and bangy. "Wood," he said out loud in a normal voice. "Someone's in the house."

"It's just me," Lindsay said, her voice higher-pitched than normal.

Keith looked to his right, and sure enough, Lindsay stood only a foot from him. She once again dropped the log in her hand, making the same woody, echoing sound that had awakened him.

"Hey, I can do it." Pure regret pulled through him. He kicked off his blankets, instantly feeling the chill in the air. The extreme chill. Then he noticed the lack of light.

The fire had gone out completely.

"I'm so sorry," he said. "I honestly didn't think I'd sleep very well." He hadn't brought up a fire-tending schedule, and he quickly took the log from Lindsay's shivering and shaking hand. "Go get back under the covers."

His shoulders shook within seconds, but he got the doors open and the fire stoked. He fed it bits of kindling instead of the bigger log Lindsay had been about to plunk down into the coals. It didn't take long, because the fireplace still held plenty of heat and some glowing coals, and the flames came licking back to life.

Keith's chest warmed, but his legs and back still ached with cold. His teeth chattered as he layered on the last of the bigger logs and closed the doors. The fan had been blowing the hot air through their space, but it had obviously been out for a couple of hours now.

"What time is it?" he asked as he turned to face Lindsay. She lay on the couch, the blankets pulled up to her chin, her eyes open as she watched him.

"Four," she said, still shaking. "Or so. I don't know." Her eyes closed in a long blink, and Keith wasn't sure what that meant.

Keith ran his hands up and down his arms, trying to make a decision. If he ran to the bathroom now, he could get warm and go back to sleep for a few hours. "I'll be right back."

He hurried around the couch, every step plunging him into even icier temperatures. That became the coldest trip to the bathroom he'd ever encountered, and as he pulled the plywood back into place, he said, "Can I climb onto the couch with you for just a minute?"

He jogged toward the furniture and around it. "Just for a minute. When we're both warm, I'll slide back to the floor."

Lindsay pulled back her covers, and Keith stooped to grab his. He then slid onto the couch behind Lindsay, the two of them both lying on their sides. He jammed his blanket down behind his back and kicked slightly to get it to cover his legs.

"Here you go," he murmured, tucking his blanket over her too, using his hand to get it between her and the couch. "Now yours." He picked up her blanket and layered it over them, some semblance of warmth starting to come back into his body.

"My feet are freezing." His voice could barely be heard above the merry fire, and he curved his legs to put his feet on hers. "Oh, yours are too."

"We'll get warm," she said as Keith slid his arm under both blankets—and over Lindsay. She wrapped her arms around his and rubbed one hand up and down his forearm. "I hope the power comes on soon."

"If it doesn't, we should see if there's somewhere else we can go," he said. "Maybe even sleeping in the barn would be better than here." He remembered it being warm out there. He thought so, at least. Right now, his mind fuzzed with cold and exhaustion. "Sorry I fell asleep so soundly. I must've been tired."

"I wouldn't have woken up, except Sabrina had to go to the bathroom." Lindsay pressed right back into him as he moved his face to the warmer hollow of her neck. She had a blanket there, but it was still warmer than where his head had been. "I got up to help her, because it was so dark. I should've realized it was so dark because the fire was dying." She trembled in his arms, and Keith wanted to pull her close and keep her safe and warm. In that moment, he realized he wore very little clothing, but Lindsay hadn't said anything.

She wore long-sleeved and long pants pajamas, and perhaps she didn't know he only wore his underwear. "The fire was still sort of going when we got back. I laid down, thinking I'd just get warm real quick, and then I could get up and get the fire blazing again. But nope."

"Sabrina's okay?"

"I'm sorry, Keith," Lindsay said, and she still shook way too much for his liking. "I shouldn't have laid back down. I didn't fall asleep, but it just got colder and colder."

"Hey, it's fine." He squeezed her arms between his and her body. "It's already warming up, and we're okay."

"My neighbors usually come dig me out in the winter," she said. "I do have an ATV with a plow on the front, but I don't know how effective it will be against so much snow."

She didn't seem to be listening to him, and Keith said, "It's okay. We'll call my dad—"

"Where would we go if they can't get the power on?" She twisted slightly, now almost lying on her back, and looked at him.

Keith couldn't really meet her gaze, so he kept his eyes on the fire still roaring in front of them. He breathed, just trying to get through this moment, which was something his father had taught him. He made it through that breath, and then another.

As he opened his mouth, the fan started to blow, which mean the fire had reached a hot temperature really quickly. The room would be warm enough soon enough.

"Lindsay," he said huskily, his mouth right at her ear. "We're okay. The fire is blazing, and I won't let it go out again. We're okay."

She nodded. "Okay."

"Take a breath with me."

She did, and that further slowed Keith's adrenaline. "Sabrina's okay?"

"She crawled back into her blankets and went back to sleep."

She turned again, and now she faced him. She wrapped her arms around him, pulling his blanket further down behind his back. Her fingers touched his bare skin, but she said nothing about it.

"I'll call my daddy in the morning," he said. "Find out who has power where. He can help get us out if we need it."

"Uncle Jack probably could too."

"Right," Keith said. "So we just have to make it a few more hours, and I'm getting warmer already."

"Me too."

"Okay." He exhaled. "So you go back to sleep. I'll keep the fire going." That meant he'd have to make a trip through the freezing utility room and outside to bring in more wood, but as Keith held Lindsay and thought of Sabrina on the love seat only a few feet away, he'd do it.

He'd do whatever it took to keep them safe and warm.

And then he'd call his father in the morning.

CHAPTER
Eight

LINDSAY KNEW the moment Keith slinked away from her. She kept her eyes closed as he tucked her back in, the blankets taking his spot between her and the back of the couch. It wasn't nearly as warm as his body, but she wasn't going to complain.

He moved about, and it took her a moment to realize he was getting dressed. She did open her eyes then, and a pale gray light accompanied the fire. "Hey," she said.

"We need more wood," he whispered. "Just stay there. I'll be back in five minutes." With that, he nodded, a fierce look of determination shining on his face in the pre-dawn light, and left the living room through the arched doorway that led into the kitchen.

Lindsay wasn't sure what time it was, nor how long Keith had been gone before he returned with the wood bag full of logs. He stacked it all, put on another piece, and got the fire roaring again. Then he took the bag and left again without a word.

Back and forth he went, bringing in load after load of wood, until the floor between the hearth and the wall held a three-foot-stack of wood, and the hearth bore as much as it could too.

Then he whispered, "I'm going to go make coffee. Stay here as long as you want." He leaned his weight into one hand against her shoulder and brushed his lips along her temple before he was gone again.

Lindsay had wanted to hear words like that for as long as she could remember. She closed her eyes, nowhere near falling back asleep and let his touch burn through her. She let his words sink into her ears.

They said things like, *I'll take care of you, Lindsay. Just relax, sweetheart, and I'll make sure everything is okay.*

She smiled softly, the real words he'd said coursing through her. *Stay here as long as you want.*

No one had ever told her that before, and his simple swipe of his lips against her skin made her shiver despite the warmth in the room.

Lindsay wouldn't really be able to stay there as long as she wanted, but she did huddle under the blankets and let her eyes rest while the room continued to brighten. All at once, she realized—"The sun."

If the room was getting brighter, the sun had to be out.

That got her to fling the covers back and swing her legs over the side of the couch. She'd thought to bring clothes into the living room from her bedroom so they'd be warm, and she kept her eye on the sheet of plywood immediately beside her as she changed quickly.

Then she grabbed her phone, which she'd turned off to preserve the power, and she pressed the button to get it to come back to life. She cast a glance to Sabrina, who still snoozed in her nest of blankets, only her nose and eyes showing. She'd even wrapped a blanket up over her head, and a pinch of love filled Lindsay's heart for the girl.

A round of relief pounded through her next, because she'd kept her alive through the long, cold night. She had to get Sabrina home today, and while she didn't want Keith to depart too, if he had to, he had to.

Lindsay decided right then and there she wouldn't stay here again if she didn't have power. She didn't have to, and if Keith and Sabrina could get off this farm and somewhere safer and warmer, so could she.

Her worries immediately reared up over her animals, but she told herself she could make the drive from a heated hotel room to the barn at any hour of the morning to feed her horses and chickens.

"If they're not frozen," she muttered as she turned away from Sabrina and slipped into the kitchen. It wasn't as light here, and wow, the cold bit at her nose and fingertips. She pulled the sleeves of her sweatshirt down to cover her hands more completely, and she found the coffee dripping into the pot, but no Keith loitering around waiting for it.

There was enough to pour into an insulated mug that she then took out onto the farm to start her morning, so she did that with two of those cups, stirred sugar into both, and called it good. After all, she had no idea how Keith took his coffee.

Something she probably should've asked him last night. They'd talked about plenty, though, and Lindsay still couldn't believe she'd told him about Porter Lewis or the arranged marriage.

She figured she'd find Keith in the barn, so she went that way. Sure enough, his footsteps in the snow had been made that morning, and she put her feet in them as closely as she could.

In the barn, she found her chickens clucking away happily, clearly already fed. One of her horses, a really pretty bay named Beatrice, blustered at her, and Lindsay smiled at the equine in return.

Keith's voice came from further down the aisle of horse stalls, and Lindsay went that way. She held up the insulated mug. "I didn't know how you took your coffee. It has sugar in it."

"Sugar is great." He smiled at her and took the mug. He took a sip of it, his eyes never leaving hers, and then he turned and set it on top of the wall separating two stalls. "As far as I can tell, everyone out here is accounted for and perfectly happy."

"It's not snowing right now."

"No," Keith said as he focused on the horse in front of him again. "But my dad says another storm is expected by lunchtime."

"Maybe we can get out of here before then," she said.

"It's only supposed to snow for a couple of hours." He twisted and grabbed another section of hay for Shadow. "So, I don't know."

"Do they have power?"

"He's in town, in Ivory Peaks," he said, feeding the horse and then moving to the next one. "They didn't lose power."

"So we can go there." Lindsay watched him, not quite sure how to tell him she'd rather stay with him than be separated— even if the power did come back on.

Keith finally stopped working and looked at her. "If we can get out of here, and if the power isn't back on, then we could go to my parents' house, yes," he said. "But I probably won't do that. Blackhorse has power too. I'll just go home."

Lindsay nodded, her voice stuck somewhere in her throat. Even a hot sip of coffee didn't dislodge it. She backed up a step and then turned and went back into the bigger part of the barn, leaving him alone to do his feeding. The barn had stayed toasty warm, but Lindsay suspected the generator currently ran on empty.

She'd need to refill that before tonight, especially if this second storm kept the power lines down. Keith came up behind her, and Lindsay realized she'd been staring into her momma pig's pen. "Are you okay?" he asked.

Lindsay felt like she'd been dunked in ice water and could barely move. She turned toward him so slowly as she said, "Would you—would you pray with me?"

The hard lines of his face dissolved into nothing, and he leaned the pitchfork against the wall. "Of course," he said quietly. He faced her fully and folded his arms. "Did you want to say it?"

Lindsay felt like she needed to, but her voice had suddenly gone on vacation. Somewhere tropical and seabreezy, where she didn't have to worry about being cold, alone, and in the dark.

She managed to close her eyes, and her fists closed around each other too. "Lord," she whispered. "I'm afraid, and I hate feeling afraid." She drew in a breath, the way Keith had coached her earlier that morning. Unfortunately, without his arms around her and the steadiness of his inhale behind her, it didn't help to calm her much.

"I can't stay on this farm if there's no power. I can't leave my animals. I know Thou can control the wind and the rain. I know Thou can calm raging seas and allow men to walk on water. I don't need any of those great miracles, but I need something." Her voice trembled, but she went on. She'd poured her heart out to God in the past, and He'd never let her down.

She tamed the emotional shiver in her voice and said, "Please bless me with the strength to refill the generator for my animals. Please bless me to get Sabrina home safe and sound. Please bless me and Keith to find more reasonable shelter. If the power cannot be restored, please guide us all off of Twilight Fields safely."

Her eyes fluttered open, and she found Keith watching her. "Amen," he said.

Lindsay nodded and murmured, "Amen."

They stood in the barn together, and Lindsay couldn't find the words. "Hey." Keith hauled her into his chest. "I'm not going to leave you here alone, okay?"

Lindsay wrapped her arms around him and held on with all her might. "Okay." She gave herself a couple of seconds of emotional shakiness, and then she pulled away and drew everything tight in her chest. "I'm going to get my paths cleared before it snows again." She touched her phone in her back pocket. "And I've got to get Sabrina home, so I'm going to call her mom once it's a more socially acceptable hour."

"I'll help with the paths and sidewalks," Keith said. "We'll make a feast for breakfast." He gave her a bright smile that still spoke of worrying things. "We made it through the worst night, I think."

"I guess we'll see," Lindsay said. She'd lived through some intense storms in her few years here, and that meant Keith had too. "Let's get to work."

Work, she understood. Work, she knew. She loved work that showed progress, so after an hour of moving heavy, wet snow, she could get from her back door to her barn without having to bully her way through snowbanks.

She could see it, see the effort, see the way she'd tamed Mother Nature this time. Inside, she peeled off her hat and scarf, both of which were wet with sweat and some snow that had fallen from tree branches and overhanging roofs.

"Sabrina," she called as she went into the kitchen. Keith had taken the ATV to try to do the lane, and while Lindsay had given him her blessing and had been silently cheering him on, she wasn't surprised to find him in the living room with Sabrina.

"The ATV couldn't do much," he said. "I got your front sidewalk cleaned up, and then Sabrina and I have been folding up everything in here." He gave Sabrina a smile, and the girl smiled back.

He finished with his blanket and said, "I checked the power company website again. They're still saying ten o'clock."

"Lindsay, I'm going to call my mom," Sabrina said.

With her attention divided, Lindsay simply nodded. "Okay," she said. "I'm going to call the Grangers and ask about their tractor." Max almost always came over to dig her out, but when she swiped on her phone, she saw the clock had barely ticked to eight.

She wasn't going to call Max this early. He had a good twenty years on her, and he'd need to get his own roads and farm cleaned up first. So she shoved her phone in her back pocket and lifted her head.

Trying to be positive, she said, "I'll get started on breakfast." She turned away before either of them could see the despair in her eyes. Lindsay wasn't even sure why she felt so shaky. She'd had a few minutes there in the early morning hours where she'd been frozen to the core. She'd warmed quickly with Keith's body behind hers, and everything had turned out fine.

"Shouldn't I be happy to see the sun?" she grumbled to herself. She *was* happy to see the sun. She just wished another storm wasn't on its way over the Rockies, and she wished the power would come back on.

As if summoned by her sheer will, as she stood in front of the fridge, reaching for the carton of eggs, everything in the kitchen started to click and hum and beep.

Keith whooped in the other room, and he came striding into the kitchen after her. "Power's on," he said, as if she didn't know.

Lindsay smiled, and it felt like the first real one since last night, when she'd seen Keith's truck rumbling down her dirt lane, his horse trailer attached.

―――――

A COUPLE OF HOURS LATER, they'd all been properly fed, the furnace still pumped, and Sabrina had just shouldered her backpack. Lindsay put her arm around her and said, "She should be here any minute."

"I hate the snowmobile," Sabrina said crossly.

"It's just to get out to the road," Lindsay said. "Five minutes, tops." She moved in front of Sabrina and took her by the shoulders. "Honey, if you act grumpy today, your momma won't let you come out to the farm with me anymore."

"I know." But Sabrina did not lighten up. She could be punishing when she got something stuck in her head that she couldn't let go of.

"Promise me you'll be nice to her," Lindsay said. "Thank her for letting you come. Take a nap today if you need to." School had already gotten out for the holidays, and Sabrina certainly didn't have animals to care for, and buildings to check on, and a neighbor to wait on to get her road cleared.

"She's here," Keith said from the front windows, and he turned toward both of them. "It sure was nice meeting you, Sabrina." He smiled with such genuineness that Lindsay felt it in her bones. "If I don't see you again, have a Merry Christmas."

"You too, Keith," Sabrina said, and Lindsay gave him a quick smile as she passed. Then she shrugged into her coat and went outside with Sabrina.

Angela, her mom, was just getting off the snowmobile, and when she turned to the house, she wore plain anxiety on her face. "Bri," she said as she sank into the snow.

"Just stay there," Lindsay said as they went down the steps. She had a three-foot high wall that curved along with her side-walk, but it had been completely buried in the snow.

"Are you okay?" Angela asked as she continued to wade through the snow until she could hop down to the cleared cement.

"I'm okay," Sabrina said. Angela took her daughter into her arms and hugged her, her smile painted on with love and relief. Lindsay hung back a few steps, and when Angela released Sabrina, Lindsay moved into her embrace.

"I kept her alive," she said. "We ate plenty last night and this morning. She seemed to sleep okay, but she was on a love seat all night." She pulled away. "She might need a nap today."

Angela nodded, her smile strong now. "Thank you, Lindsay."

"No, thank you for letting me have her." She hugged Sabrina

again. "Be good for your momma and daddy," she said. "And Merry Christmas if I don't see you again."

Sabrina hugged her back and then started climbing up the snowbank to get to the snowmobile. Angela turned to Lindsay. "They've got your road pretty socked in," she said. "Snow ten feet high on either side of the highway."

"I'm sure," Lindsay said, though the news only fired up her nerves again. "Max will come dig me out, don't worry." She just needed to call him. But she stood on the sidewalk and waved to Angela and Sabrina, her fake flight attendant smile on her face as she did.

When she returned to the house, Keith stood at the windows still, and he opened his arm and drew her into his side. His warm, strong side, where Lindsay didn't have to have all the answers.

"What do you want me to do?" he asked her.

Lindsay took a breath, and then she committed herself to her feelings. "I don't want to be here alone."

"All right," he said without missing a beat. "Then I'll stay until tomorrow."

CHAPTER
Nine

KEITH WISHED there was a way to bottle heat to use later. The power hummed along nicely now, and he and Lindsay had decided to keep the house as shut down as possible. He couldn't do anything about the high ceilings, but they'd committed to only using the living room and the kitchen.

Of course, the furnace still heated the bedrooms and bathrooms down the hall, so he didn't freeze to death when he had to relieve himself. But he really wished he could box up the heat in the bathroom to use later if the power did fail again.

"Here it comes," Keith said about midday. He wasn't hungry in the slightest, as he'd been sitting around for hours now. Lindsay had pulled a jigsaw puzzle out of a closet somewhere, and he'd found the slower, quieter morning to be absolutely wonderful.

He would've never done anything like this at the cabin had he been snowed in with the three men he lived with. But with Lindsay, it felt just right.

She looked up from trying to find a spot for the puzzle piece in her hand, the first drops of rain splattering against the window behind her. She met Keith's eye, and then turned to look outside. As they watched, the rain turned to slushy snow, and then snowflakes.

"Doesn't look as wet," she said. "Maybe the lines will hold."

Her neighbor had not come to dig her out with his tractor yet, and while Keith wasn't enormously worried yet, he would be tomorrow. He had to get back to Blackhorse Bay tomorrow, no matter what. He'd like a different pair of clothes, for one. And for another, he had to get a bag packed and everything he needed for the wedding over to his parents' house for tomorrow evening's pre-wedding family dinner.

Just him and his family—his daddy, step-mom, Britt, and their two younger half-siblings. Then Uncle Boone and Aunt Cosette were coming over with their two kids. And his cousin Gerty and her husband Mike were coming. Keith absolutely could not miss it. He *would not*.

He'd told Lindsay about his family that morning, while they built the border on the puzzle and sorted pieces into color camps. She'd told him she had just the one brother—Derrick—and Keith's nerves bubbled at him again.

He had no idea how Derrick would react to Keith's budding romance with his sister. Derrick was Keith's best friend at Black-horse Bay, and he'd known Keith was looking to date. He had not mentioned Lindsay. Not one time.

Keith could put together dots fairly well, and he simply wasn't sure how Derrick would react to Keith and Lindsay.

"We'll see how long it lasts," he said. "It feels like the wind is really scattering it around."

"A little." Lindsay faced him again, and she reminded him of slower, softer times. A lazy summer evening, where they could lay in each other's arms and watch afternoon clouds roll through the sky. A peaceful Sabbath Day, where they could sit on the back porch while dinner bubbled away in the slow cooker. A soft place to call home.

Keith honestly had no idea where these feelings came from. He'd never had them before, for anyone. "My mom used to love to do puzzles," he said, even more unsure of where those words had come from.

"Yeah?" Lindsay asked. "Did she pass away?" She watched him with open innocence in her pretty more-green-than-brown hazel eyes.

"No." Keith's jaw tightened for a moment, but he'd opened this can of worms. "I didn't mean for it to sound like she's passed." He found the piece he needed and picked it up. "She was an alcoholic." He abandoned his quest to put the puzzle together. "My daddy put her in a rehab program the summer we moved here. I haven't seen her or spoken to her since."

Lindsay's face grew sad, and she nodded. "I've been there. I mean, not for what? Twenty years? But for a year or two there, my daddy wouldn't speak to me. My momma still does, but she doesn't understand why I had to leave Texas."

Keith looked at the array of pieces in front of him. He suddenly felt like he was trying to put together the puzzle of his life. "Why did you have to leave Texas?" He lifted his gaze to Lindsay. "You don't have to tell me if you don't want to."

She sat down on the chair behind her, a sigh slipping out as she did. "It's hard to explain, but really, I just needed a fresh start. I think it can be as simple as that." She pulled her hands back and started rotating her wrists, as if stretching them.

"I think my daddy felt like that," Keith said. "Heck, I did

when I left the Hammond Family Farm. I just needed something different."

"Derrick was coming here to work for Uncle Jack, and that felt safe to me," Lindsay said. "I lived with my aunt and uncle for the first few months, while I looked for somewhere of my own. Then this place came up, and let me tell you, it wasn't in the shape it's in now."

"No?" Keith's eyebrows lifted, because he could just see Lindsay rolling up her sleeves and pouring her blood, sweat, and tears into this farm. And to think, he'd been scoffing at it on the way here with her horse.

"No," she said. "I bought it in foreclosure. No one had lived here for at least a year. Everything needed work. And luckily, I needed work to do. This place...it saved me." She looked around the house, and Keith wondered what she saw.

He saw a gorgeous woman with a big heart, strong hands, and a beautiful spirit, and he said, "Lindsay, I really like talking to you."

She seemed surprised for a moment, and then she ducked her head, that auburn hair falling over her shoulder and brushing the tabletop. "I like talking to you too."

His phone rang, and he saw his step-mom's name there. "Hey, I have to take this."

"Of course."

Keith turned away from the dining room table where he'd devoured dinner last night and moved into the living room. "Hey, Gloria," he said.

"Your father has just told me that you're thinking of bringing someone to Britt's wedding?"

"I mean, maybe," Keith said, his face growing hot for some reason. "I just met her, and I don't know. I like her."

"Is this or is this not the same woman you're currently staying with?"

"Don't make it sound scandalous," Daddy said, and Keith realized he was on speaker-phone with both of them.

"I think it's fine," Britt said.

Make that all three of them. Humiliation pulled through Keith. "I just mentioned it," he said. "I understand we have catering in place, and seating arrangements, and—"

"I think he should bring her if he wants to," Britt said, and she spoke as forcefully as Keith had ever heard her. "He wouldn't ask if he didn't want to bring her."

"It's one more place, Gloria-baby," Dad said, and that made Keith smile.

Not much riled up Gloria, but she'd been working hard on Britt's wedding with her. She normally rolled with the ups and downs of life, but maybe this was just too big of a curveball for her.

"Her name is Lindsay," Keith said. "Yes, I met her last night after slipping and falling and passing out while delivering her horse."

"You what?" Dad asked.

"Shh," Britt said. "Daddy, let him talk."

"We spent all night together, and yes, I slept here. I'm still here, and it's snowing again, and you know what? I don't have to be embarrassed for liking her. She's easy to talk to, and we've been getting to know each other."

"It feels a little fast," Gloria said. "That's all."

"I've spent the past twenty hours with her. Straight through," Keith said, watching the snow fall through the front windows. "It's like ten dates' worth of conversation. We've had three meals together. She's seen me in my boxer shorts twice now, and I've been wearing women's snow pants around her. I think we've reached the point where I can bring her to a wedding. Heck, at this point, it'll be the least embarrassing thing that's happened."

Silence rained down on him from the other end of the line, and it was a rare occasion indeed when Keith said enough to stupefy anyone. Especially his father.

"You're not going to miss dinner tomorrow, are you?" Britt asked.

"No." Keith hung his head. "Absolutely not, Britt. I'll be there, and we're staying in your cabin together one last time. That's still on, right? The farm is plowed?"

"The farm is plowed," Dad said. He cleared his throat. "Keith, bring Lindsay to the wedding. There will be a place for her at the family table, no problem."

"Yes," Gloria said quickly. "I didn't mean to say anything against it, Keith."

"I know," he whispered. "Now, can I get back to my date? We're putting together a puzzle and talking about how many babies we're going to have."

Gloria sucked in a breath, but Dad started laughing. Keith grinned too, catching part of his reflection in the glass.

"Love you, Keith," started chorusing through the line, and Keith said, "I love you guys. I'll see you tomorrow," before he hung up.

He turned to go back into the dining room-kitchen combo, but he paused in the archway when he heard Lindsay talking. "...he's a nice guy. That's what I'm saying."

"Uncle Jack and I will come get you out tomorrow." The voice on the line definitely belonged to Derrick. Keith swallowed, wondering what else Lindsay had said about him. "He could've left today."

"I didn't want to be here alone," Lindsay said. "I'm pretty sure we would've frozen to death without Keith last night."

Not true, but Keith still didn't move. He knew he should, because what kind of man loitered in archways, eavesdropping?

"He's been really helpful," Lindsay said next. "He can cook, and—"

"Yeah, helpful," Derrick said with a level of sarcasm Keith would've been able to hear from anywhere. "I'm sure he has been."

"Hey," Lindsay said sharply. "He's not like that. And besides, I can take care of myself."

"Can you? You just said you didn't want to be alone tonight, and now you've got my cabinmate staying with you."

"Are you jealous?" Lindsay asked with a light laugh.

"Linds," Derrick said. "I'm just not sure it's smart to start something with him."

"Why not?" she asked, the question echoing through Keith's mind. He really didn't want to hear who he thought was a friend disparage him, so he found the strength to push away from the wall and enter the dining room.

"I don't have a problem with it," Derrick said as Lindsay looked up. She froze, her eyes wide, her brother still talking. "Keith's a great guy. But sissy, you know Uncle Jack won't like it."

Silence filled the house now, despite the appliances humming along. Keith sat down across from Lindsay, who startled and looked at her phone. "Why won't Uncle Jack like it? He's never been overly protective of me."

"You haven't dated seriously."

"Who says this is going to get serious?"

Keith's eyebrows went up, and he folded his arms. Lindsay actually grinned at him, but he wasn't sure what was so amusing.

"I know Keith," Derrick said, as if that said it all. Great, now his best friend was giving things away Keith would rather Lindsay not know yet. "The man doesn't do anything halfway."

It was actually a nice compliment, but Keith would like this conversation buttoned up. "Is there a policy against dating Lindsay?" he asked. "Like, through Blackhorse Bay?"

Derrick pulled in a breath, and he growled, "Lindsay?"

"He just walked in," she said. "I couldn't get you off speaker fast enough." She jabbed at the phone to do that, but the damage had been done. "And you know what? Keith is right. I don't work for Uncle Jack. He can't dictate who I see and who I don't."

She rolled her eyes, and after a few more seconds said, "Okay, Derrick. I have to go. I'll see you tomorrow." She hung up and tossed her phone back to the table with some level of disgust. It took another couple of beats before she'd raise her eyes to his, and oh, Keith didn't like the guilt he saw there.

"I didn't know he was going to call," she said. "And ask about you. Things sort of got out of hand."

"Did they?"

"You heard him."

"I heard him say I'm going to lose my job if I do what I want to do."

Lindsay searched his face like he held a great secret she simply must know. "And just what is it that you want to do?"

Keith swallowed, once again his honest streak rearing up. "You know what I want to do. I want to go out with you. I want to keep getting to know you. I want to see if we have a future together."

Lindsay shone like a penny, and he definitely wanted to pick her up and keep her close. "I want all of that too, Keith," she said. "Let me handle Uncle Jack." She got an almost predatory look in her eyes, and then she dropped her gaze to the puzzle. "Oh, I just found where this piece goes."

She fitted it in and beamed at him with all the wattage of the sun. Keith couldn't help smiling at her, and while he wasn't going to ask her about babies—yet—he did lean forward and say, "My step-mom is going to put you at the family table with me for Britt's wedding."

"That's great," Lindsay said with a smile. Keith reached over and took her hand in his, their eyes meeting again. Yes, he'd only met her yesterday. Yes, he'd been interested from the get-go. Yes, they'd spent a lot of time together, even if not a lot of time had passed.

Of course he didn't know if things between them would work out. Of course he didn't know what tomorrow would even bring. But of course, he wanted more time with her to date, to talk, to explore, to find out.

So for now, he prayed for more time with her, and he prayed that her uncle's heart would be softened, and he prayed that the power would stay on so they could have a more normal evening together.

CHAPTER
Ten

LINDSAY PUT two pounds of ground beef in the pan, the sizzle so satisfying. She cast a glance over to Keith, who peeled the onion she'd given him. When she'd told him she'd planned to make cottage pie for dinner tonight, he'd volunteered to help her make it now, for lunch.

His stomach growled, and Lindsay grinned. "This is going to take a while," she said. "I can feed you lunch."

"I saw some lunch meat in there," he said. "Sandwiches? I make a mean grilled ham and cheese."

"Promises, promises," she said, well aware of how much she'd been flirting with him.

"Well, I can promise you I'll chop off the tip of my pinky if I have to cut these onions."

"Okay." Lindsay practically shouted the word, and she snatched up the knife she'd laid beside the cutting board. "You don't get to use the knife."

He chuckled, and Lindsay kept waiting for the moment

she'd be annoyed he was here with her. She'd been alone while he'd showered once the hot water had come back, and during that time, she'd figured out that if each date was an average of three hours long, she and Keith would be on their seventh date with this meal prep.

Could she kiss him after the seventh date? Would he have waited this long if their dates had been spread out, with lots of texting in between?

They'd been talking a lot; it wasn't like they sat there in silence, watching the fire burn or sorting puzzle pieces. And now, she knew he could make a grilled cheese sandwich, but cutting onions was beyond his skillset.

She suspected Keith was exaggerating, because he seemed like the type of man who could do anything he put his mind and muscles to.

He'd moved over to the fridge, and he closed the door and held up the lunch meat. "You've got ham and turkey. Which do you want?"

"Ham," she said. "It's my favorite lunch meat."

He smiled at her and put the turkey back in the fridge. He moved around her kitchen easily, and though the snow flurried outside, the sun still provided enough natural light to see his strong jaw—now covered with even more of his beard—his dark eyes, and those, very full, kissable lips.

Lindsay tore her gaze away from him. "What's your favorite lunch meat?" she asked.

"Roast beef," he said. "With provolone and avocado. Mm hm."

She grinned too, because she liked learning about him. "I'm not sure I've ever had a roast beef sandwich."

"You're not serious," he said. "You're from Texas. Aren't you born with like, a roast beef sandwich in your hand?"

She laughed, the sound and happiness just bursting out of her. She didn't try to quiet down or hide who she was. It felt so good to just be herself with this cowboy, and she found him grinning twice as wide as he'd previously been.

"I don't think you know any Texans at all," she teased through the last of her laughter.

"Oh-ho," he said. "I've met plenty of Texans. They don't let a moment pass if they can say they're from the Lone Star State."

"I'm sensing some jealousy."

"I'm just saying that really good cowboys can be from anywhere," he said. "Florida, New Mexico, Colorado, Wyoming, Montana."

"How many of those states have you lived in?"

"Just Montana and Colorado," he said. "But your uncle has good hands, cowboy bosses, and horse trainers from all over."

"And you're the agricultural manager?" she asked as she broke up the ground beef into chunks. She picked up the salt-shaker and seasoned the meat liberally. Pepper followed, and Lindsay moved over to chop the onions.

"Yes," he said.

"And you like it?"

"I love it there," he said. "I've got good cabinmates, lots of people my own age, that sort of thing."

"So you live with Derrick, Buck, and Coy?"

"That's right," Keith said. "Is that going to be a problem?"

"Why would it be a problem?" Lindsay looked over to him to find him spreading butter on a slice of bread.

"Like, have you dated any of them? Not Derrick, obviously. But Buck or Coy?"

Lindsay scoff-laughed in a burst of sound. The house had

started to smell good, and she tipped the onions into the hot pan with the meat. "No," she said.

"You say that like they're not great guys," Keith said.

"Well, Buck is a little bit of a...." Lindsay didn't know how to say it nicely. "He likes the women," she said. "And I'm not into that type of man."

"He's calmed down a little bit," Keith said, his voice soft. "He started comin' to church with me after I moved in."

"Is that right?" Lindsay asked. "That's amazing."

"And Coy?"

"Coy's been with Rachel forever," she said.

"No," Keith said. "He doesn't have a girlfriend."

"Yeah, but he's been with Rachel forever," she said. "He'll get back together with her."

"I went out with a Rachel," Keith said. "Are you telling me she was his ex?"

"I don't know," Lindsay said. "Her last name is Vernal. Rachel Vernal." She held the wooden spoon as if she'd stir her browning ground beef, but she watched Keith instead.

He swallowed and reached for another piece of bread. "Yeah, that's her," he said darkly. Everything about him turned darker and more dangerous. And dang Lindsay's pulse, but it bounced with excitement. "I'm going to kill him."

Lindsay grinned and ducked her head. "He probably just wanted to know who she was goin' out with."

"It was a really awkward date," he said. "I thought it was me. She talked about him a lot. I'm so stupid."

Lindsay finished moving the beef and onions around and put the spoon down. She stepped over to Keith. "No, you're not." She put her hand over his, and he paused in the buttering.

"Coy's the one who's stupid. Who sets up their friend with their ex, just so he can control who she dates?"

Keith blinked at her, his growly expression softening oh-so-slowly. "I still feel stupid. I can see the little pieces adding up now, and I don't like being embarrassed."

"You don't know what you don't know," she said.

He nodded, and he turned his hand over to curl his fingers between hers. "Can you really go to the wedding with me? Like, do you have a dress to wear?"

"Does it need to be something specific?"

"Britt loves silver and pink and sparkly things," he said, his smile taking over his face again. Not as wide as before, and definitely belonging to the love he had for his sister. "She chose silver, navy blue, and pink for her wedding, but you can wear anything."

"What are you wearing?"

"A black suit," he said. "The family tie. Me and my dad have matching ones. My uncle too. Lars is wearing a tux, so we don't need to be more dressed up than him."

Lindsay moved over to the kitchen sink and flipped on the faucet to rinse the potatoes. Those had to be boiled and mashed to go over the cottage pie, and she should've started them first. Perhaps having Keith in the kitchen had thrown her off a little bit.

"You have three sisters?"

"Yes," Keith said. "Britt is my full sibling, and it was just me and her for a long time. I love Alma and Roxanne too, but I was almost an adult by the time they were born."

She nodded, though she wasn't sure Keith was looking at her. He put a pan on the stove next to hers, and the gas clicked a couple of times before it lit. He laid the bottom layer of bread in first, and then started putting on the cheese and meat.

"Britt is...special," he said. "My dad took her to the doctor tons when she was younger. She sometimes would trip over her own feet. She stuttered a lot. She didn't do well in school. That kind of thing."

"No wonder you were so good with Sabrina," Lindsay said, all the dots lining up for her now too.

"Does she have autism?" Keith asked.

Lindsay nodded. "Britt too?"

He shook his head and said, "Nah. But my mom drank while she was pregnant with her, and that affected her development. She's just—she's the best, brightest person you'll ever meet." He spoke with joy now and pure love. Lindsay loved seeing and hearing him come alive as he spoke of his sister. It meant he loved deep, and he was loyal and true to his family.

She liked that, though it did concern her slightly. Would he want to get mixed up with someone like her, who had so many fractures in her family tree?

"Everyone loves her, and she loves them."

"You love her," she said quickly.

"Yeah." He kept his head down, studying the grilled cheese sandwiches like he couldn't look away from them. "I've taken care of her for my whole life. I've always watched out for her. Always been there for her."

Lindsay heard the unspoken words—Keith was going to miss her. He felt like he'd been replaced by Lars, and he hadn't reconciled where he belonged in his sister's life. She wanted to pull him close and assure him that he'd always belong to his family. His sister would always need him.

"Well," she said. "I can't wait to meet her." She walked over to her pantry and pulled out the flour. She needed gravy to go with her beef and onions, and she measured out the flour and mixed it in with the beef fat.

She added a bag of frozen peas and carrots, then poured in a can of beef broth. Once that all came to a boil, she'd have her pie filling.

Now to get these potatoes done.

———

A HALF-HOUR LATER, the cottage pie baked in the oven, and Lindsay and Keith sat down at the dining room table she'd just covered with a festive Christmas print. The unfinished puzzle still waited for them to finish it, and Lindsay wondered if they ever would.

She hoped so, but she didn't say anything. Why couldn't she have Keith over to the farm to finish the puzzle? Maybe eat another meal with her? Under different circumstances, maybe he'd kiss her when he arrived, and when he left.

She really needed to stop thinking about kissing him.

"All right," he said as he slid her plate toward her. "Are you ready for this? Britt and I used to have a contest to see who could get the longest cheese pull." His face held such life now, and Lindsay marveled at how he moved from grumpy to gorgeously happy in only a few minutes.

"You better go first," she said. "So I can see what to do."

"All right." He picked up his sandwich, which he had toasted perfectly, and broke off the corner. "It's all about how far you can pull your cheese before it breaks."

He pulled slowly, his smile growing centimeter by

centimeter as his "cheese pull" lengthened too. It broke when it was about as long as his arm, and he laughed.

Lindsay liked the sound of his voice. The way he found happiness in simple things. The shape of his face, and the breadth of his shoulders. She liked *him*, and as he messily put the bite of grilled cheese sandwich in his mouth, the long trail of cheese hanging out, she laughed too.

He nodded to her, and Lindsay's heart skipped a couple of beats. She focused on her sandwich, the competitive side of her rearing up. "I hope I win," she said. "I feel like I have a disadvantage, because my arms aren't as long as yours."

He chuckled, got the last of the cheese in his mouth, and shook his head.

Lindsay picked up her sandwich and tore off the corner, just the way Keith had. She pulled slowly, but the bread wasn't exactly super grippy. The butter he'd crisped up coated her fingers, and though she tried, she couldn't hold on.

"Blustery flibbet," she said as her piece fell, her cheese pull shrinking before her eyes.

Keith practically shouted his laughter now, and Lindsay switched her frown from her broken-off bite of her lunch to his overjoyed face. "Blustery flibbet?" He wheezed with laughter, and Lindsay finally found the humor in her form of swearing.

"Daddy was ruthless about us using good language," she said. "Derrick and I came up with whatever we had to so we wouldn't get our mouths washed out with soap."

Keith finished laughing, and his gaze grew serious. "I'm sensing some history with your daddy," he said.

"We...we've been through some patches," she said. "Let's put it that way."

"Do you ever go back to Texas?"

Lindsay took a full bite of her ham and cheese sandwich, the bread crispy, and the cheese melty, and the ham salty. Pure perfection lived in her mouth, and she didn't care what Keith asked, though she didn't want to talk about her father. Or Texas.

So she just shook her head and moaned. "This is the best sandwich I've ever eaten."

Keith's whole face lit up then. Maybe his whole persona. His whole soul and spirit. "I'm glad," he said.

Lindsay had lived here at Twilight Fields alone for a handful of years now. She'd been lonely before, of course. She'd held parties here for friends and family. Her house had come alive then, and it had felt cold and empty afterward.

But nothing—absolutely nothing—had made her realize how alone and lonely she'd been until Keith. Until she'd had *him* in her house, in her life, in her space.

And she wanted to keep him.

Now, she just had to figure out how to do that, especially once he left and their normal lives resumed.

CHAPTER
Eleven

KEITH MOVED the hay bales to the big window in the barn, hefted up one of them, and tossed it down. The pile he'd been throwing over stayed about steady, though he definitely worked faster than Lindsay could take the bales into her barn.

He wanted to make sure she had everything ready for after he left, and he wasn't sure why. This wasn't his farm. But a good cowboy checked fences, filled their barn with hay, secured their livestock, and prepared for the winter storms that came.

Lindsay managed this place alone, and Keith needed to get out of the house this afternoon anyway. The snow had stopped. The sky still held only shades of gray and white, no blue in sight, but their shoveling job hadn't been for nothing.

"This is probably enough," Lindsay called up to him, and Keith poked his head out of the window. "I'm running out of room inside." She wore sunglasses to ward off the glinting light coming from the blinding snow, her hair hidden under a woolen cap, and a form-fitting coat that only reminded Keith of holding her on the couch last night.

He cleared his mind of such things and said, "All right. "I've got one more right here. I'll just throw it down and come help you load the barn."

"Thanks."

Keith did that, and when he joined Lindsay down below, her physical strength impressed him as much as her emotional and mental resiliency.

They still had half the hay to haul inside when the grumblings of a tractor met his ears. Lindsay whipped her head up and said, "That's got to be Max."

She abandoned the hay bale she held in her gloved hands and headed for the door. Keith kept his head down and put his bale away, then hers. When he went outside, a gentleman at least ten years older than Lindsay pulled a bright red tractor to a stop. He waved, killed the engine, and got down out of the cab.

"Howdy, Linds," he said, and Keith noted the nickname. That was definitely one thing he and Lindsay hadn't had an opportunity to do—spend time together in public. He might learn about her nicknames and her friends faster if he had.

"Max, you're a lifesaver. Derrick said he'd call this afternoon, once they had Blackhorse back together."

"Yeah, I know you've got help if you need it," he said, his eyes wandering to where Keith stood on the concrete pad. "But I was out. Did the Maughans and the Yorkmans. You're next after them."

"So it's clear all the way to the road?" she asked as she reached him. She tipped up onto her toes to hug him, and he brought both arms around her.

"Yep, all the way to the road."

That was great news for Keith, as he could get his truck cleaned off and depart this farm. He thought of the cottage pie inside, how browned and beautiful the tips of the mashed potatoes had been. He thought about spending another full evening with Lindsay, as they talked more about their lives, their families, their hopes and dreams.

Fine, they hadn't made it as far as the hopes and dreams yet, but Keith reminded himself he'd known her for twenty-four hours.

It felt longer, but he told himself again and then again that it hadn't been.

"You must be the cowboy I put in bed last night," Max said, and Keith formed his mouth into a smile.

"I am," he said. "Thank you so much for your help." He stepped forward and shook Max's hand. "I'm Keith Whettstein."

"Max Granger," he said. "My wife and I and our kids live just through the forest there."

"Great to meet you." Keith meant the words, and he pulled his hand back and looked at Lindsay. Before he could think too hard about it, he pulled her to his side, his smile even more genuine now.

"Lindsay says you guys do holiday parties and stuff out here."

She looked at him, and he looked at her, and then she said, "I told him that's why my house doesn't have many Christmas decorations this year. The party is at Felicia's."

"She's not wrong," Max said with a grin as wide as Texas. "We all like it when Felicia hosts; she makes the best pecan pie."

"My aunt is a good cook," Keith said. "She's kept us Whettsteins all fed for years now."

Max looked down to where Keith had his arm around Lindsay. "Are you coming to the party then?" He gave Lindsay a knowing look, and Keith dropped his hand, feeling foolish and possessive.

"We'll see," she said. "Keith's sister is getting married this holiday, and he's got family in town."

"We're goin' to the Blackhorse Bay party together," he said.

"I thought you said I could wait and decide if I wanted to see you again after the wedding." Lindsay's hazel eyes shone like precious gems, and Keith chuckled with her.

"Well, I can see you're doing okay," Max said. "I'll tell Missy, so she's not worried about you here...alone."

"He's not staying forever," Lindsay said with a giggle. "You don't have to be so obvious, Max."

"*I'm* the one being obvious?" The older man laughed as he tipped his head back. He had a good air about him, and Keith did like that Lindsay knew her neighbors, that they took care of one another out here. "He put his arm around you right in front of me."

"I'm just saying, I met him yesterday, and he doesn't live here."

Max's eyebrows went up, and while he didn't have a stitch of hair anywhere else on his face, he definitely had dark hair on his head to match those eyebrows. "He's still here, though. He could get on home right now...if he wanted to."

Keith didn't know what to say. A hint of shame moved through him for no reason whatsoever. He hadn't done anything wrong with Lindsay. Absolutely nothing.

He looked at Lindsay and then Max. "I'm going to go clear my truck, then."

She simply said, "Okay," and let Keith walk away. He wasn't sure what that meant. They'd talked about it, and they'd decided he'd sleep there tonight. If he wasn't going to do that, Max was right—he could've left hours ago. He could've worked harder to clear the driveway. He could've called Derrick and asked him to come dig them out.

As it was, evening would arrive in the next hour, and Keith would once again be driving in the dark to get home. He thought of Derrick, Coy, and Buck back at the cabin. The questions they'd have…

He didn't want to leave now. The day felt like a waste if he up and went home now.

Who cares what her neighbor thinks? he asked himself. *You haven't done anything wrong. You can hold your head high.*

His father had always taught him to do just that, especially if he had nothing to apologize for or nothing to repent of. Keith had made plenty of mistakes in his life too, and he knew what it felt like to have to make amends, make changes, and make himself humble.

He didn't feel like that now, and he didn't have to let her neighbor make him feel like that.

He retrieved the snow brush from his truck and got to work on it. Might as well clear it now, as he'd need to get going bright and early in the morning.

He couldn't just take another day off work, and Blackhorse Bay had plenty of snow and animals to deal with too. Plus, he had the family dinner tomorrow night, and everyone there would have a metric ton of questions too.

Keith just wanted an escape, and he realized as he pushed the foot of snow from his front windshield that these past twenty-four hours with Lindsay had provided that for him. He'd gotten away from the other cowboys at Blackhorse Bay.

He'd gotten away from the annoyance of the weather. He'd found something else to fixate on other than Britt's wedding.

It almost felt like God had put him at Twilight Fields, exactly when he had, so Keith could meet Lindsay, spend time with her, and get the mental reprieve he hadn't known he needed.

"Thank You, Lord," he murmured as he continued working on his truck. "Thank You for remembering me, for knowing me, and for never abandoning me."

As he came around the front of the hood on the passenger side, he found Lindsay at the back end of his truck, a barn broom in her hand. "You don't have to go," she said. "But I understand if you want to."

"I *don't* want to," he said, keeping his eyes on the task in front of him. "I don't care what your neighbor thinks."

"Good," she said. "Because neither do I, and I wouldn't have made that cottage pie if you weren't staying."

"No?" he paused and looked over to her. "You said you were planning on making it."

She shrugged. "I just wanted you to stay, and you seemed keen on the idea of it."

"I've never had it."

"I know." She finally smiled at him, and Keith wanted to rush at her and kiss her, pressing her into the snow stuck to the sides of his truck to really make an impression.

He didn't, mostly because he hadn't kissed a woman in a while, and he had no idea if he'd be able to do it right in such a rush. He didn't want to go fast with Lindsay at all. No, when he kissed her, he was going to take his sweet, sweet time and make sure he got everything right.

"So you're staying?"

"You promised me dinner, your 'famous' caramel popcorn,

and *Romancing the Stone*," he said. "If you want to break your promise, I'll go. But I'm not going to make you break it."

"Then you're staying," she said, this time not phrasing it as a question. "I totally have to use up that popcorn before it goes bad."

"I'll bet," he said dryly. "Microwave popcorn goes bad if you don't pop it the day you bring it home from the store."

"Right?" Lindsay grinned and then started to giggle, and Keith joined his laughter to hers, glad she wanted him to stay as much as he wanted to stay.

He did leave the driver's door untouched as he went to her. "Lindsay," he said, and she looked straight at him. He slid his hand along the part of her coat that dipped in at her waist. "I like you," he murmured. "I want to see you after I leave tomorrow. More than once."

A beautifully soft smile came to her face. "I like you too, Keith." Then she folded herself into his arms, her cheek right against the breast pocket of his jacket.

Keith had never held a woman like this. Maybe his high school girlfriend, but that wasn't the same as being an adult, and being allowed to fall in love, and feeling himself do exactly that.

————

AN HOUR LATER, Keith found himself lying in the bed where he'd first awakened yesterday evening. Lindsay had claimed she wanted to take a half-hour nap, and then she'd put together the side dishes for the cottage pie.

Keith's stomach grumbled, because he was used to eating several times throughout the day, but he didn't want Lindsay to feel bad. He'd found a granola bar in his truck, but he'd eaten that the moment he'd escaped to this bedroom, and it had been a while now. Long enough for him to get hungry again.

He didn't worry one whit about what he ate or when. When he was hungry, he ate. He could barely keep any fat on his body, and he worked hard all day long. His daddy had teased him about his metabolism in the past, but Keith couldn't help that it worked overtime. He didn't caffeinate himself excessively; he simply needed more calories than other people.

The bed held him up nicely while still being soft, and he let his thumbs fly while he texted with Britt, then Lars, then Uncle Boone.

With all of them satisfied that he hadn't fallen into a snow-bank and frozen to death, he finally decided to face the music.

Blackhorse Bay. He could text Derrick, but he decided to call.

"Hey, brother," Derrick said, and he sounded cheerful enough. For Derrick that meant one of three things: money, food, or a woman. Keith didn't even want to try to guess which. It was only Wednesday, so it couldn't be payday. Money was out, unless Derrick had won some obscure bet. He wanted to wager over everything, and Keith had learned pretty quickly not to pony up even a dollar, or he'd need to get a second job.

"Hey." Keith paused for a moment. "How bad is it going to be when I get back tomorrow?"

"Well, we're dug out for the most part," he said. "Uncle Jack's got us going stable by stable to check on the horses, feed, whatever." Something blew across his speaker, and Keith assumed his best friend was outside.

Guilt pulled through Keith, because he hadn't had to do anything like that today.

"I'll be back tomorrow morning," he said. "I'll be able to do whatever needs to be done."

Derrick paused now, and Keith took a breath. "You sound like you're in a good mood."

"Uncle Jack bought burgers for everyone." A smile hid between the words.

Ah, so food. Keith smiled. "Man, I wish I was there. I could use a big cheeseburger and French fries."

"Oh, I'm sure my sister is keeping you well-fed."

Shoot. Despite Keith's attempt to deter Derrick from this topic, they'd landed there anyway.

"She's making something for dinner, yeah," Keith said. "But I made lunch, I'll have you know."

"Trying to show off your skills for your new girlfriend?"

"I mean, I do try to show them the best things up front." Keith kept his voice cool, hoping not to make too big of a deal about this. When Derrick said nothing, Keith decided to go all-in. He'd seen his best friend win lots of bets that way, and sometimes, it worked.

"I like her, Derrick," he said. "We've been getting along really well, and I asked her to go to Britt's wedding with me. She didn't even hesitate when she said yes."

"Have you kissed her?"

"I've known her for one day."

"And?"

"No," Keith said. "I haven't kissed your sister."

"But you want to."

Keith didn't like how rapidly the questions were coming. "I'm not going to deny it," he said slowly to hopefully calm down Derrick's mind. "She's gorgeous," Keith said. "I'm a man. Of course I want to kiss her."

Derrick started to chuckle. "Well, I've always said you were honest."

"To a fault," Keith said with a smile. It didn't stay long, because he thought of his boss. "Be straight with me. Uncle Jack. Is he really not going to let me date Lindsay?"

"It's not Uncle Jack you'll have to deal with," Derrick said. "Well, I mean, it is. He's pretty protective over us kids. He's my daddy's only brother, and well, they don't get along super well, but when it comes to us, they talk every week."

"Every week, wow." Keith swallowed. "Lindsay didn't make it sound like she talked to your dad that much."

"She doesn't."

"Or Uncle Jack."

"He calls her every week," Derrick said. "My daddy...well, I've told you about how gruff and firm he was. There's a reason Lindsay and I don't work the ranch in Texas."

"A few things," Keith said. "I didn't know it was to that extent."

"I only call my father three times a year," Derrick said. "His birthday, Father's Day, and Christmas." He sighed out his breath. "So I've got to do that soon. Better start gathering my chi together for *that* conversation."

Keith couldn't imagine a relationship like that with his father. He texted or spoke to his daddy every single day. Britt too. Even Gloria, who'd shown him what a good mother looked like, sounded like, and acted like.

"I'm sorry, Derrick."

"It's just my daddy, you know?" Derrick asked. "Nothin' to be sorry about."

Keith took another moment, and then he inhaled slowly again. "I can talk to Jack about her," he said. "Or should I let her do it?"

"Lindsay is a strong woman," Derick said. "She's been

through more than you even know, and she'll know what to say to Uncle Jack and when."

Let me handle Uncle Jack, rang through his mind. Lindsay had told him that, and for now, Keith had to just let it go.

"Okay," he said. "I just want you to know that I like her. There's this chemistry between us, and it's not…I don't want things to be weird between us. Between me and you, I mean."

"As long as I never have to hear about this chemistry between you and my sister ever again, I think we'll be fine."

Keith chuckled again, then he said, "Deal. See you tomorrow, Derrick."

"Bye, brother." The call ended, and Keith reached over and set his phone on the nightstand in Lindsay's guest room. He sighed and pulled the quilt up over his shoulder. He wasn't cold, but he somehow was tired, and he closed his eyes. He'd just rest them for a few minutes, and then he'd go see what Lindsay needed help with to get dinner on the table.

He dozed, his thoughts semi-aware as he fantasized about this day being his permanent reality.

No more living with other men. Or his sister. His parents. He'd have his own farmhouse, his own farm, his own animals. And there, walking beside him, helping him scrape his truck during the winter, and working right alongside him, was a pretty woman.

His wife…with gorgeous auburn hair.

The images sure did send a thrill through him, and he wondered if he really could ever have something so quintessentially perfect as a wife, family, and farm, like the one where he drifted and dozed right now.

He sure hoped so.

CHAPTER
Twelve

LINDSAY SURVEYED the spread of food in front of her, the cottage pie absolutely perfect. She'd heated it slowly to make sure it didn't burn, and she'd put together a pretty salad with yellow peppers and cherry tomatoes and plenty of shards of parmesan.

She hadn't heard from Keith in a while, and she looked toward the hallway that led down to the bedrooms. His was the first one on the left, and she could almost see it if she moved all the way back to the dining room table.

Plates, utensils, and cups already sat there, as Lindsay had fancied herself getting ready for a date with the man she'd spent so much time with.

Yesterday, she'd been so excited to get her new horse—a Christmas gift for herself and Sabrina. She'd had no idea that Uncle Jack had a cowboy like Keith, nor that he'd be the one to show up to deliver the horse.

"It could've been anyone," she murmured to herself, as she'd always wondered how two people met, fell in love, and lived the rest of their lives happily-ever-after. She knew how her parents had met, but they hadn't stayed married. Derrick wasn't married. Uncle Jack and Aunt Lenora seemed to get along and be happy, and she knew they'd met on a group hike decades ago.

But for her? She'd had no idea how she'd ever just run into someone who would be her soul mate. Could he have simply driven onto her farm because she'd bought a horse she didn't need?

What were the chances of that?

"Low, I bet," Lindsay muttered to herself now. She returned to the stovetop and picked up the tray of garlic bread she'd meant to prepare last night.

As she put the pan on the crocheted potholder one of her elderly neighbors had given her for Christmas last year, her thoughts switched.

It didn't matter what the odds were of having her soul mate drive onto her land to deliver a horse.

With God, all things were possible. Lindsay hadn't been praying for a boyfriend. She hadn't even been looking for one. But she sure wasn't going to turn Keith away. She liked holding his hand, and she couldn't name one other person she liked talking to more than him.

"Dinner's ready." She moved to the mouth of the hallway and called, "Keith."

He didn't answer, and Lindsay moved to the partially open doorway of the guest bedroom where he'd gone. He'd laid down in the bed, and he faced the doorway, his eyes closed and his chest rising and falling slowly as he slept.

He was absolutely beautiful, and Lindsay smiled to herself

right there in the doorway. Part of her wanted to let him sleep, and another part of her didn't want to make him wait for dinner any longer.

"Keith," she said, much softer than before. She moved into the room, hesitant to get too close to him. Derrick woke up badly when he was awakened, and he could flail out arms and fists. She had no idea what Keith would be like when he got awakened, and she stood a few feet back as she said, "Keith, dinner is ready."

His eyelids fluttered opened, and Lindsay held up one hand in a half-wave. "Sorry," she murmured. "Dinner's ready."

"Okay," he said, and he reached for her hand. She threaded her fingers through his, really liking the way Keith woke up. "I was going to come help."

"Not necessary," she said. "All done. Are you hungry?"

"Starved." His eyes remained fixed on hers.

Lindsay wasn't sure what she saw in his expression. She reminded herself she didn't know Keith all that well yet. "Come on, then," she said. "Come eat."

"Yes, ma'am." He removed his hand from hers and flung back the quilt. "This is a nice bed."

"My momma came and helped me pick it out after I bought this farm."

"Where's your momma?"

"She lives down in a tiny little town in the Texas Hill Country. Hondo? Her parents live there, and she does outdoor tours."

Keith grinned as he stood up. He still wore his jeans and his long-sleeved denim shirt—the same things he'd been wearing when he'd shown up with Shadow.

"I can't wait to get into some different clothes," he said.

"I bet. You can shower again if you want. I'll wash your clothes."

"And I'll wear the poncho while they dry?" He shook his head. "No, thanks."

"I thought those snow pants were pretty sexy," she teased.

Keith laughed, and she led him out of the bedroom and back into the kitchen. "Smells amazing out here," he said.

"It's the garlic bread." She smiled at it, because Lindsay loved bread of all types. "I have a lot of fun bread recipes," she added as she sat down. "I actually make a pretty amazing cranberry pistachio bread for the holidays. I haven't made it for a few years, though."

"I'd take anything you make, anytime." he sat across from her and Lindsay looked at him. He'd prayed a couple of times for them, and she wanted to voice her gratitude for the situation in front of them.

She reached for his hand and said, "I'll pray tonight."

"Yes, ma'am," he murmured, and he squeezed both of her hands and bowed his head.

"Lord," she said, her voice getting caught against the dryness in her throat. "Thank You for this day. Thank You that all of the animals stayed warm and dry in the barn, and that we did in the house as well. I'm so grateful for good neighbors to help me, and I'm grateful Keith and I were able to help Sabrina overnight." Her throat closed, but she had to keep going.

"I'm grateful to have met Keith, and please bless us as we part tomorrow that we can stay in touch. Bless our families, especially Keith's sister Britt, this winter and this Christmas, and help us to serve them in anything they need."

She paused again, and Keith's fingers tightened. She experienced a stupor of thought, so she finished with, "Thank you for this food. Amen."

"Amen." Keith pulled his hands back. "My mouth is watering."

Lindsay picked up a plate and started scooping cottage pie onto it. She handed it to Keith, and he dutifully took some salad.

"We've been getting along pretty good, right?" Keith asked.

Lindsay nearly dumped her spoonful of cottage pie onto the table instead of her plate. "Yes."

"Does it feel a little…fake to you?"

"Fake?"

"Yeah," Keith said. "I know things will change tomorrow, and I actually can't wait to see how I feel once I'm not here with you. Then I think I'll know if this…this thing between us is real, or if I've been making it all up."

Lindsay understood what he meant, even if her heart pinched at her slightly. "Okay," she said, because she didn't know what else to say.

"I think we should say something that's annoying about us," he said. "That the other would find annoying, maybe."

Lindsay's eyes widened. "You want to tell me why I shouldn't like you?"

He grinned at her and put a bite of salad in his mouth. "Here's one: I only took this salad to make you happy. I don't like salad."

She watched as he put another forkful of lettuce and veggies in his mouth. He chewed and swallowed while Lindsay sat there and stared.

"You don't have to eat something you don't like." Lindsay held her shoulders high and tight, mildly horrified that he'd eaten something he didn't like just to make her happy. She mixed her salad together with the dressing. "I guess I can say something."

Keith waited, and Lindsay wasn't quite sure how to get the words out. "I'm really competitive," she finally said. "Like that cheese pull this afternoon? I was a little upset—legit upset—that I didn't win."

Keith blinked at her, those dark eyes dancing as he finished chewing and swallowing the salad he didn't even like. Lindsay scooped up a bite of it, and she really did like the ranch dressing with lettuce and tomatoes and parm. Mm, yes. All that shaved parmesan made her so happy.

"I would never guess that about you, like, ever," Keith said.

"You didn't grow up with me in 4-H or showing goats." She smiled at him, but Lindsay was not kidding.

"Good thing we're not competing for anything."

Lindsay felt like she was in a competition, but as she watched Keith take a big bite of his cottage pie, she realized she wasn't.

"This is amazing," he said. "I'm going to eat the whole thing."

She did enjoy getting compliments about her food, so she simply smiled at him. "I have something else I want from you," she said.

His eyes met hers, something searching in his gaze. But his mouth was full, so she carried on with, "Your phone number. You realize we haven't exchanged numbers, right?"

Surprise colored his face, and he held out his palm for her phone. She put it in his hand, and he started typing into it. He swallowed and said, "Done," before handing her phone back. "The wedding is at three on Friday. I'll come get you, oh, about one-thirty? That should give us enough time to get out to the farm and for me to adequately introduce you around before I have to go walk with Britt."

"Really? How far is it from here to Ivory Peaks?"

"I'm guessing a half-hour," he said. "Let me look." He started swiping and tapping on his phone too, and Lindsay looked at hers. His name and number sat there, and she felt like she hadn't held such a great prize in such a long time.

"Shoot," he said. "It's forty-one minutes." He looked up at her, his expression open and vulnerable. She liked seeing him like this, for she felt like she could see deep inside him. "Can I come at one?"

"I shall be ready at one o'clock," she said, grinning at him.

He grinned right on back, not even making fun of her for her lame, proper wording. "Great," he said. "Can't wait."

———

THAT NIGHT, Lindsay tossed and turned, her room too hot the first time she woke up and then so cold the second time. She sat straight up, thinking the power had gone out again, but a soft light emanated from the hallway where the nightlight guided her to the kitchen on nights she couldn't sleep.

Tonight, Hamlet had sprawled on his back, and he rolled onto his side as Lindsay got out of bed. The air definitely held a chill, and her first thought was that the furnace had gone out. Of course it would.

That would be just her luck.

She nudged open her bedroom door and looked down the hallway toward the bedroom where Keith had retired. The movie had been amazing, as usual. Her caramel corn had been a real winner. She'd snuggled with Keith on the couch, held his hand, and laughed and talked with him.

He still had not kissed her goodnight after all of that, and in fact, he'd ducked his head shyly and practically shot into the guest bedroom when their evening together had ended. The familiar frustration built inside Lindsay, and she blinked as she thought she saw a reddish glow coming down the hall.

Fire.

She couldn't smell any smoke, but her adrenaline pumped out several warnings at her at once. Still, she took a step down the chilly hallway. The thermostat sat at the end of it, and the closer she got to it, the louder the crackling of a fire became.

Keith had taken the sheets of plywood back downstairs, so nothing blocked the living room from the hallway. Lindsay only glanced at the closed door to the basement as she went by. Lights in the kitchen from the microwave and a digital clock told her that yes, the power was still on.

The furnace wasn't running, because Keith had built a fire, and the air absolutely held more heat out here than it did only five feet down the hall.

Lindsay emerged into the living room, the firelight dancing and playing with itself as it licked the walls and sent shadows scurrying about. They'd moved the furniture back to its rightful place, which meant she didn't have to go far to find Keith lying on the couch, asleep.

She suddenly wanted to be where he was, and her bedroom *was* cold because of this fire he'd built....

Feeling slightly stalkerish, as she stood over him while he slept for the second time that day, she crouched down and smoothed her hand over his hair. He was sexy without the cowboy hat and definitely with it, and he stirred.

"You built a fire," she whispered.

He didn't open his eyes. "I couldn't sleep in there. The crackling put me right to sleep out here."

"My bedroom is cold now." She glanced over as Hamlet joined them in the living room, her chaperone, apparently.

"Come 'ere." Keith lifted the blanket over him—Lindsay recognized it from the bed in the guest room—and she slipped under it as she lay down on the couch in front of him.

He covered the two of them, said nothing more, and Lindsay closed her eyes and fell asleep faster than she ever had before.

CHAPTER

Thirteen

KEITH TOOK a final drink of his coffee and then got up to rinse out the mug and put it in Lindsay's dishwasher. "I have to go," he said.

She didn't groan, though he thought that would be pretty romantic. He'd never considered himself to be overly romantic, but he'd woken up with Lindsay in his arms for the second morning in a row, so he had to be doing something right.

Yeah, he thought. *Making it so hot in the house that the furnace stopped running. You froze her out of her bedroom.*

Unintentionally, but still.

"Okay," Lindsay said, joining him in the kitchen with her plate. He'd fried eggs for breakfast that morning, and they'd gotten her morning chores done together too. "I wish you didn't have to, but I know why you do."

"Yeah, or Max will really think I've moved in." He cut her a smile, but it didn't last long. He had plenty of people to face at Blackhorse Bay, and then tonight at his parents' house.

Lindsay wrapped him up in her arms. "The wedding is tomorrow."

"I'll miss you," he said, not sure where the words had come from. He'd had other girlfriends in the past, but nothing too serious. His daddy had made sure he didn't get too serious in high school, and Keith supposed some people could label him *quiet*.

He'd dated here and there in college, with only a couple of women he'd even call girlfriends. Once he graduated and went back to the Hammond Family Farm, he'd hardly dated at all.

"I'll miss you too." Lindsay held onto him and looked up at him. It felt like the perfect time to kiss her, but panic bucked against his heartbeat, and he stepped away from her before he could make a fool of himself. He'd done so often enough with her as it was, thank you very much.

"Okay." He cleared his throat. He didn't want to show up in his cabin and face Derrick, knowing he'd kissed Lindsay. The thought was stupid, but it screamed at him, and Keith had to get out of here before he did something he might regret.

"I'll call you later, okay?" he asked.

She nodded, her hair falling forward over her shoulders as she looked at the floor. "Okay."

"Okay."

Keith didn't have a bag or a toothbrush to take with him. He'd already put his flashlights back in his truck, and he literally only had to walk out the back door, start up the truck, and drive away. His feet didn't move, though, and Keith honestly felt like they were breaking up.

Nothing made sense anymore.

"Hey," he said, and Lindsay looked up. "We're going to be okay, right?"

She didn't answer right away, and her eyes harbored some fear. "I think so," she finally said, really drawing the words out.

"Why does this feel like I'm leaving and I'll never see you again?" He forced a laugh out of his throat. "It's dumb. I'm going to call you tonight, and I'll see you tomorrow at one."

"Yes." She smiled at him, and Keith took her into his arms again. He let himself take a deep breath of the scent of her hair—peaches and cream and blossoms—and he ducked his head as he whispered, "I miss you already," right in her ear. His lips may have even touched her lobe for the briefest of moments.

His pulse crashed like cymbals in his chest, echoing up into his ears. He pressed a kiss to her cheek, then her forehead. "Okay," he said. "I'll see you tomorrow." With that, he forced his feet to move, and the only reason he got out of the house and to his truck was because he told himself over and over and over again that once he left, he could get home, shower, and finally —*finally*—put on a different set of clothes.

———

HE'D JUST STEPPED into a pair of basketball shorts, one hand rubbing a towel through his wet hair, when someone knocked on his bedroom door. "Yep," he said, and he wasn't surprised to find Derrick peeking his head in a moment later.

"You're back." His best friend grinned and entered the bedroom.

"Finally." Keith smiled at him and took him into a hug. "Shower felt so good. To have more than one pair of clothes feels good."

Derrick hugged him tight and stepped back. "I'll bet." He took Keith's towel and flung it to the floor. "You'll probably need jeans, though, bro. Uncle Jack wants to see us in his office this morning."

"Perfect," Keith said, managing to keep most of the sarcasm out of his tone. "I need to clean the horse trailer too. If he sees it how it is...and I need maintenance to look at the ramp. It broke when Shadow fell on me."

"How are you feeling with all that?" Derrick asked. "Any broken ribs? Anything like that?"

"Nothing major. Just a little stiff and sore in the morning," he said. "Or whenever I stop moving."

"Oh, we never stop moving around here," Derrick said. And, unfortunately, he wasn't lying. "Well, let's get going. Get dressed. I'll grab those bags of peanuts you like." He grinned and left the room, pulling the door closed behind him. A good cowboy always leaves the fence how he found it, and Derrick was a very good cowboy. He didn't leave fences open out on the ranch, and he closed a door behind him if it had been closed when he'd gotten to it.

Keith changed quickly, and while he wore the same thing as the past three days, it was totally different too. "Just gotta get my boots," he said as he rushed into the kitchen.

"There he is," Buck said, and Keith hadn't even seen him standing in the kitchen. Looking at him, he didn't see the womanizer Lindsay had described, and he chuckled as he left his boots by the side entrance to the cabin in favor of hugging Buck.

"Where's Coy?" he asked.

Derrick, in all his redheaded glory, looked at Buck, who sported sandy blond locks. "Coy's got himself into a bit of trouble," he said with a grin.

"Hmm," Keith said. "Boss trouble or girl trouble?"

"Boss trouble because of girl trouble," Buck said.

"Oh, so he's *back together* with Rachel?" Keith glared at Derrick first, then Buck. "Why didn't either of you tell me she was his girlfriend?"

Derrick blinked, his eyes far greener than Lindsay's. His hair was a lot lighter too, almost blond like Buck's, though Keith could see the strawberry in it now. "I thought you knew."

"How in the world would I have known?" Keith scoffed and went to retrieve his boots. "Some friends you guys are. Throwing me out to the wolves like that."

"I didn't even know you were goin' out with her until you'd gone," Buck said.

"You still didn't say anything." Keith bent and pulled on one boot, then the other. "I came home and complained about how awful the date was." He faced his friends. "You don't remember this?"

Buck wore a blank look, but Derrick shifted his feet. He definitely remembered, and Keith rolled his eyes at him. "Next time you have an awkward date and want to complain about it, I'll wear my headphones."

Derrick grinned at him. "You will not."

"I'm not going to sympathize," Keith said, reaching for his denim jacket. "Now, come on. I'd rather get this reaming done sooner rather than later."

"He's not going to ream you." Derrick followed Keith outside, the snow and sun combo throwing brightness everywhere. The storms had definitely passed, leaving behind ice-cold temperatures as a high-pressure system took their place.

"Yeah? What does he want then?"

"I'm sure he'd like to see your invoices for the deliveries," Derrick said. "And get you assigned to a crew for the weekend.

He's given us all jobs through Christmas on a holiday schedule." He climbed into the passenger seat of Keith's truck. "Why do you think I'm able to come welcome you back to the ranch in the middle of the morning?"

He grinned at Keith, who decided he wasn't going to go into Jack Hollowell's office with preconceived notions. The man might not even know about Keith and Lindsay. How that was possible, Keith didn't know.

His phone vibrated in his back pocket on the drive from the cabin to the main administration building. Blackhorse Bay had two enormous buildings connected by a bridge between them. They faced the highway, with the ranch spreading out behind them. Blackhorse boasted facilities for over three hundred horses, and in the winter, their boarding stalls were at full capacity.

They bred horses, broke horses, trained horses, and lived, breathed, and worked with horses. All of those equines needed food all winter long, and that was where the nine hundred acres of alfalfa that Keith managed came in. He also handled all the pastures for the horses, and he'd devised a rotation for them this past summer and fall that had impressed his boss.

Cowboy cabins lined both sides of the stables, and Blackhorse Bay employed about thirty-five men and women full-time. Derrick was one of the cowboy bosses, as were Buck and Coy, which was why Keith had been housed with them. They had one of the biggest, nicest cabins on the property, and Keith could only pray he wasn't about to get demoted.

He worked with a team of two dozen in the spring, summer, and fall, and Jack hired a ton more seasonal help as men and women rotated out of the stables and into agriculture. All in all,

Keith had been—and still continued to be sometimes—over-whelmed with the enormity of the operation and his role in it.

Everything about Blackhorse Bay was different than the Hammond Family Farm, where he'd grown up, lived, and worked for so long. A big part of him missed that slower pace of life. The nostalgia of a family farm, not a huge commercial oper-ation. The camaraderie and the fact that he knew everyone there, and they all knew him.

"Here we go," he said as he parked outside the southern building, where Jack's office was. He and his wife lived off-site, in a big farmhouse about five miles down the highway. Black-horse Bay sat north of the city of Denver, and to make the drive south and west to Ivory Peaks took Keith almost an hour.

He got out of the truck with Derrick, and the two of them hurried up the steps and inside. Just because the sun was out today didn't mean it was warm.

"Morning, Janice," Keith said to the woman sitting at the front desk in this administration building. Jack had to cross the bridge during cowboy meetings, because they met over in the other building to get assignments, do trainings, and run team meetings. Keith had an office over there, and he often used a conference room to go over his plans. He hadn't planted the acreage last year, and weariness already weighed him down for this upcoming year.

He had so much he hadn't done, so much he didn't know, so many new things coming his way.

Janice jumped to her feet, no skirt or heels in sight. Everyone who worked at Blackhorse Bay had to be ready to get outside and get dirty at any time. "You're okay." She rounded her desk and grabbed onto him.

He grunted and fell back a step. "I—yeah. I'm fine." He

looked over to Derrick, completely bewildered, but Derrick grinned like a cat who'd caught a canary.

Oh, this had his stink all over it. Janice pulled back, true concern on her face. "Derrick said a horse fell on you, and you passed out." Her eyes—blue like the sky—searched his, then looked over to Derrick. "Isn't that right, Derrick?"

"Sure is," he drawled out, and Keith knew exactly what had happened in his absence. Derrick had gotten it in his head to get Janice to go with him to something—probably the Christmas party next week—and he'd been stopping by her desk to chat her up for the past two days.

Keith had only been here for six months, but it hadn't taken long to figure out Derrick's habits. He rolled his eyes as Derrick continued to talk about the amount of snow at his sister's, and how it was "at least twice as much as here."

There was more snow on the west side of the city, but not twice as much. Keith kept his mouth shut, and once he'd managed to pry Derrick away from Janice, he gave his best friend a glare. "What's that about?"

"You should see her in a dress," he said with a grin.

"When did you see her in a dress?"

"She showed up to church." Derrick kept on smiling. "Plus, she's nice. She works hard. Why can't I like her?"

"Because she's your uncle's secretary," Keith hissed.

"So what? You're dating his niece." He pulled open Jack's office door at the same time he said it, and Keith froze to the spot as he looked inside.

Jack Hollowell himself sat perched on his desk, his enormous black cowboy hat sitting perfectly on his head, his eyebrows drawn down, and a frown etched on his lips. "They're here," he said. "I'll talk to you later, John." He moved to hang up his phone, and then he gestured for them to come in, but Derrick was already moving.

"Talking to my dad?" Derrick asked. "What's he got to say?"

"Nothing," Jack growled. "You boys sit down now." He stood and went around the desk, sighing mightily as he took his seat too. His desk looked like a bomb filled with paper, horse supplies, and miscellaneous kitchenware had gone off, and he moved a bowl—a legit bowl with a spoon it it—out of the way.

"First up, Keith." He abandoned looking for whatever he needed on his desk. "How are you feeling? You didn't go to the hospital?"

"I'm fine, sir," Keith said. "Nothing broken. Some aches and pains when I first get up in the morning. Nothing major."

"Okay, but keep an eye on it," Jack barked. "If you notice anything different at all, we best get you into a doctor."

"Yes, sir," Keith said again.

"Second, Lenora and I put together a gift for Britt and Lars." He nodded over to a table that stood to Keith's left. The biggest gift basket he'd ever seen in his life bore bright pink and silver bows, and that screamed Lenora Hollowell all day long.

"Wow, thank you," Keith said. "They'll be thrilled."

"Okay," Jack said, the pleasantries clearly done. "So you're here today, but gone tomorrow and Saturday, is that right?" He reached for a pair of glasses and slid them on his nose. With those, he didn't seem so scary, and there'd been no mention of Lindsay at all.

"Yes, sir," Keith said. "I'm fine to work Sunday to make up for it. Christmas Eve. All of it."

"I've got you down for a full crew on Sunday," Jack said. "But we're all moving to holiday hours on Monday." He looked up. "Thursday next week, we resume our normal hours for a few days, and then it'll be the New Year."

"Yes, sir," Keith said.

"I want a plan for planting on my desk the first week of January," he said. He scrounged around on his desk for another few moments, finally coming up with a royal blue folder. "I know you've not done a planting plan before, so I pulled the last few years' worth of them."

Keith leaned forward and took them. "Thank you, sir." He had no idea when he'd have time to work on a planting plan, and he wished he'd been given more than a couple of weeks to put one together, especially with Britt's wedding and then the holidays. But he said nothing.

"Good." Jack leaned back in his chair. "Now, Derrick, we need to talk about Janice, and Keith, we need to talk about Lindsay."

Derrick started to laugh, but Keith's lungs had frozen shut at the mention of Lindsay. "No, we don't, Uncle," he said. "I've taken the liberty of pulling the interoffice dating policy, and you know what? You don't actually have one." He grinned at his uncle, completely charming and unworried. How he did that, Keith didn't know.

"I frown on fraternizing with co-workers." Jack frowned right now, his sandy beard mirroring the movement. He kept everything neat and trim, always, and Keith actually liked him a lot. He was fair, and firm, and Keith never had to wonder where he stood with Jack Hollowell.

"Lindsay doesn't even work here," Keith said.

"I know that," Jack barked. "My involvement there is purely personal."

Keith looked at Derrick, hoping he'd get a hint as to how he should respond. Derrick only grinned back at him, and Keith couldn't read Cheshire Cat, so he looked back at Jack.

"You're right," he said. "It's personal. My relationship with her, if any, won't interfere with my work. If it does, then you can talk to me about it." Keith had no idea where the words had come from. He swallowed, his throat tight and sticky. He couldn't believe what he'd just said. Was he about to get fired?

"It did," Jack growled. "You didn't come back yesterday."

"The road didn't get plowed until almost five o'clock," he said. "Fine." He folded his arms. "It was about four-fifteen." He couldn't lie to his boss and feel good about himself, and now he hadn't lied.

"Lindsay and I discussed it, and she needed help getting things put back together around the farm," he said. "I helped with hay in the barns, feeding the animals, and setting the house back to rights."

"What the tarnation does that mean?"

"It means, sir, that the first night I was there, we nearly froze to death. All we had was a fire and blankets, and one huge room to try to heat." Keith could hold his own if he had to, though his stomach trembled on the inside whenever he had to. "So, since the day was almost over, I stayed through the night again, returning to Blackhorse Bay as soon as I was able."

Jack stared at him, and Keith gazed back. He finally couldn't hold his boss's gaze any longer, and his eyes dropped to his hands.

"All right," Jack said, and Keith had the very distinct impression that he'd just been broken. "But I will be getting regular reports from Lindsay on this."

"You do what you need to do," Keith said coolly. He didn't want Lindsay talking to his boss about their relationship, and he suffered through a few more minutes of Jack trying to get Derrick to admit to something with Janice.

He never would, and that only irritated Jack until he told them, "Go on. Get."

As they walked back to his truck, he looked over to Derrick. "I never got my assignment."

"I can look it up for you." Derrick saluted Janice as they went by, and her face turned a bright red that no human face ever should.

"Something happened with her," Keith said as they left the building. "You can talk circles around anyone, but I know you."

"Yeah, of course something happened," Derrick said. "It's like you said with Lindsay. She's gorgeous, and I'm a man." He pushed himself up and into the truck, and Keith did the same behind the steering wheel.

After he started the truck to get the heater blowing, he pulled out his phone to check his messages. "My dad texted," he said. "Britt. Mike." The Whettsteins had been firing texts back and forth a lot already today, all of them about tonight's dinner.

Keith didn't need to answer any of them, and he tapped to get back to the main list of texts. His heartbeat thumped and bumped when he saw Lindsay had texted.

Uncle Jack called. Call me when you can, and I can walk you through talking to him.

"Too late for that," he muttered. He glanced over to Derrick, but he had his head bent over his phone, texting wildly. Probably with Janice.

Sorry, just seeing this, he sent to Lindsay. *I just talked to him, and it went fine. I'll call you when I'm on my way to Ivory Peaks tonight.*

It went fine? I have to know what that means.

He grinned at his phone, his thumbs already flying around to get to all the letters. *I didn't know your daddy's name was John, but guess what? I do now.*

With that, he pocketed his phone and looked over to Derrick. "So, where are we workin' this afternoon?"

"Oh, right." Derrick stopped his text-fest too, and said, "Get us over to Stable four-two-A. We've got stalls to clean there."

Keith had mucked out plenty of horse stalls. He honestly didn't mind the work, because it didn't take a lot of brain power, and he could let his mind wander wherever it wanted.

Including toward one beautiful cowgirl and her heart of gold —and what he might want to have ready to tell everyone at tonight's pre-wedding family dinner.

CHAPTER
Fourteen

MATTHEW WHETTSTEIN PULLED up to his daughter's cabin, his heart already four times it's normal size. He'd spent a lifetime of worry on Britt, his oldest daughter. He'd taken her to probably hundreds of doctor's appointments. He'd spent days and weeks on his knees, begging God to protect her emotionally, mentally, and physically.

He'd even asked the Lord to heal Britt, and while that had never happened, a mighty change had happened inside Matt. He'd learned over the years to ask God for help and strength to deal with situations, instead of insisting God fix the situation at hand.

He'd learned and grown. He'd gotten stronger. He'd learned to worry for a moment, and then he'd give the trouble to the Lord. He'd talk it out with his beautiful wife, the woman who'd taken Britt under her wing and healed her in ways Matt could've never done alone.

They shared a love for animals that Matt simply didn't

have. He'd watched Gloria and Britt bond with each other, and Britt had improved dramatically after Matt had married Gloria. She'd needed a mother, and specifically, she'd needed Gloria to take her rollerblading, horseback riding, and dog-walking.

And tonight was the last night Britt would be his little girl. Tomorrow, she'd marry Lars Hansen, and she'd become his.

"Are we going in?" Gloria asked. Matt looked away from the glowing windows of his daughter's cabin, not even realizing that his other two daughters had gotten out of the truck and gone inside.

Gloria had not, and he reached over and took her hand in his. "She's so grown up."

"She's so ready for this," Gloria reminded him. "He loves her so much, Matt."

They'd both seen it, and Matt had never dreamed that Britt would be able to find a man who wanted her so much. Who would devote himself to her care. Who would love her for who she was.

But Lars did, and Matt loved him completely for that alone.

"Let's go," he said, and he released Gloria's hand and got out of the truck. Inside, he found Britt and Lars, as well as Lars' parents, Barbara and Dennis. They all stood in the small kitchen at the back of the cabin, laughing and chatting and smiling. It made Matt smile too, because the more people who loved and accepted Britt, the happier his heart became.

Gray and Elise Hammond had arrived also, and they had both of their young adult sons with them. Tucker was home from his rodeo management job for a couple of weeks, and he spotted Matt and Gloria, and he grinned at them and tipped his hat toward them.

Tuck had a big personality, and he managed Tarr Olson, one of the biggest rodeo personalities in the world.

Deacon, who was only a few years younger than Britt, had definitely settled into his own self, and he was quieter while still being a Hammond with all that entailed.

He wanted to work the ranch, and since Matt managed the Hammond family Farm, Deac was one of his cowboys.

He came over and said, "Heya, Matt. Do you really think we're all going to fit in here?" He stuck out his hand and Matt gripped it to shake it.

"Yeah, we will," he said. "It just looks like they haven't gotten out the tables yet."

"Keith's not here," Gloria commented, and sure enough, Matt didn't see his son. Keith had agreed to get everything set up, which was why it wasn't done yet.

Roxanne and Alma, his two teen daughters, joined Britt in the kitchen, and the three girls huddle-hugged as Boone said, "Why y'all standin' in the doorway?"

Matt moved out of the way so his brother and his family could enter, and Boone held the door for his wife and two kids. He had a boy and girl in their teens, with Amy just turning thirteen.

Boone had already spent time at Matt's house, pacing and asking questions for how to deal with teenage girls, but it wasn't like he didn't have any experience with it.

He'd already raised Gerty, who'd returned to Ivory Peaks in the past couple of years, married Michael Hammond, and was due with their first baby in the next month or so.

The door had barely closed before Boone engulfed him in a hug. "How you holdin' up?"

"Good." Matt gripped his brother by the shoulders. They'd

been working this farm and raising their families side-by-side for almost two decades, and Matt felt the blessings of such a thing flow over him and through him and gather around him as he hugged his brother.

Boone and Cosette had lived down the lane from Britt and Keith—until Keith had left to work a different farm—and Matt had counted on him to watch out for his kids as they'd matured and grown and left Matt's core care.

"Sorry I'm late," Keith said, and Matt stepped away from his brother to take his son into his arms.

"You're okay," he said. He hadn't realized until that moment how much he'd been worried about Keith's safety while he'd been snowed in at a small farm on the northwestern side of the city.

"I'm fine, Daddy," Keith said. "I told you I was fine." He pulled back, a bigger smile on his face than Matt had seen in a while. So much had been weighing on Keith that he'd left this farm where he'd grown up and worked, and Matt had been praying for him a lot in the past six months.

"My boss had no problem putting me to work," Keith said as he hugged Boone and then swept a kiss across his aunt's cheek.

"Didn't you get stepped on?" Gloria asked as Keith hugged her.

"Yeah, but I'm fine." Keith shot his father a look. "I'm going to get the tables set up."

"Yep," Matt said. "Let's do it." He and Boone followed Keith down the hall to the spare bedroom that Keith used to sleep in.

Working quickly, they got the tables and chairs set up, the couches out of the way, and right before his eyes, plenty of room for this pre-wedding family dinner got created.

Gloria spread a cloth in the brightest pink across them, and

Alma came over and sprinkled silver star confetti down the middle of it. Roxane started to set the table, and Matt went behind her with plates.

Once everything was ready, Matt turned to the kitchen. "Barbara," he said, and he hugged Lars's mother. "How are you?"

"So good," she said with a light laugh. She was a shorter, stockier woman, and she always had a smile and a laugh for everyone she met. Matt had learned where Lars got his sunny personality, and where he'd learned to work hard and devote himself to his family. That came from his daddy, and Matt seriously couldn't ask for a better man for Britt.

Lars worked at his daddy's hardware store in downtown Ivory Peaks, and he'd be taking it over in the next year or so. Dennis wanted to retire, and Matt moved over to hug him too.

"You guys ready for tomorrow?" he asked.

"I think Lars has been ready forever," Dennis said.

Matt smiled and finally faced his daughter, who held Lars's hand fiercely. She glowed like the North star, something she'd always done. At the same time, Matt had seen that light turn dark when Britt got frustrated or upset about something. Especially math. Or his questions about how she felt. Her health and strength. Her abilities.

Matt's emotions quaked. Hard. His chin wobbled, and Britt said, "Daddy, don't cry."

Oh, he was going to cry. The love he felt for his daughter could not be quantified or described, and he opened his arms for both of them, and Lars and Britt stepped into his embrace.

He wanted to be the powerful, almighty man who could protect them both from the winds and hails and tsunamis of life. But he couldn't. He could thank God that He'd given them each other to rely on during those storms, so he held them tightly and did that.

The noise in the house finally came back into his ears, and Matt stepped back. Gloria hugged them both too, and then Matt watched as Keith took only Britt into his arms. He probably said something to her, as Britt's eyes were closed and tears started to leak down her face.

Matt had to turn away, because he knew his kids shared such a close bond. This marriage was an amazing, glorious thing, but it was hard for him. And really hard for Keith.

"All right," Barbara yelled in her loud, small-town momma voice. "Food is done and hot. Let's eat."

Matt moved to the mouth of the hallway, hoping to fall back out of the way. He ended up next to Gray Hammond, and he leaned into the man's side-hug. "I think I'm gonna die when Jane gets married."

"Two more months," Matt said.

"She's ready, but I'm not." Gray lowered his arm and gave Matt a small smile. "We haven't always seen eye to eye, but she's my only daughter."

"Cord is a good man."

"The best," Gray murmured. "I thought they were coming tonight too."

"Gerty's not here yet either," Matt said.

The cabin door opened, and both couples came inside, and Matt wanted to lunge toward his niece to make sure she didn't topple forward. Her baby belly seemed to poke straight out from her body, as she only had a month left before she'd deliver her baby boy.

Boone stood right there in the next moment, and he greeted his daughter and son-in-law.

Jane and Cord edged to the side, their hands locked, to get out of the way.

Lars raised both hands above his head. "Everyone. We're all here now, and the food is hot."

The conversations died down, and everyone looked at Lars and Britt. He shone with a bright light too, and Matt found himself experiencing a supreme sense of contentment. What a blessing that was, not to be nervous or worried about this wedding.

"Thank you so much for coming," he said next, his eyes fixed on Britt, who wouldn't speak. If she did, Matt would likely fall down dead.

"Britt and I love our families, and if this dinner was the only thing we did to celebrate our wedding, I think we'd both be happy." Lars looked around at the crowd then, his eyes landing on Matt for a moment before moving to his momma.

"Momma?"

"We need to pray," she said in a quieter voice, and Lars nodded.

"Sure, right." A blip of panic worked across his face, and Matt stepped forward and raised his hand.

"I'll say it."

"Thank you, Matt." Lars nodded and bowed his head.

The storm inside Matt had already blown itself out, creating a perfect eye of calm for him to pray.

"Dear God," he said. "We thank Thee for being our Heavenly, divine Father. We're grateful for the moisture we're receiving now, though we won't need it for several more months. Thank You for giving us patience, and help us to enjoy the blessings we have now and anticipate the blessings You'll provide for us later."

He had no idea why he'd said any of that. This night was about Britt and Lars.

"We thank Thee for the gift of marriage. We're grateful Lars and Britt have met each other, and that their love for one another has brought us together as family tonight."

They didn't have to share blood to be family, something Matt had learned over his years with working for and with Gray and Elise.

"We dedicate tonight and tomorrow to Thee, and we ask Thee to bless the details of Britt and Lars's wedding. Bless us all to travel safely, and for hearts to be softened and turned toward each other or toward Thee." His eyelids shook, and he decided to wrap this up. "Bless the food tonight, and thank You for those who prepared and provided it." He cleared his throat. "Amen."

"Amen," chorused through the cabin, and Matt faded back to Gloria's side.

Since there were no little children, a beat of silence filled the house before Barbara called and said, "Don't be shy now. We've got barbecue chicken, mashed potatoes, and the best baked beans this side of the Rocky Mountains."

That got people to laugh and the silence to break, but Matt still didn't make a move to be the first person to grab a plate and start filling it with food.

Britt and Lars led the way past the casserole dishes, and Matt found himself standing next to Keith in line.

"Tell me about Lindsay," he said.

Keith's smile finally brightened the way Matt had been praying and hoping it would. "She's great, Daddy," he said. "I really like her so far."

"We'll get to meet her tomorrow?"

Keith nodded as he picked up a plate and glanced to Gloria. "Yes, she'll be there. I think you'll both really like her."

"What do you like about her?" Gloria asked.

"She's really pretty," Keith said. "I know it's not always about that, but she is." His face turned slightly ruddy, which was how Keith blushed. "She volunteers with kids," he said. "She has this calmness about her that helped keep us all calm during the storm. She's a good cook."

Gloria looked past Keith to Matt, and so much got said. Matt smiled and nodded, breaking eye contact with his wife. "That's great, Keith."

"She has a hobby farm," he said. "I don't know how big it is, but she's got seven horses, and a bunch of chickens, and a big ole momma pig—and she loves them. She has a generator just for her barn." He chuckled as he loaded a drumstick onto his plate. "Not her house. But for the barn."

"She sounds great," Matt said. "I can't wait to meet her."

"Maybe we'll have two matches made in heaven this year," Gloria said with a smile.

"I don't know," Keith said. "Her brother is my best friend at Blackhorse. It's Derrick."

"Oh." Matt didn't know what else to say. "Is he…would he not approve of you dating his sister?"

"He says it's okay," Keith said with a shrug. He loaded mashed potatoes onto his plate, as it was one of his favorite foods. "It just feels a little…I don't know. They definitely have some family issues with their daddy. I don't know."

"If Derrick is her brother, then her uncle must be your boss." Yes, Matt could navigate family trees, and the way Keith's eyebrows fell into a frown confirmed what he'd said. "Well, just see how it goes."

"That's the plan, Dad." Keith finished filling his plate, and Matt did the same. He found a spot for him between Gloria and Britt, and Matt pulled her to his side after he'd sat down. "Love you, my girl."

"I love you too, Daddy." She squeezed into him, and then they started eating. Matt told himself over and over that this was the day he'd been preparing Britt for over the past twenty-seven years. He couldn't be upset it had come.

It's an accomplishment, he thought, and he seized onto that, because it felt better than experiencing a loss.

Now, he just had to get through tomorrow without breaking down and becoming a blubbering mess during the ceremony. If he could pull that off, it would be a miracle, and Matt figured he better start praying for such a thing.

Gloria smiled at him, and he knew tomorrow would be fine —rain, shine, enough food, not enough food, ripped dress or wilted flowers—because she stood at his side.

CHAPTER
Fifteen

LINDSAY FINISHED TWISTING her hair and she reached for the claw clip to hold it in place. The curls rained down over her shoulders as she adjusted the clip until it felt like it would hold for longer than a few seconds.

She lowered her hand, and her hair stayed in place. Satisfied, she sprayed it, tightened the clip one more time, and turned to leave her master bathroom.

"Hamlet," she chastised as she very nearly tripped over the dog. "When did you come in?"

The blue heeler looked up at her with his keen, blue eyes, and Lindsay couldn't stay irritated with him for longer than three seconds. She even bent down to pat him, then moved into the bedroom to finish getting dressed.

She currently wore her full slip, which covered the best push-up bra she owned. Her dress wasn't made of bubble-gum pink sequins, but she'd taken a picture of the dusty rose gown and sent it to Keith. He'd deemed it "perfect" and said he "couldn't wait to see her in it," and Lindsay experienced the same ooey-gooey feelings now as she had when he'd texted this morning.

She'd done her makeup and hair without wearing the dress, as she didn't want to drop powder onto it, and now she stepped into the gown and struggled to reach behind her and zip it up.

So many things were harder to do alone, like put a leaf in the dining room table for a large group dinner, or moving her horses from pasture to pasture.

She didn't have anyone to help her do up dresses like this, or move vehicles around in the barn, or hold a horse while she checked its hoof.

She finally managed to get the zipper up by reaching around herself and pushing it up as far as she could and then putting her arms over her shoulders and pulling it up further. Back and forth she did that until the zipper reached the top, and Lindsay pulled the dress down and smoothed her hands over the sequins to make it all lay the right way.

She felt a little winded, but she turned to put on her shoes, hoping the walkways would be clear and even for today's nuptials.

Keith had told her Britt and Lars were getting married out on the Hammond Family Farm where he'd grown up and lived—with his sister—until he'd moved to Blackhorse this summer.

Her phone chimed as she minced her way into the kitchen, Hamlet on her heels. She pulled it out, because she'd assigned "Cowboy Keith" the high-pitched, whippish sound.

On the way, he'd said, and Lindsay smiled at the prospect of seeing him again.

Of course, he'd only left yesterday morning, but after being with him so continuously for a couple of days, her time alone yesterday had felt so lonely. So silent. So long.

She hadn't even realized how big and quiet her house was without him in it, and even the cold winter, which she normally didn't mind, had felt far too chilly for her to withstand.

He'd introduced life into her that she hadn't known she'd been missing, and she wanted to see him again to find out if that spark and attraction that had been so hot and so immediate still existed.

"I sure hope so," she whispered to herself.

This afternoon held a wedding and a post-wedding dinner, but Lindsay pulled out a box of peanut butter crackers and mindlessly ate one.

The knots in her stomach didn't dissipate, and before she knew it, her doorbell rang. She hadn't heard it for a while—probably years—and Hamlet perked up instantly but didn't bark.

Lindsay hurried through the living room to the door, and she once again paused to smooth down her dress before she opened the door.

Keith, in pure cowboy goodness and good-looking-ness stood there, and Lindsay actually sucked in a breath loud enough to be heard next door. "My, my," she said as she drank in his broad shoulders in that black suit coat. His body tapered to a narrow waist, where he wore a silver belt buckle as part of his suit.

Black cowboy boots. Black cowboy hat. Dark beard and hard, dark eyes. He was absolute perfection from head to toe, and that boiling bubbling attraction definitely roared through her again. Louder now. More insistently. So much stronger.

"You are so beautiful." He smiled at her, and that action

really made his face come alive. "I'm going to steal the show at this wedding with you at my side."

"Don't say that," she said. "It's your *sister's* wedding."

His grin stayed stuck to his lips. "Are you sure you want to go with me?"

"Keith." She cocked her head and gestured for him to come in. "I need to get my jacket, and it's cold."

He stepped into the house and closed the door behind him. Lindsay started to turn, every inch of her skin burning to touch him but not knowing how. "Wait a second," he said, his hand sliding down her forearm. "I just mean...."

"I am not out of your league." She figured she might as well address what he'd texted her last night. "I want to go to the wedding with you. Has it occurred to you that I consider myself the lucky one to be on your arm?"

"No, it has not," he drawled out, drawing her closer. "I just feel a little inadequate."

"Why? Because your own good looks have blinded you?"

His smile, which had slipped away, came back softly. "No," he murmured.

Lindsay's gaze dropped to his mouth, but she quickly forced it back to his eyes. Then she couldn't look there either. Her mind whizzed, and she didn't know what else to say. The moment to tease him had passed, and this mood between them felt intense, heated, and absolutely wonderful.

Keith's other hand came up and slid along her shoulder, eliciting sparks and heat in her throat. He kept moving it to the back of her neck, and Lindsay looked up at him again.

"I want to kiss you," he murmured. "Can I?"

Yes! shouted through her head, but she couldn't get her voice to work. Thankfully, the heat of his hand allowed her neck to work, and she nodded slightly.

A smile tugged at the corners of his mouth as he moved closer, and Lindsay's heartbeat flopped and flipped beneath her breastbone. Her eyes drifted closed, and Keith had flattened his lips by the time they touched hers. A bright pop of light exploded behind her eyes, and Lindsay sank into the warmth and strength of his kiss.

She kissed him back, her hands sliding up the front of his suit coat and then slipping inside, where his body heat continued to filter into her system.

Kissing him felt magical, like she'd stepped into a dream, and this cowboy wasn't real. Because he couldn't be real. Men like him didn't exist, and yet, she could smell his spicy, wood-scented cologne, and she definitely felt the stroke of his mouth against hers, and the burn of his skin along the bareness of her shoulders.

He pulled away, and Lindsay took the first breath of her new life. The life where she'd kissed Keith Whettstein. This brand-new life, where she'd just been changed by a kiss.

"I feel better now," he said as he stepped back and gave her back her personal space. "Can I get your jacket?"

"Sure," she said, still trying to get her legs to go back to being able to support her weight. "It's...somewhere."

Keith smiled at her and said, "Kitchen?"

"I think so."

He walked that way, and Lindsay pressed one hand to her forehead and one to her heartbeat. She needed to get her bearings back, because she had to meet his family very, very soon.

He returned with her fluffy black faux-feathery jacket, and he held it for her while she slipped her arms into it.

"The barn should be heated," he said.

"So we will be outside."

"Sort of," he said. "The Hammonds have plenty of money, and all of their buildings are immaculate." He smiled. "I don't think you'll be cold, and if you are, it'll be only be from the time you have to walk from my truck to the barn."

"Okay," she said.

"Like right now." He reached for the doorknob and opened the door. He guided her through it with his hand on the small of her back, and Lindsay felt so taken care of. She hadn't even realized she wanted someone to take care of her the way Keith currently did.

He opened her door for her, and when he got behind the wheel, he said, "This is my high school truck."

"Wow," she said with a chuckle. "You don't want to get a new one?"

"I don't really need one," he said. "She takes a minute to get up to speed on the highway, but she's sturdy and dependable."

"You weren't driving this truck when you delivered Shadow." She turned toward him. "Oh, and he took the saddle just fine today."

"You rode him?"

"Around the farm," she said. "Just for a minute. I wanted him to get acclimated."

"I use a truck from Blackhorse Bay when I deliver horses. I had eight equines that day. My truck can't do that."

"Maybe you do need a new one then," she teased.

He grinned and rolled a shrug through his shoulders. "Maybe."

Lindsay liked the easiness of the drive and the chatter on the way to the farm, but when Keith turned the corner and the enormous pine trees gave way to the land, a big, red barn appeared.

Cars and trucks had been parked out front, and there seemed to be one reserved for Keith close to the barn while others were parking down the fence toward the farmhouse.

Keith looked at her and said, "My heart is beating so hard right now."

"Come help me down," she said. "I'll be fine. I've met mommas and daddies before." She gave him the most reassuring smile she could, and he nodded, swallowed, and got out of the truck.

With her arm linked through his, and the cold afternoon air skating over her legs, she walked with Keith toward the barn. Sure enough, when he opened the door, a rush of heat flowed over her face.

She entered first, and it didn't seem like a loud or busy place. Her heels clicked against the cement, and she let Keith hold her hand and lead her down a hallway and then into another stable.

Ah, the party opened up here, with an altar in front of the windows, which let in plenty of light. Pink and white flowers hung in an arch, and the altar had obviously been constructed by someone with extreme talent.

"Wow," Lindsay said as she went by it. "I love this."

The altar stood straight and tall, and it rose to her waist. The top had been upholstered in soft fabric that resembled horse hair, and the front had an L and a B carved and stained into it.

Tea lights ran everywhere, and Lindsay couldn't count chairs fast enough, but this was definitely a smaller family wedding.

"My parents are back here," he said. "I want you to meet Britt too. Then my uncle Boone said you could sit with him while I walk Britt down the aisle."

"Okay," Lindsay said, not sure why everything felt so blurred all of a sudden.

Keith took her into a smaller room down the aisle, and she took in the few people standing there. A dark-haired man with salt in his hair—that had to be Keith's daddy. They looked almost identical.

Another man wore a bigger beard and had slightly lighter hair. That had to be Uncle Boone. Two other women lingered in the room, both of them fluttering around Britt.

"Guys," Keith said, and all activity ceased. Lindsay suddenly felt completely out of sync with her own heartbeat, like she was the inadequate one now.

Keith beamed at her and the world shifted again. She was worthy to be here with him. She could meet his family. "This is Lindsay Lewis," he said. "We just started seeing each other, like yesterday."

"Maybe today," she joked. "It is our first time actually out together."

"Today, then." Keith spread one arm wide to indicate the other people in the room. "My daddy, Matt," he said. "Who I call my momma, Gloria."

The dark-haired woman at Britt's side nodded once, her smile lovely and glorious.

"My sister, Britt," he said, and she started moving toward Lindsay. "My Uncle Boone and Aunt Cosette."

Cosette had auburn hair like Lindsay's, though hers was a touch darker than the older woman's.

"Howdy," Boone boomed, but Lindsay switched her gaze to Britt as she arrived in front of her in her wedding dress.

"Lindsay," she said. "It's so great to meet you." She hugged

Lindsay, and she knew instantly why people liked her. She only radiated goodness, without a shred of judgment or pause.

"You too," she said. "Keith's told me a lot about you."

"I have not," Keith said quickly. "If I did mention you, sissy, it's only the good things."

Britt shone like a lighthouse. "He does always say the good things." She reached for her daddy's hand as he joined her.

"Mister Whettstein," Lindsay said.

"Oh, ho, you can just call me Matt." He shook her hand, and Lindsay did the same for Gloria, Cosette, and Boone. She took a breath, because this wasn't so bad. Five people, all dressed like celebrities.

She glanced over to Keith and then moved into his side. His arm came around her, and she saw all five pairs of eyes see it too. Oh, okay. This was something, and it was more for Keith than her.

He hadn't mentioned his previous dating history too much, and it sure looked like maybe he didn't have much to mention.

"Your dress is beautiful," Lindsay said to Britt, and she seemed to shine brighter.

"Isn't it? Cosette made most of it." She looked over to her aunt while Lindsay continued to enjoy the scallops along the neckline and the lace that seemed to cover every inch.

"Come on, baby," Matt said as he raised his watch. "It's ten minutes until we walk down the aisle."

"All right," Boone said, and he spoke with the loudest of voices out of anyone in the room. "That's our cue to leave." He hugged Britt and waited for Cosette to do the same. Lindsay felt the loss of Keith before she even stepped away from him, but she went.

Boone and Cosette went down the aisle hand-in-hand while

Lindsay trailed along behind them. The barn smelled like horses and wood and hay, and she loved it. Out in the bigger room, which they surely hadn't built just for weddings, the scent of lilac and honey filled the air.

More guests had started to arrive, and Lindsay sat next to Cosette, who gave her a somewhat shy smile. "Keith says you own a farm north of here," she said.

"Yes." Lindsay reached up to tuck her hair, only remembering when she didn't have much to tuck that she'd done an up-do for the wedding. "It's a little hobby farm. About forty acres is all. I have a few horses and chickens and a pig."

"What do you do?" Boone asked, leaning forward to see past his wife.

"I raise a couple of cows every year," Lindsay said. "I do horseback riding lessons in the spring and summer. I show my pig and sell her." She knew it wasn't an exciting life, but for her, it meant freedom. "I work with my uncle Jack sometimes, and I grow alfalfa that I sell to other farmers in the winter."

"Ah, there's the income," Boone said.

"Sometimes," Lindsay said, though she did well enough with her vegetable garden and her cow to reduce her grocery budget. The hay did bring in the most money, and Lindsay had already planned to plant as much as possible this year.

"Sounds wonderful," Cosette said. "If you ever need something a little extra, come out here and see us. Molly is always looking for horseback riding instructors."

"Do you guys do a lot of that here?"

"Yep," Cosette said. "Camps, counseling, all of it."

"A hundred and fifty kids come through Pony Power every week," Boone said. "We always need help with the horses, the barns, and the lessons come summertime."

"Good to know," Lindsay said.

Gloria slid onto the seat in front of her, and the music changed. The wedding began, and Lindsay watched as two girls dressed in pale pink dresses came down the aisle first.

"That's Roxanne and Alma," Gloria whispered, her face aglow now. "They're mine and Matt's daughters."

Lindsay nodded to her, then looked at Keith's half-sisters. Another boy and girl came down the aisle too, and they moved onto the row with Boone and Cosette, clearly belonging to them. So Keith's cousins.

Then, finally, the barn doors opened, and Britt entered from outside, alone. Keith came to her side on the left and her father on the right.

They both kissed her cheek, and they all had her light shining from them as they faced the crowd and started down the aisle.

Lindsay knew she should probably be staring at the bride, but she couldn't take her eyes off Keith.

She also couldn't help wondering if he'd ever want to get married, and if so, where and when and how.

Their eyes met, and he radiated happiness through his smile now, a side of him she'd only seen a few times. Oh, how she liked it—how she liked *him*—and she couldn't wait to dance with him after the I-do.

CHAPTER
Sixteen

KEITH TOOK Lars into a hug and crushed him to his chest. "I love you, brother," he said to the man. He'd had the opportunity to get to know Lars over the past year or so, and he did love him like a brother.

"Love you too, Keith." Lars pulled back, his joy so full it couldn't be contained inside him. "I'm going to take good care of her."

"I know you are." Keith smiled, schooled his emotions, and stepped back. He turned away from the altar where he'd just delivered his sister to her about-to-be husband, and he felt completely lost for a moment.

Then Lindsay's fingers slid between his, pulling him down the row toward her. He belonged there, and he went easily. Daddy took his place on the end of the row, and then guests started to sit down now that the bride had arrived at the altar.

Keith sat next to Gloria, Lindsay beside him, and Roxanne and Alma on her other side. They all looked at Britt as she leaned forward and let Lars kiss her on the cheek. Their romance story was so sweet and so good, and Lars had played every single card right.

He and Britt had never broken up and gotten back together. He'd become her friend first, and then her boyfriend later. He treated her like a queen, and he let her be herself, and he'd been working on his grandfather's house for the two of them to live in for months now.

Lars had built the altar where they currently stood too, and Keith shifted in his seat while the pastor came forward and took his place behind it. "Just wow," he said with the light of heaven shining from his face. "Isn't witnessing two young people in love the most amazing thing in the world?"

A few people twittered, and of course, Uncle Boone had to call, "Yeehaw!" as if he didn't already attract enough attention with his larger-than-life personality as it was. His wife and Gerty shushed him, but several more guests laughed.

Britt turned and looked at him, pure goodness flowing from her. She didn't mind Uncle Boone's loud voice, and she grinned at him.

"Marriage is such a special thing," the pastor continued. Keith had always liked his sermons—at least after he'd grown up enough to sit still and listen to them—and he missed Pastor Milligan's lectures. He went to a church closer to Blackhorse Bay, but he didn't make it every week.

As the pastor talked about ceremonies and covenants, Keith's spirit burned at him. He needed to get to church more often, and he needed to grow the faith he'd always had inside him. Determined to do that, he focused on the wedding again.

"I believe our bride and groom wrote their own vows." Pastor Milligan smiled at Britt, and she pulled her hand out of

Lars's. She turned to Gloria, who handed her a simple three-by-five-inch card.

Keith's heartbeat hammered at him, hard. Britt did not like public speaking. Sometimes, when she got nervous or afraid, she still stuttered, and it was horribly embarrassing for her. He prayed with everything inside him that she could do this, because he knew how badly she wanted to.

He'd heard these vows already, because she'd practiced them with him last week. She hadn't made a single mistake, though she had needed the card.

She looked at it now, and he could see her pulse throbbing in her neck. *It's okay*, he thought. *Calm down, sissy. You're okay.*

He'd sat with her at school when she'd been teased. He'd shown up after he'd graduated to make sure she had what she needed for the first day of school. He'd driven her to school, helped her with her homework, and encouraged her to calm down plenty of times. Britt didn't like being told she couldn't do things, but at the same time, she knew she couldn't do some things.

As he'd walked her down the aisle, he'd sensed no weakness in her legs or her step, and he prayed for that same strength to be in her heart and in her voice now.

"Lars," she said, and she looked up at him, her eyes wide and bright. She had more of their mother's fairer features than Keith, and he really wished his mom would've come. At the same time, Britt had not even invited her. She'd sat down with Keith and Daddy and Gloria, and after a long talk, good food, and plenty of chocolate cake for dessert, Britt had made the decision not to tell her.

She said she'd send her a card afterward, but that she barely knew or remembered her mother, and she didn't want to reunite simply because she was getting married. Keith had strong doubts that his mom would come, but none of them had been sure. Thus, Britt had not invited her.

He wondered if he'd invite her to his wedding. He'd sent her his college graduation announcement, and she'd sent him a hundred dollars. Not much else over the years. No birthday or Christmas presents. No cards. It was like she was a ghost who sometimes existed somewhere out there.

"I love you," Britt said in a clear voice. "The first time we m-m-met in the grocery store was a really scary day for me."

Tears filled his eyes as she stuttered over the M. But only the one. She'd said "me" just fine.

"I wasn't sure what you wanted or why you liked me." She looked down at her card. "You became my best friend, and I love spending time with you, whether that's to catch butterflies, or ride horses, or to help you with our house."

Keith squeezed Lindsay's hand, glad when she squeezed back. Listening to Britt speak in such a clear, steady voice once again told him how ready she was to truly live on her own. Down the row a couple of seats, Daddy sniffled, and that nearly undid Keith's composure too.

"I think we will build a wonderful life togeth—togeth-ther," she said, looking at her card again. She paused, like she'd gotten lost, and Keith's muscles tensed again. As the seconds ticked by, he wanted to take the card gently from her and tell her to simply look at Lars.

To his surprise, Lars reached out and covered the card with his hand. He said nothing, but Britt looked up at him. He smiled at her, not in a patronizing way. Not like she was a problem either.

"We will build a wonderful life together," he said.

Britt's eyes shone with tears now too, and Keith sincerely hoped they were happy ones and not embarrassed or sad ones. "I will do my best every day," she said, her voice turning tinny. "I promise."

He nodded, and tears splashed down her face. "I love you, and I'm so glad I get to be your wife."

Gloria wiped her face with her hand and then stood to collect the card. The altar, Lars and Britt, and the flowered and lit arch blurred as Keith's eyes filled with water. He had only seen Gloria cry a couple of times, and both were when she'd been physically hurt. She was tough as nails and yet perfectly soft and maternal too, and seeing her cry over this wedding made Keith so emotional.

He put his arm around her, and she leaned into his chest for a moment. Daddy wept openly as Lars lifted his hands and brushed away his bride's tears.

"I love you, Brittany Rose," he said, using her first and middle name. "For me, it was love at first sight, and when you wouldn't go out with me, I begged God to tell me what to do. How to get you into my life."

He held no note card and read from no paper. He simply gazed at Britt with pure, unadulterated love on his face. "He told me to be your friend. I have tried to do that every day since, and I'm so happy that I get to marry my best friend today. I will work hard every single day of my life to give you what you want and need, and to be the man you want and need."

He took both of her hands in his and pulled her closer and closer until he leaned down and his forehead touched hers. They both closed their eyes, and Keith wanted to pause time and look at the sweetness of this situation over and over and over.

"I love you," he said out loud despite how close they stood.

"I love who you are, and how much you love dogs, and that you'll come sit with me at the house while I rebuild the cabinets or fix a leak in the roof. We are going to be so happy together, okay?"

She nodded, and Lars turned back to the pastor, tucking Britt against his side. She held onto him too, and Keith couldn't see her face as Pastor Milligan asked them to pledge themselves to each other.

When she said, "I do," Uncle Boone whooped. When Lars did, several more people cheered. And when Pastor Milligan finally said, "I pronounce you husband and wife," the roof got lifted off the barn from the applause and cheering, Keith's included.

———

A COUPLE OF HOURS LATER, Keith stood on the edge of the dance floor, watching Britt and Daddy sway back and forth. The wedding had transformed into a dinner in the stable, and then they'd come back to this part of the barn for the dance. His feet ached, and he was ready to get out of his constraining white shirt and tie.

He wanted this to be over, so he could say he got through it, and he could face the future with Britt as a married woman. He'd tried to tell himself over and over that things wouldn't change, but of course they would.

Keith knew that better than most.

Lars cut into the dance, and Daddy grinned as he spun Britt in her bright pink party dress into the arms of her husband. She squealed, and he laughed, and the whole scene was just farm-perfect.

Gloria moved into Daddy's arms, and they'd had their first real love connection at another wedding during the dancing portion. Hunter and Molly's, and they moved onto the dance floor too.

Keith turned to Lindsay and smiled at her. "Can I have this dance?"

"Yes, you may." She smiled back at him, put her hand in his, and let him lead her onto the dance floor.

Taking her into his arms felt natural now, but Keith still looked around to see if anyone was watching them. It felt like every person in the room had zeroed in on them, and he found his father and Uncle Boone watching. Cord and Mission—the latter staring openly until Cord swatted his chest and Mission practically jumped out of his own skin.

So Keith hadn't dated in a while. It wasn't *that* big of a deal.

Gerty watched him too, casually lifting her cup to her mouth but her eyes never leaving him. Even Travis and Gray, who stood together, looked his way.

"Everyone is staring at me," he muttered.

Lindsay leaned closer. "I'm sorry?"

"Everyone is staring," he said louder. He'd sat at the family table with her during dinner. Hadn't everyone gotten their fill of them then? He'd introduced her to Mike and Gerty there, as well as his younger sisters and Uncle Boone's younger kids.

He certainly hadn't thought he'd need to go around to everyone who'd ever worked on the farm and give them a formal introduction. He moved with Lindsay, and she said, "It's fine, Keith. They're your friends, right?"

"Yes," he murmured.

"Mine acted the same way, remember?"

He stopped swinging his gaze around the crowd and focused on her. "Max did seem very interested in us," he said.

She gave him a smile. "Right. So tell me about your favorite Christmas movie."

Keith's mind blanked. "I'm supposed to have a favorite Christmas movie?"

Lindsay laughed, tilting her head back slightly as she did to reveal more of that slender, kissable neck. He couldn't believe he'd kissed her before the wedding, but then again, he couldn't believe he'd left her farm yesterday *without* kissing her.

"Okay, cowboy," she said. "A favorite Christmas tradition?"

"Okay." He swallowed, his focus narrowing to just her. "My daddy, when we first moved here to the farm, wanted us to feel like we were still in Montana. It always snows before Christmas in Montana, and my parents always made hot chocolate and Belgian waffles for breakfast on Christmas morning. Well, it didn't snow that first year we lived here full-time, and my daddy bought a bag of the fake stuff and figured out a way to get it to fall down gently when we woke up in the morning. So it looked like it was snowing, and he had hot chocolate and Belgian waffles ready for us."

Keith grinned at the memory, the scent of chocolate actually coming into his nose. "He doesn't make it snow anymore, but we still have hot chocolate and waffles before anyone opens a single present on Christmas Day."

"Will you do that this year?" Lindsay asked. "Your first year at Blackhorse?"

Keith already had plans to be at his parents' house for their Christmas Day celebration. "Yeah," he said. "But I'll be back at Blackhorse in time for the dinner there. It's not until four o'clock." He peered at her through the dim light and shadows cast by the fairy lights that had been hung in the rafters. "Right?"

"Right," Lindsay said.

"Keith," someone said, and he looked up.

Gerty stood there, something sharp and knowing on her face. "Dance with me for a minute."

"I—"

"Tucker will take Lindsay." Sure enough, she'd brought Tucker Hammond with her, and sure enough, he eased Lindsay into his arms on the next step Keith took.

His feet came to a halt as the other cowboy whisked her away, and he frowned as he looked at his cousin. "What is going on?"

"I just want to talk to you for a minute." Gerty put her hands on his shoulders, and with her big baby belly, he certainly couldn't hold her too closely.

"When is this baby coming?" he asked. "You're enormous."

"Not fast enough," she complained. "Mike's making Tag watch me twenty-four-seven. My momma comes over all the time now too, and I swear, I can't even lift a fork without someone gasping." She rolled her eyes, but Keith found her distaste for being babied—in her condition—quite funny.

He chuckled, but Gerty did not. She could be a little sour sometimes, but it was only because she had such strong opinions. "Listen, I don't really want to talk about Lindsay all that much. I met her a couple of days ago, and I was snowed in with her, and it's really new, okay?"

"Yeah, so new, you've kissed her already." Gerty's eyebrows went up, and Keith's face burned.

He leaned closer to her. "How do you know that?"

"I just do," she said. "So not that new."

"Yes," Keith said. "We just happened to spend a couple of nights together on the couch during the storm, that's all. It was like...speed dating."

"A couple of nights together on the couch?"

"The power was out." For one of the nights, anyway. "It was something like forty straight hours together. That's got to be the equivalent to ten dates or whatever. It's fine that I kissed her tonight." And that he wanted to do it again.

Gerty gave him a dubious look but didn't argue.

Keith realized the gold mine he currently danced with. "You and Mike fell in love fast," he said.

"We'd been together before," she said.

"So you're telling me you waited all this time to kiss him?"

"I'm not telling you anything," Gerty said.

"But how fast is too fast to fall for someone?" Keith glanced over to Lindsay and Tucker, and she currently smiled and said something as if she was having a grand time.

"Ah, so you're falling already."

"Yeah," Keith murmured, because he wasn't a child and saw no reason to hide it. "She's...I don't know. There's something about her that makes me smile."

Gerty didn't say anything as the song ended. She dropped her hands and said, "Keith."

He looked at her, only realizing then that he'd been staring at Lindsay and ignoring his cousin. She smiled at him anyway. "I can see you really do like her. That's all I wanted to know."

"I think you could see that from the sidelines," he said.

"Yeah, but this bought me a few minutes away from my babysitter."

"Hey, baby," Mike said, joining her. He put his arm around her and smiled at her, then Keith. "Howdy, Keith."

"Heya, Mike." Keith shook the man's hand and smiled at Gerty too. She loved her husband fiercely, he knew that.

Another song came on, and Gerty turned to him. "Dance with me, baby."

"Fine, but this is the last one."

"I'm fine, Mike," she said as they swayed away from Keith. He sidled up to Lindsay, who now stood talking to Deacon and Tucker, and she grinned at him when she turned toward him.

"Tucker's a rodeo manager."

"Yes, he is," Keith said, looking at the other cowboy. "Did you do rodeo, Linds?" The nickname just rolled off his tongue, and she didn't even blink at it.

"No," she said with a laugh. "But I dated a couple of rodeo guys in high school." She looked over to Tucker. "No one famous, though. No one who went on to do anything."

He nodded, and Keith tugged on her hand. "Let's get some cake." He looked at the Hammond boys. "Excuse us, guys."

"Yeah, sure," Tucker said, and Keith led Lindsay away from them. He took her toward the cake, sure, but then past the table where cut slices awaited them.

"Keith," Lindsay said as if he'd gone blind and couldn't see the cake. He kept going, finally getting to the end of the barn that led into the attached stable. He pushed through the door there, glanced over his shoulder to the brightly lit party behind him, and then closed the door once Lindsay had joined him in the dimmer, cooler barn.

"What are we doing?" she whispered.

"I just needed some fresh air," he said, also in a lower voice.

"It was kind of hot in there."

The sound of gentle horse movements and snuffling filled the quiet air here, and Keith paced away from Lindsay for a couple of strides and then turned back to her. "Thanks for coming to the wedding with me."

"It was a beautiful ceremony," she said. "Your sister is amazing."

"She is." He nodded as he took her into his arms. "I think you're amazing."

"Thank you."

"Tell me what I should expect things to be like on Christmas Day," he said. "You'll introduce me to your aunt and uncle as your boyfriend? Or...we're just showing up together? Or...." He trailed off, his nerves about the upcoming holiday warring inside him. "I've never been to the thing at Blackhorse."

And he just needed to breathe for a minute, until he had a plan for Christmas Day dinner with Lindsay—and everyone else at Blackhorse Bay.

"I think I know what you really wanted to do," she said, ignoring his questions.

"Oh, yeah?" He took in a deep breath of her hair, getting something fruity and a little acidic. Probably her hairspray. "What's that?"

"You wanted to get me alone so you could kiss me again."

"Guilty," he murmured, pulling back enough to look down at her. He didn't ask permission this time. He didn't need to. He simply lowered his head and touched his mouth to hers. She caught on, and she kissed him with more movement and passion than he'd started with.

He caught up quickly, and yeah, he could definitely get used to kissing this bold, beautiful, breathtaking woman.

So much for getting more air—or answers to his questions about the Christmas Day celebration on her uncle's farm.

CHAPTER
Seventeen

LINDSAY GLANCED AROUND THE KITCHEN, her eyes landing on Hamlet in his red, white, and green-checkered bandana. She smiled at the heeler and said, "You're adorable." He came trotting toward her, his head down, and his eyes delighted.

She gave him a scratch and then pulled down her skirt. It fell to her feet in waves of dark green, and she'd paired it with a white blouse that had holly berries embroidered on the collar. A little old-fashioned, but she liked dressing up for the holidays.

Her neighborhood party last night had been fun and festive, but she'd missed Keith. She did her work in the barn with her horses and chickens, but she missed Keith. They'd been texting, and she'd even video-chatted with him yesterday as he drove to his parents' house for Christmas Eve, but talking to him and texting him wasn't the same as being in the same space as him.

She drew in a deep breath and moved over to the counter to pick up his Christmas gift. It could possibly be lame, but it could also be a homerun, and she wouldn't know until she showed up at Blackhorse Bay and gave it to him.

Still, she didn't rush for the exit. With seeing Keith, she'd also have to confront Derrick face-to-face, as well as Uncle Jack and Aunt Lenora. Keith had asked her if she'd introduce him as her boyfriend, and she hadn't answered before he'd kissed her.

Her stomach growled; she thought of the delicious spread of food Uncle Jack always had for his cowboys at the ranch; she picked up her phone and started a text to Keith.

I'm on my way, she typed out. *And I've decided I'm going to introduce you as my boyfriend unless you have a problem with that.*

The cowboys at her uncle's ranch had their phones attached to them and on all the time. She knew, because she'd worked at Blackhorse plenty of times. Uncle Jack wanted to be able to get ahold of anyone, everyone, with one text. Sometimes he had to call everyone in off the ranch for safety reasons, and sometimes he just needed to get in touch with someone to let them know he appreciated their work.

No matter what, phones were closeby with the volume up.

So it didn't surprise Lindsay to see Keith respond with, *No problem with me. See you soon.*

She couldn't read any emotion in those words, and that was another reason she wanted to be in the same space as Keith. Then she could read his body language and see his expression. The cowboy didn't hide much behind those eyes, which made her smile as she looked down at Hamlet.

"Come on, bud," she said. "It's time to go."

He trotted ahead of her to the utility room exit, and she followed him across the deck, down the steps, and then into the garage. It was attached to the house, but she didn't have a direct entrance. No matter what, she had to go outside from the garage to get into the house. She'd thought about having someone come do an appraisal of what it would cost to put in a door, but she'd never done it. Such a project lingered on her list, much the same way the remodel in the basement did.

Hamlet jumped into her truck, and Lindsay set the gift bag on the console between the two front seats. Then she and Hamlet started their drive across the northern edge of the city of Denver to Blackhorse Bay.

Keith had spent the morning with his family, and he'd sent her several pictures with his parents, his siblings, their Christmas breakfast feast, and their tree. He'd gotten new gloves and new boots and new bedding for his cabin. His sisters had given him his favorite candies and treats—and now Lindsay knew he liked barbecue potato chips, Twix candy bars, and peanut butter M&Ms.

She hadn't gotten him any of those things, and her stomach cinched. "It's fine," she said to Hamlet. "He'll like this too."

Before she knew it, she'd made the turn off the highway to Blackhorse Bay, and the enormous boarding facility spread before her. Two big buildings blocked the view from the highway and kept the vehicle noise at bay.

She went between them and watched the stables bloom before her. Horses did make her happy, and Lindsay smiled at the hundreds of stalls which protected the equines, the immaculately plowed roads and paths, and the few cowboys she saw moving about.

The party would be in the administration building now on her right, and Lindsay glanced at it to find three big, brightly lit, Christmas trees dressed and glowing out on the patio area. Pure joy struck her in the chest, and Lindsay's eyes filled with tears.

She loved Christmas, and it was hard to feel isolated from

her core family. Thoughts of her momma and daddy ran through her mind. Childhood memories of Christmas trees just like those, with white lights and plenty of presents underneath. The scent of hot chocolate and hot coffee and hot maple syrup filled her nose, reminding her of family meals around her childhood dinner table.

She hadn't had one of those in a long, long time.

"This is that," she told herself firmly, blinking back the tears. "You have that with Uncle Jack, Derrick, and Aunt Lenora."

And now, maybe Keith too.

The cowboy cabins started around the corner and across the lane from the stables, and since Keith held a managerial position here, his came into sight pretty quickly. His driveway sat cleared too, with four trucks parked in a single row in the driveway. Lindsay had been to this cabin plenty of times over the past several years, but today, everything felt different.

She felt like a new and changed person, and she couldn't believe a snowstorm had altered so much in her life.

As she brought her truck to a stop, Hamlet put his paws up on the cusp of the door where it met the window, his face practically smashed into the glass.

Lindsay looked that way too, and she found Keith leaning against the porch railing, smiling in her direction. A grin popped onto her face too, and she couldn't call it back even if she'd wanted to.

With the truck in park, she slid from the driver's seat and turned back for Hamlet. "Come on, bud. This side." She never went around to let her dog out, and she wouldn't tonight either just because Keith loitered over there.

Hamlet nearly jumped into her, but she managed to avoid him as she reached for the gift bag. With everything she needed right now in her hands, she headed around the front of the truck to greet her very real boyfriend.

The porch only had one set of steps leading up to it, and Keith came down them as she approached along the sidewalk.

"Hey, you." Keith grinned as he crouched to greet Hamlet. Her dog sat down and took his love from Keith's big hands, and Lindsay smiled as she kept walking.

She arrived, and Keith rose to his full height. His smile only increased, and he eased her into his arms without another word. Without any awkwardness at all, without the tension she felt radiating through her whole body.

"You're not wearing a coat," he said as his hands slid down her barely-there sleeves. "Let's go inside."

"I got you a present," she said as she lifted the holiday bag.

He looked at it and then her, and she noted that he hadn't kissed her. She wondered where her brother was, and what, if anything, had been said between him and Keith.

Lindsay slid a glance to the cabin, didn't see anyone, and then smiled up at Keith again. "Merry Christmas."

"Mm, Merry Christmas," he practically purred, and then he turned and they went up the stairs together.

Inside the cabin, she didn't see any of his cabinmates anywhere. Not in the kitchen, the dining room that held a table for six but only had four chairs, or the living room that held two full-sized couches and a bean bag.

Keith didn't pause or turn back to her. He stepped over to a short, probably only six-foot-tall Christmas tree and pulled something from the branches. His eyes skated past hers as he took her hand again and led her down the hall now.

Her heartbeat bumped strongly against her ribs, because the only thing down here was bedrooms. Keith glanced left and right, like he was looking for traffic as he crossed the street, and he practically ducked into the last room on the left.

She nearly ran into the room after him, and the door closed almost before her second cowgirl boot had entered. "What is going on?"

"Derrick is going to be here soon," he said.

Lindsay searched his face. "Are we hiding from my brother?"

"No."

"Isn't he going to see me come out of your bedroom?" Not only that, but her truck sat out front. So did Derrick's for that matter.

"I just wanted...a minute." Keith took her gift bag then and he set it aside. Where, Lindsay didn't know, because she couldn't tear her eyes away from her handsome cowboy boyfriend.

Something soft finally melted into his expression, and he slid one hand along her waist and around to her back so beautifully slowly. She felt every inch of his touch, and he pulled her gently closer. "I don't like that I don't see you every day," he said just before his mouth touched hers lightly.

He flirted with kissing her without actually doing it, and Lindsay wanted so much more from him. She leaned into his chest, into his touch, and she kissed him fully in the next moment.

His lips curved up for half a heartbeat, and then he wrapped his other arm around her and held her the way she expected her boyfriend to hold her.

When she pulled away, she ducked her head, trying to catalog her heartbeat, her adrenaline, the way her breath slid through her nose and easily down into her lungs. She opened her eyes and looked up through her lashes to see his face.

"I didn't want an audience for that," he whispered. He drew in a quick breath and stepped back. "Let's do presents." He stepped sideways and picked up her bag and handed it to her. "Mine isn't anything special."

"Neither is mine." Lindsay wondered if Keith wanted big celebrations or not. "How was your Christmas morning?"

"Amazing," he said.

"Do you have big parties?"

"If we meet up with my uncle," he said. "Or the Hammonds. But my daddy just wanted it to be us this year, since Britt is gone."

"How's he doing now that she's married?"

"Good." Keith reached up and ran his hand through his hair. He picked up his cowboy hat and reseated it on his head. Lindsay hadn't even noticed it had fallen off.

"You have great hair," she said, not sure where the words had come from. "I spent Christmas morning making cinnamon rolls for tonight's party," she said. "I talked to my mama, but I haven't called my daddy yet."

Keith watched her, something caring moving through his eyes. "When are you going to do that? I've heard this party takes the whole night."

Lindsay wasn't sure, and she shrugged. "I don't know. I was going to talk to Derrick about it and see if he's called yet. Maybe we could put in our ten minutes together."

Keith drew her into his chest again, his embrace warm and comforting. "I'm sorry about your daddy."

"I don't know what to do about him," she said.

"Is there something to do?" Keith asked.

"Get a therapist?" she joked. Keith did not smile, and Lindsay's faded from her face too.

"Have you ever seen a counselor?" Keith asked.

Lindsay turned away from him, but there wasn't a big space to hide in. "No," she admitted.

"Maybe you should." He put one hand on her elbow, just a touch, and then it disappeared. "I've seen a therapist, and it helped a lot."

"Do you still go?" she asked, looking at his made bed. Keith had almost everything he owned in its correct spot, and she saw how neat he was. Or maybe he'd cleaned up because he'd planned to bring her in here and kiss her.

"No," he said. "But it was helpful when I needed it."

She drew in a deep breath. "Okay," she said. "Open my gift."

Lindsay turned and thrust it toward him, her smile back in place. Keith studied her for a moment, all seriousness on his face. Then that mask broke, and he gave her that sexy, almost crooked smile, ducked his head, and took the bag.

She'd stuffed it with tissue paper, and he pulled it out. Lindsay pulled in a breath and held it as he took out the puzzle.

His face lit up, and he looked from the box to her face. "It's the town of Ivory Peaks."

Lindsay nodded and pointed to the corner. "I'm pretty sure those are those big pine trees out on the Hammond Family Farm."

Keith gazed at the box, then lifted his hand to the side of her face. "Thank you." He kissed her again, another sweet, slow kiss that didn't last as long as their first.

"There's more," she said as he pulled away. Keith dipped his hand back into the bag and pulled out the coupon book. Lindsay wanted to rip it out of his hand, because it suddenly felt like a gift a ten-year-old would give to their daddy.

"These are coupons to come out to Twilight Fields." he raised his eyes to hers, stars and lights dancing in his. "To do puzzles."

"Read the fine print," she coached.

"The bearer of this coupon will also be treated to a dinner of his choice, a fun dog to curl up with, and a movie and caramel corn."

Keith started laughing, and he wrapped her up in his arms again. "I can't wait to use these." He kissed her sloppily, and then he stepped back and retrieved the gift he'd pulled from the tree.

"I haven't had much time to get to town," he said. "I hope you're not disappointed."

"We just started dating," she said as she looked at the square envelope. It bulged with something hard in it, and Keith had scrawled her name on the front of it.

She flipped it over and lifted the flap, which had only been sealed at the very tip. She pulled out a pin shaped like a horse, and she looked at the eye, which was a tiny diamond.

"It's a pin for your boots," he said, as if she didn't know.

She looked at him, pure wonder streaming through her. "I've seen these," she said. And they weren't cheap. "I love this." She bent quickly and started to attach it to the top of her boot.

She straightened and pushed her foot out to see it. "It's so stinking cute." She looked up at Keith. "I love this. Thank you." She touched her lips to his just as Derrick called, "Keith? You here, buddy?"

Lindsay turned toward the door and moved to Keith's side as it opened, and her brother stood there.

"We're ready to—" Derrick cut off as his eyes landed on Lindsay. "Oh. I didn't know you had company."

"Company?" Lindsay snorted and moved over to her brother. "Hey, Derrick." She swiped a kiss across his cheek and settled back onto her feet. "We were just exchanging gifts."

"Is that right?" Derrick looked over to Keith, who said nothing.

"Look at the boot pin Keith gave me." Lindsay showed Derrick her boot, and he glanced at it briefly.

"Nice," he said. "We're headed over to the party." He hooked his thumb over his shoulder. "You two comin'?"

"Yep," Lindsay said as Keith nodded. "We're comin'." She followed her brother down the hall and found Buck and Coy dressed in their holiday finest too. Every cowboy wore red or green, mixed with black, brown, white, or silver, and Lindsay found them all so adorable.

Keith slipped his hand into hers and said, "You guys know Lindsay, right? We've recently started seeing each other."

Buck grinned at the two of them while Coy simply nodded. "Merry Christmas, Linds," Buck drawled, and Lindsay smiled at him but didn't move over to hug him.

"Let's go," Derrick said. "Uncle Jack likes everyone to be there for the big speech." He led the way out of the cabin, and Keith followed him with Lindsay at his side.

She'd parked behind him, so they loaded into her truck, and she drove them all over to the administration building with the big Christmas trees.

Cowboys were lining up to park, and they joined the throng. She got a spot, took it, and the five of them, plus Hamlet, spilled from the truck, and Lindsay walked beside Keith to enter the building.

Uncle Jack and Aunt Lenora stood at the door, greeting every single cowboy as they arrived.

"There you are," he boomed to Lindsay. "I wondered when you'd show up."

She couldn't help grinning at him. "Uncle Jack." She stepped into his arms, and it really was like hugging her daddy. She let herself sink into him, into the cologne that smelled exactly like her father's, into the roughness of his skin, into the father figure-ness of him.

This was *home*, and it was okay that she'd only heard her mother's voice this morning, and that she and Derrick hadn't had time to do a joint call to their daddy. She could call him on her way home after the party.

"Uncle Jack," she said. "I know you know Keith, your agricultural manager." She fell back to Keith's side. "He's my boyfriend now too."

"Is that right?" Uncle jack looked over to Keith, not a single stitch of a smile anywhere in sight. "Keith?"

"Yes, sir," Keith said. "It's pretty new, but it's goin' well." He looked down at Lindsay, and they smiled at each other.

"Well, there's eggnog over at the drink station," Uncle Jack said.

"Merry Christmas," Aunt Lenora said. "Lindsay, baby, come give me a hug." She pulled Lindsay into her arms and held her tight. "You two make a handsome couple."

"Thanks, Aunt Lenora," she said as she pulled back. Her smile felt too tight on her face, but she moved with Derrick, Keith, Buck, and Coy further into the party.

The whole place held Christmas lights in white, and someone had put up wreaths, Christmas balls on ribbons, and pine garlands. Window clings stuck to the glass, and two more trees had been set up and decorated inside.

Long tables took up half the room, and salt and pepper shakers and plates of butter sat every so often.

The buffet took up the back wall, and Lindsay took the sheet pan of cinnamon rolls that way. Somehow, a spot had been left for the treats, and she slid them onto the table.

That done, she turned to face the party. Cowboys and cowgirls mingled together, talking and laughing. Most of them held something to drink, and she looked at Keith. "Coffee? Eggnog? Hot chocolate?"

"I'm not sure who drinks eggnog," he said. "But I'll see what else they've got."

Things felt a little stilted, but the moment Lindsay slid her hand into his, everything aligned. The world righted, and while Lindsay wasn't sure of her place quite yet—here at Blackhorse Bay, inside her own family, or even in her own life—with Keith at her side, she felt certain she'd find her way.

"Not so bad with Uncle Jack," she murmured, glancing over to him.

"No," he whispered back. "Not so bad."

The word *yet* wasn't vocalized, but Lindsay somehow felt it hovering in her head. She pushed it away as she picked up a glass of eggnog, held it up in a silent toast to Keith, and then took a drink while his face transformed into one of disgust.

CHAPTER
Eighteen

MICHAEL HAMMOND REACHED both arms up above his head and stretched to the right and then the left. A yawn filled his chest and came out of his mouth, and he looked over his shoulder to the open doorway of his home office.

Gerty was due with their first baby today, and he'd been working remotely for a week. He couldn't be more than an hour away from her if she went into labor, and they had no idea when she'd have the baby.

Something smelled like dinner, and he got to his feet. His bones and joints felt a little rusty, and Mike took another moment to move through the range of motion in his shoulder. He'd had it replaced about a year and a half ago, and the cold certainly didn't do it any favors.

He and Gerty lived on a beautiful farm that had thrived under his wife's care. She'd allowed Mike to hire a full-time foreman, and Tag ate dinner with them almost every night. He did have his own cabin here at the farm, and so did Gerty's grandparents.

Mike wasn't surprised to find Carrie bustling around the kitchen, pulling cornbread out of the oven and putting it next to a big pot of what smelled like beef stew.

She slathered butter over the top of the cornbread, and Mike's heart grew happier with every step he took. "Is Gerty sleeping?"

"I'm right here," Gerty said, her voice a monotone rising from the other side of the couch. Mike grinned as he leaned over the big cushy thing she'd bought to fill their farmhouse, and Mike loved cuddling with her and watching movies on long, cold dark weekends.

She lay flat on her back, her baby belly rising up and up and up, seemingly forever. If she'd had any fat on her body before she'd gotten pregnant, she wouldn't look so strange. But she hadn't, and Mike loved her so dearly.

"Are you resting?" he asked.

"Yes," she said. "He's moving so much tonight, and it's not pleasant."

"Maybe he'll be born today."

"It's evening," she said. "He'd have to be in a hurry to get out, and I don't think he is."

Mike smiled and reached over to stroke her hair back. "Are you warm enough?"

"No," she whispered. "But Grandma says dinner is almost ready."

"Dinner's ready," Carrie said as if on cue, and Gerty's eyelids fluttered open. Their eyes met, and Mike smiled at his beautiful wife. He leaned over the back of the couch and touched his lips to her forehead, expecting her to sigh.

Not gasp.

He pulled back, not sure what she needed. "Gerty?"

She rolled, pulled in a breath, and tried to sit up. Every movement of hers seemed to take so much effort, and Mike hurried around the couch to help her.

"Tag's not coming in," Kyle said as he came through the back door. "He's excited about somethin' on the TV."

Mike smiled at Kyle's use of "the" TV, as his grandfather had always put "the" in front of TV too. Mike helped Gerty all the way up, and she braced both hands against her belly.

Behind them, Carrie and Kyle chit-chatted, and the house held heat and light and hope and happiness.

But when Mike's eyes met Gerty's, a bolt of fear struck through him. Her face held only paleness, with wide eyes filled with anxiety. Mike had seen this look on her face before, and he did not like it.

"Are you okay?"

She shook her head. "I think I may have had a contraction." She gripped his fingers. "How do you know? It's not like I've had one before."

"You've read books," he said, as if they could adequately describe what it felt like to go into labor.

She sat very still, and some color started to come back into her face. "Maybe I just need to eat," she said.

"Let's go eat." Mike got to his feet first, and he offered his hand to Gerty. She got to her feet with some struggle, and he helped her over to the table. A moment later, her grandmother put a bowl of stew in front of her and smoothed her hair back.

"You look a little peakish," she said to Gerty.

Gerty said nothing, and Mike waited until they all had a

bowl of stew and a big platter of cornbread sat in the middle of the table.

"I'll pray," he said, only looking away from his wife for a moment. Gerty gave him a couple of short nods, and Mike bowed his head.

"Dear God," he said. "Thank you for this good day. We hope we have worked sufficiently to show our gratitude for all of the blessings Thou hast given us. We're grateful for this farm Thou has entrusted us with, and we're grateful for Carrie and Kyle's help this winter. Bless this food and those who made it. Amen."

He prayed over his job at other times, and over Gerty all day long, and for his parents, his siblings, and every farm animal Gerty had brought to this place at still other times.

But right now, he wanted to see his wife's face again. Mike immediately looked at her, and he found her leaning her head into her hands. Her eyes opened slowly, and she'd lost her color again.

Something told Mike not to sit there, and he said, "I'm taking Gerty to the hospital," as he got to his feet, his stew forgotten.

"What?" Carrie looked over to her and pulled in a breath. "Goodness, she's gone white."

"Can you grab our baby bag?" Mike stood and took Gerty by the elbow. The fact that she hadn't protested spoke volumes, and her grandfather came to her other side.

"I'll grab your keys," Kyle said, and together, they helped Gerty into Mike's truck, which sat parked outside.

Kyle passed Mike his keys, and Carrie rushed the bag down the front steps. "We're praying," she said, and Mike thanked her and got behind the wheel.

He started the truck and got it moving before he looked over to Gerty. "You tell me if you're going to pass out," he said.

Gerty looked at him. "What if they turn us away?"

"Then we'll come home," he said. "But I don't like the look of you. You're not responding, and you're not talking. And you keep losing your color."

She nodded, and Mike reached over and took her hand in his. "Squeeze if it hurts, okay?"

She nodded again, and Mike made it off their property and onto the highway. Only a minute later, her hand in his tightened and tightened, and he looked over to her.

"This is definitely a contraction," she gasped out. She groaned, and Mike suddenly wanted to be in her place. He'd do anything to protect her from discomfort, heartache, or pain, and he felt absolutely helpless as she went through the contraction.

It subsided, and she relaxed in the seat beside him, her strong fingers relaxing in his.

"It's too far to the hospital," he said.

"Well, keep driving, Mister," she said. "I'm not having this baby in the dark on the side of the highway."

"Tell your son that," Mike said, but he pushed the truck to keep moving faster and faster. Unbeknownst to Gerty, Mike had driven this road before, just to time it to see how long it would take him to get his wife to the hospital.

Thirty-nine minutes, and Mike prayed for every single one of them. Gerty's contractions continued, and they came closer together before he pulled up to the brightly lit hospital.

He jumped from the truck and hurried around to help her down. "Can you walk?"

"Yes, for now." She waddled for certain, but they moved into the building without a problem. He grabbed a wheelchair, and she sat. He got her up to labor and delivery, and he said to the nurse sitting at the desk, "She's been contracting for about forty-five minutes. They're coming every three minutes or so, and she almost loses consciousness with every one."

"Mike," Gerty said, and he spun to her just as she started to slump forward over her baby belly.

"We've got her," a nurse said, and more seemed to appear out of nowhere.

"Walk with me," one said, and Mike got separated from Gerty as another started to push her ahead of them. "What's her name?'

"Gertrude Hammond," he said.

"Date of birth?"

Mike continued to give the personal details the hospital staff needed, all while keeping his eye on his wife. Nurses helped her change, and then they put her back in bed.

Finally, Mike went to her side, kissed her forehead, and held her hand in both of his. "Maybe he will be fast," he murmured.

"No one has their baby on their due date," she said back, and there was his salty Gerty.

"Well, you went into labor," he said. "I'm counting it."

"Did you text anyone?"

"Nope."

"I'm sure Granny did." She sighed, then sucked in a breath. The monitors she'd been hooked to started making way more noise, and Mike looked at them, alarmed.

"It's fine," a nurse said as she came in to silence the machines. "But a nice contraction."

"For who?" Gerty growled, and Mike had to agree.

Things moved quickly for several minutes, as Gerty got put on an IV, and then a doctor came in to give her the epidural. She hadn't wanted to do anything naturally, and as Mike watched his wife start to relax now that she wasn't in so much pain, he was so glad he'd brought her in when he had.

He stood out of the way until he could return to Gerty's side, and then, everything slowed down. A doctor came in and checked her. "Looking good," he said.

"Really?" Gerty glared at him. "I've been here forever, and I'm still pregnant."

Mike stifled his smile, but the doctor didn't. "I'm sure it feels that way." He stood. "I'll come check on you again."

He came every half hour, and on the third time, he said, "Okay, Gerty, we're gonna get you moving a little bit."

A nurse put something in her IV, and the doctor didn't leave the room. Gerty got raised to sit in the bed, and Mike moved to stand behind her, shoring her up.

"All right," Doctor Tasman said. "It's time to push."

Gerty did what was asked of her, and with every moment that passed, Mike loved and appreciated her more and more and more.

"Here he is," the doctor finally said, and a tinny, high-pitched wail of a baby followed. Mike couldn't look away from the red infant as he got lifted up, and instant love filled him.

And filled him and filled him.

"I'm going to go...." He walked over to the nurse who'd taken his baby and wrapped him up. She took him over to a scale and weighed the baby, then put an ID band around his skinny little ankle. She wiped him all up, cleaning him thoroughly, and then wrapped him in a pale blue blanket.

"Here you go, Daddy," she said, passing the baby to Mike.

He gazed at the infant, pure joy and happiness pulling through him. "Look at him, Gerty." He looked over to his wife, still several paces away in the hospital bed.

She looked at him earnestly, and Mike took the baby over to her. "Look at him. He's perfect—and blonde. Gerty, he's blonde like you."

Everyone had expected the baby to be a Hammond through and through. Mike had dark coloring—dark eyes, dark hair, dark everything, and Gerty was his opposite.

"Look at him."

"He's beautiful," she whispered as Mike slid him into her arms. "We can still name him after your daddy, right?"

"As long as you think yours will be okay with it." They'd kept the name of their baby a secret from everyone, not wanting any opinions on the matter.

"He'll be okay," Gerty whispered. "He'll be thrilled to meet West Michael Hammond." She leaned over and touched her lips to his son's forehead, and Mike leaned forward and kissed hers.

He loved her; he loved that baby; he adored his family.

"God is so good," he murmured. "He is so good."

CHAPTER

Nineteen

HUNTER HAMMOND PULLED up to his house, the word *home* moving through his body, mind, and spirit. "Home," he even whispered. He'd been up in Coral Canyon for the past couple of days, without his wife and family, and nowhere could truly be home without them.

This farm meant a great deal to him, even snow-covered and monotone in the winter as it was. Brown dirt roads. Deep green, almost black pine trees. And white, white snow for miles, only broken by more brown houses, brown barns, and brown branches.

He'd grown up here on this farm, and he had a lifetime of summer memories in the sunshine, with green pastures, rolling clouds, and blue skies overhead. He'd ridden horses here, and gone to school here, and fallen in love here.

Now, he raised his family here, and soon, his sister would start her new life with a cowboy who'd worked here for years as well.

Cord and Jane's wedding sat only a week away, and Hunter had gone to Coral Canyon to get a whole slew of cousins to come down for the wedding.

Of course they would. Hunter had really gone to show them they could drive the road between Coral Canyon and Ivory Peaks in the winter. And to visit them, too. He liked getting away every once in a while, and Molly was kind enough to take on the entire family responsibilities, much the way she had when he'd been CEO of HMC.

He got out of the truck and went up the front steps of the farmhouse. Inside, he called, "Daddy's home," and cheering happened from the back of the house, where the large kitchen, living room, and dining room sat.

"Daddy!" Charlotte called, and Hunter grinned as he strode down the hallway and into the kitchen. He swept his darling girl into his arms and kissed her cheek.

"Hey, princess." He looked over to Molly, who sat at the kitchen table with Clay. The little boy slid from the chair and ran toward him, and Hunter set down Charlotte to pick up his youngest son.

"Why are you home, Char?" he asked. Molly home-schooled Clay for now, but Charlotte had gone to school this year.

"She missed her ride," Molly said dryly, and Charlotte turned her back on Hunter and skipped into the kitchen.

"Momma said I could make you some welcome-home cupcakes."

Hunter met his wife's eyes, and so much was said. *Yeah, cupcakes*, Hunter thought. *To keep her busy.*

"Hey." Keith walked in the back door, and neither Molly nor Hunter were surprised. People came in and out of the farmhouse all the time. His daddy had warned him of such a thing, and Hunter had grown used to it. Mostly.

He did grin at Keith, and he looked at the auburn-haired beauty who followed him. "Hey," he said.

"This is Hunter and Molly Hammond," Keith said, and Hunter wondered if this was some kind of tour. "Guys, this is my girlfriend, Lindsay. She wanted to see the farm, because she's got a hobby farm too, and—"

"It's so much smaller than this," Lindsay said, shooting Keith a look filled with apprehension. "But yes."

"My daddy said we could come today," Keith said. "Since the weather's been so good."

"Bright, sunny, and cold," Molly said. "Are you guys hungry?"

"Yeah," Keith said. "I maybe bribed her out here because my uncle said he'd feed us. But we just went by there, and my aunt is dealing with a dishwasher flood."

"Oh, boy," Hunter said. "I just got back, and you know what I have in the truck?"

"It better be the pizzas I asked you to get," Molly said, and she put her hand on Hunt's chest and leaned in to kiss him quickly.

"Pizza my wife asked me to get," Hunter said. "Feels like the Lord knew about the dishwasher leak." He smiled at Keith and Lindsay, noting how shiny and glowing they seemed.

"How long have you two been dating?" he asked. He was only about a decade older than Keith. A dozen years maybe. Not quite another generation, but not quite the same one either.

"Couple of months now," Lindsay said. "I can help with lunch. I'm pretty good in the kitchen."

"I'm not going to say no to that," Molly said. She gave Lindsay's free hand a squeeze. "Are you the one Matt told me I should recruit for horseback riding lessons this spring?" She looked between Keith and Lindsay, and Keith started nodding.

"I don't know about that," Lindsay said. "But I love this farm."

"She does her own riding lessons," Keith said. "About forty minutes north of here."

"Mm, I see." Molly grinned at Lindsay and gave her a look that Hunter knew well. She was already thinking about how she could get Lindsay to come over to Pony Power. She walked past her and into the kitchen. "I'll get the ovens going. We can put a couple of pizzas in your momma's kitchen."

Hunt set down his son and said, "All right. I'll grab the pizzas." They were take-and-bake, and Molly hadn't wanted to cook tonight, not after Hunt had been gone for a week and he'd just be coming home. He'd entertain them all with stories and tales of Coral Canyon, and Hunt grinned as he walked through the cold to the back seat of the truck.

Keith had come with him, and Hunt passed him a stack of pizzas. "Are you sure there's enough for us?" Keith said. "I can just take Lindsay for lunch somewhere."

"Up to you," Hunter said. "But we have plenty." He lifted a stack of pizzas too and hipped the door closed. "I have a dozen pizzas."

"So you were going to feed the farm anyway."

"I don't know what my wife and momma are up to," Hunter said. "I just do what I'm told." He grinned at Keith. They went back into the house, and Hunter slid his stack of pizzas onto the counter alongside Keith's.

"Is Jane all ready for the wedding?" Keith asked, his eyes over on Lindsay as she did something with Charlotte at the table.

"Yeah, I think so," Hunter said.

"It's going to be beautiful," Molly said. "We're having it in our old backyard, actually."

"In February?" Lindsay asked.

"You would not believe what they can heat these days," Hunter said with a grin. He did not judge Jane for what she spent her money on. He'd started two charitable foundations, bought Molly as many horses as she wanted, and still gave donations to the businesses he'd helped fund and start over the years he'd been CEO at HMC.

If Jane wanted to have the backyard where she'd been living with Deacon cleared of all snow, and tents brought in that went all the way to the ground, and heat pumped through the entirety of it, she could.

And she wanted to, so Hunter had simply listened to Molly tell him about the plans she'd been helping his sister and momma with for the past several months.

Cord was the type of cowboy to fade into the woodwork, and Jane had promised to keep the wedding small. That meant a venue opposite of what Hunter had rented for his wedding, and fondness moved through him.

Yes, he'd done what he'd thought society expected of him, but he'd still enjoyed his wedding greatly.

So as Keith settled down with Lindsay and the kids at the table, he grinned at them too. To his knowledge, Keith hadn't dated a whole lot, but as Lindsay looked at him and laughed about something, they sure looked happy together.

Hunter moved into the kitchen, feeling tired and a bit travel-worn as he said, "Put me to work, baby," as he put his arm around his wife.

Molly smiled up at him, and Hunter took the moment to kiss her better than he had earlier. Mm, he loved kissing his wife, and he couldn't wait to tell her all about the house he'd found for his daddy in Coral Canyon.

Later. For now, he just wanted to help her get all these pizzas baked so they could feed the cowboys and then get them out of the farmhouse.

Then, finally, he'd have her all to himself, and they'd come up with a plan to present—really present—the idea of Daddy and Momma making the move to Coral Canyon permanently.

He knew they wanted to, but Hunt also knew Daddy would never pull the trigger. So Hunt would do the work for him, and then he, Molly, and Deacon would go over how they'd take care of the farm, and Daddy would finally be…released.

———

HUNTER WALKED into the house where he'd started raising his family. He and Molly had lived here for over a decade, actually. Maybe a dozen years or so. A long time, Hunter knew that. Now that he wasn't CEO anymore, he didn't have to keep track of time as much as he'd used to.

Jane came around the corner, wiping her hands on a towel. "Hunt." Her smile broke across her face, and Hunt wondered about the worry he'd seen.

"Just me," he said, his cowboy boots clacking on the tile the same way they always had. Jane tossed the towel onto the counter and turned back to Hunter in enough time for him to take her into a hug.

"You're getting married tomorrow," he whispered in her ear. "Are you ready?'

"I've been ready for this my whole life," she said.

"Are the other brothers here?"

Jane had invited her brothers over for dinner tonight, this last night of her single life. They'd held a rehearsal dinner last night, and Hunter could still see Cord's square jaw tightening over and over again. His momma had come to town, but he hadn't invited his brother. Hunter knew the man's history, and he'd been a proponent of Cord establishing the boundaries he needed to establish to keep himself safe in every way.

Hunter had had to do that with his own mother, and sometimes a hint of guilt or regret—something—pulled at him. But also, every time, Hunter got confirmation from the Lord that it was okay to keep a firm boundary between him and someone who could hurt him.

He'd forgiven his mother, but that didn't mean he had to willingly invite her into his life. Not everyone got a seat at his table, and she hadn't earned hers.

"Tucker landed about a half-hour ago," Jane said. "Deacon picked him up, and they're on their way."

Hunt nodded as he pulled back. He sat at the island in the kitchen and looked around. "Did you cater?"

"Of course I did," she said. "Deacon's moved out to the ranch, and Cord and I are moving in here after we get back from California."

"I still don't know anyone who takes a road trip for their honeymoon," he said, grinning at her. "Especially when they're a billionaire."

"Yes, well, it means something to us," Jane said. "And I don't want to deal with dishes and whatever for tonight when we're leaving tomorrow."

"What did you get?"

"I took a leaf out of your book," she said." And I got something for everyone."

"What does that mean?"

She gave him a grin, and Hunter loved Jane's smile. "You'll see."

Over the course of the next thirty minutes, dinner arrived—times four—and Hunter laughed and laughed when his showed up. He took Jane into his arms and said, "You're the best sister in the world."

"It's a sandwich, Hunt," she said.

"It's the gyro I love," he said. "Molly never lets me get this, because she doesn't think gyro meat is real meat."

Jane simply smiled and opened the door for the last item—a pizza that had Tuck's name all over it. The other brothers arrived a few minutes later, and their voices joined together as they all greeted one another, hugged, and laughed together.

Tuck traveled a lot for his job, as he managed a pro rodeo career for one of the bigger names out there right now. Deacon adored Tucker, and he looked at his older brother like he'd been dipped in gold. Hunt could agree that Tuck definitely had a big personality, but just because Deacon was a little quieter didn't mean he didn't have value too.

"All right, all right," Jane yelled over them. "Let's pray and eat, okay? We have a few things to discuss." She tossed a look to Hunter, but this was her house. He wasn't going to dictate things. "Hunt?"

He would pray, and he folded his arms and lowered his chin. "Lord," he said. "We're real grateful to be united as siblings tonight." His throat closed instantly, because Hunter didn't have full siblings. None of these people here with him tonight came from the same mother he did, and yet, their bond still felt as solid as steel.

"Thank you that Tucker could travel safely, and bless us that we can put Momma and Daddy right in the middle of our discussion tonight, not our own selves. Thank you for the good fortune you've always rained down on us, for a new baby in the Hammond family who was born healthy and strong. Bless Jane and Cord as they get married tomorrow, and bless all those who'll be there to be on their best behavior. Amen."

He opened his eyes and cleared his throat as his siblings echoed the end of the prayer.

"I got y'all's favorite things tonight," Jane said. "So there wouldn't be any squabbling." She picked up the pizza box. "Tuck, that Alfredo pizza you like with the artichoke hearts."

"Thank you, sissy." He took the whole box over to the table and then came back into the kitchen while Jane handed Hunt his Styrofoam container full of the best gyro in the city. Deacon got a grilled cheese sandwich made out of a waffle, as well as a big bowl of tomato basil soup to dip it in. Jane had ordered for herself a chicken bacon ranch salad, and she poured the dressing all over everything, closed the clamshell top, and shook it to coat the lettuce and veggies, meat and croutons, in ranch dressing.

Tucker handed out cups with ice, and Jane said, "There's soda and lemonade in the fridge." Tuck got what everyone wanted, and he became the last person to sit down at the table.

Hunter knew he'd lead out on this conversation. He wanted

to do so with a full belly and a happy heart, so he started eating, and he let Jane get the younger boys to give reports on what they'd been up to lately. Hunt could listen to them talk about their lives all day long. It was still miraculous to him that all four of them had lived and continued to live on such different tracks.

With his gyro gone, and Tuck's pizza box almost empty, Hunt finally dusted off his hands. "All right, guys," he said as he tapped on his phone. "I found the perfect house for Mom and Daddy." He glanced up as the website loaded. "It's close to town, but it's not in a fifty-five-plus community. I don't think Daddy will ever want to live there."

"Land?" Deacon asked. "He won't leave without a horse or two."

"Or five," Jane said with a snort.

"It's got a pasture, yes," Hunt said, and he turned his phone around. "It's a big house, because houses with pastures and big driveways to hold trucks, trailers, and motorhomes usually come big." He looked at the phone screen too as he started to swipe through the pictures. "But it's not as big as it looks. No basement. Three bedrooms, three bathrooms, three-car garage. It's flat parking, and the landscaping is done and mature."

"And it's for sale?" Jane asked, taking his phone. "How close is it to Uncle Wes? Or the other uncles?"

"It's on the west side of Canyon Street," Hunter said. "North of Main, but only a couple of blocks. The house is only a decade old, as the land used to be owned by one person. They had a huge lot, and they sectioned it up and sold it off a while ago. It's about in the middle of things, so they'll be close to Uncle Wes and Uncle Colt, but Cy and Ames are on the north side, right? They're gonna be further no matter what."

Hunter lowered his phone and looked around at his siblings. "Jane, I know you've said it, but we have to ask again."

She started waving her hand. "We don't want the farm."

"Cord too?" Hunt asked. "You're the next oldest, Janey. He's worked there for almost two decades. He's earned it, if you want it."

"We don't want the farm," she said again. "Cord and I are working on his mechanic shop, and he thinks we'll be able to open later this spring." She smiled at Hunt. "I swear. I'm not going to come back in a year, upset."

"Well, even if you do, it won't matter," Hunt said. "I've got Darla at HMC drawing up the contract." He grinned at Jane and then Deacon. Then he switched his attention to Tucker. "Tuck."

"I don't want the farm," Tucker said. "I like doing the rodeo thing, and I'm making good money."

"Rodeo careers don't last forever," Hunt said.

"No, but I'm a manager," Tuck said. "I'm not the one getting beat up by bulls and getting bucked off horses." He surveyed the siblings. "If I do want to come back, I can work the farm. Fine. But I don't want to own it. I don't need to manage it."

Hunter nodded, and then turned his attention to his youngest brother. "Deac."

"Sounds like it's mine," he said, and that was as good as him saying—again—that he wanted it. Hunter technically owned the farm right now, but Matt ran it, the same as always. Hunter loved living on the farm; he loved raising his children out in the country; he enjoyed driving them to school, to sports lessons, to piano, to whatever. He didn't need the money generated by the farm, and he wanted to spend his days doing what he did now.

Go fishing. Help his wife with the equine therapy unit they ran. Be a father.

Deacon was only twenty-five years old, and he wanted the farm. He'd always loved being a cowboy, and as he wasn't married yet, whenever he found someone, they'd know what they were getting.

Hunter shifted in his seat. "I want my son to have a place there," he said. "If he wants it." Ryder was only ten years younger than Deacon, and he worked around Pony Power every single day. "He might not want to be there long-term. He might simply take over Pony Power once Molly decides she's had enough of it. But I want him to have a place if he wants one." He watched Deacon. "So that'll be in the contract, unless there's some objections I need to know about right now."

"Anyone sitting here, or anyone we add to our family, kids, whatever, will have a place on the farm, whenever they want it." Deacon had grown up so much, and he reminded Hunt so much of their daddy. He hadn't gone to law school, and as far as Hunt knew, Deacon had done nothing with his inheritance yet.

Of course, not everyone needed to start two charitable foundations in their twenties, the way Hunt had done. He didn't judge his brothers at all. Everyone had their own journey, and he knew they worked through their decisions with their parents, and with God.

He put his hand out into the middle of the table. "All right," he said. Jane put her hand in, then Tuck, and then Deacon.

"Love you guys," Hunter said.

"Love you all," Jane said.

"I love you guys," Tucker said, and Deacon added, "Love y'all."

Hunter pulled his hand back and looked at his siblings in age-order. "I don't hear any ideas for how I should bring up this house to Mom and Daddy. So get talkin'."

"You never said if it was available," Jane said.

"It's not," Hunt said. "Because I bought it last week." He grinned around at everyone, his eyes landing on Jane. She shook her head even as a smile filled her face. Hunt waved both hands as if gathering big armfuls of snow toward him. "Ideas, guys. I need ideas."

CHAPTER

Twenty

GRAY HAMMOND TURNED toward his wife and let her fix his tie. "Our baby is getting married today," he murmured.

"She's actually our oldest," Elise said with a smile. She'd brought such a calmness to his life. She'd been his partner for just over thirty years, and he loved her with his whole soul. She patted his collar flat and backed up a couple of steps. "And she's been dying for this day for a long time. So we will not act like we're upset in any way."

"I'm not upset in any way," Gray said. "I love Cord, and I especially love Cord for Jane."

"Yes, I know."

"Jane knows," Gray said, reading between the lines of Elise's words. She reached up and touched the hair she'd already braided. It had only faded in color as she'd aged, and now that she was sixty-two, her white-blonde hair had really started to pale.

She tugged on the neckline of her mother's dress and turned her back on him. "Come help me with my necklace."

"Yes, ma'am," he murmured, and he moved behind her. He loved the flowery scent of her skin, and the way his body still reacted to hers. "I love you, Elise."

She laughed lightly and ducked her head. "I love you too, Gray."

He put on her necklace and ran his hands down her arms as he leaned down and pressed a kiss to the back of her neck. "Okay, so let's go see what they need our help with."

"No, sir." She turned and faced him. "You're going to stay right here until I bring you our daughter. She needs you right here, Gray." She smoothed her hands down the front of his suit coat, and Gray simply watched her. "Promise me you're going to stay right here." She looked up at him, and he nodded.

"All right," he said almost under his breath.

Elise took a big, deep breath. "Okay, I'm going to go help Jane with everything. It's not long now."

It definitely wasn't too far from the start of the ceremony, and Gray watched Elise as she slipped out of the bedroom they'd been assigned to get ready in. Jane would be in the master bedroom, where she'd been living for the past few years, since Hunt had moved to the farm with his family.

Gray honestly wasn't sure where he belonged. He and Elise had moved into the generational house without complaint. It was plenty big enough for where they were in their lives, with Hunt right next door, and now Deacon living in a cowboy cabin on the farm, and Jane here.

But all of his brothers were getting close to the same empty nester status where he and Elise were. Wes and Bree were there too, as were Colt and Annie. The twins were still raising their teenagers, but they'd be there in the next few years.

And with Daddy gone, Gray knew now more than ever that his family was up in Coral Canyon. He simply didn't know how to leave the farm that had been such a prominent thing in his life. In his children's lives.

He and Elise had talked it all to death, and no answers, no solutions, ever presented themselves. It was as if God had slammed the door in his face on the matter, and Gray was trying to find the right thing to do while stumbling around in the dark.

He paced over to the window and looked out. Whiteness blanketed the backyard. White snow. White tent, reaching up into the sky. It actually steamed, as Jane had brought heaters to keep the guests warm. They entered on the opposite side from where he stood, and Gray had attended plenty of weddings. With the ceremony set to start in only another fifteen minutes, the tent would be filling with guests.

Gray hadn't had much of a hand in planning the wedding, but Jane and Molly had spent hours with Elise at their dining room table, pouring over plans, plates of food, and the guest list. The Hammonds were a big family, well-known in the area, but Jane wanted a smaller, more intimate affair.

Cord required such a thing, and Jane would do anything to alleviate some of the stress and anxiety Cord had over becoming an official part of the Hammond family.

Thinking quickly, Gray moved over to the door and cracked it. Down the hall, he heard voices, and he switched his gaze the other way. Toward more bedrooms. He knew where Cord was, and despite his promise to his wife, he darted down the hall a couple of steps and knocked on the door across the hall.

Then he slipped inside and pressed his back to the closed door.

"Gray," Cord said, and he turned from the mirror. Travis Thatcher stood in the room with him, as did Mission Redbay and Keith Whettstein. They'd all been cowboys at the farm, and their friendship with Cord made a lot of sense.

"I just wanted to come say hi." Gray's heartbeat thumped in his chest. He knew Cord still looked at him as a father figure. He knew Cord worked as hard as possible to impress Gray. He hadn't always given the man the credit he deserved, nor the feedback that would've lifted him up.

He didn't want to spend the next few minutes apologizing. He just wanted Cord to know how very worthy he was to be Jane's husband. So while he'd heard Keith was dating someone new and he wanted to ask about that, and he had an inkling to make a dad-joke about how Mission was now one of the only single cowboys left on the farm, he stuffed all of that away.

He strode toward Cord, who was fully dressed in his black tux, shiny black boots, and big, wide, black cowboy hat. He grabbed onto the cowboy and pulled him right into his arms.

"I love you, Cord," Gray said, the words just there. The other man's arms came around Gray, and though the man had worked for Gray for a lot of years, this felt like the first time they'd truly bonded.

"I love you too, Gray," Cord said, his voice soft and rough. He clapped Gray on the back, and he stepped back.

"She loves you so much," Gray said. "And there has been a hole in our family just for you for so long."

Cord nodded, sniffed, and reached up to wipe his eyes. "I love her, Gray. I'm gonna take real good care of her."

"I know you are, son." Gray nodded to him, then Mission,

and then Keith. "Okay, my wife is going to fillet me alive if I'm not back in my appointed room when Jane's ready." Before he could turn to leave, the door opened again, and Elise stood there.

"Gray Hammond." She put her hand on her hip. "What are you doin' in here?"

"Leaving," he said, moving toward her now.

She gestured for him to go, and then she waved the others forward too. "Cord, Wes is going to take you out to the altar now."

"Yes, ma'am," he said, and he followed Gray out of the room. Gray ducked back into his room, but he didn't close the door as the others walked by. He pressed his fingers together, trying to get his mind back where it needed to be.

After all, he only had one daughter, and this would be the only time he'd get to walk someone down the aisle.

He rolled his neck left and right, finally looking heavenward. "Lord, bless this wedding to be exactly what my daughter wants."

God had answered plenty of Gray's prayers over the years, and he had no reason to think He wouldn't answer this one too.

————

CORD BEHR ROLLED his shoulders the moment before he stepped out of the house where he'd be living with Jane when they returned from their road trip to California's National Parks. Everything he owned had been packed in the past couple of days, including his bag which currently sat in the back of Jane's SUV.

He'd be driving it, and they had their case of water, plenty of food, and both of their bags.

Jane had planned for a mid-day wedding, with a luncheon to follow, and then he and the love of his life would be on their way. They planned to stop in Green River tonight, and Cord's excitement about the rest of today bloomed to life as he followed Jane's uncle Wes across the deck and down the steps.

The tent had a single doorway at the back, and Wes ducked through it. Cord followed him, and they walked side-by-side down the aisle. Cord nodded to the cowboys and cowgirls he knew from the farm, from Pony Power, or from the other ranches surrounding the Hammond Family Farm.

The altar waiting for him at the end of the aisle had been carved by Travis, and the man himself waited in the front row. When Cord arrived, he hugged Wes, then Jane's uncle Colt. Mission and Keith stood there, both with dates—Keith actually had a girlfriend now, but Mission had just invited someone for this wedding only, so he didn't have to attend alone.

Cord knew what that felt like, even if he'd never done such a thing. He'd always had Mission, to be fair.

Travis gripped Cord and said, "This is it, cowboy. Everything you've ever wanted." That was so true, and Cord prayed he wouldn't mess up too badly. He knew he couldn't be perfect, and Jane had already been so kind and so patient with him. He'd done the same for her, and in that moment, he experienced the sweetest feeling of...adequacy.

He belonged with Jane Hammond, and she belonged with him.

"Thank you, Trav." Cord stepped back and drew a deep breath before the broad-shouldered cowboy moved back to his spot in the row. That way, no one could see how nervous he was.

Who was he kidding? Every eye focused on him as Cord took his place, and he was sure his nerves showed plainly on his face. He watched that single doorway at the back of the tent, and he noted that none of the guests sat down. Jane had to be moments away from entering the tent.

He cleared his throat, trying to remember the vows he'd written for her. He hadn't wanted to recite them; he'd preferred the pastor say something meaningful about covenants and marriage, but Jane really wanted them to do their own vows.

Cord had written his, then had Trav go over them with him. Then he'd shown them to Jane, and she'd gone over them with him too. The last time he'd said them, he'd had every word memorized.

Right now, he couldn't remember a single word. His stomach swooped and swung, like a swing that had had one chain cut.

To make matters worse, Jane appeared in the doorway, an enormous bouquet of flowers held in front of her. They boasted the color of sagebrush, crimson, and ivory, and they matched the off-white color of Jane's gorgeous wedding dress.

It only had one strap that went up and over her left shoulder, leaving her other one completely bare. Somehow, she held the blooms with only one hand, and her other one reached down and pinched a piece of her dress, lifting it out to the side.

Her daddy entered through the side door, grinning for all he was worth. Gray wore a neatly trimmed beard the same color as his name, and he seemed so big and so radiant in his tuxedo. Cord wanted to be half the man Gray Hammond was, and it had meant the world to him to have his almost-father-in-law come to his room only minutes before the wedding and say he loved him.

His smile formed on his face as Jane looked at her father and then leaned into his kiss. Her hair had been swept up into an elegant knot, with flowers and gems along the seam of it. Gray slipped his arm through hers and held the flowers with her, and they both looked down the aisle.

Cord's pulse pounded and pounded and pounded, because they didn't move. Jane smiled at him from the end of the aisle, and Cord couldn't look anywhere else.

Why wasn't she moving?

The wedding music piping through the tent came to a halt, and Cord looked up into the rafters of the tent as if the reason why would be there.

When someone started playing a guitar, clearly into a mic, Cord's pulse seized. He looked at Jane, who glowed with a smile —but she still had not moved a muscle.

"Well, howdy, folks," a country music twang said, and Cord knew that voice. He looked around for Tex Young, and sure enough, he found the man walking down one of the aisles close to the front.

Country Quad was here.

Jane had brought in *Country Quad*.

Cord grinned and grinned, especially when he saw Travis throw a guitar strap over his shoulder and move to the end of his row. Keith did the same, then Mission, Hunter, Tucker, Deacon, Michael, and every single one of Jane's uncles.

They all wore smiles as they moved to the end of the aisles, creating an aisle of guitar-wielding cowboys as Tex's guitar got joined with another one.

Trace Young joined him, and then Otis, and then Luke.

Cord had met them last summer in Coral Canyon, and he couldn't believe Jane had done this for him. She truly, truly loved him, and Cord shifted his feet and looked back to Jane.

She still had not moved a muscle, and Cord really wished she'd come toward him. His fingers itched to touch her, and he somehow could imagine the floral, expensive perfume she'd smell like.

"Jane has loved you for a long time, Cord," Trace Young said. "She's looking forward to building a life together with you, right here in this house."

"And at a mechanic shop just down the road," Otis said. "Every day, she's praying for the chance to work alongside you, help you, champion you, cherish you, and love you."

They took a break to play a little riff, and Cord realized they were reciting her vows. He wished he'd thought of something like this, because he still couldn't remember a single thing he'd rehearsed. Not with Country Quad here.

"She'll sacrifice for you," Luke said. "Go through thick and thin with you, and she can't wait to build a family legacy with you at her side."

The cowboys of Country Quad kept playing, but they took a couple of steps back, allowing a better view of Jane.

She finally took a step, and relief painted through Cord. Then her uncle Wes said, "Jane, Cord has been working his whole life to be standing here at this altar today, with you walking toward him."

Those were Cord's vows, and somehow, Wes had them.

"His prayers are being answered right now," Hunter said. Jane stepped again, her dress held out to the side, and her daddy helping her with those flowers.

"He's not the smartest man on the planet, but he knows what love feels like and looks like," Deacon said.

Another couple of steps brought Jane closer to him.

"And he loves you," Tucker said. "He loves you with his

whole soul, and he's looking forward to building a life with you."

"A family," her uncle Colt said. "He's hoping to build a family, a life, and a business with you."

"He'll support you," her uncle Ames said. "Through highs and lows, through road trips and long days right here in Ivory Peaks."

"He'll do whatever he has to in order to make sure you're cared for and happy," her uncle Cy said.

Jane had been walking down the aisle this whole time, and she stood only a few paces from Cord right now.

Travis took one more step out into the aisle, but Cord thought his vows had about run out. He smiled at Cord, his fingers moving along the strings of his guitar just fine. Only the Country Quad instruments were miked, but since Trav stood so close to Cord, he could hear the notes.

"He loves you, and you love him so much, and this is the most amazing showcase of love between two people—a marriage. Now...." He looked around, his smile growing as he lifted the neck of his guitar.

Everyone else did too, and then they all said, "Let's get this I-do done!"

Jane arrived in front of Cord, and Gray passed her to Cord while everyone finished up the song they'd clearly rehearsed just for this.

Guitars then disappeared; cowboys took their seats; Jane pressed her lips to Cord's cheek. "Surprised?"

"Beyond," he murmured.

"Are you mad you don't get to say your vows?"

"Not even a little bit."

Jane smiled prettily, and she faced the altar, so Cord did too. The pastor stood there now, and Cord could only think one thing. The same thing Travis and the other cowboys had said last.

He couldn't wait to get this I-do done.

CHAPTER
Twenty-One

KEITH STOPPED at the end of the row and bent down to get the soil samples he needed. He'd been out every afternoon this week after his work in the stables to do this. He hadn't been around last year to know why some fields had been left dormant, some had held alfalfa, and others corn.

He knew he needed to keep the journals and make the decisions this year, and that meant he needed to know what the soil could tolerate this year. A farm couldn't grow anything without soil, and the soil was the lifeblood of any plot of land.

This afternoon, the sun beat down, heating Keith's shoulders and his back while the air still held a definite spring crispness. April sat right around the corner, and as Keith walked a hundred yards and stopped to take another soil sample, he thought about his relationship with Lindsay.

They'd been together for three months now, which for Keith, was one of his longest relationships in the past several years.

He didn't see her as much as he'd like, to be certain. Blackhorse Bay sat a good forty-five minutes from Lindsay's little hobby farm, and while he'd redeemed a few of his coupons for dinner, a movie, and putting together a puzzle, they still hadn't finished one.

He didn't have time to sit around and do puzzles. Lindsay didn't seem to either, and she didn't seem to come to Blackhorse Bay very often.

"Ever," he said under his breath as he started walking further into the field. He took samples from various places from all the fields, as the inner areas seemed to have more soil and better soil.

Maybe you should've made her some coupons, he thought when he realized how poisonous his thoughts had been. At the same time, he understood why he went to her house. She lived alone; he did not. She had ultimate control over the kitchen, the living room, everything. They could be alone, and Keith could admit that one of the reasons why they still hadn't finished a puzzle was because he maybe spent too much time kissing Lindsay when they got together.

He finished up the soil samples on this field, meticulously marked them all, and headed back to the administration building where he could conduct his tests. He kept his phone on and nearby, but when he got working, he tended to ignore it even when it chimed.

So, by the time he finished testing the samples and recording the results in his notebook, his mind pinged at him that his phone had gone off several times. He picked it up, instantly overwhelmed with all the messages waiting for him.

Britt had texted a few times, wondering if he knew the recipe for the ham and cheese sliders their daddy made. *I can't get in touch with him*, she'd said. *Lars and I want to try to make them tonight for dinner.*

When Keith hadn't answered right away, she'd added, *You could come too, if you want. You can see the house and how it's coming along.*

With the melting of the snow and the thawing of the earth, Keith hadn't left Blackhorse for a couple of weeks. That meant he'd only been texting his parents, texting Lindsay, and texting Britt too.

Did you get it? he asked. *Sorry I was up to my elbows in soil samples.*

No, she said. *I know it's butter and brown sugar, but I can't remember what else.*

Mustard, he said. *Just a teaspoon.*

Perfect! He could just see Britt shining like a star, and that made a small smile tug at the corners of his mouth. *Do you think you might be able to come for dinner? I didn't use the gross Swiss cheese.*

Keith smiled even more, because he happened to like Swiss cheese. Only Britt didn't like it, and since he hadn't seen her for a while and he was tired of eating something he'd thrown in the microwave for dinner, he thumbed out, *I can be there in about an hour.*

That's fine, Britt said. *Wait'll you see the new cupboards in the kitchen.*

Keith actually couldn't wait, and he headed back to his cabin to shower.

"There you are," Derrick said. "I was just about to come over to that office of yours and make sure you hadn't died."

Keith had forgotten about his other messages, and he didn't take his phone out now either. "Yeah, sorry," he said, glancing over to Coy, who sat at the dining room table with half a sandwich on his plate and the last bite of the first half going in his mouth. Keith's stomach growled at him, but he ignored it. "Busy afternoon, and I got lost in the testing."

"I'll bet," Derrick said good-naturedly. "Janice and I are going out, and I wondered if you wanted to go." He scanned Keith down to his cowboy boots and back. "But I'm leaving right now, and I don't think you've answered my sister's texts either...." He let the words hang there, his eyebrows going up.

"Yeah, I got talking to Britt," Keith said. "I'm going over to her place tonight."

"I see."

Keith didn't like how Derrick said that, and he also couldn't fathom double-dating with him and Janice. He liked the woman who sat behind the desk in the admin building just fine. But Derrick out on a double-date with his younger sister? Keith wouldn't even be able to draw a full breath.

Which didn't speak super well for a long-term relationship. Why couldn't he go out with Lindsay when her brother was there?

Keith didn't have room for all these thoughts and questions. "I'll call her," he said. "I have to go shower and get over to Britt's." He nodded to Derrick, who nodded back. Keith glanced over to Coy again. "Howdy, Coy."

"Keith," he said. "You need help in the fields tomorrow?"

"Yes," he said, pausing. "Are you offering?"

"Jack told me to ask," he said. "So I'm at your disposal after lunch."

"He wants a report by the beginning of next week," Keith said. "Thanks, Coy."

"Anytime." He picked up his second half-sandwich and took

a bite. Keith glanced over to Derrick again, who wore a slightly calculating look on his face. He didn't know what to make of it, so he ducked his head and continued toward his bedroom.

He showered without calling or texting Lindsay. He brushed his teeth as he thumbed through her messages. *Derrick wanted to know if we wanted to double-date with him tonight.*

I think it'd be fun.

What do you think?

She always sent super short messages, one right after the other, and if Keith had seen these as they'd come in, he honestly wouldn't have known how to answer. He really liked Derrick. They'd never had a problem in the cabin in the past nine months since Keith had moved to Blackhorse Bay.

But he wasn't sure why Derrick wanted to double *now*.

He got dressed, grabbed his wallet and keys, and headed out. Buck had returned to the cabin for the evening too, and Derrick had gone. "Going to my sister's," he said. "Be back later."

"Drive safe," Buck called from where he stood in front of the stove, frying eggs.

Keith jogged down the front steps to his truck, and he got everything connected before he put the vehicle in gear to back out of the driveway. Once he hit the highway, he dialed Lindsay.

"Hey, you," she said when she answered. "I was beginning to think you'd dropped your phone in a hole and buried it."

He smiled at the teasing quality of her voice. Everything that had gotten misaligned since he'd spoken to her last fell back into place. "Hey," he drawled out. "Sorry about this afternoon. I just have a big deadline, and I get a little lost inside the work sometimes."

It wasn't the first time Keith had become fixated on something. When he did something, he did it deep, and he'd missed calls while studying for tests in college, while working with a horse out in a pasture, and while simply watching a movie. He could get sucked in sometimes, and it was hard to get out.

"So no double-date tonight," she said. "Derrick says you're going to Britt's."

"Yeah," Keith said. "She invited me for dinner and to see the progress on the house." Lars had inherited his granddaddy's house in Ivory Peaks, and he'd been fixing it up for months. He'd tried to get it done before the wedding, but it hadn't worked out, what with supply issues, his full-time job, and spending time with Britt.

Lindsay let a healthy pause go by, and Keith shifted in his seat. "What did you make for dinner?" he asked.

"Chili and cornbread," she said.

He chuckled. "You realize we're moving *out* of soup season, right?"

"Don't even say that," she said. "It's *always* soup season."

He chuckled with her, glad he'd been able to cover over a slightly awkward spot. It wasn't lost on him, however, that there even was a slightly awkward spot.

"I feel like I haven't seen you forever," Lindsay said.

"Yeah." He sighed. "I know. Listen, Linds." He sat up straighter, ready to be honest with her. "We're moving in planting season. Then I have to monitor the growth. Every field will need something, all summer long."

He suspected she knew that, but she didn't really *know* it. There was a reason he got hired really quickly last year, and it was because Jack had lost his agricultural manager and needed another one. Fast. Growing crops wasn't just standing around while the sun shone.

Fields could get too much water, and then they didn't produce properly. That had to be adjusted according to what Mother Nature dropped on them too. There were pests to deal with, and fungi, and birds that could eat their crops.

He didn't want to say he had the most important job in the world, but agriculture was more than just a few rows of corn planted and forgotten about. Keith was in charge of *nine hundred acres* of crops. The planting, the maintenance, the harvesting. Alfalfa, corn, and more. All of it fell on him.

"Maybe you could come to me for dinner one night," he said when she didn't say anything.

Still, Lindsay didn't answer, and Keith wasn't sure what to do. "I mean, I didn't make a fancy coupon booklet, and I certainly can't cook as well as you, but I bet I could do something."

"Yeah?" she asked. "Like what?" She sounded halfway to laughing, and Keith wasn't sure why.

"I can cook," he said, swallowing. "Well enough." He seized onto the dinner he'd be eating that night. "I could make these ham and cheese sliders I think you'd like."

"Ooh, that does sound good," she said. "Do you cook for the whole cabin?"

"No," he said. "Not always. Tonight, Coy had a sandwich. Derrick and I left. Buck was making eggs when I left."

Lindsay didn't commit to coming to Blackhorse Bay and his cabin for anything, and instead, she said, "Interesting. Okay. I want pictures of Britt's house."

He smiled, because she had shown a lot of interest in Britt. "I'll be sure to take some."

"You're driving right by me, aren't you?" she asked.

"Yes," he said. "But I'm already late, and I'm not stopping."

"Come on," she said. "What are they having for dinner? I bet some cornbread would be nice to go with it."

Keith warred with himself. He really wanted to see Lindsay, but if he stopped, he'd be late for dinner at Britt's. And if he told her what they were having for dinner that night, he'd never convince her that he'd made the sliders if he ever made them for her.

"Lindsay, do not tempt me," he warned.

She laughed, and that made Keith smile too. Perhaps he was worried about nothing. Perhaps he simply wished the days had more hours in them. Perhaps he should be satisfied with his amazing job and his gorgeous girlfriend and be content for things to move a little slower.

Their relationship had just gotten off to such a fast start, and Keith couldn't help feeling like there was something between them.

Yeah, he told himself. *Forty-five minutes and your busy lives.*

"Maybe you could stop by after dinner," she suggested, her voice a bit on the coy side now. "Twenty minutes, for coffee. I know I'm not that far out of your way."

She wasn't, and he said, "Okay. Let me see what time I'm wrapping up, and I'll text you if I'm not dead-dog tired."

She giggled again, and Keith really wanted to see her. He determined that he'd stop by no matter how tired he was, but he kept that to himself for now. "See you later, cowboy," she said, and the call ended.

Keith reasoned for the rest of the drive to Britt's that he didn't have to go fast for a relationship to be meaningful. He *wanted* to see her all the time. It just wasn't possible.

Still, a touch of guilt moved through him. If he truly liked her, wouldn't he *make* time?

"She could make time too," he said as he turned and rumbled down the street toward a century-old home in the middle of the block. Britt's house was surrounded by tall trees and thick grass. Well, in the summertime, it would be thick. Right now, it sort of sat halfway between gray and brown, though someone had recently cleared the flowerbeds.

He pulled into the driveway behind Britt's car. She didn't drive much due to some of her health problems, but she had been driving herself out to Pony Power since the wedding.

Keith put his truck in park and killed the engine. Then he got out and headed for the door. It opened before he got there, and Britt spilled out into the evening sunshine. "Keith," she said. "I'm going to plant bulbs here this year."

"That's great." He truly grinned for the first time that day. "You know those won't bloom until next year, right?"

"Right." She hugged him and Keith held on tight. "So I'll plant some other stuff this year, and then we'll be ready for next year."

"That's great." Keith pulled back and met his sister's eyes. Britt had been so happy since she'd married Lars, and Keith's chest pinched.

Her face fell slightly. "Are you okay?" she asked.

"Yeah." He sighed. "I just have a lot going on right now."

"How's Lindsay?" Britt turned and went back into the house. "She should've come."

"Honestly, I'm not sure she would," Keith said, not even sure where the words had come from. He stepped into the house too and paused to take in all the changes. Lars worked on it every day after his job at the hardware store, and Keith drank in the freshly painted walls in this front living room.

"Wow," he said. "This is so open now. So much brighter."

"I think so too," Britt said. "L-look at the fireplace."

Keith looked, and sure enough, it had been cleaned until it gleamed. His eyes widened and he looked from it to Britt. "You're never going to use that. It'll get too dirty."

Britt laughed and pulled him through a triple-wide doorway and into the kitchen. They'd wanted to knock down the wall there, but it turned out, they couldn't. So they'd just made the doorway as wide as possible to open things up as much as they could.

"Look at the cabinets." Britt laced her arm through his. "I love them. They're red."

"I see that," Keith said. The new kitchen cabinets were a cherry-woody type of red, but red nonetheless. "They look great in here." This old house had high ceilings, and the colored cabinets made it seem like the room had been filled.

"I'm going to add some handles to them," she said.

"You are?" he asked. "Or Lars is?"

"I am." Britt dropped her hand and moved further into the kitchen. "Lars just called and said he's on his way home."

Keith knew when Britt didn't want to be questioned on something, so he didn't press the issue of her adding handles to these cabinets. He wasn't sure she had the capability to do that, as he'd never seen his sister use a power tool before. She didn't have a ton of upper body strength either.

But he said nothing as he settled at the half-bar in the kitchen. "Do you love it here?" he asked.

"So much." Britt bent and pulled a pan of sliders out of the oven. "I hope these aren't sick."

"Why would they be sick?" He chuckled and shook his head. "Have a little faith, sissy."

She tossed the oven mitts next to the pan of food and faced him. "Why wouldn't Lindsay come for dinner?"

Keith hadn't expected Britt to backtrack to that conversation. "I—I mean, I don't know. She just—" He cut off when he realized what he'd been about to say.

She just never leaves her farm.

Or he could've said, *She just likes to cook for others.*

Both were true, and one was definitely more positive than the other.

Britt folded her arms and glared at him, and Keith honestly didn't know what he'd done to deserve that. "Are you two still dating?"

"Yes," Keith said with a sigh. "I mean, I think so? I haven't seen her in a couple of weeks. We call and text. I'm really busy at Blackhorse right now, and she's got her hobby farm she has to get planted for the summer too."

Britt softened like butter melting in the microwave. "Oh." She moved over to the bar and sat on the only other stool available. "Do you want to see her more often?"

"Of course," he said. "She never comes to my cabin. I always have to go to her farm, and I just haven't had time."

"Lars used to come to the grocery store to spend time with me."

Keith smiled and nodded, his love for his sister filling him time and again. "I know, Britt, but he lived here in town. He could literally stand at the front window of the hardware store and watch you drive by, then hustle over there to catch you."

"That's exactly what I did too," Lars said from behind them.

Keith startled, because he hadn't heard the man come in, and Britt slipped from the stool to go greet him.

"Hey, baby." He grinned at Britt and kissed her hello. Keith watched them, because they were so good to each other. "Heya, Keith." He tucked Britt against his side and looked at her, then him. "You're alone. Could Lindsay not come?"

"I didn't think to invite her," Britt said.

"You didn't, Keith?" Lars moved into the kitchen and pulled open a drawer. "Or maybe she was too busy to come tonight."

Honestly, Keith hadn't thought of it either. So he wasn't entirely used to having a girlfriend, especially when he went weeks without seeing her. "Listen," he said. "Can I ask you guys some questions?" He looked between Lars getting out plates and utensils, and Britt standing there with a blank look on her face. "I might need some help with Lindsay, and I don't even know where to start."

Britt gaped at him. "I can't help you."

"Sure we can," Lars said as he moved the dish of hot sliders over to the dining room table. "Come on, guys. Let's sit over here and eat—and we'll work out whatever you need help with, okay, Keith?"

"Yeah," he said. "Okay." Maybe he was making things too complicated, and sitting down with two of the least complicated people he knew might just help him tremendously.

Because he didn't want to lose Lindsay, and if he didn't figure out how to see her more often and curb his irritated thoughts about how she didn't seem to want to sacrifice to see him, he knew that was exactly what would happen.

CHAPTER

Twenty~Two

LINDSAY LOOKED over to Hamlet as he perked his head up. Twilight had come and gone, and the day had moved into dusk. Full dark would arrive in the next few minutes, and as Hamlet got to his feet and jumped up onto the couch to see through the front windows, Lindsay knew that someone had arrived on her farm.

Her pulse bumped and jumped, and she got to her feet and surveyed the mess on the end table next to where she sat, watching TV. She had no less than three empty Diet Pepsi cans, several candy wrappers, and two coffee mugs. Used coffee mugs.

She grabbed as much as she could carry, because while Keith hadn't texted, she couldn't think of anyone else who'd be coming to her hobby farm. She dropped everything into her deep farm sink, wishing she'd invested in the feature that would allow her to pull a lid over the top to hide what was inside.

But Lindsay operated on a budget, and she hadn't. She ran

back into the living room, smiled at Hamlet with his paws up on the windowsill, and gathered as many candy wrappers as she could. She'd just tossed them in the trashcan in the kitchen when her doorbell rang.

She hadn't seen Keith in a couple of weeks now, and as she rounded the corner to get to the front door, she glanced down at her clothes. A groan immediately came out of her throat, and she wished he'd texted the way he'd said he would.

Still, she couldn't be upset with him for coming, so she marched onward, her red-and-black plaid pajama pants notwithstanding. A white tank top completed her lounge outfit, and she supposed Keith had seen her in worse.

Or rather, she'd seen him in a poncho and nothing else.

That brought a smile to her face, and she wished she could go back to being stuck in a house with him. It felt easier than trying to make a relationship work when they lived as far apart as they did.

Her reluctance to go out to Blackhorse to see him didn't help, and she wondered if he'd picked up on it. *Probably*, she thought as she reached for the doorknob and pulled open the door.

The porch light haloed Keith in soft yellow light, and he looked up from the ground when the door swung in. "Evening," he said, his voice nowhere near loud. He hadn't raised his head all the way up, and he barely looked past through the brim of his cowboy hat.

"Well, howdy, cowboy." Lindsay leaned into the doorjamb. "What brings you to these parts?"

Keith straightened all the way and took a tiny step toward her. "I miss you." He made no move to reach for her, but his words had gone right into her heart.

"I miss you too."

"Two weeks is too long to go without seeing each other."

"I agree."

He reached up and swiped his hat from his head. He had not asked to come in, nor had he tried to kiss her hello. He hadn't even attempted to touch her, and he usually swept his hand flirtily along hers or up her arm.

"I could've invited you to dinner at my sister's house tonight," he said.

Lindsay merely blinked at him. She hadn't thought of that, and now that the idea sat in her mind, she realized it would've been something a couple—a serious couple—would do together. Without an invitation.

"Why didn't you?" she asked.

"I didn't think of it. Britt told me I should've." He took a step up into the house, pressing right into Lindsay. "If we were spending more time together, I would've."

She nodded, her eyes closing. He stood so close, she couldn't look at him right now.

"You won't come out to Blackhorse Bay," he said. "And Linds, I *can't* come here all the time, even if I want to. So I need to know if this is it for us."

Her eyes flew open. "No," she said quickly. Lindsay put her hands on Keith's chest and used his body to steady hers. "No, this isn't it for us."

"Can I come in, then?"

"Are you going to break-up with me?"

"I think we need to talk," he said, inching her backward into her own house. She let him, and when he passed the door, he toed it closed with his cowboy boot. "But I will say I don't *want* to break-up."

Lindsay's blood hummed through her veins now, as if his

presence didn't do that all by itself. Confronted with the possibility of not seeing him again, never catching his name as it brightened her phone, forced her to realize how close she was to losing him.

All because she didn't want to drive forty minutes to a place that felt like home to her.

She shook her head. She couldn't believe she'd done this.

"Coffee?" she asked.

He shook his head. "I'm already too keyed up, and I need to sleep tonight." He edged past her. "I can make us some hot chocolate if you want."

"I'd like that." She turned as he walked into her kitchen, Hamlet on his heels. The dog sure was happy to see him—and Lindsay was too. She hurried after him to find him setting a pot on the stove and lighting the gas burner. "I wanted to avoid the whole you-work-for-my-uncle thing."

He glanced over to her but said nothing.

"And my brother." She scuffed her toe along the kitchen floor.

"I thought you and Derrick got along," he said. "Just tonight, he said you two were planning a double date."

"We get along, sure," she said. "I just keep thinking it'll be weird if I show up there as your girlfriend."

"You've shown up there lots of other times."

"Yeah, that's why it's different."

"Then it sounds you don't want to be my girlfriend."

"Keith." Lindsay moved toward him, her desperation spurring her on. "Stop saying stuff like that. It's not true."

He poured milk into the pan, and then Lindsay took it from him. She set it on the counter and grabbed onto his hand. "Can you look at me? Forget about the hot chocolate."

Keith did what she asked, and he didn't seem uncomfortable. "There are plenty of places we can be alone out at Blackhorse. I'm going to be real honest, because Britt told me I should be, and I think she's right. I can't come here all the time. I need to see you more than once every two weeks. More than once a week. I'd like to see you every single day."

Lindsay started nodding about halfway through his tiny monologue, and she waited while he swallowed. "I want that too," she said.

"But I'm moving into an extremely busy time. I know you are too. Maybe it's just not the right time."

"Well, that just makes no sense." Lindsay took a step back now that he'd slowed down enough to look at her, talk to her. "If we end up together, and I'm not dating for fun. This is serious for me."

"It's serious for me too," he said. "That's why I'm here tonight, when it's past my bedtime."

Lindsay swallowed, because he wouldn't just talk and run, and he still had to make the drive home afterward. She could just pad down the hall to her bedroom and fall into bed. "So if we end up together, we can't just be married in the wintertime."

"No, we can't." A smile touched his face, and he fought against it until it hibernated again. "And I want the record to show that you brought up marriage."

Lindsay ducked her head to hide her smile, but it came anyway, and she was sure Keith saw it too. She let it fully form on her face, and then she lifted her eyes to his. "We better start seein' each other a little more, I think."

"Yes, I think so." He took her into his arms again, despite the fact that he'd put the fire way too high under the milk, and it was probably boiling out of control about now. But with

Keith's gaze on her, nothing else mattered. Not Hamlet sniffing her knees, and not bedtime, and not milk about to overboil.

They moved toward one another at the same time, and as Lindsay kissed him, she knew she'd been making a huge mistake by insisting he come to her farm so they could be together. She also knew the real reason why.

Keith didn't kiss her long, and after he pulled away, he kept her close to his chest. She wrapped her arms around him and buried her face in the cottony, earthy, country scent of his shirt, his skin, his very spirit.

"Keith," she murmured.

"Yeah, baby?"

"I didn't mean to put so much on you," she said. "But I did, and Uncle Jack and Derrick are only part of it."

He moved back, met her eye, and then turned to tend to the hot chocolate. He pulled the pan off, which only confirmed her suspicions that the milk had been boiling away, and she took a deep breath.

"I did it, because I was trying to make you prove that you want to be with me."

He poured the hot milk into two mugs. "Why? My texts and calls weren't enough? The way I kiss you didn't tell you that?"

"I don't know," she whispered. "Sometimes I think there's something a little broken inside me." She drew in a steadying breath that only made tears press behind her eyes.

Keith stirred both mugs and held them, one in each hand, as he faced her. He said nothing, but the expression on his face was an open invitation for her to keep talking.

Instead, she took one of the mugs and headed into the living room. Keith and Hamlet followed her, and she settled into her preferred spot next to the end table, beyond grateful she'd had twenty seconds to clean up.

She set the mug down and wiped her hands through her hair. "Nothing was ever good enough for my daddy," she said. "He made Derrick and I do things over and over if we got one little thing wrong, and after a while, I felt like my entire existence was wrong."

Keith sat on the other end of the couch, stirring his hot chocolate, as it was way too hot to even sip.

"Then, when I found out he'd arranged a marriage for me, I felt even more useless. He told me it was the opposite—that I was finally good for something."

Her chest felt like someone had just cleaved it into two parts with a giant maul. All of the childhood and young adult hurt she'd endured gushed out, and she couldn't stop it now.

"I've only ever wanted him to love me, and I feel like he never did."

"Lindsay," Keith said quietly.

She shook her head, because she didn't want an empty reassurance that her daddy loved her. She wasn't sure he did, and she'd left Texas so she didn't have to be around that scrutiny and disappointment so often.

Ever, now.

"So I didn't realize it until just now, but I was making you prove to me that you want me. That you want to see me and be with me. It's stupid, and I'm sorry." She looked up from her hands and turned toward him. "Really."

"Did I pass the test?"

Frustration filled her. "It's not a test." She turned and picked up her hot chocolate, though it was still way too hot to drink. She tried anyway, burning her tongue and the roof of her mouth.

As pain seared through her, Lindsay couldn't hold back the tears. One slipped down her face, and she nearly dumped her entire mug of hot chocolate down herself as she hastened to wipe it away.

"Oh, you can't be crying about this," Keith said kindly. Miserably. He set aside his hot chocolate and took hers too. He set them both on the recently cleared end table and knelt in front of her. "Hey, I'm not mad. Don't cry."

"I'm not crying over you," she said, her voice so embarrassingly tinny. Her eyes met his and danced away. "I'm sorry. I don't know why I did this."

"Yes, you do," he murmured. "You just told me."

She nodded, and her tears started to abate. Thankfully.

He threaded his fingers through hers, his eyes fixed on where they connected. "I'm really sorry about your dad. You should come spend some time with mine. He's one of the best out there. Best cowboy. Best boss. Best daddy." He smiled and looked up at her. "Would you? I can call my mom and ask her to make us dinner at the house one night. Us and my parents, the girls. Maybe even Britt and Lars."

Lindsay sniffled and nodded. "That sounds a lot better than me eating mini candy bars and watching reality TV by myself."

Keith frowned. "I don't like thinking of you doing that." He pulled her into his arms. "Load up Hamlet and come see me. I'll feed you. We can ride horses. At least walk through the fields and talk while I collect samples or try to get the soil to hold together the way I want."

Lindsay looked at him with new, clear eyes. "You want the soil to hold together?"

"A little, yeah," he said. "That means it has some clay in it, and clay keeps water in the soil, but clays aerate well."

A smile came to her face. "You're really sexy when you're talking smart."

Keith burst out laughing, and he got to his feet. He left their hot chocolate where it was and pulled her to her feet too. "Can we just lay together for a minute? Then I have to go."

"Sure."

He lay down on the couch first, and Lindsay folded herself into his arms. "Mm, yes," he murmured. "This is so much better than me doing it in the cabin while Coy and Buck bicker about which game show rerun to watch."

Lindsay giggled, and she focused on the TV in front of her. She'd turned it down earlier, and she didn't mind that she could barely hear it, nor that she didn't really know what had come on at the top of the hour. Behind her and around her, Keith existed, and life was far better with him here than without him.

A few minutes later, he snored softly, and now Lindsay's biggest problem would be determining when to wake him up.

It was a far better problem to have than him breaking up with her. Her heartbeat boomed out one, then two beats, and she couldn't imagine how different the night would be if he hadn't shown up to have this talk.

Where they'd be next time she saw him—if she'd ever have seen him again.

She felt like she'd dodged a bullet, and while she hadn't seen a counselor in a long time, she knew the steps to take to get herself out of the fearful flight response that dating Keith had triggered.

She also knew she needed to get out to Blackhorse Bay tomorrow—yes, tomorrow—and talk to her uncle and her brother. They *were* part of why she hadn't wanted to see Keith there, and that air needed to be cleared as fast as possible.

Cleared, not avoided.

"Thank you, Lord," she whispered while her boyfriend slumbered. "Please help me to meet him halfway. More than halfway, if possible. Don't allow me to make him prove himself —he has nothing to prove to me."

She continued to pray until she felt sufficiently calm, and only then did she turn in Keith's arms and press her lips to his. "Time to wake up, cowboy," she murmured as he stirred.

"Mm, not yet." He kissed her again, definitely awake, but Lindsay had no complaints about that.

CHAPTER
Twenty-Three

KEITH FOUND Lindsay's truck in his driveway a couple of days later, and he smiled as he pulled his vehicle in beside hers. He certainly hadn't meant for her to come up to Blackhorse every single time, and it felt like she was trying to make up for the couple of months where she'd made him come to her.

He honestly hadn't minded, back then. He was just busier now that the snow had melted, the days were longer, and so much more was expected of him.

Planting wouldn't be for another month, at least, and Keith's plan was to get in an establishment crop by the third week of May. It shouldn't snow by then, and the moisture content and temperature of the soil should be right.

At least according to the journals Keith had inherited. He wasn't sure why the agricultural manager before him had left so suddenly, because the man kept good records, and the crops last year had been done well.

This year, Keith would plant alfalfa in the early fall months too, and he couldn't wait to see if that would yield something higher for him.

In the meantime, he had plenty more acreage to test, fields to assign to specific crops, crews to put together to manage the planting, and stock to order. He'd been down to the IFA twice this week already, and his heart sure did a happy jig when he found Lindsay sitting on his bottom step.

"You didn't want to go in?" he asked, sighing as he sank down beside her.

She grinned over to him, leaned toward him, and kissed him quickly. Keith sure liked that they were comfortable enough to do that, that while the first touch was thrilling and amazing—and he still felt his skin turn combustible with this woman's touch—there wasn't any of the awkwardness or shyness.

"Buck said he was making omelets, but it smelled like he was boiling shoe leather."

Keith chuckled and looked out over the lawn. It had started to green, but it wouldn't really come out of its dormant state for another couple of weeks. And only if those weeks kept getting warmer and producing sunshine, which Keith hoped they would.

"So we should plan on eating out tonight," he said.

"I brought dinner," Lindsay said. "It's packed and loaded." She leaned into his bicep. "I mean, it's in my truck. We could drive somewhere and eat on the tailgate, or we could saddle a couple of horses and go for a ride."

Keith wasn't sure he wanted to deal with finding two horses they could ride on such short notice. He had said they could do that, and he had no doubt they could. But it wasn't a task he wanted to complete tonight. "Drive?" he suggested. "There's a great place just down the road, and it has amazing views of the mountains."

"Sounds perfect," she said, but she didn't move.

Keith didn't either, because he could honestly sit right there on his east-facing steps and let the sun go down behind him. The sunset would be better, and the romantic inside him told him to get moving before they missed it.

The Rocky Mountains were huge, towering spikes to the west, and the sun went behind them fairly early.

So he groaned as he got to his feet and offered her his hand. "Come on. If we hurry, we can catch the sunset."

Lindsay smiled up at him, and she was the most gorgeous creature in the whole world. She slipped her hand into his and got to her feet. "I got the horses out to pasture today. You should've seen Shadow. It was like he'd never been freer."

Keith grinned and tucked her under his arm as they headed for her truck. "That's great, baby. Do you want me to drive?" He didn't particularly love calling her "baby," but he hadn't been able to come up with another, adequate pet name for her.

Sweetheart felt contrived too, though when Lars said that to Britt, it sounded completely natural. Keith hadn't dated enough to truly find something he liked, and it had to suit Lindsay too.

She handed him her keys, and she made her way along the passenger side of the truck before he could follow and open her door for her. He hurried to be there to close it, and she gazed at him with only half a smile on her face. "What?" he asked.

"You look like you have something on your mind," she said.

"Nope," he said. "Unless you count wondering what you packed for dinner."

"It's a surprise." She faced the front. "Let's get going, because the sky is already stunning tonight."

Keith closed her door and went around the front of the truck, taking in the beauty and breadth of the sky. "You're right," he said as he dropped into her driver's seat and moved the chair back. "Look at the orange."

"That'll settle into a nice pink," she said. "How far is this place?"

"Not far." Keith backed out and left Blackhorse Bay in favor of a tiny park about four miles down the road and then one up into some bluff-like foothills. He'd hiked up there with Coy a couple of weeks ago, and while they hadn't been there for sunrise or sunset, Keith had a great imagination and knew it would be spectacular.

"Oh, this is Cactus Grove," she said when he made the turn.

"I didn't know it had a name." He went past the two garbage cans that marked the road. "Coy and I came here a couple of weeks ago. Before that, I didn't even know it existed."

"My uncle brought me here a couple of times," she said. "One time, he did an Easter egg hunt here for the cowboys. Lots of crevices and cracks to hide those eggs." She grinned, and Keith could just see the bland landscape of mostly brown, beige dirt broken up with pastel eggs.

"Sounds fun," he said. "And it reminds me that my daddy said they'd love to have us all over for Easter dinner."

"Does your momma make ham?" Lindsay asked, almost teasing him.

"No," he said. "But my daddy does."

They laughed together, the evening lazy and easy, exactly the way Keith wanted it to be. He pulled into one of the handful of parking spaces and got out. The picnic basket with their dinner in it sat on the floor behind him, and he picked it up while Lindsay dropped down from the truck.

They met at the hood, and he led the way down a path toward a picnic area he'd seen on the hike. "Should be…right—yep, there it is." Good thing, too, because whatever she'd packed for dinner weighed a decent amount.

Keith lifted the basket on to the table and stepped back so she could go through the food. He'd learned that she liked doing that. Lindsay was a talented cook, and she liked telling him about what she'd made, why, and how she'd learned to make it.

"All right," she said. "Tonight, I brought barbecue tortillas." She pulled out a wad of aluminum foil that Keith would've probably mistaken for garbage. "My aunt used to make these when we'd go to the park for the fireworks."

She unwrapped the top of layer of foil to reveal a stack of small, six-inch, flour tortillas. "She called it 'hands-free barbe-cue.'" She grinned as she set the tortillas on the table, then lifted them off to reveal a big old pile of messy meat. "The idea is, you take a tortilla here, and you use it to pick up the meat. Now."

Lindsay reached back into the basket. "I brought slaw and hot sauce as condiments. Same principle."

"Better demonstrate," Keith said. "I'm a cowboy from Montana, not Texas." He grinned at her as he took a seat facing the sunset.

She did too, the picnic basket still down by her. "All right, it's not hard." She picked up a tortilla and turned it over, pinching it up into the palm of her hand. "You use it to grab the meat." She pinched up some of the saucy, glazed meat, and then turned it over. "See? Then I can add slaw like a lady."

After pulling out a plastic fork and popping the top of the plastic container of cole slaw, she did just that. She handed him the tortilla, which was a little messy around the edges and said, "Try it."

The scent of the sauce—sweet with heat—hit his nose, and Keith's mouth watered. He folded the tortilla even more and took a bite. "Mm, yes," he said around the mouthful of barbecue taco. "It's perfect."

Lindsay laughed and pulled out another container. "This is loaded baked potato salad. It's cheesy, and bacony, and delicious." She opened that and set it between them. "And I made pea salad too. My mama always made pea salad in the summer. For everything."

To Keith, that just looked like peas with mayo on them, with chunks of Colby jack cheese and more bacon. "You can never have too much bacon," he said, echoing something Lindsay had told him previously.

She beamed at him. "Now you're thinking like a Texan."

"Are there eggs in that too?" Keith asked, not sure about this pea salad.

"Yes, sir," she said proudly. "They're from my chickens too. Some of their first eggs this spring."

"Nice," Keith said. "Why did your momma like pea salad so much?"

"It's a recipe her mama won with at the State Fair," Lindsay said, and Keith enjoyed these windows into her life. She always spoke with pride about her mama, her granny, and the recipes and cooking she'd learned from them.

He prayed that she'd be able to find the same peace and closure about her daddy, as she hardly ever spoke of him in a complimentary way. Keith hadn't told his parents about it either, and he wondered if maybe he should before Easter, just so they knew where Lindsay was coming from.

At the same time, he wouldn't expect it to change his parents, so maybe they didn't need to know.

"That's it," she said. "Hands free barbecue and the two best sides."

"Three," he said. "The slaw counts, I think."

"Oh, the slaw counts," she agreed. Then they both dug into the barbecue again, Keith with a fresh tortilla. Somehow, the meat still held some warmth, and Keith especially liked it with the slaw.

"What do you think about me getting wild?" he asked as he pinched up his third tortilla's worth of barbecue.

"Wild?" Lindsay looked at him, a smidge of barbecue sauce in the corner of her mouth. Keith wanted to kiss it away, but he held himself back.

"Yeah." He turned over his tortilla, but instead of forking on some slaw, he added a spoonful of pea salad. He looked at her and found her eyes glued to the container of peas, eggs, and cheese. And all that mayo. It was practically slaw. Sort of.

He put on another spoonful. "It's meat and veggies all in one." He folded over the edges of his tortilla, met her eye, and took a big bite.

She sat there, mouth open, eyes wide, as he chewed. She seemed to realize it a couple of moments later, because she turned abruptly away from him. "How is it?"

"So good," he said around all the new flavors. "The cheese is so good. The mayo is way creamier than the slaw dressing."

"That's because slaw is not made with mayo." Lindsay shook her head as if Keith's taste buds needed to be chastised, but he only grinned.

"I'm pretty sure there's mayo in that," he said as she properly forked on another pile of slaw to her barbecue. "You've got to admit—you want to try this."

"I do not." She gave him a disgusted look, but that only fueled Keith's desire that she try it. "And there's only a little mayo in this. It's cut by the vinegar." She eyed his pea salad barbecue. "That's got to be so heavy."

"If you'd try it, you'd know." He took another bite, and oh, he could read Lindsay pretty well. She so wanted to try this. He held it out for her, and after he swallowed, he said. "I'll even hold it for you, so you don't have to touch it. Just one bite."

He moved the half-tortilla closer, and Lindsay leaned in. He fed her a bite, and somehow that was one of the most intimate, hottest things he'd ever done with a woman. She chewed, and the look in her eyes seemed more thoughtful than anything else.

"Not bad, right?"

She swallowed and wiped her mouth with a napkin. "You know what, Keith? I'll give you 'not bad.'"

He laughed again, polished off his third hands-free barbecue tortilla, and rested his arms on the table in front of him. The metal radiated heat, which was great, as the sun had just dipped below the mountains, stealing the light-warmth from them.

"There she is," he murmured, the very tips of the mountains stunningly illuminated by bright yellow-white light. It spilled over the tops of them, and shot out other hues as the sky went up and sideways.

Light purple, pink, tangerine. Keith could name colors forever and not get every one his eye could see. "I love the sunset," he said. "It reminds me to reflect on the day I've had."

"Yeah?" Lindsay scooped up another bite of plain pea salad. Before she put it in her mouth, she asked, "And how was today?"

"Good," he said as he nodded, his eyes still roaming the skies, trying to find every last hue God had created for him. "I did good work today. I think the Lord would be happy with me."

"Is that what you worry about?"

He looked over to her. "Yes," he said simply. "I want to be right before God. I want to treat my friends and co-workers right. I want to do a good job for my boss."

"It's the cowboy code," she said.

"Family," he said. "Grit. Hard work. Determination. God."

"You forgot love of country."

He nodded, his gaze back out on the sunset. "That's important too. Honor the land you've been blessed with. Love those around you. Work hard for all you have. Give praise to God above."

"Amen," she whispered. She finished eating and laid her head against his shoulder, and together, they watched the sunlight fade and fade and fade, until Keith finally said, "We should go, so we don't trip on the way back to the truck."

Lindsay said nothing as she got up and started cleaning up their dinner. He carried the basket, and back in the truck, he faced her. "I really enjoyed that, sweetheart."

"Me too."

Keith wasn't sure what lasting marriages and what eternal romances looked like or felt like. He'd never been in love before. He wasn't sure if a picnic dinner, carefully prepared by Lindsay, with stories shared about her family, her heritage, added to such a thing.

He wasn't sure if something as simple as a watching a sunset counted. He wasn't sure about any of that, but he was sure he was falling for Lindsay Lewis as he took her face in his hands and kissed her.

Now, he could only pray to string together enough small, sincere, simple moments like this and hope they were what true love was made of.

CHAPTER

Twenty~Four

LINDSAY LOOKED at herself in the mirror and quickly got out her vanity face razor for women. She'd been living the cowboy way of life for decades, and one thing her daddy had taught her that she still believed was that she had to be okay with the woman staring back at her when she shaved each morning.

She'd heard him give that lecture to Derrick plenty of times, and it was always about who he was looking at in the mirror while he shaved. So while Lindsay didn't whisk off her light blonde hair along her chin and upper lip very often, she did have to look at herself in the mirror and make judgments every single day.

She'd been thinking a lot about what Keith had said a week or so ago about how the sunset made him contemplate how he'd done that day. Lindsay had never given it much thought. Of course, she tried to be kind to those around her. She volunteered with the Ranch Sisters program—and she had three of them coming out to help her with her garden plot prep this week. She took good care of her belongings. She did her best with her animals and her farmland.

Her church attendance had been spotty over the winter, but they'd had a lot of snow this year, and plenty of people hadn't been able to get off their farms in time for the sermon. She couldn't be the only one.

Still, sitting on that picnic table bench with Keith had taught her something: She needed to make sure she was on the same page with God every single day. Or at all.

So she finished with the facial razor and tossed it back into her drawer. Lindsay looked into her own eyes, trying to see something. What, she didn't know. The house sat in complete silence, and she let it inside herself. It seeped into every corner, refusing to let anything hide.

Lindsay wanted it all to come out anyway. All the darkness inside her. All the insecure thoughts. All the secrets and other things she was hiding from.

She'd been putting off praying, because she knew from personal experience that God answered prayers. And if she asked, and she didn't like the answer...no. It was better if she just didn't ask.

But now, the time had come. She couldn't hide from herself any longer, and she couldn't hide from the Lord either.

"Am I doing okay?" she asked. "Is there more I can do? Is there something You want me to do that I'm not doing? Are there things I should quit doing to be closer to Thee?"

She'd asked a lot of questions, and she didn't expect answers to all of them. In fact, most of the time, she didn't get a tangible to-do list from God. Shockingly. She normally got a feeling, good or bad, and then as she pondered on that, she'd get impressions for what she could do to satisfy that feeling.

Today, as she stood stock-still and silent in her bathroom, nothing came. She wasn't sure what she was doing right, if anything. She had no idea if she needed to fix something.

"I haven't shut You out that much, have I?" she whispered next, and the slightest glimmer of hope entered her mind. So, no. God was still there. Perhaps He just wasn't ready to talk to her yet.

She understood that, as she seemed to be perpetually in a state of not being ready to talk to someone. Her daddy. Her brother. Uncle Jack.

She'd been spending more time at Blackhorse Bay, and surprisingly, when she didn't go track down Uncle Jack, she hardly ever saw him. He was an excellent overseer, and he trained his cowboys well, so he didn't have to be out in the stables and stalls, monitoring them.

She and Derrick had seen each other, of course. That double date had never happened—*yet*, she told herself—but they'd not spoken about Keith. She couldn't fathom Derrick being upset about her relationship with him, but if there was one thing she and Derrick had learned from growing up in the same household together, it was that when something was wrong, silence prevailed.

"When something's wrong, silence prevails." Her eyes grew slightly wider in the mirror, because she's just realized God had been silent with her.

Just like her daddy wouldn't talk when things got tough, and her mama had left her husband, her kids, her home, and her community rather than stay and hash it all out, perhaps God was letting Lindsay know that yes, she had a little bit of a problem she needed to fix.

She turned away from the mirror and went to get dressed. Keith was taking her to church today, and then they were going to his parents' house for Easter family dinner. Lindsay had not been able to stop herself from making something to bring, and after she pulled on the pale pink Easter dress with lots of splashy, yellow, baby chicks across it, she went to pack up the hot cross buns.

She'd made them yesterday—not technically Good Friday, but she hadn't wanted them to sit for too long once baked. Even now, she wondered if she could take them, and she picked up one of the fruit-filled, spiced buns. It gave a bit under her fingers, telling her they were still fresh and highly consumable.

Keith had educated her a lot on soil in the past few weeks, and she smiled to herself. She could tell if a baked good was going to be delicious just by touching it, and he could tell if the ground was ready to be planted by doing the same thing.

Since she'd made two dozen buns and Keith had six people in his family, plus the two of them, Lindsay pinched off a bite of the roll and put it in her mouth. A moan seeped out instantly, because she'd spiced these perfectly.

A hint of the warmth from the cinnamon and nutmeg. The sugar, the ginger, clove, and allspice. She could taste the lemon zest, and the light syrup she'd brushed over the buns the moment they'd come out of the oven.

She'd filled hers with golden raisins and dried apricots, and they were absolutely divine in the sweet dough. "Yep," she said as she ripped off another piece. "They're going to love these."

She'd piped on the crosses, and she covered the basket with the light blue cloth she'd moved aside to check on them. Check what, she didn't know. What she did know was that she stood there in her kitchen, eating a hot cross bun, when Keith walked in. "Hey, Linds," he called.

"In the kitchen," she yelled back to him. "Come try these hot cross buns." She had about half left, and she held it up slightly as the cowboy walked around the corner and into the kitchen.

If she found him attractive in jeans, boots, and a cowboy hat, his church attire dang near stopped her pulse. He wore black slacks and a white shirt, with a bright pink, white, and gray paisley tie. *How very Eastery*, she thought.

Shiny black boots, check.

Silver, gleaming belt buckle, check.

Big, wide, delicious midnight cowboy hat, check, check, check.

He stole her very breath, and Lindsay knew with one look at him that she needed to up her game to be worthy of him.

"Wow," she said as she passed him the half-bun she had left. "You look amazing. You must go to church all the time."

"Every chance I get," he said. "But it's not all the time." He took a bite of the bun, which was almost like a crime for Lindsay. She couldn't imagine mashing the bread down like that, but Keith's face lit up all the same. "Wow," he said. "This is fantastic."

She grinned at him. "You're doing that talking-with-your-mouth-full thing again."

He smiled and finished his bite of bun. "I can't help it," he said. "Everything you make is so good." He took another bite, still grinning.

"Let's go," she said with a laugh. "How hot will it be in the car? Do I need to bring these into the church?"

"You're going to bring hot cross buns in with us?"

"If it means they'll melt otherwise, yes." Lindsay picked up the basket and gave him a look she hoped told him not to argue with her. "My mama once brought in a jar of wild berry lemonade, because she thought it might ferment in the heat."

"Well, I'll be," Keith drawled out at her. "I kinda wish I could've seen that. Your mama carryin' in a vat of wild berry lemonade." He laughed, the sound carefree and amazing, and Lindsay loved hearing it in her house.

She grinned at him and led the way toward the exit. "It was a sight to see," she said over her shoulder. "My basket of bread will be nothing."

Now, if she could just make it through the sermon without God frying her to a crisp, that would be great. Oh, and then, she had to go to dinner with Keith's family, and surely they'd see how much she was sure to sweat during church.

Be positive, she told herself. Just because she knew she had something to fix didn't mean she was one step away from the devil himself. In fact, Lindsay felt herself being slowly reeled back toward the Lord, where she wanted to be, as she deemed Keith's truck too hot to hold the buns she'd spent so long creating.

So, armed with the blue-linen covered basket in one hand and her other one in Keith's, she headed for the chapel doors.

————

AN HOUR AND A HALF LATER, Keith now carried the hot cross buns while he led her up the sidewalk to his parents' house. They lived in Ivory Peaks, in a nice suburb, with a big pasture out front. A couple of horses grazed there, and Lindsay enjoyed the sight of them there.

"How big is this place?" she asked.

"Five acres or so." Keith went up the steps and pulled open the screen door. He held it for Lindsay and nodded. "Just go on in. We're the last ones here."

They'd been swamped after church, which he claimed his family attended too. But the pastor hadn't seen Keith in a while —since he'd moved north to Blackhorse Bay—and it seemed like every congregant wanted to exclaim over him as well. Lindsay had stood at his side, letting him introduce her around, smiling, and shaking hands, asking small talk questions, and defending the basket of hot cross buns in her arms.

In Texas, everyone would've understood. Here, Lindsay felt a little out of sorts, but not so much that she wouldn't go back to church. Maybe not with nearly two dozen buns in tow, but she had liked the sermon and the reminder that Christ was risen.

She hadn't gotten any answers to her ponderings over what specifically she needed to fix, but she could be patient. She could keep taking steps into the dark until the Lord decided to illuminate her path.

Now, Lindsay took another unknown step into the house where Keith's parents lived, and the scent of good meat and salty bacon filled her nose. "Oh, wow," she whispered to herself as she saw all the way to the back of the house, where all six of Keith's relatives stood.

They all turned toward her at once, some version of a smile coming almost simultaneously to their faces.

"Hey, everyone," he called needlessly as he brought up the rear. "Lindsay made hot cross buns, and I've already sampled one, and they are going to blow your mind." He looked at her, fondness residing in those pretty eyes, and moved past her toward the back of the house.

This place was bigger on the inside than it looked from outside, and he had to walk past the length of a full-sized couch, the dining room table, and an island to reach his family. They celebrated his arrival, and Lindsay suddenly knew what she needed to fix.

The broken pieces of her family.

From her and Derrick, to her and her daddy, to her and her mama. She couldn't make them all carefully glue back together what had been broken over the years, but *she* could do more to make sure *her* relationships with them were rock solid.

She could, and she would.

"Linds?" Keith asked, and Lindsay got moving away from the front door. Her chick-covered skirt swished around her legs as she arrived, and Keith took her right under his wing. "You remember everyone, I'm sure."

She looked around at them all—his momma and daddy, his sister and her husband, his two younger sisters. They all held light in their eyes and love in their hearts—for each other. And for her.

Her next breath quivered as she felt their love for *her*, this near-stranger they only welcomed because their son and brother told them it was okay. That spoke of how much they loved and trusted him, and Lindsay could only look at him with wonder in her eyes and say, "Yeah, of course I remember them."

"It's wonderful to see you again, Lindsay," Gloria said, her voice full of pleasantness and grace. Lindsay wanted to learn more about her, spend more time with her, and be better friends with her. One look at Britt confirmed the same thing, and she felt the same instant connection to Alma and Roxanne.

She looked at Matt, Keith's daddy, and her stomach vibrated in a strange way. She had no idea what Keith had told his parents, but Matt Whettstein drew her into a hug, his smile absolutely shining and genuine. "Welcome to our home, Lindsay," he said in a gravelly, cowboy voice that struck her heart like a gong.

Vibrations moved through her, and she knew—she absolutely knew—she had to do more to repair the road between her and her daddy.

She'd been this bonded with Keith almost immediately too, and she acknowledged silently to herself that God had brought these people into her life for a reason.

Now, she just had to remember why—and act on it.

CHAPTER
Twenty-Five

JANE BEHR STOOD in a huge garage, the scent of oil somehow already hanging in the air, though Cord had not completed a single car repair here yet.

Her husband would, though. Soon. Very soon.

She held a clipboard in her hand and wore blue jeans and a tank top the same color as the oil she could smell. "Socket set," she called. "Times three."

"Got them," Cord said.

He had given her a checklist of tools and items he wanted in this garage, and Jane had been reading them to him for the past twenty minutes. They'd done the same in the office, in the waiting room, and in the oversized garage, where he'd work on everything from farm equipment to motorhomes.

This garage could house four cars across, but only Cord would work here. For now. They'd talked about him hiring other mechanics, but he'd wanted to start slow. Everything Cord did got done absolutely right, and he never rushed into anything. It was one of her favorite things about him, actually.

She brought the big ideas, and he tamed them into bite-sized pieces he could handle. He brought his excitement and enthusiasm for opening this mechanic shop, and she shaped them into business tactics and marketing endeavors.

They'd only been married for three months, and yet Jane felt like she'd been with him forever. They'd been working on this shop for longer than they'd been married, and a certain giddiness pulled through her too.

I'm so grateful this is happening, she thought, her form of a prayer. She'd been trying to list the things she was grateful for as she felt them, thought of them, or noticed them. And coming closer and closer to her husband's life-long dream of owning and opening a mechanic shop felt like such a huge blessing. Such a big, giant thing to be grateful for.

Jane let the feeling move through her as she called out the next piece of equipment.

"Got it," Cord said over his shoulder, and she made the obligatory checkmark on the list attached to the clipboard. Once the list was completed, Jane took the clipboard over to the long counter that ran along the back of the shop.

Cord had sketched out everything he'd wanted in a shop, and Jane had bought him everything he'd needed through her foundation. It had come in big boxes all at once, then in slower periods with tiny tools in small cases.

Her husband had gone through every piece meticulously, catalogued it all, and placed it where he wanted it here on the mechanic shop complex. Jane felt like God had directed their feet every step of the way in this operation, and as Cord started flipping through his packet of notes—something he'd done countless times in the past five months, Jane simply watched him.

"Are you staring at me, because I'm so beautiful?" he asked without looking over to her.

"Yes," she said with a smile. Cord was a beautiful man, and she was so glad she'd calmed enough to be at his side.

"Jane."

"Cord, how many times are you going to go over that packet?"

"Just one more," he said without missing a beat.

She put her hand over the pages, and Cord had no choice but to stop reading them. He wasn't reading anyway. He had the whole thing memorized. He'd written it all out, and that meant so much, as he wasn't the smartest with reading and writing.

"We're ready," she said. "*You're* ready, Cord."

He finally met her eyes, but he only moved his to do it. She could barely see him past the brim of his cowboy hat, and she had half a mind to nudge it up. Cord—most cowboys, in fact—didn't like it when someone touched their hat, and Jane fisted her fingers to keep them to herself.

"It's opening day in four days," she said gently. "You're going to shine like a *star*." She grinned at him, glad when his mouth twitched. He liked to hide his emotions from her, even now, but it wouldn't last long.

"You're going to cut the ribbon, right?" he asked. "I don't want to do it."

"We have a plan," Jane said. "I don't deviate from the plan." She cuddled into his side and removed her hand from the packet of papers. Thankfully, Cord didn't go back to them. "All right, baby," she said. "I want you to show me how you're going to flip the sign from closed to open after I cut the ribbon."

He looked at her out of the side of his eye, but he wasn't seriously questioning her. He didn't want to demonstrate flipping a sign, but Jane would insist, and he'd do it.

"I don't have any customers," he said. "It's going to be so anti-climatic." He straightened and tucked her arm against his side. "Maybe we should just cancel the grand opening and just start taking appointments."

A sense of pride filled Jane, because she'd quit her job at her family company at the end of the year, and she'd spent the last five months working on this shop. Cord had kept his job at the farm, and he'd only quit a few days ago.

Hunter was looking for someone new, and he'd known Cord would be gone before summer. Thankfully, it wasn't too hard to find cowboys willing to work in the summertime. In fact, a couple of Jane's cousins had committed to coming down from Coral Canyon to help out at the farm.

"You have a look on your face," Cord said.

"A look?" Jane asked innocently. "I don't know what you mean."

"Janey."

"I told you I was going to handle the marketing," she said. "I'm running the office, Cord. The books. Everything."

He said nothing, because this wasn't anything new. They'd gone over and over how to work together so they didn't drive each other nuts. Really, so *she* didn't drive *him* crazy. They'd drawn clear lines in the sand—she would run the financial aspects of Behr's Automotive Restoration, and he'd dominate all of the shop spaces.

They'd brainstormed the name together, and he'd really liked the word "restoration." He said it made him feel like he'd finally set his life right. He'd restored what had been damaged previously.

"So what did you do within the scope of your job?" he asked.

"I have been advertising the grand opening." Jane shook her hair over her shoulders as they walked toward the big bay doors. "As part of that, I have been taking appointments for opening day."

Cord came to a complete stop. "You have?"

"People now know we're going to be open, and yes, I've got a…." She cleared her throat. "Few clients."

"A few clients? And they're willing to wait to bring in their cars for several more days?"

"Yes," she said.

"I hope you haven't been overpromising on delivery dates," he said. "You promised I would get to look at a car before you told anyone when they'd have it back."

"I have promised nothing outside the bounds of my job description," Jane said haughtily. "I rather like you, and I'd like to stay married."

"Mm hm."

"You doubt me?" She grinned at him, and they got moving again. They stepped out of the shop and into the sunshine, and Jane released her breath, closed her eyes, and tilted her head back toward the sky.

"The bays will be full on Saturday," she said to the backs of her eyelids. She straightened and turned into her husband's arms. "But I told everyone that you wouldn't be working that day. They could leave their cars—or trucks. Or tractors—and you'd look at them first thing on Monday and get back to them."

Cord gazed down at her, his cowboy hat now shading both

of them, especially the closer he dipped his face toward hers. "I love you, Jane Behr."

"I love you, Mister Behr." She barely managed to get the words out before he covered her mouth with his. She loved kissing Cord, and she loved being his wife, and she loved the way he loved her.

———

SATURDAY MORNING CAME, and Jane wore a black pencil skirt that matched a sleeveless top. She'd bought the suit in a department store downtown, and she carried the clipboard with a new sheet of paper on it now. Cord wore black from head to toe as well, but he sported jeans and a polo with his cowboy boots and hat.

He also wore a look of complete anxiety, and Jane took a peek out the front windows to see more people arriving. Only she and Cord had hidden themselves inside, and she found her momma and daddy right up front. She smiled to herself, because Momma's minivan would be taking up one of the four bays in an hour.

Travis had scheduled one of his tractors, and then Tyrone Watters had said he had a truck he couldn't get to stop squealing no matter what he tightened or replaced. Jane had assured him Cord would find and fix the problem, because her cowboy husband could practically speak Vehicle, and she'd seen him find and fix so many problems in his life.

"It's getting close," she said over her shoulder.

"I think I'm going to throw up." He'd been threatening such a thing for the past hour, since they'd arrived ahead of the crowd.

Jane turned toward him and clicked across the cement floor in her heels. She slid herself onto Cord's lap, glad when he put his arms around her and held her. "Sweetheart," she said. "I want you to enjoy this."

Cord looked at her, his quiet strength one of his best qualities. "I'm not trying to be nervous."

"I know, but I don't want you to be so anxious that you don't enjoy it." She nodded toward the windows. "The people out there? They love you. You, baby. It's not for me."

"I guarantee your daddy is out there," he said. "And that's for you."

"No." She shook her head. "He's here for *you*. Trav is here for *you*. They're all here for *you*." Besides Daddy and Travis, she had three people from the community leaving their cars, trucks, or tractors, and then the last spot had been taken by Keith. He'd called with a truck from Blackhorse Bay that needed new tires.

Cord could do it all, and Jane had tried to bring him a variety of projects for his first several out of the gate.

"Thank you, Jane," he whispered.

"Please, please try to enjoy this."

"I'm enjoying myself right now." He tipped a half-smile at her, which earned him a kiss. Her phone alarmed, and Jane pulled back to silence it.

"It's time, baby." She met his eyes. "Come on, now." She stood and used both hands to pull him to his feet. "We're just going to make a short speech, cut a ribbon, and flip a sign." She smiled at him, her own excitement about to overflow. "And then, people will drive in their cars, and I'm going to make you stand by them for a bunch of pictures, so prepare yourself, and then we're going to go eat lunch with everyone on the farm, and then—"

"Then we get to go home." Cord kept both of her hands in his. "Just me and you."

"That's right," she said matter-of-factly. "Just me and you, and your favorite steak dinner, and an early bedtime. All the things you love." She backed up a couple of steps, pulling him with her. "It's opening day, baby! Come on."

He stumbled forward for a step or two until he righted himself. "All right." He chuckled. "All right."

Jane led the way outside, her hand locked in her husband's. The crowd started to cheer and applaud, and a smile popped onto Jane's face. She waved to the crowd, who were mostly people she knew and loved. She did see a few faces she didn't know, and that made her happier than she could describe.

She'd tied a bright blue ribbon from bay to bay and tied a bow right in the middle of the building. She'd set up a mic with a portable speaker, and she headed that way. Cord did not want to speak, and Jane said she'd handle it all. He did for her what she didn't want to do, and she'd do this for him.

"Welcome," she called into the mic once she'd arrived. "Thank you so much for coming to this grand opening of Behr's Automotive Restoration!"

More cheering. More clapping, and Jane turned toward Cord and applauded him too.

"We've been working physically on this mechanic shop for months. Cord's dedicated almost his whole life mentally and emotionally to this shop, and I am thrilled and so proud to be at his side today."

She pressed against the pinch in her vocal cords, because she did not want to cry here. Not today. This was a happy day, and while happy things did make Jane weep, Cord wouldn't like it. And everything about today was about Cord.

"We're thrilled to open the doors to the community of Cherry Creek, Ivory Peaks, Canyon Gulch, and all surrounding towns. Cord can fix cars, trucks, vans, ATVs, RVs, and any piece of farm or ranch equipment." Pride started to creep into her voice, and Jane needed to wrap this up.

"Thank you again for coming," she said into the mic. "Cord?" She turned toward him, and her momma stepped forward with an enormous pair of scissors. Cord took them without dropping them, and Jane stepped back as he moved to cut the blue ribbon.

He posed like a champion, and Daddy took plenty of pictures with his phone. When he gave him a thumbs-up, Cord clamped the two blades together, and the ribbon fluttered innocently to the ground.

The crowd went wild, and Jane laughed up into the sky. Cord handed the scissors back to Momma, and he moved over to the door right in the middle of the four bay doors. He walked through them, and Jane used both arms to display the windows that sat just above her head.

A large CLOSED sign hung there, and as they all watched, Cord flipped it to OPEN. That caused another surge in whooping, and then, Cord hit the magical button inside that lifted all four doors at the same time.

Jane laughed as her momma swooped her into her arms, because this grand opening was like starting a new chapter after planning to take this step for *such* a long time. "Thank you, Momma."

Her mom held her by the shoulders. "I'm so happy for you, Jane."

"I meant thank you for the money for the foundation, so I can do things like this." She glanced over to where Cord hugged

Travis, with Mission, Keith, and Daddy all waiting to do the same. "Even if it was for my husband."

"Baby, I just married into the money." Momma grinned at her. "But you are a Hammond, through and through. Generations of them would be so proud of you and all you've done here."

Jane gazed around the large bays and the people who'd come. Her cousin Opal approached, and Jane moved over to hug her. She'd been such a big support leading up to the wedding too, and Jane loved her.

"How long will you be here?"

Opal grinned and then sighed as she pushed her thick, dark hair out of her eyes. "Well, Momma finally went back to Coral Canyon, and she's worried that Mike—who literally runs a billions-dollar company with hundreds of employees—and Gerty—who brought a dead farm back to life—won't be able to keep their baby alive." Opal rolled her eyes. "Their four-month-old baby, who literally never cries."

Jane nodded along, but she knew Opal secretly loved her new nephew. "So you took time off work. How long are you staying?"

"All summer," she said with a grin. "I love that baby."

Jane laughed, but she nodded. "I love that baby too." She nudged her cousin with her hip, marveling that they were related but looked so different. Opal was like a woman dipped in midnight, while Jane had been made of the night, but had moonlight in her hair, skin, and eyes. Her lighter features came from Momma, who'd moved on to chat with Cord's momma.

"I got to babysit West a couple of weeks ago." Jane grinned at Opal. "I know you're jealous."

"I am," Opal said. "I'm hoping to get her to go stay in the

city for a couple of nights. My mom says she simply takes West everywhere with her. Straps him in and goes out onto the farm."

"I've seen her do it," Jane said with a nod. Cord caught her eye, and she lifted her hand to tell him she'd seen him. "Opal, let's have lunch or dinner while you're here. As many as times as we can."

Opal followed her gaze, and said, "Go on over to your hot cowboy mechanic husband."

"I'll be right back."

"Yeah, I'm sure you will." Opal waved and turned to go stand by Tucker and Deacon.

Jane moved over to Cord, sliding her hand into his. He squeezed, just once, but that was enough for him to tell her how very grateful he was that she stood at his side. How much he loved her. And how glad he was that they were on this journey together.

Jane squeezed back, just once.

CHAPTER
Twenty-Six

TUCKER HAMMOND STOOD on the bottom rung of the fence separating the crowd and the cowboys from the arena. The tractor had just finished raking and smoothing the dirt. The crowd sat mostly dormant, but they'd perk up the moment movement started happening in the gates next to him.

The announcers bantered back and forth, and Tucker could admit he was growing tired of the same jokes, the same filler, the same noise. It was all just *noise*.

This noise paid his bills quite well, and Tuck pushed aside his weary thoughts. He got down on his knees every night, no matter where he'd landed or how late it was, and he thanked God for his career. He hadn't been able to cut it in the rodeo, not with his times, but he loved the sport with his whole heart.

He still loved to rope and ride, and managing the career of another cowboy who could do things he couldn't allowed him to do both. He'd been working with Tarr Olson—*only A's and O's in his name*, Tuck thought—for five years now, and the man was like a brother to him.

They traveled together, they dined together, they'd even been out with women together. Tuck hadn't found much luck in making a love connection, and he grinned into the dark night at the words *love connection*.

His younger brother would tell him never to say or think them again, but Tuck couldn't help it. He had an old soul, and he loved things of yesteryear. He did want a sweeping romance with someone. Someone who would pull him away from the announcers, the late nights in arenas, the noise.

He'd been back to Ivory Peaks and the family farm where he'd been born and raised a couple of times this year. Once for Jane's wedding, and once when his cousin Mike had had his first baby, and once when Cord, Jane's husband, had opened his mechanic shop.

Now that rodeo season had arrived, he, Tarr, and the horses —Checkers for Tarr and Freckles for Tuck—traveled from rodeo to rodeo, training wherever Tuck could find them room on the off days. They drove. They bought burgers. They rode their horses and threw ropes.

They soaked up the endless blue skies, the heat of a long, warm day, and the brotherly banter between best friends. Tuck couldn't even dream of a better life, even if he grew tired of the day-to-day from time to time.

Like right now. The next event started, but Tarr wasn't on until the bull riding a little later. Tuck had everything set for his ride, and he'd texted Tarr that he'd drawn Thunder and Lightning for tonight's ride, and Tarr had sent back several pairs of clapping hands.

On a bull like Thunder and Lightning, Tarr should win, hands down. The bull didn't have that high of a rating, and Tarr had ridden him successfully twice in the past couple of years. He'd have to show his skills and really kick Thunder into high gear to score well, but Tuck believed in his boss's ability to do so.

Sometimes Tuck rode as a pick-up man during rodeos, but tonight, he stayed on the ground and let others assist the cowboys off the backs of the broncs through the bareback and the saddled events.

The night wore on, and Tuck found himself wondering what was happening back home. He normally didn't, and he told himself it was because he'd been home so much this year. He'd stayed for an extended time in December as well, being able to go to Britt Whettstein's wedding too.

Finally, the bull riding event arrived, and Tuck tuned back into what he needed to do. He met Tarr behind the gates, finding the cowboy dressed in his thick, leather chaps and the required padded vest. He currently wore his midnight-colored cowboy hat, but he'd swap it out for a helmet when he mounted Thunder and Lightning.

He wanted to win, and he wanted to look good doing it, but Tarr wasn't stupid. He was about four years older than Tucker, and he wanted a long career in rodeo. He wasn't flashy. He spoke to reporters, had a quick smile, and grinned at Tuck as he approached.

"Goin' sixth," he said. "That should tell you about where you'll be, I'd think." Tuck kept his voice down, as he didn't need to insult the four riders who'd follow Tarr. But Tuck studied everyone on the circuit, every entry at every rodeo. He knew who Tarr was going against, and sometimes he entered him in only the bull riding—like tonight—and sometimes he did the saddle bronc as well as the bull event.

Tarr loved to rope, and Tucker had put him in the tie-down roping plenty of times. If he could get his rope to cooperate with him better, he could be Tarr's heeler in team roping, but Tuck wasn't the most consistent with his loop.

Everything else, he excelled at, and one day, maybe he and Tarr would be able to enter a rodeo together.

The first five bull riders rode their beasts, and only two of them made the eight-second bell. Tuck helped Tarr up onto the bull, and he pulled the rope across his best friend's hand while Tarr tightened the helmet strap under his chin.

The adrenaline flowed like molten lava, making the night hotter under the bright lights in the arena. Tuck could taste the excitement on the air, especially when the announcer in this small Utah town yelled into the mic, "Ladies and gents, we have a high roller here with us tonight. All the way from Stephenville, Texas, we have a three-time PRCA bull-riding champion, as well a two-time PRCA World All-Around Champion with us tonight. Put your hands together for *Taaaaarrrrrr Olllllsonnnnn!*"

The crowd sure did, and people began stomping their feet against the metal bleachers too. They whooped and hollered, and Tuck leaned in close to Tarr, who had the exceptional ability to tune everything out when atop a bull—even Tucker.

"Tarr!" he yelled. "He spins, brother! Spur him hard and lean into the left spin!"

Tarr nodded in short little bursts as cowboys vacated the fences where they'd been helping get him into position. He sat with his knees up, and Tuck had no more advice for the man. It was almost like he moved into superhuman mode when riding, and he'd come back to earth when the bell rang.

Tuck's boots hit the dirt, and he jogged the few steps to the fence. He jumped up and clung to the top rung as the only cowboy in the arena boogied backward, pulling the gate open with him.

Thunder and Lightning bolted out of the chute where he'd been contained; the crowd only increased in intensity; the world narrowed to Tarr.

The cowboy raked his spurs up the bull's sides, and Thunder totally went into his death spin, going left and left and left and left.

Tarr leaned into it, then pulled out on the way up. He seemed to absorb the bull's jarring landing as he leaned in close again. And again.

Tuck sometimes took the split-second to look over to the clock, just to see how close Tarr was to meeting the required eight seconds. Tonight, he didn't need to. This event was as good as his, and they'd add more points and more money to their totals.

Then Thunder and Lightning went unexpectedly to the right. Out of nowhere. In the hours of film Tuck had watched on this bull, he'd never done that. Ever.

The announcer shouted something; the crowd went silent for a painful, terrifying moment; Tarr flew to the left—the first law of motion required it. He'd been moving left, and suddenly the bull went right, but Tarr *still* went left, and that meant he wasn't on the bull any longer.

He hit the dirt hard, and the crowd sent a up a collective gasp. The clowns ran toward the bull, hoping to distract it, while the blue heeler who'd been driving them toward the exit gate sprang into motion too.

Tuck saw all of that from his peripheral vision, because he

couldn't look away from Tarr.

He hadn't moved. Not even a little bit.

All cowboys, no matter if they were hurt or not, sprang back to their feet after getting bucked from the bull. They knew to run for the fence line, lest the two ton beast came at them with his horns down.

Tarr had been knocked out cold. Tuck knew it, but his body had frozen.

Then the announcer said, "It looks like Tarr's down, folks. Let's get our hats off and take a breather."

The arena went silent, and that got Tuck up and over the fence. He wasn't the only one running toward Tarr, but he felt certain his heart was sprinting the fastest. "Dear God," he said right out loud. "Don't let this be too bad."

Dear God, don't let this be too bad.

Dear God, don't let this be too bad.

Dear God, don't let this be too bad.

"SO THIS IS IT," Tucker said a handful of days later. He glanced over to the passenger seat of his truck. Rather, it as Tarr's truck, but Tucker was driving it. He'd been driving them everywhere since Tarr's accident last weekend.

"Right around the bend here, the farm opens up." Tucker smiled, because he'd been telling Tarr about his family farm for years. "You're going to love it here."

The rodeo champion had been benched for the rest of the year. He had a Grade 2 concussion, and he'd been unconscious in the dirt on the arena floor for twenty minutes before the paramedics had gotten him to wake up.

He'd broken his ankle after landing on it completely wrong, because he'd been knocked out by the bull's shoulder while he was still atop it. So he'd flown through the air like a ragdoll, his body landing just…however it had landed.

Still, Tarr wore a smile as he gazed out the windshield. The pine trees curved with the road, and the big red barn that housed Pony Power's administration office came into view. A couple of stables sat behind that, with pastures for miles on either side.

Well, sort of. To the north, across a wide pasture, sat a row of cabins where the counselors met with kids as part of the equine therapy unit that Tucker's sister-in-law owned and operated. The farmhouse sat down the fence as well, and Tucker's heart rejoiced to once more be coming home.

He loved coming home.

So he too wore a huge grin as he trundled along the dirt lane past the big barn. A couple of horses grazed in the near pasture and a few more walked in the training circles. A cowboy crossed the fields down the way, and everything spoke of a slow summer night, a beautiful country evening, and the absolute peace of God.

"I love this farm," he said. And Hunter, his oldest brother, had two cabins that were completely empty right now. The one Britt and Keith used to live in, and Cord's former cabin, as he'd just quit at the Hammond Family Farm a couple of weeks ago.

"It almost feels like God has prepared a place for us here," he said.

Tarr nodded and said, "It sure does," as Tuck went past the house where he'd grown up and continued past it, past the family garden plot, and past the bonfire pit. He made the left turn, the cabin community opening up back here.

"My parents will already be up in Coral Canyon," he said, catching sight of the generational house. "Depending on how you're doing, we can go up for the Fourth of July. That's when Hunter is surprising them with their new house."

His momma and daddy had bought a house in Coral Canyon many years ago, when Jane was first born. They went every single summer—earlier than ever this year, in fact—without fail, but now that Daddy had hit seventy-five, and combined with decades of marathon running, his knees couldn't quite handle the steps at the mountain home.

Hunt had found them one that would suit them better, and since it wasn't up the canyon, it had better year-round access. Tucker's heartbeat actually fired at him at the thought of his momma and daddy not being here in Ivory Peaks. To him, they always would be.

At the same time, he knew it was time for them to move up north. Daddy wanted to be with his brothers. Momma had friends up there, and she'd sold her landscaping business to someone else. They could make the trip down here for babies or reunions, weddings or special events, the same way Tuck's aunts and uncles did.

He pulled up to Britt's cabin, where he and Tarr were going to be living for the foreseeable future. Tarr could rest here. Recover. Recuperate. He could keep training here once the doctor cleared him. And Tucker could be there to help him, the way he had been for the past five years.

"All right," he said. "Let's go check it out. Hunt said he came over and opened the windows and made sure things were ready." He got out of the truck and went to help Tarr with the crutches.

They moved slowly up the walk, and Tarr struggled with the

steps, finally getting up the seven or eight of them to the front porch.

Tuck had stayed behind him, and he still had two to navigate before he'd reach the porch and could move around his best friend to open the door.

"What are you guys doing here?" a woman asked, and Tuck looked up prematurely. The toe of his boot caught on the front of the step, and he stumbled forward. Horror crashed through him as he tried to avoid Tarr. Ramming into him would not be good, and Tuck managed to avoid him.

He didn't manage to catch himself, so his cheekbone cracked against the wooden floor of the porch, and stars blitzed through his vision as pain exploded through his jaw, mouth, and skull.

"Whoa." The woman dropped to her knees. "Are you okay?"

He pushed himself up, humiliation making every inch of his skin burn. "Yeah," he muttered. His eyes met hers, and she'd knelt down only a few inches from him.

He froze; she did too; the whole universe just came to a screeching halt.

She couldn't be much older than him, if she was at all. She had dark, soft green eyes filled with concern, and hair the color of Freckles's coat. Tucker would never, ever tell her that, but he sure did like the shiny, deep, rich honey color of it. Like raw buckwheat honey, which had a darker color, and a deep, rich taste Tucker suddenly wanted in his mouth.

"I'm Bobbie Jo," she said as she stood. She extended her hand to Tucker, and he put his in it. Crackles and flames burst to life, and he pulled back as soon as he had his feet under him.

"Tucker," he said, touching his chest, which did sting a little. "Tarr. We're movin' in here today."

Bobbie Jo's eyebrows puckered in confusion. "You are? That's weird."

"Why's it weird?" Tarr asked. He didn't seem to have frozen, but he also hadn't taken an embarrassing header into the porch planks.

"Well," Bobbie Jo said as she folded her arms and cocked out a curvy hip. "Because I live here."

CHAPTER
Twenty~Seven

BOBBIE JO HANKS didn't mean to call on her redheaded fire within the first five minutes of meeting the first people she'd encountered on the Hammond Family Farm. She'd just been hired, for crying out loud.

Curb your temper, she told herself, and she tried to get her tongue and mind and body to align by un-cinching her arms. Both cowboys standing in front of her had been dipped in the Handsome For Days Pool, to be certain. The one on her right—Tarr—balanced on one foot and seemed to look to the other for guidance and direction.

Tucker, he'd said his name was, and the flush that had deliciously stained his face drained away as confusion took over his expression. "That can't be right." He looked over to the other cowboy, then out toward the road and down to the next cabin over. "I talked to Hunt about it just this morning."

"Hunter Hammond?" she asked.

"Yes, ma'am," Tucker said. Out of the two of them, Bobbie

Jo's heart skipped and hammered at the same time for Tucker. "Let me just call him real quick, okay?" He flashed her a smile, and Bobbie Jo turned her attention to Tarr. "Do you want to come in and sit down?"

"I've been sittin' for a while now," he said. "If I can just lean here for a sec, that would be just fine."

He spoke with a total Texan accent, and Bobbie Jo had known plenty of cowboys like him throughout her lifetime. Cowboys like him were responsible for the loss of her family ranch, thank you very much. That alone gave him a strike, and Bobbie Jo once again told herself not to be so quick to judge.

She'd done too much of that in the past, and it wasn't really her job. Before she'd come west from Oklahoma, she'd gone to church one last time with her folks. All of the friends and neighbors she'd known for her whole life. Everyone she'd thought she'd spend the rest of her life ranching and farming beside.

Her throat narrowed as Tucker said, "Hey, Hunt, we're here, but there's someone in our cabin." He'd turned his back on her, and he started down the steps he'd just come up as he added, "Yeah, a real pretty woman. Bobbie Jo? What's goin' on?"

A real pretty woman.

His words buzzed through her ears, cleaning out every bad and hard and negative that had been accumulating over the past year.

Tarr cleared his throat, and she yanked her attention to him only to find him hopping on one foot as he turned away from her. His smile couldn't be missed, nor the low chuckle that he somehow managed to keep in his throat.

Surely he'd seen something funny on his phone, but the cowboy didn't have the device out. Blast him. Was it funny that Tucker found her pretty?

Bobbie Jo reached up and tucked her hair behind her ear. She'd been driving a lot today too, and she'd started to come outside to go grab some dinner and check on her truck. It had started making a noise about a hundred miles from here, and she'd made it to Ivory Peaks by gripping the steering wheel with two hands and praying right out loud.

She'd stopped by the mechanic shop closest to the farm, talked to the cowboy there—why Colorado had all cowboys so far, she wasn't sure—and pulled her bike out of the trailer. She'd ridden the last five miles to this farm, and her stomach wasn't happy about it.

"Yeah, sure," Tucker said as he started back up the steps. "We're starving for sure, and I don't think Tarr is gonna be upset about your wife feeding us dinner tonight."

Bobbie Jo wanted an invitation to that dinner too, but she wasn't sure how to get one. Tucker arrived on the porch again and shoved his phone in his back pocket. "Sorry, Bobbie Jo. Hunt told me we were in this cabin, but we're actually down the road in that one." He turned and pointed back down the lane, closer to the main farmhouse. Tucker looked over to his friend. "That's where Cord lived, and Hunt says it's bigger, but he didn't know it until after he talked to me, and then he forgot to text me."

Tarr nodded, his smile perfectly pleasant. "Well, get me loaded up again, Tuck. Did I hear we're getting fed tonight?"

"Yeah." Tucker hooked his thumb over his shoulder. "Molly's been cooking for us all day, Hunt said." He turned back to Bobbie Jo, and oh, those dark eyes complimented his lighter, sandier hair, and she wanted to know why he was half-light and half-dark. "Do you have food here? Hunt said you just came in today too. From Oklahoma. Said he meant to text you too, about dinner."

Bobbie Jo's first thought was to deny him. She could ride the five miles to town and find something to eat just fine. But her heart just wanted someone to take care of her, and a home-cooked meal fit that bill perfectly.

"I was just going to go to town," she said. "That's why I came outside when I did." And a good thing too. She could've been walking around the kitchen, naked. She wasn't, of course. But she *could've* been, and the front door wasn't locked.

Tarr started down the steps, and Tucker lurched after him. "Dude, give me two seconds."

"I can do it," Tarr growled, and Tucker fell back and watched him for a moment.

When he faced Bobbie Jo again, he said, "There's no car here. Did you come with someone?" He looked to the cabin next door, which did have two trucks parked out front.

"I was, uh, just going to ride my bike," she said. "My truck was having some problems, and I left it at the shop in town."

"Oh, no," he said, shaking his head. "No. Nope. You're not riding your bike to town for dinner on the first night you're here. No way." He grinned at her and offered his arm. "Do you want to come with us? We just want to take in our bags for tonight, and we'll unpack tomorrow. Then we'll go over to the farmhouse."

Bobbie Jo looked at Tarr, still laboring down the steps. "I could help him with his bag."

"I would love you forever if you do," Tucker said, almost under his breath. "He gets a little crabby when he's hungry." A smile filled his face, revealing straight, white teeth to go with his perfectly trimmed beard—also in those same half-light, half-dark good looks he had going on.

Her heart did another flip, this time adding a twist and telling her she definitely felt some attraction to this cowboy. She hadn't expected that, and not only because she was so heart-broken over the loss of the life she'd thought she'd have.

But because she'd left a boyfriend in Ryerson. The plan was for her to work here for the summer, then reassess. She might stay here, but she might return to Oklahoma if an opportunity existed there for her to buy her own place. And of course, Lawson lived there.

He was a dentist, which was about as far from the well-dressed cowboy still standing in front of her.

"My sister-in-law is a really good cook," Tucker said. "I'd be willing to bet she's made something just for you."

"You think so?" Bobbie Jo asked.

"Don't let him bet you," Tarr called from the bottom of the steps, and both she and Tucker looked down to him. "And he hasn't stopped talking about Molly's cooking, so I'd definitely do that over riding my bike anywhere."

"That's because you have a broken leg," Tucker called to him.

"It's my ankle," Tarr fired back, without slowing, stopping, or looking at them. "Not my leg."

Tucker grinned widely and looked at her, his eyebrows up now. "So? Dinner with my brother and his family?"

All of the pieces now fell into place. "Hunter is your brother."

"Yes, ma'am," he said. "The oldest of us Hammonds. I've got a sister older than me too, and a brother younger. Deacon lives here too."

Bobbie Jo didn't know why him owning this farm mattered to her. And he didn't own it, besides. His brother did. *Yeah, and he's the next oldest son,* she told herself. Then she backed off mentally, telling herself not to make assumptions about things she knew nothing about.

The constant back and forth inside her really was exhausting. She reminded herself that she was supposed to call her boyfriend tonight to let him know she'd arrived safely. With that barrier securely in place, she could nod to Tucker and say, "I'd love to have dinner with your brother and his family."

She could only hope she didn't live to regret this evening and what might come out of her mouth.

CHAPTER
Twenty-Eight

KEITH WALKED into the administration building, a thick pad of papers stuck to the clipboard he carried everywhere with him. He ate breakfast with it. He kept it on the dashboard of his truck and looked at it, made notes on it, and took it out into every field with him. Heck, he slept with the thing, as he'd woken up an hour ago with it on his chest—where it had settled after he'd fallen asleep while looking at it.

Today was their first planting day of the year, and the only thing keeping Keith here was the fact that Lenora would be feeding them all throughout the day. In fact, as he smiled tersely at Janice and walked by her, he smelled the scent of fruity jams and freshly toasted bread.

"There he is," Jack practically bellowed, and Keith wished he wouldn't. He'd be in the spotlight all day long—and in plenty of other instances—and he didn't need the boss calling more attention to him than necessary.

Jack meant well, Keith knew. He stuck out his big hand to go with his big personality and his enormous voice. Keith's smile relaxed a little as he shook his boss's hand. "Morning, sir."

"We ready for this?"

"Yes, sir," Keith said, resisting the urge to lift up his clipboard to find the answer.

"Well, we've got the boys here." Jack indicated the twenty or so cowboys milling about. "Just tell 'em what you want them to do."

"Yes, sir." Keith looked at the others waiting there. They all looked at him, and Keith honestly had no idea how he'd come to be in this position. He'd never been the one in charge. He was much more comfortable as one of the crowd, one who simply waited for someone higher than him to tell him what to do.

He was that person this year. He'd been back and forth with Jack for months now, but he'd finally approved it all last month. Grudgingly, Keith could admit. But he'd approved it, and Keith wanted to get the cowboys divided up into three groups and get going.

"We're ready?" he asked.

"Waitin' on you." Jack clapped his hand on Keith's shoulder, and he very nearly went to his knees.

He cleared his throat and stepped away from his boss. "All right, everyone," he called. The chatter died down, and he lifted his clipboard, ready to dive in.

"I need these people over on my right," Keith said. "You'll be on the tractors, planting our largest bulk of fields with alfalfa." He started naming people, including Derrick and Buck, and people started weeding themselves out of the group.

"In front of me," Keith continued. "These people will be planting cover crops in a few fields." He cleared his throat, because Jack had never planted cover crops before. Keith had found several fields with suffering soil, and one of the better ways to get it back to full health was to rest it. More than that, plant something in it that he'd then till into the soil to replenish it. The practice was done all over Iowa and other midwestern states, and he saw no reason not to do it here at Blackhorse Bay.

"We're planting mustard and buckwheat in these fields, and while I wish I could place them where I want, I can't. These crops are going in fields that need to be refreshed, but Jack has assured me that our beehives will be producing some amazing honeys with these plants." He cut a glance over to his boss, where Jack nodded.

"It's nine fields," he said. "And we'll have to monitor them, and we'll be tilling the crops under before they're fully grown—and definitely before the mustard goes to seed—to get the fallow dirt to rejuvenate. We may then plant alfalfa, but we might simply swap our cover crops. I'm going to be testing a lot this summer."

Keith felt a little in over his head, actually. He probably shouldn't have taken on three things his first summer here, but his passion for agriculture couldn't be contained. He wanted to honor the land here, and some parts of it had been neglected in recent years. Or rather, it had been overworked. It needed to be rested, and he couldn't wait to see the gorgeous waves of yellow flowers and bright yellow-green leaves.

It would suppress the weeds, add nutrients to the soil, and bring him—and hopefully others—great joy.

"We won't be tilling these fields," he said. "Oh, wait. My cover crop cowboys are...." He listed the people he'd put on that, and they clustered in front of him, a couple of them exchanging glances. He did his best to ignore them, and he focused on his clipboard while feet continued to scuffle.

"And finally," he said. "We won't be tilling the fields I didn't take to ground last winter to prevent erosion and water loss. Half of these will be corn, and the other half alfalfa, because I want to see how our production compares between tilled and no-tilled fields." He called the rest of the names, but most people had already moved to his left.

He lowered his clipboard. "I've got all the seeds sorted in the long lane by the greenhouse, and we'll need people on refilling, and two people in our bigger tractors. Jack's rented and borrowed the machines we need, and if you don't know how to drive something, say something."

Jack stepped next to him and said, "I've spoken to you if you're driving the planters today. If I didn't, you're on refilling duty and making sure we get every inch done. You can ask me or Keith anything, at any time." He nodded, and Keith did the same.

"Some of you thought I was crazy for planting winter wheat last year, but there's a reason. We're going to be using those fields for more wheat, but we won't be tilling them under. We're doing a no-till method, where we're simply cutting down the stalks of winter wheat that are still there—I had them cut high—and we'll be using roller crimpers to mow them down a bit more and plant the wheat at the same time. Again, two people on these fields to make sure we're cutting and planting evenly."

He nodded to his left-side crew, where Coy stood. He had his arms folded but a big smile on his face, and it gave Keith a bit of courage. "That's it, everyone," he said. "Lenora has breakfast this morning, and it's my understanding there will be something to eat anytime you come back here."

People started to move, and those who'd been spoken to by Jack came to him to get the keys to their machines. A sixteen-row planter could do about fifteen acres per hour, so over the course of the next ten hours, one hundred and fifty acres would get seeded.

Blackhorse Bay owned three planters of their own—two of which were only twelve rowers—and Keith had arranged to rent two roller crimpers and two more sixteen-row planters. He'd also secured a massive twenty-four-row planter, and he noted that Derrick had gotten the key to that one. Buck went with him, and Keith didn't worry one ounce over that pair. They'd get the job done, and then they'd all gather at their cabin that night, where Lindsay had said she'd bring dinner for all four of them. Five, counting her.

Jack had borrowed three other planters from colleagues around the area, and that brought their planters to ten. That meant Keith could plant fifteen hundred acres today, and he only had nine hundred to do.

If the seeds held out, and the cowboys got along, and his meticulous planning actually went according to plan, the farm would be fully planted by evening.

Such a sense of accomplishment flowed through him, and Keith started to truly smile at those moving past him. "I love this idea of no-till planting," Coy said. He was an environmentalist, and Keith had really enjoyed talking with him about erosion and evaporation concerns, and how they could prevent them. No-till planting also allowed for far more organic farming, as the use of herbicides for weed control wasn't nearly as necessary.

That would reduce the manpower Keith needed for a mid-season spraying, and he said, "Me too," as he fell into step with Coy.

Outside, the sun shone, and Keith took a moment and

inhaled way down deep into his lungs. "Yes," he said almost to himself. "It's a good day for planting."

Down at the greenhouse, cowboys were loading bags of seeds into the backs of trucks and the rumble of tractor engines filled the air. All of it made Keith enormously happy, and he sat behind the wheel, his truck off and his window down. He pulled out his phone and texted Lindsay.

Planting is underway!

He took a picture of the activity nearby and sent her that too.

I need you to come do my forty acres, she said.

He chuckled and shook his head, because she'd borrowed a planter from her uncle a few days ago, and her crops were all already in.

Can't wait to see you tonight, he said. Things between them had been going so much better since his intervention into her absence, and while he wasn't sure if she'd actually gone to see a therapist, she certainly made more of an effort to come to him.

A picture started to come in, but it was still processing when her next text arrived. *Guess what I'm making for dinner?*

The picture arrived, and it was a deep stock pot with what looked like onions and celery sautéing. *That could literally be anything,* he said. *Give me a hint.*

You said it was one of your favorites.

"Keith," someone called, and he abandoned his flirt-fest with his girlfriend to go see what his cowboys needed for planting day.

He'd spoken true, and he couldn't wait to see her that night, because it meant this day would be over. Whether things went well or they didn't, it would be done, and Keith really needed this to be done.

And if he could kiss Lindsay and eat her delicious dinner on top of that? His life would be about perfect.

Now, he just had to figure out what was one of his favorites —that he'd told her—and get through this day. His planning would pay off, he was certain.

Then Derrick said, "Keith, brother, we can't find the mustard seeds."

CHAPTER
Twenty~Nine

LINDSAY PACKED up the chicken enchilada soup first. It had been done for a few hours now, so the threat of it being boiling hot and steaming had passed. She could easily heat it up at the cabin and feed the four cowboys who lived there.

She hummed along with the radio as she ladled the soup into a big plastic container, covered that with plastic wrap, and then snapped the lid on. She covered that with plastic wrap too, a transport secret she'd learned from her granny.

This soup recipe had come from her too, and with another equally as large container of soup filled, covered, and lidded, Lindsay moved on to packing up the toppings. Avocado—which she'd chunk up once she got to the cabin. Tortilla strips, which she'd fried herself, thank you very much. Sour cream, cheese, and cilantro. They all went in the box with the soup, and Lindsay turned back to the kitchen to get the three bags of chips, the salsa, and the guacamole.

Mexican food was easy to serve for a crowd, and she hoped

Aunt Lenora hadn't opted for that too. Besides the soup and chips, which were both appetizers, Lindsay had spent some time this morning making ground beef patties the size of sliders. They waited on a tray, as Derrick had confirmed the cowboys had an operating grill at the cabin.

Lindsay had buns, cheese, tomatoes, lettuce, and bacon to top the sliders, and she carefully placed all those toppings in the box with the soup goods. The tray of sliders came out of the fridge and on top of the box, and Lindsay lifted that to take outside to her truck.

Hamlet trotted outside with her, stayed nearby while she loaded everything onto the floor behind the driver's seat, and then headed back inside with her too.

She needed the grand prize of what she'd made that day— one of Keith's self-proclaimed favorites: baked beans.

When he'd told her that a couple of weeks ago, this planting day menu had popped into her mind immediately. Appetizers, so she could feed the boys as they staggered into the cabin after a long day of working outside in the wind and in the sun.

Then, once everyone had arrived, sliders cooked up quick, and it was easy to assemble them, scoop on baked beans, and sit down to eat.

She'd told Keith at the time that her granny's recipe for baked beans was a little unconventional, and in her opinion, the best. Of course. They had meat in them too—ground beef and bacon—as well as three different types of beans that added great texture and mouth chew over a regular can of baked beans.

Lindsay had been simmering them since that morning in her slow cooker, and now, she simply unplugged the appliance, picked up the whole thing, and headed back to the truck. Out and in Hamlet went, and he sat by her feet as she stood in the kitchen, looking around to make sure she hadn't forgotten anything.

"Let's go, Ham," she said to her heeler, and together, they headed out again. She made the drive to Blackhorse, and the farm possessed an energy unlike anything she'd felt here before. The air teemed with...excitement Purpose. *Life.*

She drove past the upper stables, seeing a few horses out, their tails switching and twitching in the afternoon sunlight. She turned, and down the lane, she found the most activity at the greenhouse. Men worked there, and as she watched, a tractor with a huge attachment set out for its field.

Lindsay's excitement for farming and growing things, for spending time outdoors with plants and animals, rose up in a way it hadn't in a long time. Since she'd left Texas, actually. She parked as close to the sidewalk at Keith's as she could, and she let Hamlet down. He barked and ran down the road toward the greenhouse, and Lindsay watched him go. Only a blip of worry moved through her, because she knew Hamlet would come back. He wouldn't cause a problem—hopefully—and she turned her attention to carrying in the food she'd been preparing all day.

Then, she moved her truck, so the cowboys could park closer to the house, and she went inside and got her slow cooker plugged back in. She put all the toppings in the fridge that needed to be, and she dug around in a couple of cupboards before she found a pot she could put one of the containers of soup in.

She left the sliders out, because she liked to grill meat from a room temperature stage, and as no cowboys had walked in yet —and she expected Keith to show up last—she started to set their table. They only had four chairs, but she borrowed one from the built-in computer desk in the living room, and she'd just checked the time when the front door opened.

Coy walked in, and he brightened when he saw Lindsay. "I've never been happier to see you," he said. He looked like someone had sprayed him down with a firehose and then forced him to roll in dirt. He stepped right over to her and gave her a quick hug-squeeze. "I'm gonna go shower. Buck and Derrick are right behind me."

"And Keith?" Lindsay asked as Coy stepped back.

"Haven't seen him for a minute," Coy said. He left, taking the strong earthy, muscly, sweaty smell with him. Lindsay didn't entirely hate it, because it signaled a really good, hard day of work.

Her daddy valued hard work above all else, and Lindsay once again found herself thinking of her father at the most random of times. It almost felt like God was slapping her across the face, and she found herself standing in a cabin that wasn't hers, with nothing to occupy her time.

She spun and marched out the back door. This cabin butted up against a long corridor of grass, and thirty yards away sat the back of another house. Lindsay pulled out her phone and practically stabbed at the buttons.

"I have nothing to say to him," she grumbled to herself. But she'd been putting this off for far too long. She wanted to enjoy the vibrancy of this farm, the meal she'd put together tonight, and every other day of her life.

"Hullo," her daddy barked, and Lindsay flinched. She forgot who she'd called, but her heartbeat raced from her scalp to the soles of her feet.

"Who's there?"

"Daddy," Lindsay said, the word almost a shout as it came

out of her mouth. She drew a breath, the enormity of the sky pressing down on her, crushing her lungs. "It's me, Lindsay."

"I know," he said, and she wanted to roll her eyes. He clearly *hadn't* known, but she didn't say so.

"I just—I guess I just wanted to hear how you were doing." That wasn't exactly why she'd called, but the problem was, Lindsay didn't know why she'd called. "I mean, they're planting here at Blackhorse Bay and I got my fields planted a few days ago, and I've just been thinking about you and how things are going down at Sagebrush."

Lindsay forced herself to stop talking. She hadn't said anything that wasn't true; she had been thinking about her daddy a lot lately. He said nothing, and Lindsay paced down the slight decline, going past the cabin next door while she waited for her daddy to say something.

"You helpin' at Blackhorse now?" he asked, his voice rough and gravelly.

Out of everything Lindsay had said, she hadn't expected him to completely ignore it all. "No," she said slowly, her mind moving slower now too. "I'm just here to deliver dinner to my boyfriend. He works here and lives with Derrick." She turned around and started back toward the cabin where she wanted to be. "Did you hear me say I got the planting done on my own farm?"

"Y'all are a little behind, aren't you?"

"We live in Colorado, Daddy," she said. "It's actually a bit early, but it's been warm this year."

"Well, I suppose," he said.

"How's the farm?" Lindsay asked, because if there was one thing her father could talk about for hours, it was his farm. That blasted farm was the whole reason he'd treated her like a piece of property and tried to marry her off to the "right man."

"We're pluggin' along," he said.

"How's the duck pond?" She hadn't given the pond where she'd once gone to find peace and solace any thought whatsoever until that moment.

"Still there," he said.

Lindsay sighed. "I'll let you go, Daddy. It's clear you don't want to talk to me."

"It's not that," he said.

"Then what is it?" she asked, more proud of herself in that moment than any other in her life. Maybe not when she'd stood up for herself, refused to marry the man her father had chosen for her, and left the state. "I'm asking you easy questions just to get you to talk, when you should be asking me why I'm calling. You should be asking me about *my* farm, and how *I'm* doing it all by myself, and if *I* need any help."

She took a breath and then started again. "Or, you could ask me who I'm dating now. I just said I have a boyfriend, and he lives with Derrick. He works here with Uncle Jack, and I'm tired of you getting the details of my life—like you deserve any of them—from your brother. I called you. The least you could do is give me more than three words about your life."

Her chest heaved, and Lindsay would like it to be because of the slight uphill hike she'd taken back to the cabin. She tried, but she failed, and still her father sat there, silent. He hadn't hung up yet, not that he'd ever done that to Lindsay before.

She rolled her eyes and her neck at the same time, then turned and focused on the mountains in the distance. "I have to go," she said. "I hope you're happy. I hope the ranch is exactly what you want it to be." Her throat started to close, but she still managed to squeeze out, "I love you, Daddy," before she pulled the phone away from her ear and tapped to end the call.

She didn't cut off her father mid-sentence, which meant he hadn't said anything. Still.

Maybe Lindsay was expecting too much of him. Even growing up, she'd not heard very many affirmations from the man. He only told her and Derrick that he loved them on their birthdays, and he'd let Mama handle all the things of the heart. He was the stern taskmaster, the one barking about backpacks left by the back door and too much laughter during dinnertime. He expected chores to be done right the first time, and by the time Lindsay was ten, she was convinced her daddy expected her to be able to read his mind.

"So that hasn't changed," she muttered to herself. Another giant sigh pulled through her chest and out of her throat. "Why did I need to do that?" she asked the Lord. The breeze kicked up, but it didn't hold the answers she needed or wanted. She faced into it and closed her eyes. She breathed in slowly through her nose, trying to find the happier version of herself she'd been earlier today, while cooking, in her own kitchen, on her farm. The one she owned, the one she worked, the one she'd found and paid for all by herself.

"Linds," a man called, and she opened her eyes and turned toward the cabin. Buck stood in the doorway, waving, and she lifted her hand to acknowledge that she saw him. "Derrick and Keith are back too."

"Great," she called, and she got moving back to the cabin. She just needed a slow, easy evening with people who would tell her more than two words about the past five months of their life.

She went up the steps and through the still-open door to find

Derrick standing at the kitchen sink while Buck disappeared down the hall.

"Amazing day," Derrick said, his back to her. So he couldn't be talking to her.

"It went okay," Keith said, and Lindsay's eyes flew to where he'd collapsed on the couch. He faced away from her too, his boots up on the far arm. "We got all nine hundred acres done in one day, and that was my goal. You know, sometimes I wish I just ran one of those tiny little farms like your sister's. A silly little operation that doesn't mean anything, you know?"

Derrick turned off the water and said, "Yeah, I get it."

Lindsay stood there, dumbstruck. Her heartbeat bobbed up into her throat, then crowded into her ears. Thankfully, it drowned out anything else that Keith or Derrick could've said. She looked over to Derrick, who met her eye.

His mouth moved, but she didn't hear him. Keith sat up, and his movement drew her attention back to the living room. He finished swinging his feet down to the ground, and he did look tired. Dirty, tired, and sexy. He was likely waiting for the shower, and Lindsay could probably time the grilling of the sliders to the very moment he walked back out into the dining room, fresh, clean, and smelling like soap.

She suddenly didn't want to be there at all. So while both Keith and Derrick looked at her, she spun on her heel and marched back out the door she'd just come through.

Sometimes I wish I just ran one of those tiny little farms like your sister's. A silly little operation that doesn't mean anything, you know?

Keith's words grew sharp points and jabbed, jabbed, jabbed at her heart as she walked away, and walked away, and walked away.

CHAPTER

Thirty

KEITH WATCHED Lindsay stomp out of the cabin, and he looked over to Derrick. "What's going on?"

"I don't know." Derrick frowned at the open door and went to look outside.

Exhaustion pulled through every single one of Keith's muscles, but he placed his palms on his knees and pushed himself to a stand. "Had she just walked in?"

"I don't know," Derrick said again. "I was washing all that dirt off my hands." He looked over to Keith as he approached. "She went down the hill."

Keith's stomach roared, and he tried to think through what he'd said right before he'd heard Derrick say, "There's my beautiful sister, and she's brought all this delicious food."

Lindsay hadn't said anything, and she'd taken one look at Derrick, one at Keith, and promptly left again. He hadn't been able to get a close enough look at her face to see if she was upset or not.

He left the cabin and trotted down the steps, muttering, "Of course she's upset." She wouldn't have marched off if she'd been thrilled to see him. He turned left and saw Lindsay's slighter frame ahead of him.

"Linds," he called.

She turned and looked over her shoulder, but she kept right on going. He wasn't sure how, but he broke into a jog to catch up to her. The land flattened out soon enough, but they had to go back. Keith had already been thrilled to walk through the door of his cabin, and he hadn't planned on leaving again.

"Hey," he said when he reached her. "Hey, hey, what's goin' on?" He strode with her step for step, his breath hitching in his chest.

She stopped suddenly and faced him. "You think my farm is a silly little operation that doesn't mean anything?"

Keith's mind blanked. "I—what? No."

"That's what you said." She reached up and ran her hands through her hair. He recognized that it held some curl, which meant Lindsay had put it there. Her hair normally hung straight down, or she ponytailed it, or she braided it. When she curled it, she'd put special effort into her appearance.

"I—didn't."

"I *heard* you," she said.

"I didn't mean it like that," Keith said. "I was just saying nine hundred acres is a lot, and having a smaller place would be a relief."

"Forty acres is not a tiny little farm."

"I didn't say it was."

"You did!" Lindsay swiped at her face and shook her head. "You know what? I don't need you to approve of my farm."

"Lindsay." Keith felt her slipping away from him rapidly.

"Can I...?" He gathered her into his arms, and she collapsed against his chest. "Baby," he soothed as she started to cry. "I didn't mean it like that. At all. I love Twilight Fields. You planted those forty acres yourself in a single day."

He honestly wasn't sure why he'd compared Blackhorse Bay and what he and twenty other cowboys had achieved that day to Lindsay's farm.

"I didn't mean it like that," he whispered again. "I don't know why I said it. I was just feeling like trash, and I couldn't believe my plan worked and we got all nine hundred acres planted in a single day."

Keith wasn't sure why he was talking so much. And all the wrong things too.

"Jack said they've never done this before. It's been so much pressure, and I just meant that a smaller place—like your amazing farm—would be less stress. That's all." He ran his hands up and down her back. "I'm sorry. I didn't mean Twilight Fields was silly, or that you're silly, or that what you do isn't valid."

She melted into him now, her tears about gone. "I called my daddy tonight."

"You did?" Keith smoothed his hand down through her hair. "Why?"

"I don't know," she whispered to the waving grass and the sun as it continued to sink toward the mountains. "I just keep having these feelings about him. I keep thinking about him, and I figured I had a few minutes."

"It didn't go well," Keith murmured, and he wasn't asking.

"No, and then I walked in on you saying my farm was 'silly.'"

Keith pressed his eyes closed as regret streamed through

him. "I did *not* mean it like that, Lindsay." His stomach growled again, but Keith ignored it. He opened his eyes and watched the sun sink and sink. "Derrick told me there were baked beans in the house."

"Mm."

"You made them for me?"

"Mm."

"I'm really sorry," he murmured. He pressed his lips to her forehead and prayed that she'd accept his apology. "I can grill the sliders. Give you a break. You've been working as hard as us today."

She stepped away from him slightly and looked at him.

"Oh, I hate that I made you cry." Keith wiped her eyes. "I'm so, so sorry, Linds." He hung his head, his cowboy hat somewhere in the cabin.

"Did the planting go well?"

Keith swallowed and nodded his head. "Best day ever," he said. "I mean, once we found the mustard seeds, everything flowed like clockwork." He looked up, but not at her. "I knew the answer to every question. I had the perfect plan. Everyone did their job flawlessly, and it was a really, really good day."

He managed a smile. "Exhausting, and by the time I came in for lunch, there was this little nub of a sandwich, and those baked beans smelled so dang good."

She nodded, and Keith reached up and tucked her hair behind her ear. "You're the most beautiful woman in the world." He leaned closer to her, finally touching his forehead to hers. "I'm sure you were working all day too, and I just want to have dinner with you, and kiss you, and please, please forgive me for being insensitive and saying something that sounded so cruel."

"Keith, it's okay."

"It's not, but you can still forgive me."

"Okay," she whispered.

"My mom taught me that," he said. "My step-mom, but my mom. She said I didn't have to say things were okay when someone apologized. That I should say, 'I forgive you,' because it probably wasn't okay, but I could still forgive someone."

Lindsay pulled back and met his eyes. "I forgive you." She drew in a breath, her gaze pulling to the mountains. "My dad said maybe seven words to me," she said. "I asked him about the farm, asked him how he was doing, about this silly duck pond I loved as a girl, and told him I had a boyfriend."

Keith said nothing, because this wasn't about him. Lindsay stepped into his side, and he wrapped his arm around her. "I got seven words from him." She exhaled and faced him again. "You gave me so much more. Thank you." She touched her lips to his in a sweet kiss. "I'd just gotten off the phone with him when I came back inside. Maybe I was already frustrated and irritated."

"You don't need to make an excuse," he said. "I said something that upset you, and that's all I need to know."

"Hungry?" she asked, clearly ready to move on to another topic.

"Starving."

She grinned at him, all traces of her tears gone now. "I brought sliders and appetizers and baked beans."

"There aren't going to be any leftovers, you know." He found a smile, and he still needed to find his way into the shower. He stifled a yawn, because Lindsay had worked hard to make them all dinner, and he'd already made a mess of the meal she'd planned.

"I'm sorry," he whispered.

"You've already said it," she said. "Let's go eat."

"Yeah," Keith said. "Let's go eat." They started the walk back to the cabin, and Keith's fingers slid easily between hers. With only one more cabin until his, he said, "Lindsay, coming home to you is pretty fantastic."

She didn't say anything, and Keith wasn't sure of the feelings flowing through him. He'd never been in love before, and he couldn't articulate everything inside him. "If we—I mean, you know—if we got married, I wouldn't be able to live in this cabin."

"No," she said slowly.

"Do you think—would you ever be able to share your house with a guy like me?"

"You'd move to my little hobby farm?"

He dropped his eyes to the grass at his feet. "If you're there, I'd want to be there, yeah."

She veered toward the steps to the little back porch, and he let her go up them first. He followed, and in the kitchen, he found his three cabinmates eating chips and salsa.

"Oh, you found the appetizers," she said. "The soup goes with the chips, guac, and salsa."

"I'm going to go shower," Keith said, but no one answered him. Lindsay brought the soup pot to the table, and more toppings came out of the fridge. He quietly slipped down the hall, hoping his cabinmates had left him some hot water.

As he stepped into the warm spray, he let the tension in his muscles, in every cell of his body, seep away. "What a great day," he said as he smiled into the stream of water. "And Lord, I could use some help with Lindsay Lewis. Am I falling in love with her? How will I know?"

He couldn't stand in the shower, waiting for God to answer his prayers. After all, he'd already delayed dinner, and he really was starving. Plus, he wanted to get back to Lindsay, because maybe then, he'd understand the depth of his feelings and what they all meant.

———

"YEAH, IT WAS GREAT," Keith said a couple of days later. Beside him, Taggart Crow pulled out a bale of hay, turned, and tossed it behind him. Mike Hammond stood there, wearing blue jeans and a long-sleeved plaid shirt instead of the suit and tie he normally wore to the office.

He'd come for breakfast at the invitation of Gerty, and had he known he'd have to move a bunch of hay first, he might have declined.

"You rented those big rollers?" Tag asked.

"Yeah," Keith said. "They weren't cheap, but everything got planted in one day. It was incredible."

Tag looked over to Mike. "Not cheap," he said.

"We can afford it," Mike said without pausing. He picked up one of the bales Keith and Tag were tossing toward him, and he hauled it out the window. "Rent them if you want, Tag."

"It'll get way more acreage planted," Tag said.

"It's your head with Gerty," Mike said.

Tag exchanged a glance with Keith, and his heart skipped a beat. "Uh, I can talk to her," Keith said. "About planting day and how great it was. How much we got done." He looked back to Mike, but he'd bent over. "Sometimes when it's coming from someone else, she'll listen."

Mike laughed, and Tag smiled, and while Keith didn't really want to get in between Gerty and well, anything—the woman had strong opinions and didn't hesitate to voice them—he could talk about planting all day long.

"Do you guys have fields that need to be mown down?"

Tag nodded. "A couple is all. There's two of us here, you know?"

"It's what? Eighty acres here?" Keith asked. "With a big planter like that, it's six hours of work. I could even come help."

"I can take a day off work and do it," Mike said.

"Do we have to reserve the crimper in advance?" Tag pulled down another bale.

Keith copied him, his back protesting the weight of the hay bale. He tossed it anyway. "Yeah, but I don't know how far out they're booked. It's...." He trailed off, because he didn't want to tell Tag it was late in the planting season. But it kind of was.

"We know we're behind," Tag said.

"Which can also help push Gerty toward using this planter," Mike said, his voice winded.

"I can call and find out."

"Oh, I can call," Tag said. "If you text me the info, I'll call."

"And I'll talk to Gerty at breakfast." Keith caught sight of Tag nodding, and he reached for another bale of hay. "This has to be enough, right?"

"Yeah." Tag clapped his gloved hands together and grinned at Keith. "Thanks, Keith. You're the best."

Keith tossed his bale of hay, only to turn and see that Mike hadn't been able to keep up with them. Obviously.

"I wanted to ask you something," Tag said, and Mike started to chuckle.

Keith looked between the two of them. "What?"

"Are you going to ask him about my sister?" Mike gave Tag a hooded, almost disapproving look, but Tag only grinned.

"Yeah," he said, holding his head high. "Do you know Opal, Keith?"

"Yeah, sure," Keith said. "I mean, not as well as *her brother*." He shot a look over to Mike and peeled off his gloves. Tag went to help Mike keep tossing bales out of the upper window of the barn. "You're sweet on Opal?"

"Well, she's gorgeous, number one," Tag said. "She's smart as anyone I've ever met."

"She doesn't live here," Mike said in a deadpan.

"Yeah, that's a strike," Tag said good-naturedly. "But she sort of does live here right now. Says she doesn't like cowboys, though."

"That's crazy," Keith said, grinning at Mike now. The three of them looked at one another, and then all three of them burst out laughing.

"Maybe just put in a good word for me," Tag said. "Everyone seems to like you, and if Gerty will listen to you about the planter, then surely Opal will give me a chance."

"Sure," Keith said. "I'll do my best." He had no idea why Opal Hammond would have any problems with cowboys. She'd grown up in the cowboy-est of states, and she'd come to Ivory Peaks and the farm a lot on top of that. Her daddy was a cowboy; all her uncles and cousins were too. Heck, she'd come to help Gerty with West and the farm, and Gerty was as cowboy as they come.

Surely she'd give Tag a chance, and if she wouldn't, there must be a really good reason why.

CHAPTER
Thirty-One

"THIS IS SO EXCITING," Lindsay said as she rode alongside Keith.

"We came here for my sister's wedding." Keith looked over to her, his smile wide and oh-so-handsome.

"It was winter," she said. "This is so different, and the event is much less formal."

"Sure, okay," Keith said.

"You grew up here, right?" she asked, though they hadn't made it to the Hammond Family Farm yet.

"Sort of," Keith said. "We moved here full-time when I was fourteen, but my daddy had been bringing us every summer for about five years. He sold our farm in Montana, because he needed a change." He shifted in his seat. "It was a lot more than that, but I didn't know much as a teenager."

"Do you know more now?"

"Yeah," he said. "My mom had gotten drunk again. I mean, I knew that. But not just one time. All the time. Dad needed to protect Britt. Us. He needed to protect us." He cleared his throat. "He checked Mom into a treatment facility, and we dropped her off on the way to the farm the last time we came from Montana. Never been back."

"Never?"

Keith shook his head, and Lindsay waited. She'd gotten better and better at giving Keith a moment, and he said, "There was nothing for me there." He glanced over to her. "And everything for me here."

She smiled at him, and her anticipation for tonight's bonfire only grew. Something magical existed in summer nights that seemed to stretch for hours before it grew dark, and a group of men and women who loved horses, dogs, farming, good food, and each other.

"Will your family be there tonight?" she asked.

"They've all been invited," he said. "My mom is a bit sick, so I'm not sure if she and Daddy are coming. Roxanne will drive out with Alma if they come, but I heard she has a new boyfriend, so I don't know."

"Ooh, juicy. A new boyfriend."

"Yeah, my daddy's not really happy about it," Keith said with a chuckle. "He never liked me having a girlfriend in high school either, and apparently, the boy works out here."

"Is he older than her?" Lindsay didn't get to have many normal conversations with teenagers like Roxanne. "Sabrina told me about this boy that moved in at the end of the school year, but she said she didn't even know if he was cute or not." She grinned out the windshield. "Can I invite her next time? I think she'd love it out here."

"She should come do the equine therapy," Keith said. "It's an amazing program for kids like her."

"I've mentioned it to her mom," Lindsay said. Her excitement faded slightly. "Do you think it would be okay for me to talk to Molly about doing riding lessons?"

Keith looked over to her, his eyebrows going up. He wore a cream-colored cowboy hat tonight, and a light blue polo with his jeans, and Lindsay found him so darn attractive. "Keith, do you think you could really live on a small farm like mine?"

He blinked and said, "I wasn't expecting that." He took a breath. "First, yes, you can talk to Molly about horseback riding lessons anytime you want."

"No, I want a job," she said. "There's a difference."

"I think you could start tomorrow," Keith said with a chuckle. "And second, yeah, I love Twilight Fields. I'd have no problem living there."

"It doesn't make much money," she admitted. "Thus, me asking if I can ask Molly for a job."

"Maybe we'd get a different place," he said. "Or maybe I'd keep working at Blackhorse, and we'll keep the farm and work it together."

Lindsay considered the options. "Do you ever think you might want a place of your own? Maybe something bigger than Twilight Fields? Somewhere where we could make better money?"

Keith drove, which meant Lindsay could watch him while he had to keep his eyes on the road. Even in profile, she could see the raging indecision and then the smile as it touched his mouth. "My daddy's asked me the same thing. Suggested I'd like a farm of my own. Or somewhere I could be foreman, the way he is." He looked over to Lindsay. "I told him a year ago the same thing I'm going to say now: I don't know."

He reached over and took her hand in his. "I like how you keep saying 'we,' though."

A soft smile spread Lindsay's lips too, and she had more questions, but she wasn't sure how to ask them. Instead, she said, "Uncle Jack and Aunt Lenora don't have any kids."

Keith chuckled. "Sweetheart, I'm pretty sure Jack's been priming Derrick to take over Blackhorse Bay for him. Not me."

"But if we're together." She didn't say anything more.

Keith looked over to her, his eyebrows up again. "This sounds like something you're going need to talk to your uncle— and your brother—about. I'm not going to bring it up." He shook his head, his smile and chuckle making a reappearance.

Lindsay didn't want to think too far down the road either, and tonight was supposed to be made of chocolate, graham crackers, marshmallows, and hot dogs. There would be laughter and storytelling, plenty of cowboy hats and food and just good energy.

She and Keith had plenty of time to talk about their future together, and Lindsay could scarcely believe the fact that they'd started having these conversations at all. Warmth filled her despite the blowing air conditioning, and she grinned out the windshield as Keith kept driving.

At the Hammond Family Farm, he went past the big red barn where Britt had gotten married, and kept driving down the pretty white fence that led to the farmhouse. An oversized SUV sat there, but not the amount of trucks she'd expect for a family and farm bonfire.

Keith kept going around the house, and Lindsay found the family firepit quite easily. A couple of people moved about it, setting up chairs and calling her attention to the area. The fire hadn't been started yet, but two long tables had been set up, and

Molly Hammond herself carried a tray of treats and slid it onto the first one she came to.

Her husband and a couple of their kids followed her with more trays, and she directed them with what to do. As Keith pulled up next to another truck, more cowboys came walking down the lane in front of them.

The sky held shades of gold, amber, and coral, and it made Lindsay so, so happy. "My mama grew tulips that look like this amazing sky," she said. "They were mostly yellow. Sort of creamy in some places, like freshly churned butter, and deeper gold like the sunset tonight."

She turned her head and looked at him as he put the truck in park. "Then, there was all this pinky-carnation, coral-type color throughout. It almost looked like someone put a drop of red food coloring in a bowl of golden water. It just seeps through it as it gets watered down, right?"

"I can see it in my head," he said.

"Those tulips. They looked just like this sky." She looked out the front window again, the world so beautiful and so open with possibilities in a way Lindsay had never imagined, in a way she hadn't known possible...until Keith had delivered Shadow to her farm, fallen, passed out, and then had to stay the night at her house.

"Maybe we could plant some tulips like that here," he murmured.

Lindsay loved that he didn't just dismiss her story. Didn't just say it was a sweet story. She reached over to him and squeezed his hand. "Yeah, maybe," she said. "But tonight, I want a hot dog fresh from the flames, and you're going to show me how you can make a golden brown marshmallow nine times out of ten." She grinned at him.

"Maybe only eight out of ten times."

"Oh-ho," she said with a laugh. "Yesterday, you said nine times out of ten." She unbuckled her seatbelt. "I'm holding you to that. You can't walk it backward now." Laughing, Lindsay slid from the truck, and she collected the peanut butter rice crispy squares she'd made. The chocolate might melt all over, but if sliced thin and placed on a graham cracker, with a hot marshmallow, the peanut butter and crispy rice cereal elevated the s'mores to a new level.

She wouldn't say anything about it. She'd simply do it, and feed one to Keith, and then she'd see if anyone else thought slicing a peanut butter rice crispy treat with chocolate ganache on top would make a leveled-up dessert, perfect for a bonfire.

Lindsay managed to find a spot for her treats, and she slid the heavy dish onto the table. Then, since she didn't really know many of these people, she slid her hand into Keith's.

He, of course, knew them all. He'd left this farm almost a year ago in favor of Blackhorse Bay, but all the cowboys acted like he'd been out fixing fences and finding lost cattle with them earlier today.

He laughed with them; he talked with them, always good to bring her into the conversation; and finally, they found seats around the now-raging bonfire. Lindsay had not seen who built it, but currently, Cord Behr and Hunter Hammond tended to it, turning over logs on either side of it.

Hunter called, "There's real nice coals here now." He stepped back and set the poker he'd been using way out of the way. Then he started helping his daughters thread their hot dogs onto a stick. His youngest, a boy, came over to him, and Hunt took the boy onto his lap and started turning his hot dog roaster for him.

Molly didn't seem to leave the food table, and she helped anyone from age two to eighty find what they needed.

"You want me to make you a hot dog?" Keith asked.

"Yes, please." Lindsay nodded, and he moved away. She tucked her hands in her back pockets and found herself almost instantly surrounded by Gerty Hammond and Jane Behr. A couple of teenagers hung around by them too, but Lindsay didn't know their names.

"They're doing it again," Jane said, her eyes across the fire on a couple. Lindsay followed her gaze and found Opal Hammond sitting between her brother on her right and Taggart Crow on her left.

"He is so stinking cute," Gerty said. "I don't understand why Opal won't go out with him."

"She's always saying she's got a doctor boyfriend in California," Jane didn't sound convinced, and Lindsay really had no idea. Keith had pointed out Opal and Mike Hammond, and she could see the family resemblance. Opal definitely had more feminine features, and she was dark-haired and dark-eyed, but with a really pretty pair of pink lips.

Tag couldn't seem to look away from her, and he leaned over and said something that made her laugh right out loud.

"They are cute," Lindsay said. "She won't go out with him?" She looked to Gerty and then Jane, both of them shaking their heads. "Because it kind of looks like they're already together."

"I'm so going to tell her that," Gerty said.

"What about how cute Mike is with that baby?" Jane said next.

Lindsay smiled at the man with the baby on his lap. She knew Mike was a big-shot businessman who worked long hours in a high-rise in downtown Denver. But tonight, he just looked like a cowboy dad, enjoying the evening with his family.

"I love them," Gerty said quietly. "Do you and Cord want kids, Jane?"

"Yeah," Jane said just as a couple of men joined them.

"Gossiping about Opal?" Tucker Hammond asked. He had another cowboy with him, this one in a walking boot. They both stood head and shoulders taller than Lindsay, and she smiled at the one who hadn't spoken.

"You must be Tarr," she said. "Keith told me you two were working here this summer." She stuck out her hand as Tucker made the quick introductions. Since no one else said anything—so they clearly weren't gossiping about Opal—Lindsay took a deep breath. "What are the chances of me getting hired on here? Are y'all full-up?"

Every eye moved to her, and she swallowed as she shifted her feet. "I mean, Keith said Molly's always looking for horseback riding teachers. I do that on my own farm...." She trailed off, not sure why this many eyes bothered her.

"I'd say it's a great idea," Tucker said. "Let me grab Molly."

"Oh—"

"Don't grab Molly," Gerty hissed. "I want Lindsay to come work for me."

"Mols," Tucker called, ignoring Gerty completely.

Jane only grinned as she shook her head. And Tarr said, "You sure you want to work here? It gets a little crazy sometimes."

"Crazy in a good way," Jane said. "Don't listen to him. He's just used to riding a bull for living. Some cowboys actually work for a living."

"I work, sweetheart," Tarr said, but he remained as good-natured as usual.

"Who works?" Opal asked, her eyes landing on Tarr. And oh, Lindsay could see the instant attraction between them. Perhaps she wouldn't go out with Tag, because she already had eyes for Tarr.

"Howdy, ma'am," he said, actually lifting his cowboy hat an inch or two. Lindsay hadn't gotten that luxury, and she turned away as she hid her smile.

"What's goin' on?" Molly asked. "I don't like the look of this huddle." She had to be maybe ten or fifteen years older than the rest of them standing there, but she had the Mom-look down pat.

Everyone stilled and went silent. All eyes came back to Lindsay. "Uh, it's my fault," Lindsay said. "I was hoping you might have a job opening here."

"Yes," Molly said without hesitating or asking another question. "I'm always in need of good people." She stepped aside as yet another woman joined them, and Tucker actually grabbed ahold of his sister's shoulders and moved her to his other side so he now stood next to the pretty woman with the deepest honey-brown hair Lindsay had ever seen.

Oh, so there was something fizzing there too.

"Heya, Bobbie Jo," he said. "Haven't seen you tonight."

"Oh, brother," Tarr groaned right out loud. "The woman has a boyfriend, Tuck. Leave 'er be."

Bobbie Jo smiled at Tucker, her face blooming a bright red. She did nod over to Tarr and say, "He's right."

"But do you really?" Tuck asked, and that made Opal and Jane giggle. "I mean, he's not here. I'm not even sure he exists."

He grinned at Bobbie Jo and then around the group, obviously not shy about his crush.

"I've called him on the phone and let you speak to him," Bobbie Jo said.

Lindsay listened to them bicker, really enjoying herself as they all seemed to know each other so well. She found Keith with Britt and Lars, all of them around the fire roasting hot dogs, and a moment later, he looked over to her. He lifted the roasting stick, and Lindsay could read that universal language.

"My dinner is ready," she said to Jane at her side. She found Molly's gaze again. "I really would like to come work here if possible. Should I call you?"

"I'll find you in a bit," Molly promised, and then she added in a much louder voice as she stepped out of the huddle they'd formed, "Everyone, come get as much as you want. I can't have all these desserts leftover."

With as many cowboys here as there were, Lindsay really didn't think that would be a problem, and pure joy filled her when she walked past the table and found her rice crispy treats almost gone. She joined Keith and let him put ketchup and brown mustard on her hot dog for her.

Then she sat with him and Britt and Lars and all the others, the night absolutely perfect.

Her mind flew back twenty years, to a family party so much like this. But it had taken place in Center, Texas, and her daddy had built the fire. Mama had supplied all the food, and while they'd eaten walking taco dip and then had roasted corn on the cob with steaks, the feeling of it was the same.

She remembered feeling so loved back then. At ten years old, she didn't realize her father was grumpy and unkind sometimes. She just figured that was how he was.

She belonged to her family, even if they were small. Daddy employed a lot of cowboys too—five or so at any given time—and Mama had fed them all, much the way Molly currently was.

Something similar, and yet so foreign at the same time. Now, she knew what true love looked like and felt like. She knew it wasn't as hard to be kind as her father made it seem. She knew that sometimes life didn't always work out the way she wanted, but that if she kept her sights squarely on God, she'd be okay.

She knew that sometimes families were formed not through blood, but through shared experiences. So gathering around this bonfire, with all these people who worked this land, worked together, and gave something of themselves to one another—that formed a bond that could grow into something as powerful as DNA.

She finished her hot dog and smiled at Keith. "I like it here," she whispered.

"Me too." He leaned over and kissed her quickly. "Maybe we'll have a place like this one day."

"This is a big place," she said as she snuggled into his chest. "You want something this big?"

"Wait for it…." He grinned toward the glowing coal, the shadows flickering across his face.

"I don't know," they said together. Lindsay didn't know what the future held for her and Keith either. She didn't know where they'd end up. But she fell further in love with him sitting right there in the country night air, friends and family surrounding them—and she knew.

Wherever this life took her, she'd be all right if she was at his side.

CHAPTER
Thirty-Two

KEITH RODE up to Lindsay's barn, the horse beneath him moving just fine. He swung down out of the saddle, and Honeybear just stood there. "She's great," he said to Lindsay, who came out of the barn wearing gloves and carrying a hammer. "What's next?"

He reached for the reins on Honeybear. "I'll put her away and make sure the barn's stocked with hay?"

"Yes, please," she said. "I'm going to go fix that back door hinge." She started along the barn as the wind kicked up. "Then we'll get all the gates latched and closed, and I want everything in the equipment shed we can get inside."

"Yes, ma'am," he called after her. A summer thunderstorm threatened the Denver area, and some forecasters were even saying there could be the threat of a tornado. With the mighty Rockies overlooking them, Keith had never actually seen or lived through a tornado, and he had his doubts now.

But a good cowboy was always prepared. He found himself

throwing hay bales on another farm that wasn't his, but this time, he didn't mind the service. He stocked Lindsay's barn while she fixed the back door, rode out and closed and latched all the gates, and then started moving in chickens.

"I don't want them to get blown away," she said. "The wind is already putting up a fight." She wiped her hair out of her face and exhaled heavily.

"I'll push the coop in."

"Thank you."

Her chicken coop stood on wheels, and it actually took both of them to get it moving from where it had been all spring and summer. It barely cleared the top of the doorway in the barn, but in it went. He looked around, a keen sense of déjà vu hitting him. "Feels like I might be staying the night again."

She grinned at him but shook her head. "No, you won't," she said. "It's just summer rain."

"Could be a gale," he said. "A hurricane. People don't drive home in hurricanes."

She laughed, because a hurricane would never make it as far inland as the Denver area. Lindsay's farm actually resided in another little town just north of Ivory Peaks—Mountain Glen. Blackhorse Bay was further north still and then on the eastern outskirts of Boulder.

"Come on, cowboy," she said. "The skies are getting dark, and we can pretend it's cold enough for hot chocolate."

"Deal." They closed up the barn with all the animals inside. Lindsay made sure her garage entrances were locked tight, and then they entered the house. He pulled that door closed and locked it too, because he'd leave through the front door in a couple of hours.

He'd almost brought his last coupon for a dinner of his

choice and a puzzle, but then she'd called and asked him to come help her batten down the hatches. So he'd get to use it another time, a thought that made him smile.

Of course, at this point, Keith didn't need a coupon to come see Lindsay. They'd started talking about marriage and buying a farm together, and while it all sounded like wildflowers and rainbows, Keith wondered if any of it would ever come true.

As Lindsay set about making the hot chocolate, he settled at her bar and watched her. When she finally put a cup of the warm, rich drink in front of him, she said, "You've been staring at me for ten minutes."

"I'm just admiring the view." He lifted his cup to his smiling lips, but it was still far too hot to actually drink. He blew on it instead, using that action to straighten his smile.

"No, you have something on your mind," she said. "I know you well enough to know."

"I'm glad you do," he said. "Did you know this is the longest I've had a girlfriend? Well, in my adult life. I dated this girl in high school for a while."

"It's been six months," she said.

"So let's do some serious talk, but without long explanations. One or two word answers." He looked over to her, unsurprised to find her eyebrows up and her hair pressed flat down. She'd been wearing her hat outside all day as they prepped for the storm. "You're so pretty."

"Is that a question?" she teased.

He grinned and shook his head. "If you were planning your dream wedding, where would it be?"

"Outside," she said. "Maybe at Blackhorse."

"What month would it be in?"

"I...April or May, when all the flowers are out."

Keith nodded. "If you could own anything you wanted, what would it be?"

"More horses."

He laughed then, because Lindsay did love her horses. She braided their manes and talked to them like teenage girls. She gave them special treats and bought saddles she didn't need, just because they looked good with This Horse's coat or That Horse's mane.

"Do you want kids?" he asked as the last of his laughter died away. He swallowed, and since his throat felt like tar paper coming together, he dared to take a sip of his hot chocolate just to wet it. The hot liquid worked, and he managed to draw another breath.

"Yes," she said. "My turn. Do you want kids?"

"Sure do," he said. "Did you see Mike with that chubby baby on his lap a couple of weeks ago?" Keith grinned. "He was really cute."

"Yeah, but they're really rich. Sometimes having kids is expensive."

"True," he mused. "We're young. We don't have to have kids the day we get married."

"True," she said. "Be honest, you want a bigger farm than Twilight Fields."

Keith set down his hot chocolate and stirred it. "It's not about the size of our place," he said. "It's about us being able to pay our bills."

Lindsay leaned her head against his bicep. "I know."

"I do like Blackhorse," he said. "I can talk to Jack about living there after we're married. You're his niece. He has married cowboys who work for him." They didn't live on-site, though, and part of Keith's pay came in the form of room and board.

"So let's talk to him," Lindsay said. "I mean, I like working at Pony Power too."

"That's a long haul from Blackhorse Bay," he said. "If we did that—split up and I work at Blackhorse and you're at Pony Power, we'd need to find somewhere in the middle to live."

"Like Twilight Fields," she quipped.

"Yes," he agreed. "Like right here at Twilight Fields." And even then, that was a longer commute than he wanted. Her too, especially in the winter.

The questions stopped, and they sipped their hot chocolate together for a few minutes. Keith did love this farm, and this house, and every moment he spent with Lindsay, he fell more in love with her too.

They did have to make their own way in the world. No one was gifting him two billion dollars on his twenty-first birthday, and Keith had really enjoyed the agricultural work at Blackhorse Bay.

"Let's go watch a movie," Lindsay said, and she picked up her mug and headed for the living room. Hamlet heaved himself up and trotted after her, pausing when the hardwood of the dining room turned into the carpet in the living room. Then, he turned and looked over his shoulder at Keith.

"Yeah, I'm coming," he said to the dog, and he got to his feet too. The air conditioner still pumped throughout the house, but Keith looked over to the fireplace for some reason. It held such fond memories for him—he'd started to fall for Lindsay right there in front of it, months ago, on a much different night than tonight. But it also felt kind of the same.

Lindsay held the remote and she flipped through channels. "What are you feeling like? Action? Western? Romcom?"

"Feels like a western day." Keith set his hot chocolate on the end table next to Lindsay and then laid down on her couch, using her lap as his pillow.

"Oh, I see how it's going to be. The cowboy's going to sleep while I watch a movie all alone."

"You can fall asleep too," he said, his eyes already drifting closed. He smiled to himself. "I've been workin' hard this summer, sweetheart. I'm tired."

"I know you are, baby." She ran her hands through his hair, and a shiver squirreled down Keith's spine. And to think, this was his reality. A year ago, he'd been depressed and angry that he didn't have this reality, and he'd done something incredibly hard for him to try to find a perfect day like today.

Maybe not the rain part, but every other thing. Getting called for help. Working around his girlfriend's farm. The hot chocolate. The cool house. The gorgeous woman.

Oh, the gorgeous woman.

"Linds," he murmured, his mind already turning spongy and soft, and she hadn't even started the movie yet.

"Mm?"

"I'd like to marry you in the springtime."

"Okay, Keith," she said, and he fell asleep with visions of tulips, roses, and wildflowers lining both sides of the aisle, littering the altar, and sewn into her dress as she walked toward him, about to become his wife.

———

HE WOKE to the sound of something pattering. Then clattering. Then downright shattering. His eyes popped open and he sat up. It took him a moment to come to consciousness and realize he'd just awakened in Lindsay's house.

"It's raining," she said. "Just started." She moved over to the window and peered through the drapes. Keith couldn't have been asleep for long, but the light coming through the windows had definitely turned dimmer.

"Sounds like hail," he said as the noise intensified. It seemed to come from everywhere—the roof, the walls, the fireplace, even the floor.

"It is hail," she said. "Wow. And it's big."

Keith got up and joined her at the window. His mini-truck sat in her driveway, and as he saw the quarter-sized balls of hail bouncing off the sidewalk and ping-a-linging all over, he hoped his vehicle wouldn't end up dented. "Good thing we moved all the chickens inside. One of those looks like it could kill a bird."

"This is wild," Lindsay said. "I'm glad we put away all the equipment too."

The hail started to subside, and in the next few moments, it turned to rain. "Not cold enough to stay hail for long," he said, but all the white balls on the ground sure did look a little creepy. The rain would wash them away soon enough, and Keith fell back to the couch. "How much did I miss?"

"Just the first half-hour," Lindsay said. "Want me to start it over?"

"Pretty sure I can follow the plot." He grinned at her and picked up his hot chocolate. It was lukewarm chocolate now, but he didn't mind, and he drank the whole thing in a matter of minutes. He'd just set his mug on the floor beside his feet when another loud, unexpected noise filled her house.

They both jumped, and Lindsay cried out.

Once again, it took Keith's brain, as fast as neurons were, a moment to recognize the sound. "Someone's knocking?"

That someone started to yell too, and the knocking became more than knocking. It was downright pounding.

"Maybe someone's broken down in the storm." Lindsay flew from the couch and jogged to her front door. Keith wanted to tell her to check first, to be careful, but he didn't have time. She unlocked and pulled open the door so fast, his brain had once again come in second.

A cold wind fluttered through the house, and Keith kept his eyes trained on his girlfriend's back.

"It's pouring out here," a man said in a harsh, deep voice. "I'm comin' in, Lindsay." And he did just that.

Keith stared as a tall man in a black cowboy hat, a black leather jacket, and deep dark blue jeans crowded right past Lindsay. Something told him to get to his feet, so he did. The man's eyes scanned the house, up to the ceiling, along the walls, over to the fireplace, past the TV, and then finally settled on Keith.

He quickly switched his gaze to Lindsay, and Keith felt like he'd been reprimanded without a word being spoken.

Lindsay gaped at the man, and while Keith had been slow picking up on cues in the past few minutes, he already knew who this was.

So he wasn't all that shocked when Lindsay asked, "What on earth are you doin' here, Daddy?"

Terrified, sure. But not all that shocked.

CHAPTER
Thirty-Three

LINDSAY'S HEARTBEAT sputtered in her body, almost like an empty truck gasping for more gas. She didn't have enough blood returning to her heart, so it couldn't pump out more oxygen and life to her body.

She stood numbly in her own doorway, the front door still open, the percussion of the rain on the porch roof echoing in her ears, and her daddy taking off his cowboy hat and shaking the water from it.

It sprayed all over the walls, the carpet, and Lindsay, and then he covered his silver hair again, seemingly oblivious to what had just happened.

"Hello, sir," Keith said, and Lindsay's gaze shot to him. She wanted to throw herself in front of him the way a bodyguard would put himself between his charge and a speeding bullet. Her daddy could have his gun with him, for all she knew. Either way, Daddy could be worse than a bullet, because at least bullet wounds healed. The things he said could inflict damage and pain for decades to come.

Lindsay turned and pushed the front door closed. She locked it again, and when she turned, she found Daddy extending his hand over the back of the couch where they'd just been lying, and he and Keith shook hands.

She'd hallucinated. That was what this was. She'd entered some dimension where her reality had been tilted, shifting, blended into something that wasn't real.

"...nice to meet you," Keith said, his eyes roaming to Lindsay. She had no idea what to say or how to act. She couldn't believe her father was here.

"What are you doing here?" she asked again.

"I came to see you kids," he said matter-of-factly, like he regularly drove a thousand miles to see his children. Every summer, in fact. *Duh, Lindsay.*

"Did I miss a call? A text? An email?" Her daddy didn't email, so she hadn't missed that.

He glared at her. "I didn't have solid plans until last night."

"Then you send a text last night," Lindsay said before she could censor herself. At the dark, growly, unappreciative look on her father's face, Lindsay laced all of her manners back into order. "Sorry," she murmured.

"I have a hotel," he said with a frown of epic proportions. "I was thinking you and I could go to dinner tonight, but I haven't seen a single place open."

"There's a big storm," she said needlessly. She reached up and wiped her hands down her arms, but the tiny water droplets had already dried. She looked over to Keith for help, but he couldn't get to her. She and Daddy stood in the alley between the back of the couch and the wall, and he remained in the living room.

"Lindsay is a phenomenal chef," Keith said, his smile appearing. She wasn't sure if it was manic or friendly, because it only stayed for point-three seconds. "I can help you make something for dinner, sweetheart."

"Okay," she chirped. She squeezed past her father, realizing she hadn't hugged him hello. They hadn't even said hello. "Daddy, do you—?" She stopped when she realized she'd been about to ask if he wanted to bring in his bags. But he wasn't staying here.

"Do you have any allergies?" she asked instead, pure humiliation filling her. This man was her father; she should know if he had life-threatening allergies.

"Allergies?" he asked like they were made-up things like unicorn horns and pots of gold at the ends of rainbows. "I don't have any allergies." He scoffed like such a thing would be physically impossible for a man of his stature.

"Okay," she said meekly, and then she practically ran for the kitchen. Keith entered it from the dining room, his eyes wide and filled with a touch of panic as she opened the fridge.

"Do you want me to stay?" he asked.

She spun from the fridge, worry mingling with panic inside her too. "I don't want to be here alone with him."

Keith's face grew fiercely protective, and he said, "Okay, then. I won't leave you here alone with him." He took her into his arms, and Lindsay felt like such a rag doll—a baby, wimpy, whiny rag doll—as she sagged into his strong chest.

"Got any coffee?" Daddy barked, and everything in Lindsay went ramrod straight again. She took a moment with her back to her father to close her eyes. She drew in a long, deep breath through her nose.

Lord, she thought. *He's here for a reason. He's my father. Help me to be kind to him. Help me to serve him, and through that, find a way to love him.*

She didn't know where the prayer had come from, but it was exactly what she needed to do. So she turned toward her father and watched as he shed his wet leather jacket and hung it on the back of a dining room chair.

"Sure, Daddy," she said. "Do you want cream and sugar too?"

"Whatever you've got," he said, and when he looked at her again, some of the frown in his expression had softened away. Because he'd lived so much of his life growling and judging, frowning and yelling, his face had permanent lines worn into it, shaping into that wolfish expression she'd seen so many times in the past.

Lindsay moved toward him, ready to hug him hello now. "It's good to see you, Daddy." She stepped into him, but they were so out of practice with embracing, it was awkward and stilted. She almost banged her chin on his shoulder, and his arms came around her late, almost getting stuck between their bodies.

Then, they managed it, and Lindsay did appreciate and enjoy something she hadn't had in *such* a long time: a hug from her father.

———

HE JUST SAID *he doesn't know when he'll go back to Texas.*

Lindsay's heartbeat bobbed around in her throat, then her

chest, then down into her stomach. She'd escaped the house, where her daddy had just shown up for "an early breakfast." He'd been dropping by at his convenience for meals, to help around the farm, to help move the chicken coop back out, to ride her horses.

She sent the text to Keith, not sure how he'd react. He'd stayed as long as she'd wanted the first day her dad had arrived, but it had been hard for them to get together since. He said he didn't mind, that he had plenty to keep him busy at work, and that she could call or text anytime.

Lindsay minded, but she didn't know how to tell her daddy he needed to return to Texas. She, Derrick, and Daddy had gone out to dinner a few times, but he seemed to migrate to Twilight Fields more than Blackhorse Bay. He had spent a whole day there, and Lindsay had escaped to Pony Power and stayed there almost all evening, hoping her dad wouldn't be waiting for her at home.

He hadn't been, and guilt had sliced through her for hours, making it hard for her to fall asleep. She felt like her life had become a ball of nerves or barbells of stress. Her shoulders weren't strong enough to endure this for much longer, and she tilted her head back and looked up into the sky.

"Lord," she said. "What am I doing here? Why is he here? What does he need? What does he need from me?"

God had been mysteriously quiet on the matter, and Lindsay had been doing her best to talk to her father, who would never, ever be categorized by anyone on this planet as a chatterbox. She wasn't sure what she was supposed to learn from him being here, and she didn't know why her father could leave the ranch in Texas for weeks at a time.

Fine, it hadn't been weeks. It only felt like a decade.

Lindsay sighed and opened her eyes. The late-June sky held a deep blue, and it should've soothed her and reminded her of how grateful she was to have this farm, this land, in a place like this.

Today, all it did was remind her that it was still daytime, and her daddy was still here.

"Linds," he said, and she stepped away from the house. She walked out from it and looked up the few steps to the deck. "You want to help me with that mid-season spray?"

"Daddy," she said. "You don't have to do my ranch chores."

"It's gotta be done, don't it?" He frowned, surely not sure why he wouldn't do her farm chores while he was here.

"Yes," she said.

"Great." He came down the steps. "Let's do it, then."

Lindsay went with him, not sure how to get out of doing so. She'd have to be in the cab of the tractor with him all day, and she sure hoped he'd showered and used a lot of deodorant this morning.

She opened the big bay door of the equipment shed, and she let Daddy take the lead in getting the tractor out. She'd used the sprayer a couple of weeks ago, and he got it all hooked up before Lindsay moved toward him.

Keith still had not answered her text, and she wasn't sure what that meant. He'd been so good about responding immediately. He'd call her and talk in a low, soothing, slow voice, and she couldn't wait to see him again.

"So, Dad," she said once she'd climbed up into the tractor. "Who's taking care of the ranch in Center?"

"I've got someone tendin' to it."

"Who?" she pressed. She'd been tiptoeing around him for

over a week, and she felt like she'd earned the right to ask him a few questions.

"Honestly, Linds, it's the Freeman boys." He wouldn't look at her, and it was no wonder.

Once again, her blood stream spluttered and stuttered, for everything had just drained away. Daddy drove the tractor, seemingly at ease with everything in the world. Lindsay somehow kept breathing, and the sprayer kept spraying, and the clock kept ticking.

"Did you sell the ranch?"

"Yes."

The breath left Lindsay's body. "Daddy."

He sighed, but it didn't sound as insufferable as it had every other time he'd made the noise. "I've been holdin' on too hard for a long time, Lindsay." He spoke in a far quieter voice than Lindsay had ever heard him use. "And to what end?"

"I—"

"I lost your mom," Daddy said. "I lost you kids. It's just me there, and for what?" He glanced over to her then. "When you called, I—" His throat worked, and Lindsay's tears burst onto the scene.

The field continued to roll by. Daddy said, "I knew I needed to stop holding onto the past. That ranch has been a big part of my life, but it can't be my *whole* life anymore."

"Are you moving here?"

"Eventually, I think I'd like to," he said in almost a whisper. He looked over to her. "Would that be too hard for you? I don't want anything to be too hard for you, Lindsay. Heaven knows you've put up with so much from me, and I apologize for that."

Her jaw might as well dropped off her face. Shock moved through her, and she had no idea what to say or do. Number one, Daddy had never apologized to her. About anything. Number two, he'd be moving here "eventually," and that meant Lindsay had to figure out how to deal with him on a more permanent basis.

And with a man who could apologize, maybe she wouldn't have to find a coping mechanism at all. Still, it wouldn't be easy, and Lindsay already had plenty on her plate. Summertime on a ranch, plus her own horseback riding lessons, the lessons at Pony Power, and her relationship with Keith.

At this point, that felt like a long-distance relationship, and she wondered how this news would affect the two of them. She needed to call him as soon as possible, and she could only pray her father wouldn't be the reason she and Keith didn't make it.

CHAPTER
Thirty-Four

KEITH SAT on his front steps, his frustration barely contained behind a thin veil of patience. He hadn't seen Lindsay in almost two weeks now, and he wanted to give her the time and space to deal with her father.

He'd spoken to her every day, but a phone call wasn't the same as holding her hand, seeing her smile, or kissing her. Keith *missed* her, and he wasn't sure what to do.

I'm so sorry, Lindsay had just said, in answer to his question about whether they'd be going out that night, as planned. *Daddy has found a horse he thinks I'd like, and I don't know how to tell him no.*

"She knows how to tell me no." Keith set his phone aside, because he didn't want to be frustrated with Lindsay. She had a lot on her plate, on her mind, and happening on her farm. He didn't mind being a support, but he'd rather see her in person to support her than be sitting here on his front steps, the summer evening in front of him—and nowhere to go and nothing to do.

The front door opened and Derrick came outside. His boots thunked against the wood porch and steps, and he said, "Hey. No dinner tonight either?"

"She just canceled." He swiped his phone from the step so Derrick could sit down. "You and Janice are headed out?"

"She's on her way home," Derrick said. "I'm gonna go pick her up in a little bit."

"Are you guys serious?"

"Getting there," he said. "I know you and Lindsay are. She's said a lot about you in the past couple of weeks, with Daddy here, and as we've met with Uncle Jack."

"Oh, you've been doing that?" Keith looked over to Derrick. "Lindsay has talked to Jack?"

He nodded, his gaze set out on the horizon. "Yeah."

Keith's curiosity reared up, and he wanted to know what had been said in these meetings. Lindsay had told him they'd had dinner out at Twilight Fields a couple of times, but he wasn't sure he knew Jack had been there. Derrick didn't say anything more, and Keith didn't want to get the news from him.

He wanted to see Lindsay. He wanted to talk to her. He wanted to know if she'd been talking to her uncle about a future here for herself, or for the two of them. They hadn't landed on any plans whatsoever, and Keith didn't mind that so much.

It wasn't like they were engaged, and at the rate things were now going, Keith didn't think they'd be getting engaged any time soon.

He sighed out all his cares and got to his feet. "Well, I'm gonna go grab Buck and see if he wants to be my date tonight."

"Okay, brother," Derrick said, and Keith went up to the front door. Inside, he didn't see Buck, but he could hear the shower running. He was hungry now, and he wasn't sure he had any more patience to give.

His phone rang, and Lindsay's name sat there. Instead of going back outside, where her brother sat, Keith answered the call on his way toward the back door. "Hey," he said.

"You didn't answer me."

He sighed again, unable to keep the irritation out of it. "I didn't have anything to say."

"You're upset."

"I'm not going to deny it." He went down the steps to the lane of grass that ran between the backs of the cabins. A few cowboys had come out tonight, and they threw a football to one another. Keith turned his back on them and took slow steps in the opposite direction.

"I don't know how to manage him right now."

He hung his head. "I know." He didn't want to break up, but he didn't want to be upset when he couldn't see her. "I'm trying to be patient, Lindsay. I really am."

"I know, and you're a saint," she said. "Honestly. I'm going to find my way through this."

"I'll be here when you do," he said, and it sounded like a final statement. Like something he'd say to someone when he wouldn't be seeing them for a while. Like a mutual break up when someone had a better opportunity in another state, and they'd decided to take it, but if they ever came back…he'd be right there waiting.

"Okay," Lindsay said. "I'll call you after, okay? Maybe I'll send you some pictures of the horse, too."

"Okay," he said.

She hung on the line for a moment, and then she said, "I'll see you this weekend for sure."

"You will?"

"Church," she whispered. "I got Daddy to agree to go to church with me."

His heart ballooned a little bit, filling with the tiniest rays of hope. So he said, "Great, I'll see you both there."

"Keith."

"I'm fine, Linds. Buck and I are gonna go get burgers. I'm going to Britt's tomorrow after work." He skipped Friday and Saturday—date nights—and said, "And I'll see you Sunday."

Finally.

"Lunch at my house, okay?" she asked.

"Sure," he said. "Sounds great." Keith knew her daddy would be there, as would Derrick, and while he wanted Lindsay to himself, so they could truly talk, and he could hold her hand, and tell her he thought he might—just might—be in love with her.

How was he supposed to keep that to himself?

"Just take it a day at a time," he muttered to himself. Sunday. With Lindsay. Keith wasn't sure why his chest pinched with more tension than excitement, and he shoved his phone in his back pocket and turned back to his cowboy cabin.

CHAPTER
Thirty-Five

MOLLY HAMMOND RODE in the passenger seat on the drive to Coral Canyon, much the same way she had several times before. Hunter drove, but instead of packing up their four children and making the trip, this time, all the other passengers in the SUV had packed their own bags.

Tucker, Tarr, and Deacon rode in the long bench seat in the middle, and Cord and Jane had taken up residence in the way-back, and as Molly looked at herself in the mirror, she caught the two of them talking with their heads bent.

To get Cord away from his newly-opened mechanic shop meant a great deal. Of course, the Hammond siblings had been planning this Fourth of July surprise for their parents for months now. Molly was ready to turn the keys over to Gray and Elise, if only so Hunt could find some peace—and something else to talk about.

He'd been obsessing over the house he'd bought months

ago, because his heart was made of pure gold, and he just wanted everything to be perfect for his parents.

The house they'd lived in during the summers simply didn't serve their needs any longer. Hunter had told her he wanted to purchase it from them, because this new house wasn't nearly as large, and he and Molly still enjoyed going to Coral Canyon in the summer months too.

With their family of six, and the location of the house on the mountain lake, it was the perfect property for them. Molly had no reservations about it, because Hunter had been a billionaire since birth. He was generous and smart with his money too, and that only meant he had more money now than he'd started with almost twenty years ago.

As the city limits of Coral Canyon neared, Molly turned to the boys in the backseat. "Are y'all going to the rodeo over the holidays?"

"Yes, ma'am," Tarr answered first, while Tucker pulled his attention from the window and nodded. Deacon had his head buried in his phone, but he looked up too, his eyes a little bleary.

"Yeah, we have tickets," Deac said. "With all of Uncle Cy's and Uncle Ames's kids."

Molly nodded, as both Cy and Ames had four kids each. Chris and Lars were Ames's twins, and they sat between Tucker and Deacon in age. They had two daughters too—June and Jill— and Jill was the youngest of the Hammond cousins.

Cy had a set of twin girls, and Ava and Ella were almost as old as Jane. Their two younger boys—Tom and Wade—also still lived in Coral Canyon, as Cy and Patsy owned a huge apple orchard there, and they all worked in the family business.

Ames ran a dog training facility, and his youngest was a

junior in college, with plans to become a computer scientist. Out of all of them, Jill seemed the most inclined to come work in Denver at the Hammond family company one day.

Otherwise, Ames's kids helped with the dogs, and Molly could admit she always loved a trip to Ames's ranch on the north side of town. Just watching him—a former cop—work with his dogs was a sight to behold.

All of Hunt's uncles lived in Coral Canyon too, and Molly did enjoy spending time with Wes and Bree and Colt and Annie. Whenever they came to town, the uncles and their wives hosted a big dinner, and this year, it was at Cy and Patsy's orchard-surrounded house.

She looked over to her husband, and Hunt smiled. They hadn't taken too many trips without their children, but Molly's parents had taken them for this week. "You ready for this?"

"I might be able to sleep tonight," he said.

"Do we want to go over it again?" Jane asked from way in the back.

"No," all three of her brothers said, and Molly hid her smile by turning toward the passenger window.

"I just think Daddy might need some extra convincing."

"I don't think so," Molly said. "Your daddy has always been really good about knowing his limits. He's ready for this; he just doesn't want to admit it." Molly loved Hunter's parents, because they'd welcomed her into their lives a couple of times now.

No, his daddy hadn't been thrilled with their pre-teen and early teen romance. Truth be told, Molly's parents hadn't been either. She'd broken up with Hunter when they were both only fifteen, and when they'd come back together almost eleven years later, Gray and Elise Hammond had once again welcomed her with open arms.

As adults, they definitely approved of the relationship, and now Molly lived in *their* house. She ran her children's equine therapy program on *their* family farm.

It's your house, she told herself as Jane and her brothers continued to squabble a little bit. She and Hunter had bought the farm, the house, the cabins, all of it. It wasn't like Gray and Elise needed the money, but they'd made the cash change hands anyway. The Hammonds had a huge family fortune to continue to build and protect, and Hunter did a lot of money management, investing, and portfolio work when he wasn't out on the farm.

He wanted their kids to have the same benefits and life he'd been given, but they didn't quite have enough money to make all four of their children billionaires when they turned twenty-one. Close, because Hunter had worked at HMC for almost two decades as the CEO, and that had a hefty salary and stock options.

He'd already started priming Ryder, their oldest, for his role at the helm of HMC, as none of the other Hammond cousins seemed all that keen to make the move from Coral Canyon to the Denver area to run a company they hadn't grown up around.

Molly brushed her hair back off her face, watched Jane and Cord talk quietly to each other, and observed the three cowboys in the middle row bent over their phones. "How's Bobbie Jo, Tuck?" she asked, just to stir up the beehive.

Hunt glanced over to her, a small smile on his face and diamonds in those dark eyes. "Just fine, Mols," Tuck said in a deadpan.

"No luck on getting her to break-up with her boyfriend?"

"Nope."

"He's going out with Hadley," Tarr said, and that got Tuck to look up from his phone. "What? You are."

"So? I don't need you tellin' everyone. How about if I tell them about your crush on—?"

"Don't you dare," Tarr growled out, his face turning a deep shade of burgundy.

"Oh, ho," Hunter said. "This ride just got so much better. Who's caught your eye, Tarr?"

"Absolutely no one," the rough, tough rodeo cowboy said. He wasn't quite so rough and tough, and Molly found him to be a softie at heart, with plenty of sunshine that got sent out through his smile. He worked hard; he never complained; he was handsome as the day was long.

And he had money. He should have no trouble getting a date. And yet, he'd been on the farm with Tucker for a couple of months now, and he hadn't been out with anyone that Molly knew of.

"Deacon?" Molly asked. "Who are you texting?"

"Mission and Charlie," he said. "Not a girl."

"If you could text a girl, who would it be?" Jane asked.

"Absolutely no one," Deac said, mimicking Tarr. They grinned at one another and bumped fists while Tucker scoffed.

"It's okay to like a woman. I don't get what's embarrassing about it."

"Well, maybe I'll video you with Bobbie Jo," Tarr drawled out. "And then you'll see how embarrassing it is for you."

Tuck gaped at him, his own face turning more and more scarlet. "Is it really?"

Tarr's expression instantly turned to sympathy. "Brother, I

know you like her. I'd make her go out with you if I could, because yeah, you two would be super cute together. But, Tuck." He shook his head. "She has a boyfriend. It's a little embarrassing, yeah."

"People break up with their boyfriends all the time, Tuck," Jane said. "Give her some time."

Molly didn't want to say that God would lead Tucker to who he should be with, though she did believe that. It wasn't what he wanted to hear, and instead, she said a silent prayer that he would have the blessings he needed.

"Here we are," Hunt said only a few minutes later. "Ah, Coral Canyon."

"I love this place," Molly said with a contented sigh pulling through her soul too. It was cooler here than in Ivory Peaks, and while they both had mountains and forests and big, blue sky, there was something magical about Coral Canyon.

"Are we going straight to the orchards, baby?" She reached over and ran her fingertips along Hunt's longer hair that stuck out of his cowboy hat.

"Yeah," he said, really strangling the steering wheel. "I need this done, and then maybe we can escape to the house for a bit."

"Which one?" Molly asked, smiling at him.

"Ours," he said. They already owned a house in Coral Canyon, and Hunt would have to sell that to buy the one on the lake from his daddy. "Then, maybe we can help Momma and Daddy move this week."

"Maybe," Molly said, not quite sure what to do with herself without her kids. "Or maybe we can just go out on the lake or for a walk through the trees, and just...be." She met his eye and lowered her voice. "Without the kids."

Hunter nodded, his expression blazing now. She loved being with him, just holding his hand and talking about the farm, horses, their life, what they both wanted.

The apple orchards lined the northwest side of town, and Molly fell silent while Hunt drove through town to the highway that led up to Dog Valley. Soon enough, he turned left, drove down a tree-lined lane and past an enormous building where Cy Hammond built motorcycles for veterans.

He and Patsy also had a house out here in the trees, and Hunt pulled up to find several other SUVs and trucks already there. Chris, Lars, and Thomas threw a football around in the front yard, while Opal, Ava, and Ella hung out on the front steps. They had glasses of what looked like frozen lemonade in their hands, and Molly's mouth puckered up instantly.

"Here we go," Hunter muttered as he put the SUV in park and doors started opening left and right. Molly got out to help Deacon with the seat that had to be slid and bent so Jane and Cord could get out of the way-back, and she did that while he rounded the SUV.

"Looks like Mike and Gerty beat us," Hunter commented. "Not sure how they did that."

"They flew," Molly said. "Of course they're going to beat us."

"Even with the wait-times at the airport?" He shook his head. "I always thought it was about sixes."

Opal had flown with them, and they'd left the farm in the capable hands of Taggart Crow. He had an open and obvious crush on Opal, who acted like she didn't like the cowboy. Molly knew she secretly did, but she didn't know how to admit it—especially after she'd said no the first time he'd asked her out.

She'd told Molly she'd just been so surprised, and she hadn't known what to do. Her medical training had kicked in, and she'd made a fast decision. Said no. Didn't mean it was the right one, but at least no one's life was on the line.

Molly left her bag, because this wasn't their final destination, and she linked her hand with Hunt's as they approached the house. More Hammonds started coming outside, and soon, Molly had been whisked away into hugs from Aunt Bree, Aunt Annie, and Aunt Patsy.

Apparently, Sophia and Ames weren't here, and Hunt threw her a panicked look. He just wanted to get this house thing done, and he'd wanted everyone here to do it. The rumblings of a very loud motorcycle started, and Molly swore it shook the very foundation of the house.

Cy pulled up on a big, loud bike, as did Ames and Sophia. They all looked so...*cool* riding the motorcycles, and while Molly had gone with Hunter before, it wasn't her favorite thing to do. He loved riding with his uncles, and when she looked at him again, he'd relaxed.

The motorcycles got switched off, and the orchard silence returned. Hunt said, "Jane, let's do this," and led the way up the steps.

Molly exchanged a glance with Patsy and asked, "How are Gray and Elise doing right now?"

"Why?" Patsy asked, a knowing look in her eye.

"Molly," Deac called. "Let's go. Hunt's got them in the living room."

As if he needed to cage his parents somewhere to talk to them about a house he'd purchased for them.

"This is going to be good," Patsy said as she took off for the front door.

Molly sighed, then she cast her eyes heavenward. "Lord, please bless Hunt that this will go exactly the way he needs it to go." Then she met Opal's eye, and they linked hands and went up the steps to the house too, where Hunt apparently had his parents in the living room.

CHAPTER
Thirty-Six

OPAL HAMMOND COULD ADMIT she missed Coral Canyon. But only to herself. Maybe her momma. No one else. She'd been spending time with Gerty and Mike on their patch of land in Ivory Peaks too, and she loved it there as well.

Anything was better than the hustle and bustle of the city in California. She'd been telling everyone she was on sabbatical from her residency, but the truth was, she'd quit.

Opal didn't need the money. She needed clarity. She needed time to figure out who she was and what she wanted. She'd just turned twenty-eight years old, and she'd been so driven to be a doctor, she'd forgotten about everything else inside her.

She'd forgotten to feed her spirit. She'd forgotten to just be herself. As a doctor, she didn't get to be herself. She had to be calm and collected all the time. She had to know every answer, to every question. She had to be a leader for the other doctors on her team.

In truth, Opal was tired. She had billions in the bank, and

she'd been charged to do something good with it. Instead, she'd used some of it to go to medical school, and then she'd worked herself almost to the point of a break-down.

Now, she crowded into Aunt Patsy and Uncle Cy's house, and she remembered how much fun she'd had growing up and coming to this orchard. She had female cousins her age, and she missed them.

Ava and Ella were Cy's oldest children, twins, and they were a year older than Opal. They wore jeans she'd never dream of wearing, and cowboy hats with their long blonde hair spilling over their shoulders.

They both had boyfriends, and they both worked for their momma on the orchards. Ava had gotten an associate's degree in farm management, and Ella had taken several secretarial classes. They simply wanted the skills they needed to keep running the orchards, as that was part of their momma's family legacy.

Apparently, Aunt Patsy had fought hard to own the orchard after her daddy had stopped being able to do much with it. She'd brought it back from the brink of extinction, and now it thrived over five hundred acres of land that spanned both sides of the highway.

Opal could get a job here in Coral Canyon, and as she looked at her father—her eighty-two-year-old father—her heartbeat screamed at her to do that. He was getting so old, and while Momma was quite a bit younger than him and could take care of him, Opal knew how tiring it was to be a constant caregiver.

So she was keeping her options open, for now. She'd given serious thought to moving closer to Mike and Gerty. She loved their little boy, and she could do some good charity work in a city the size of Denver. She could dedicate whole wings to their hospital, and she could probably guest-lecture at a community college.

Part of her wondered about helping her brother at HMC too. She hadn't gone into business or law, but she was smart. Trainable. A good problem solver. She could learn and do anything— at least that was what her momma and daddy had always taught her.

"Daddy," Hunter said, and Opal clued in to the happenings in the living room. Everyone had gathered, and Uncle Gray looked at his oldest son, a hefty dose of wariness in his eyes.

"What is this?" he asked. "Is this some sort of intervention."

"Yes," Jane said with her whippish tongue. "Now just listen to him, Daddy." She nodded to Hunter while Opal tried to hide her smile. That didn't really work, and she wasn't the only one grinning.

Hunter swallowed, and he looked at his younger brothers. When he faced his parents again, he drew a deep breath, and his boxy shoulders rose up. They reminded her of Taggart Crow's, and a flush instantly started to sweep through Opal's very being.

Why did cowboys always have such broad shoulders? Why was she thinking about Tag? Better question: When did she ever *stop* thinking about Tag?

The answer to that was never, and Opal had never wanted to go back in time to a single moment as badly as she did the time Tag had asked her out and she'd turned him down flat.

"It's time for you and Momma to move to Coral Canyon permanently." Hunter fished in his pocket and pulled out a set of keys. "I found you the perfect house, and we all walked through it virtually." He held up the keys, but neither Gray nor Elise made a move for them.

Daddy reached out and took them, and Hunter gaped at him for a moment. Then he pulled himself back together. "It's in town, right close to everything. It's a single level, so no stairs. It's got gorgeous, mature landscaping, and yes, there's still plenty of room to park the boat. It's not lakeside, but Daddy, you can't even go up and down those stone steps to the lake anymore. Admit it."

"I'm not going to admit anything," Uncle Gray said stubbornly.

"Boo," Uncle Ames said good-naturedly. "We all know you need a knee replacement, and you're too stubborn to get one."

"I—"

"Need a knee replacement," Elise said over him, something she rarely did. Opal loved her mild-mannered aunt so much in that moment. She'd watched Aunt Elise champion everything Uncle Gray did, always standing solidly at his side, cheering for him, then the kids, as they lived their lives. They'd done the same for her, coming together to help her with her landscaping business and clients whenever she needed them. She rarely spoke over Gray in public, and he looked at her with fast-blinking eyes.

"One level?" she asked. "Close to town?"

"It's only a few miles from Uncle Wes and Aunt Bree," Hunter said. "Jane?"

"It has a beautiful yard, Momma." She turned her phone toward her parents. "These were taken just a few days ago, by a neighbor I've been texting. They own a landscaping company here in Coral Canyon, Momma, and they've been keeping up the yard this summer, so it's move-in ready for you."

"Wait, wait, wait," Uncle Gray said, waving both hands in front of his body. "When did you buy this house?"

"February," Tucker said without missing a beat. "We've had it since February, and we all think it's time for you to move here." He looked at Deacon, then around at all the other cousins and aunts and uncles.

"Daddy," Deacon said, and while he'd been a rambunctious kid growing up, he was more of a silent giant now. "You want to move here. Admit it."

Uncle Gray looked at his youngest son. "I want to see you flourish on the farm too." His voice choked on the last word, and tears flooded Opal's eyes. She was so tough in so many ways, but the moment one of her uncles started getting emotional, it was like she had zero control over herself.

"I want to see Jane have babies," he said. "I've lived on that farm for my whole life."

Hunter sat down on the coffee table, and Jane crowded in beside him. Opal prayed it wouldn't break under their combined weight.

"Daddy," Hunter said quietly. "I know this is the right thing for you and Momma." He looked over to Aunt Elise, who swiped at her eyes with a tissue Momma had given her. Opal had watched Aunt Elise and her own mother for her entire life. They'd been friends before the Hammond brothers had come into their lives, and they'd stayed friends after marrying them.

"All of your brothers are here," Jane said. "You can come visit Ivory Peaks and the farm anytime." She looked up to Cord, who stood out of the way, as usual. "Besides, Cord and I don't have any announcements yet. It'll be at least nine more months before there will be any babies from us."

"And we're done," Molly said.

"And Bobbie Jo won't go out with me," Tuck said.

All eyes moved to Deacon, and he simply shook his head.

Laughter filtered through the house, and Opal let a little giggle out of her mouth too.

"Daddy, I want you to think about it." Hunter squeezed his father's hand and stood. "And Mols and I can take you to see the house right now, if you'd like."

Elise looked at Gray, and Gray looked at Elise. She raised one shoulder, her blue eyes hopeful. "Might as well go look at it, right?"

"Jane got to you with those rose bushes in the front yard, didn't she?" Uncle Gray grinned at his wife, and it took a moment for what they'd both said to sink into every ear. Then, the family started cheering, and Gray laboriously got to his feet.

"Fine," he said. "We'll go look at it."

Daddy handed his brother the keys, and then the house started emptying. Apparently, it wasn't just going to be Uncle Gray, Aunt Elise, Molly, and Hunter going to look at the house. But everyone in the Hammond Family.

"That's about how we do things," Opal muttered to herself, and that was just another reason why Ivory Peaks appealed to her more than Coral Canyon. Yes, there were Hammonds there, but less of them, and in this case, less was more.

———

"AND YOU SHOULD'VE SEEN Grandpa moving stuff for Uncle Gray." Opal smiled at the sleeping baby in her arms as she eased out of the rocking chair. "But they're all moved now, and they love the house."

Her parents were thrilled Gray and Elise would be living in Coral Canyon full-time, and every Hammond who could lift a box would come in September to help them pack up what they had here and move it north.

Opal laid baby West in his crib, bent over and kissed his forehead, and then tiptoed out of the nursery. Mike had gone back to the office after their trip to Coral Canyon, and Gerty had gone to her mother's to do some canning. She claimed not to be very domestic, but she wanted to spend time with her parents, and if that meant she had to make strawberry jam, then she'd go make strawberry jam.

Opal was far more stubborn than Gerty, if that could be believed. But marriage and motherhood had softened Gerty, and she'd settled into who she was. Opal was still trying to figure that out.

She picked up the baby monitor that could be worn as a wristwatch, and she slipped it over her hand. The afternoon had started to turn golden, and Opal wanted to bathe in it. She stepped out onto the porch and moved to the railing to drink in the view.

A dirt lane led toward the highway and then on past the house and onto the farm. The sun sat behind her, behind the house, so its golden rays lit up the scene in front of her. The trees boasted bright, green leaves, and the sky held a lot of white, puffy clouds today.

They'd been moving all day too, chasing each other here and there. Opal had watched them from indoors, but now, she switched on the watch and went down the steps. She should be able to go out to the barn and back and still be able to hear West if he woke from his nap.

He wouldn't because the baby was practically perfect in every way, and he still slept twice a day. He'd taken a short nap this morning, and when Gerty had left, she'd told Opal that meant he'd likely take a longer one this afternoon.

She'd held him in the rocking chair for twenty minutes before finally laying the six-month-old in his crib, and as Opal meandered toward the barn, she could admit she wanted a baby. Only to herself, though. Because a man and a marriage came before a baby, and Opal needed to find herself before she could find a man and get married.

Noise came from the training pen behind the barn, and Opal went that way, expecting to find Tag. Her heartbeat increased, and she could hear the beeping such a thing would cause if she'd been hooked up to a machine in a hospital. Sometimes, she still heard those machines. Still smelled the antiseptics. Still got jolted awake at night, thinking someone had paged her for an emergency.

There were no emergencies here, but she did find Tag in the middle of the training ring, holding a pole with an orange flag on it, and tutting at the horse circling the rail.

He looked over to her, and Opal raised her hand in a friendly hello. It wasn't flirting to wave to a cowboy. Tag's face split into a grin, and oh, that should be illegal. Why couldn't he be dating someone else, the way Bobbie Jo was? Then, he wouldn't have ever looked at Opal.

At the same time as those thoughts entered her mind, a wave of jealousy for Tag's non-existent girlfriend raged through Opal. No, him having a girlfriend would be far worse.

"He's doing great," she said as she stepped up onto the bottom rung of the fence and rested her arms on the top one.

"Yeah," Tag said. "I'm gonna get him to let me saddle him today."

"That's great." Opal smiled at him, because Tag ate dinner

with Gerty, Mike, Opal, and Gerty's grandparents about half the time. She knew about this new horse Gerty had bought, and how Tag had been working on breaking the pony for the past couple of weeks.

"Yeah, Florence is a good horse." Tag smiled at the equine, who'd completely stopped moving once his attention had shifted to Opal. "Aren't you, Flo? Get goin', now." He dragged the flag on the ground and moved it toward her, and Flo got moving again.

Opal loved watching cowboys work. Her mind did not function on Horse, but Tag's so did. The man could work and work and work too, and Opal just wanted to rest. "Why'd they name her Florence?" she asked.

"Apparently, they name all their horses after places," Tag said. "All right, Flo. Right there." He held up one palm and took a step in toward her. The horse froze immediately, and he murmured something to her Opal couldn't hear with his back turned. "I'm gonna go get her tack." He peered over his shoulder to Opal. "You okay here with her?"

"She's in a pen," Opal said. "I'm fine." Still, it was sweet of him to ask. He smiled again and went into the barn. He came out with a saddle and a blanket, all the strappy things that Opal didn't know where they went.

He'd looped a rope around Florence now, and he'd tied her to the gate, so she stood still for him. That was one thing Opal had learned in the past few months of living here with Gerty and Mike. Gerty always secured her horses before she tried to do anything, either in cross-ties or by tying them to a post. She said that was their cue to know they just stood there. They let her check their hooves or brush them down, give them a bath, or saddle them, the way Tag currently did.

He successfully got the saddle on and tightened down, and he unlooped the rope from around the top rung of the gate. He faced her, a twinge of a blush in his cheeks. "You gonna stay and watch?"

"I don't have to." Opal stepped down off the rung, her own embarrassment heating her face.

He clearly didn't want an audience for this, and she gave him another friendly wave before he said, "You don't have to go."

She faced him, now undecided about what to do. Her decision fatigue couldn't be described, and she simply didn't want to make any more choices right now. She was just too burnt out. So she nodded and stayed where she was.

Tag put one foot in the stirrup, and Flo danced away from him. "Come on," he coached. "We've talked about this." He tried again, and Flo skittered away from him again. He edged around the ring, getting closer and closer to Opal, before, he just went full-send and launched himself into the saddle.

He landed hard, with a grunt, and Opal noticed how tightly he gripped the reins. "All right," he said a bit breathlessly. "Good good, Flo. Just like that."

Except not, but Opal suspected the horse would get better and better with time and practice.

"Let's walk." Tag aimed the horse toward her, keeping her right against the fence. Flo tossed her head, and her ears seemed pinned to her head, but she walked. Opal, for some reason, stepped back as Tag went by her, and she smiled up at him.

Oh, with that golden sun haloing him, he was cowboy perfection, and Opal really wanted to go out with him.

The baby monitor on her watch squawked, and she jumped.

Florence did too, a whinny coming from her mouth as she kicked out. "Whoa!" Tag yelled. "Come on, Flo, whoa!"

The pounding of horse's hooves met Opal's ears, but it didn't matter. The feedback from the baby monitor didn't matter. She wanted to help Tag as he tried to get a bucking and rearing and running Florence under control, but she couldn't do that either.

For she'd been kicked somehow. Flo's hooves had gone right through the breaks in the fence, and Opal could not get a breath.

She wheezed. Her vision started to cloud.

She bent over, knowing she had at least one broken rib and suspecting it had done some major damage to her left lung.

She fell to her knees, now hearing shouts in Tag's voice.

She tried to look up, and failed.

She cradled her ribcage as she fell onto her elbow and then rolled onto her back. The sky was all gold now, and Opal got what she'd originally wanted: she bathed in it.

CHAPTER
Thirty-Seven

"THEY'RE ALMOST HERE, OPAL." Taggart Crow hovered over the woman, he knew. But someone had to, and there wasn't anyone else out here today.

Carry and Kyle, yes, but Tag had already called on Gerty's grandparents to go be with West. They'd said they'd call Gerty and Mike too, and Tag had called the ambulance.

"Five minutes," he said aloud to himself. "Opal, honey, can you hear me? Can you wake up for me, please?"

She'd been unconscious for five minutes, and they'd been the five longest minutes of his life. She was the doctor here, not him, and he didn't know what to do but keep stroking her silky dark hair away from her face.

She finally groaned about the time Tag heard the faint strains of a siren. "There you are," he said. "Come on, honeybee. Wake up. It's Tag, and you're okay."

Flo had just gone nuts in a split second. He'd managed to jump from her back without hurting himself too badly. A sprained ankle he could barely feel because of how Opal had fallen to the dirt.

All he'd been able to think was, *Get to Opal. Go help Opal. Make sure Opal is okay.*

She had blood seeping through her blouse, but Tag didn't dare move her. It didn't seem like a whole lot, and he couldn't see any more anywhere else.

"Tag?" she moaned.

"I'm right here," he said. "You got kicked, Opal. It's okay. The ambulance is almost here, and we're gonna go together."

"Yes," she said, her tongue thick against her teeth. "I'll go to dinner with you."

"No—" Tag cut off and stared at this gorgeous woman he'd had a crush on for months now. Since the day she'd shown up on this farm, in fact. "You want to go to dinner with me?"

Their eyes met, and she sure seemed lucid to him. Maybe a hint of pain in her eyes. But she nodded. Said, "Yes, I'd like that."

Tag's entire life just got brighter. Finally. He'd asked Opal out three times before he'd decided to back off. The first time had been flirty and fun, and he thought he'd taken her by surprise. She'd shut him down fast, but he'd kept trying.

But a cowboy's ego could only take so much, and he'd clammed up around the pretty woman who was his boss's little sister.

"Here they come," he said as the siren got louder. "Can you tell me where it hurts?'

"My ribs," she said in short bursts of words. "I got kicked in the ribs. I can feel it. My lung might be punctured. I'm having a hard—time—breathing." Her breath stuttered then, and Tag didn't know what to do.

"Do I sit you up?" His big hands fluttered around uselessly.

"No, let—" She sucked in a tight breath. "Them." She sounded like she'd inhaled helium, and Tag got to his feet as the siren became deafening.

He jogged away from Opal, hoping that wasn't the biggest mistake of his life, and waved both hands above his head. "Back here," he yelled. "She's back here."

The paramedics didn't move with as much urgency as Tag felt propelling him forward. Then back to Opal. He stayed right beside her, answering questions as to what had happened, and he didn't look away when one of them took a pair of scissors from his kit and cut her blouse straight up the middle.

A deep purple bruise sat on her left side, covering almost her whole stomach and up under her bra. "Yep, looks like she got you good here," the man said.

"What does it look like?" Opal gasped. "Pink?" She pulled in a short breath and held it. "Purple? Blue? Is my skin bro-bro-broken?"

Tag said, "Shh, Opal. You don't have to talk."

Her eyes met his again, this time with plenty of panic in them. She become more and more alert, and he just wanted to take every ounce of pain and discomfort from her. He looked over to the paramedic. "She's a doctor in California."

"It's mostly pink, ma'am," the paramedic said as he nodded at Tag. "Some redness, swelling, and yeah, it's deepening to purple pretty quick."

"I feel—like—my—lung—"

"Let's get you goin'," the paramedic said. "They can do x-rays at the hospital."

Tag rose as they lifted the stretcher, and he walked with his hand in Opal's over the bumpy dirt to the ambulance. They loaded her, one paramedic got in, and then he climbed in the back too. Double-checking to make sure he had his phone, he sat on the narrow bench in the tiny space beside her.

"I'm going to call Mike," he said.

"No," Opal gasped.

Tag stared at her, trying to make her understand. In her pain and panic, she probably didn't. "They're taking you to the hospital." He spoke slowly, but he hadn't seen her hit her head. The paramedics had even said her pupils looked great. "That means a ride all the way to Caster Falls." He glanced over at the man in the ambulance with him, and he nodded. "It's not Ivory Peaks, Opal. There's no hospital in Ivory Peaks."

Her eyes got wider, more afraid. "This—place," she muttered.

"It's only another ten minutes to Caster Falls," he said as he looked at his phone. Mike had already called him once, and Gerty had texted to say she was on her way back to the farm.

"I'm going to put you on some pain meds," the paramedic said. "Something light, just so you're not in so much pain."

"Yes," Opal gasped. "Okay."

Tag really hated hearing her talk like that, and regret pulled through him. He should've just let her go when she'd gotten off the fence. Why had he called her back? Why had he said she could stay?

You wanted to show off, he thought, and that was the truth. Tag was very good with horses. Just the fact that he hadn't hit the dirt when Flo had gone into bucking bronco mode proved that. Not that Opal had seen that.

Yes, he'd wanted to show Opal that he was a worthy cowboy. Now she had broken ribs.

The ride to the hospital didn't take as long as Tag thought it would, what with him updating Gerty, Mike, and then Hunter. He accompanied Opal inside, got her checked in though he didn't know her middle name or her birthday. He did have the address at the farm, and he knew her phone number, and that seemed to satisfy the nurse.

Then, she slept in a hospital bed while Tag waited. And waited. And waited. Finally, a doctor came in after an hour and said, "We're taking her for x-rays now." He looked over to a still-sleeping Opal. "Has she been asleep this whole time?"

Off he whipped his stethoscope, and Tag got to his feet lest he be in the way. "Uh, yeah," he said. "I didn't know she wasn't supposed to sleep."

"Did she hit her head?" He listened to her chest, then her stomach. What he could hear there, Tag had no idea.

"No," Tag said. "Broken ribs. The paramedics gave her some pain meds. They said they might make her sleepy."

"No," Opal whimpered, and then her eyes fluttered open. Tag had helped her into the hospital gown, but he didn't think she'd remember that. Their eyes met, and Opal blinked. "Mike?"

"I'm Tag," he said.

The doctor looked between them, growing alarmed again. "Oh, right, Tag," she said with a sigh.

"We're taking you for x-rays now," the doctor said. "How are you feeling? Can you breathe better?"

Opal used her hands to push herself up, a gasp like a shout of pain coming from her mouth. "I could lying down." A parade of pain crossed her face. "Up here, no."

"Lay down, honeybee," Tag drawled. "Let them do the work."

She nodded and lay back down. A couple of nurses came in, and one of them said, "You'll have to stay here."

"How long will you have her?" he asked, his stomach telling him enough time had passed for it to be dinnertime.

"Forty minutes or so." The nurse smiled at him, and Tag knew interest in a woman's eyes when he saw it. "You her brother?"

"No," he said, but he didn't elaborate as to the status of his relationship with Opal. He had to be insane for wanting another girlfriend. The last few he'd had sure had done a number on him, and the emerald-eyed nurse had caused a flood of memories to resurface.

"Tag," Opal said as they started to wheel her past. "Don't leave, okay? Will you wait for me?"

"Right here, ma'am," he said with a tip of his hat, and then she left the room. He remained with the doctor. "How bad is it?"

"Looks like two broken ribs," he said. "The lung...." He flipped a page on her chart. "EMTs say it could be punctured or collapsed, but I don't know about that. I think she'd be breathing way worse if she had any lung issues." He lowered the chart and looked at Tag. "Are you her boyfriend?"

"No," he admitted. "We work on the farm together. I was there when she got kicked."

"Ah, I see. Well, she wants you here, so you can stay," he said. "You've called her family?'

"Yes, sir," he said. "Her brother is coming over from the high-rise."

"Mm, yes, Hammond. Of course." What that meant, Tag didn't know. Mike worked for his family company in downtown Denver, he knew that. He and Gerty had a lot of money, Tag knew that. When he'd first been hired to work the farm with Gerty, he'd named an astronomical salary, mostly because he wanted a reason that wasn't him being pathetic to stay in his current situation.

Mike hadn't even batted an eyelash. Not a single one. He'd agreed, and he'd paid to move Tag over from the ranch outside of Green River. Tag thanked the Good Lord Above every day for that man and his generosity, and that Tag had dug down deep enough to find his self-respect and bravery.

He could never go back to Green River, which was fine. It wasn't like he had to drive through town to get gas or groceries. Green River sat on the Colorado-Utah border, a good three hours away, and Tag never had to go back there if he didn't want to.

He settled back into the hard plastic chair and pulled out his phone. He'd exhausted the news about Opal for now, and no one had texted for updates. Mike had said he'd be there in a half-hour, and Tag decided to use that time to plan the perfect dinner date.

Excitement built inside him, though he should be worried about Opal. He reasoned he could be excited about a forth-coming date and worried about her health at the same time, and he found a great little bistro further from the city and closer to the farm that looked like something Opal would like.

The restaurant decided, now all Tag had to do was nail down a day and time, and he'd be on his first date with the lovely Opal Hammond. He sighed and leaned his head back against the wall. He took a breath and cleared the afternoon from his mind. He ignored a text as it came in, because his fantasy of kissing Opal on the first date had just started, and he just needed a few more minutes before he could face reality again.

CHAPTER
Thirty-Eight

LINDSAY FINISHED WASHING the pots and pans from dinner, put all the dirty silverware in the dishwasher, and pulled a pod out from under the sink to start it. She'd been cooking and cleaning so much more since her daddy had come to town.

Now, her daddy *lived* with her, and Lindsay started the dishwasher and then leaned against the thin strip of countertop in front of the sink. She gazed outside, the summer evening still holding plenty of promise. The sun wouldn't go down for ages, and she could slip away and drive over to Blackhorse Bay to see Keith.

The problem was, she wasn't sure he'd see her. He'd missed church a couple of weeks ago when an "emergency" had come up at Blackhorse. Later, Derrick had told her that Keith had volunteered to stay back and deal with the fences. He'd volunteered to go out and round up the horses who'd gotten out. He'd volunteered to miss church, miss sitting with her, miss seeing her.

Volunteered.

Tears pressed into her eyes, because it felt like they'd broken up. She still called him, but she'd noticed that he didn't call or text her first anymore. She had to initiate all contact with him, and while that didn't bother her, it definitely spoke volumes.

"You did this," she whispered. Her daddy was the most demanding man on the planet, and she'd let him boss her around. She'd let him dictate to her what they did, when they did it, what they ate, and where they went.

He'd been talking to his brother about getting on at Black-horse Bay, but Uncle Jack wasn't stupid. He'd dealt with Daddy his whole life, and he wouldn't let him step foot on the property as an employee without legal paperwork in place. "Otherwise," he'd said right to Daddy's face. "You'll take this place over as if you own it, John, and you do *not* own this place. I do."

The paperwork had not been completed, and while Daddy had only been here for a month, it sure felt like a lot longer. Lindsay had watched the fireworks display with him, Uncle Jack, and Aunt Lenora. She'd had no idea how to get Keith to come, and she hadn't yet found her strength reserves to tell her father no.

"You have in the past," she said to her partial reflection in the glass. "Why can't you now?"

Maybe because she already had in the past. Maybe because it was because of her that Daddy didn't have the ranch anymore. If she'd married Carter Freeman, they'd all be living on the ranch in Center, happy as clams.

"You wouldn't." Lindsay turned away from her thoughts, from her reflection, from her monologue with herself. She'd already cleaned up dinner, so she headed outside to feed her chickens. Daddy didn't do any evening chores, and Lindsay counted that as a blessing. Then, she got to go around her own farm and do things her own way, just the way she usually did.

Daddy had been critical of her big mama pig. He didn't like the way the stall doors hung in the barn. He had something to say about This Fence and That Silo and everything in between. He didn't like her dating Keith, but she wasn't sure why. He just said, "I don't trust anyone named Keith," and Lindsay had scoffed mightily.

At the same time, she hadn't invited Keith over much after that first night her daddy had arrived, and it was out of protection. She didn't want Keith to know what he was like. She didn't want him to get hurt by what Daddy said or did.

Even if her intentions were good, the result was the same. She wasn't with Keith Whettstein anymore, and tears blurred her vision. She threw the chicken seed, and her birds warbled at her as they came over to eat.

"There you go, ladies," she said to them, her voice hardly sounding like her own. "Lord, how do I fix this?"

I'll be here when you do.

Keith had said that, and he was such a good man. What felt like love moved through her, and Lindsay wondered if she could really show up on Keith's cabin porch and apologize profusely. Explain everything about how she simply didn't want to let her daddy hurt him. Beg him to forgive her. Profess her love for him.

If it even was love. Lindsay wasn't one hundred percent sure on that.

She felt like God had thrown her back in time six years, and she was living on the ranch in Center, totally and utterly trapped. The only way out was through extreme measures, and back then, Lindsay had taken them.

Everyone had taken them, and they'd all left the ranch within a couple of months of each other. Her, her momma, and Derrick. They'd all left Daddy there to deal with the mess he'd made.

Deal with the mess you've made.

The thought came into her mind like someone had spoken it into a microphone. She glanced around, only seeing chickens and fields and fences. Over by the barn, her horses grazed, as they'd be put in their stalls in a few minutes, and they knew it.

She hurried through the rest of her chores, because she couldn't just abandon her animals, even if she did want to go straight to Keith and tell him how much she missed him. How badly she'd messed up. How much she loved him.

"I do love him," she murmured, and that feeling grew and expanded, reached way down deep inside her and made everything that had gone cold in her life warm again.

That love spurred her somehow, made her move in a way she hadn't before. Of course, she'd never been in love before either, and she'd never understood the weight such a feeling carried. It felt like she'd bottled gravity and couldn't lift it, couldn't get her feet to move fast enough, to get to Keith quicker.

Inside, she washed her hands and called, "Daddy?"

"Watchin' TV," he yelled back. And he wouldn't be happy she'd interrupted him. He hated it when anyone talked during a TV show or movie. He'd pause it, make a big show of turning it up really loud, or simply start ranting at someone if they dared to so much as yawn or sneeze during his TV-watching.

Lindsay didn't care tonight, whereas all other times, she played by his rules. Better to have Daddy happy than not, because an unhappy Daddy created an unhappy world.

However, fueled by the way she felt about Keith, her strength and will rose up. She loved him, and she wasn't going to play by anyone's rules anymore. She needed to get to him quickly, and while she still wasn't sure what she'd say or how he'd react, she had to do it.

I'll be here when you do.

Moving through the confusing path that had dropped into her life the moment her father had arrived on her doorstep had to be the right thing to do. Lindsay had been standing still, and she disliked herself for allowing her father to stall her so completely.

And now, Daddy was living in her house, and he could turn off the blasted TV while she spoke to him. She entered the living room, saying, "I'm headed over to see Keith."

"Keith?" Daddy threw her a glare. "I thought you broke up with that boy."

"He's not a boy, Daddy, and no, I didn't break up with him." She put her hands on her hips, dangerous words foaming in her mouth. "You can't live with me forever."

"I'm not gonna live with you forever." He rolled his eyes like she was the insufferable one here.

"Good, because Keith and I are going to get married, and this is going to be our farm." Maybe. She wasn't exactly sure on that, because they'd talked about a lot of different things. Living here. Finding somewhere else. No matter what, the more Lindsay thought of it, the more she wanted to be wherever he was. Among the still expanding and growing affection she felt for him, started a kernel of pain. She couldn't believe she'd allowed herself to be kept separate from the man she loved.

"Married?" Daddy scoffed.

"That's right," Lindsay said. "I get to choose who I marry, Daddy, and I love Keith."

"Does he love you?"

Lindsay drew a breath, unwilling and unable to lie. "Maybe," she said. "We've...I'm going to see him tonight."

"I thought we were *go-ne* watch this archaeology thing together."

"You started it forty-five minutes ago," she said. "While *I* cleaned up dinner. While *I* did the dishes. While *I* worked on the farm."

Daddy slumped back into the couch, his frown etched in place, and that was just fine with Lindsay. When he didn't have a defense for himself, he just stopped talking.

"Don't wait up for me," she said. "And I'm going to need proof that you're looking for somewhere else to live. Tomorrow."

"Proof?"

"Remember how you used to make me and Derrick give you proof that we'd done something? Proof that I'd saved half my babysitting money, though it was *my* money. I'd earned it, and you really had no right to tell me what I could and couldn't do with it." Lindsay really wasn't interested in going over every detail of her childhood that now haunted her. She had other examples of Daddy asking for proof, but she pushed against them.

She definitely needed to talk to someone who could help her unpack everything, especially because it sure seemed like Daddy was moving here to stay. For good. Not a visit.

"Proof I'd washed the car. Proof I'd paid my lunch money with the twenty-dollar bill you gave me."

"I was trying to teach you responsibility."

"And you did," she said. "And now, I'm going to need to see you exhibit some of that. I expect to see you leaving to go look at apartments or condos or houses—something—tomorrow."

"You can't just go see whatever, whenever," he said.

"You absolutely can, Daddy." She could look up rentals and for-sales on her phone, but her father didn't use a smart-phone. She wondered if he could even use a computer. "You can use my laptop while I'm gone tonight. Search for something. Call or text someone. It's not even late yet."

"It's six-thirty," he said.

"It's summertime," she shot back. "Three places, Daddy. You need to move out."

He harrumphed and said something under his breath. Lindsay used to quake in her shoes when he did that, but now, armed with this new well of strength that seemed built on the foundation of her love for Keith, she simply turned and headed back into the kitchen to get her car keys.

"Again, don't wait up for me," she called over her shoulder. Then she left him alone in her house for the first time.

Panic reared up before she even made it to the end of the lane. "Keep going," she told herself. "What do you think he's going to do? Burn it to the ground?" She looked left and then right, and she needed to pull out and go left—east—to get to Blackhorse Bay.

No, Daddy wasn't going to burn the farm to the ground, if only because then he wouldn't have anywhere to stay either.

Lindsay made the turn with shaking hands and arms, praying with everything inside her that she could find Keith quickly, that he'd forgive this weakness inside her, and that they could be together again.

Oh, yeah, and she had to tell him she loved him.

Her throat turned to dust, and when she opened her mouth to practice saying those three little words, they wouldn't come out. Lindsay had never dreamed she'd ever want to say them to someone else. For her, love and marriage had turned into a poof of dust when she'd learned she'd basically gone to the highest bidder in Center, Texas.

But Keith had brightened it all again. He'd brought the concept back to life. He'd brought *her* back to life.

And then she'd gotten derailed by the same man who'd blown up her life previously. Why hadn't she learned?

"Please, please," she begged. "Please don't let it be too late for us. Please give him a soft heart and a forgiving spirit. Please help me to say the right thing, at the right time."

Lindsay drove, hardly seeing the road in front of her, the words she needed to say on repeat in her mind.

I love you.

She still couldn't get them out of her mouth.

"When you see Keith, you will," she promised herself. *You will, you will, you will.*

CHAPTER
Thirty-Nine

KEITH CAME out of his bedroom and walked down the short hall to the kitchen. "Well?" He spread his arms wide and turned in a circle for his cabinmates. "Do I look good enough to ask for a raise?"

Derrick whistled as if Keith were a runway model, and they grinned at each other. "He called you in," he said as he got to his feet. "He's going to give you the raise, no questions asked." He took Keith's hand in his, pumped it, and then pulled him into an embrace. "Uncle Jack loves you, man." He spoke the last sentence with fondness and conviction, and when they parted, Derrick nodded.

"The farm has never produced this much," Buck said from where he stood at the counter making a sandwich. "So I agree with Derrick. You've got this in the bag. Nice shirt, though. Can I wear that for my date with Regina this weekend?" He licked the peanut butter off his finger and slapped the two slices of bread together.

"No way," Keith said. "It's blue and purple. A week ago, you said you wouldn't be caught dead in purple."

"Yeah, but it looks nice." Buck grinned and lifted his PB&J to his mouth. "I can retract my statement."

"You'd stretch it out," Coy said.

"Are you calling me fat?" Buck asked around a mouthful of bread and peanut butter. He was a tad on the stocky side, but it suited him.

Keith grinned as Coy and Buck got into it, and he picked up his wallet and truck keys. "I'm gonna go," he called over them. "I'll report back in a bit."

"Good luck," Coy called.

"He doesn't need it," Derrick said. "You've got this."

Keith left the cabin. Almost on autopilot, he drove up the road to the admin building. He parked and went inside. He could do so much with Lindsay on his mind now that he didn't even stutter over the stairs on the way in.

He missed her fiercely. More than he'd missed anyone before, even Britt. His breath hitched, but he tightened every-thing down as he smiled at Janice. "I'm supposed to see Jack at six," he said.

"Yes, he's ready for you." She handed him a manila folder that couldn't have more than a few sheets of paper in it, and Keith's surprise moved through him.

"Thanks." He didn't know what he needed this folder for, but he moved past Derrick's girlfriend and entered his boss's office. He knocked on the door once and opened it in the next breath. "Mister Hollowell?"

The tall, tough, no-nonsense cowboy boss turned from the windows, where he'd been standing and looking out. If he'd been standing there long enough, he'd probably seen Keith park and walk in. "Keith, come in." He gestured him forward. "Come in, son."

Keith did, closing the door behind him. He now gripped the manila folder, hoping there wasn't anything too breakable inside. Jack moved toward his desk as Keith did, but he was closer and thus sat down first. Keith scrambled into a plush chair in front of the desk only a moment later.

He didn't know what to say. He had been summoned for this meeting; he had not asked for it. Once he'd scheduled it, he had talked with his cabinmates about asking for a raise. They'd all been at Blackhorse Bay longer than him, and they'd all had regular check-ins with the boss, wherein they'd asked for and received raises.

But now, Jack just stared at him. Keith gazed back, wondering what went through the other man's mind. In his brain, he fought a battle over fleeing the office, staying in his seat, leaving the state, or running to Lindsay.

He'd been in the war for a month now, since her daddy had shown up during a rainstorm and caused a hurricane of grief in their relationship. Sort of. Keith wasn't sure if he should be blaming John Hollowell or Lindsay, and he'd only talked to Derrick about his sister and father one time.

He'd said, "They have an extremely complicated relation-ship, and if I were you, I'd stay out of it."

So Keith had. But now, he could barely swallow when he thought about Lindsay, and she plagued him in all seconds, minutes, and hours of the day and night.

"Keith," Jack finally said. "How are you feeling about your job here? It's been just over a year."

"Yes, sir." Keith cleared his throat, the emotion and nerves there making it hard to talk. "I really like it here. The cabin is great. The horses are great. I've increased the field production by twenty-three percent, and I—" He squirmed, not sure he should say the next thing.

Jack only tilted his head, and that made Keith believe that he wanted to hear it.

"I love these fields," he said. "I love this land. If you'll have me, I want to stay here."

A smile spread across Jack's face. "That's great, Keith. I'd love to keep you." He nodded to the manila folder. "Let's go over your new contract."

Keith looked down at the folder in his hands. He'd forgotten about it, but now a rush of adrenaline surged through him and he slapped it on the desk, scooted to the edge of his seat, and opened the folder.

Sure enough, a new contract sat there, and Keith wasn't much for legal jargon. He could scan for his name—spelled right, which was a miracle in itself—his address, which was right here at Blackhorse Bay, and his email address and phone number.

Another number sat below that, in the first row on compensation, and Keith dang near threw up. "Jack." He looked up, awe threading through him and touching the end of his boss's name.

"That's a thirty percent increase," Jack said without missing a beat. "I think you're one of the better cowboys I've ever had at Blackhorse Bay, Keith, and I want to keep you."

Keith looked at the number again, then back into Jack's eyes. "Yes, sir," he said.

"Also." Jack leaned back in his chair. "I don't know what Lindsay and Derrick have told you...." He let the words sit there, and another moment passed while Keith marveled at the number on that contract. It was as big as what the Hammonds had been paying his father, and Keith couldn't believe it.

"What have they told you?" Jack asked outright now.

Keith shifted and sank back into the chair behind him. "Oh, uh, nothing. Lindsay and I, well, uh…." He might as well just tell Jack. It wasn't like secrets could be kept around here. "We're not really…together? anymore. I don't know. Her daddy came back to town, and she's been dealing with him. I guess it's a full-time job."

Jack scoffed, his expression darkening. "That it is. My brother is one of the prickliest, meanest men on the planet."

"Yeah, so, he's living with her, and we—we haven't exactly broken up, but we're not exactly dating anymore either. It's…weird."

Jack smiled. Actually smiled. "I think Lenora and I went through that once or twice. Then, and I can remember this as if it happened this morning. She got me over to her place for break-fast—I can't remember how—and she sat me down and said, 'Jack, if you don't want to marry me, just say so. But if you do, then let's do it. Then, we won't be goin' back and forth, and you won't have an excuse for why you can't see me.'" He chuckled, but Keith reeled.

"You lived far apart?" he asked.

"She was working down in Colorado Springs," he said. "I was just starting this place. It was a long haul across a big city." He grinned and put his hands behind his head. "Ah, those days. I proposed right there in her kitchen. We got married three months later, and it was the best decision of my life."

He gazed evenly at Keith. "That woman has been at my side since, and I'll tell you what, there's nothing better than going home to a good woman."

"I bet not," Keith said quietly, his eyes dropping to the contract again. He didn't know what to say, so he read.

The salary.

The cabin accommodations. Access to a garden plot. A stall for up to two horses.

The ability to buy into Blackhorse Bay as a partial owner.

Keith yanked his gaze up.

"You got to that part, did you?" Jack smiled at him again, and he leaned forward this time. "I've been meeting with my brother, my son, and my niece," he said. "It hasn't been pretty, or easy. I asked them not to say anything to you, and it looks like they honored my wishes."

"You want—? What is this?"

"I want to know how serious you and Lindsay are," he said. "Derrick wants Blackhorse, and he's as good as my son. Of course, he's *go-ne* to run it someday, and he'll do a heckuva job. But I've been watchin' out for Lindsay since the day she was born. If she wants part of this place, I want her to have it."

Keith swallowed, because he knew all of that. "Does she?" he asked. "Want part of it?"

"She told me she'd have to ask her very serious boyfriend," Jack said. "I negotiated with her and said the two of you could have partial ownership. Nothing to derail Derrick. But enough to keep you here, keep you comfortable. Enough to raise your family and have a house of your own—off-site." His eyes blazed and his smile had vanished completely. "You've got to get off the farm sometimes, Keith. It's not healthy to be here all the time."

He nodded, so many things happening at once. "Is that why you and Lenora live in town?"

"I have to 'go home' every night," Jack said. "Lenora insisted on it, and she was once again correct."

Keith looked at the contract again. "I need to talk to Lindsay."

"I'd say that's about right," Jack said.

He looked up at his boss, nerves and worry and anticipation clouding all together. "What about John?"

"He's *go-ne* have a place here if he wants it," Jack said. "But his role will be extremely defined, and every cowboy on this farm will know what it is." The tough-boss cowboy glared back at him now. "My brother tends to take things over that he has no right to take over."

"Like me seein' Lindsay."

"Sounds like it, yes." Jack gave him a fleeting smile again. "Keith, that's fixable. Don't let my brother come between you two if you love her." His eyebrows went up. "You do love her, don't you?"

Keith hadn't truly confronted those feelings yet, but when faced with the bold question, he had to deal with the apparent answer. He nodded miserably. "Yes, sir," he whispered. "I think I do."

"Well, I'll let you go, then." Jack got to his feet, his hand already coming across the desk for Keith to shake. "You better get over to Twilight Fields and talk to her."

Keith flipped the folder closed and stood. He shook Jack's hand, their eyes meeting. Jack wouldn't let go, and his intensity shone throughout the office. "I sense some hesitation here. Don't hesitate, son. If she's for you, now's the time to tell her."

"Yes, sir."

Jack pumped his hand one more time, and then fell back to

his side of the desk. Keith picked up his folder, said, "Thank you, sir," and turned to go.

"You're a good man, Keith," Jack said. "An excellent cowboy. It'll all work out."

Keith nodded and waved before he ducked out of the door. He moved to the side and pressed his back against the wall just to catch his breath. He started making a list of everything that had just happened behind that closed door.

He'd gotten his raise.

Jack liked him and thought he was a good cowboy.

He'd been offered partial ownership of Blackhorse Bay.

He'd admitted to his boss that he was in love with Lindsay Lewis.

A fierce determination entered Keith's entire being, from the tips of his toes to the top of his head, front to back, side to side. He pushed away from the wall, said, "Good night, Janice," as he stormed by, and practically ran to his truck.

He tossed the folder onto the passenger seat and yanked open the glove box. His last coupon for dinner, a puzzle, and a movie sat there, and he wondered if he could just show up at Lindsay's house the way her daddy did and completely disrupt her life again.

He stared at the slip of cardstock in his hand, his heartbeat banging at him and so many thoughts moving through his head.

It was time to step up. Time to step in. Time to live his life again.

"No more waiting," he told himself. He put the coupon on top of the folder too, then buckled his seatbelt and started the truck. He rolled the windows down, because it took a minute for the AC to get working in the minitruck, and then he hit the highway.

Every mile that went under his tires added to his nerves, but Keith gripped the wheel and kept going. He thought of Lars and how he'd waited and waited for Britt to be ready to marry him. He hadn't given up. He hadn't gone anywhere.

So if Lindsay wasn't ready, if she couldn't marry him right now, that was okay. But Keith couldn't disappear again. He couldn't just throw the ball into her court and walk away. He couldn't believe he'd done that in the first place.

She needed him more than ever right now, and he'd been blind to it. He'd heard the stories about her daddy, but he hadn't been listening.

He was now.

He neared a turn that required him to slow way down, and a truck came around it from the other direction. Something buzzed inside Keith. "I know that truck...." He stared at it as it neared, and he tried to get a glimpse of the driver as she went by.

Auburn hair falling over her shoulders. Those sunglasses Lindsay always wore....

Stop!

The shout happened through his whole soul, and Keith jammed on the brake and pulled to the side of the road. With fumbling fingers and a trembling pulse, he pulled his phone out and called Lindsay.

"Keith, oh my goodness, I need to talk to you," she said in a rush when she answered the phone.

"Are you driving to Blackhorse Bay?" he asked. "Like, did you just go around the Black Fork turn?"

"Yes," she said slowly. "I—well, I'm coming to see you. I have to talk to you, and you just have to listen. I'll explain everything, I swear."

Keith started to laugh, and when Lindsay didn't join in, he realized she probably didn't think any of this was funny. "I'm on my way to see you," he said.

"You—are?"

Thinking quickly, Keith checked the road in both directions and started to swing around. "Let's meet at Cactus Grove," he said. "I'm probably four minutes behind you now."

"Okay," she said, but she didn't hang up. He didn't either.

"Linds," he started.

"No." She sniffled. "I have to talk first. This is all my fault."

"None of this is your fault," he said gently. He was the one who'd stayed away. He was the one who'd created distance between them.

"I have a lot of work to do with my daddy," she said. "I knew it, but I didn't see it. I can see it now, but I can't do it without you."

A smile touched his lips. "I can't do anything without you."

She sniffled again and said, "Okay, we are not making up over the phone. I'm hanging up and I'll see you in a few minutes."

"Right behind you, sweetheart," he promised, and then he quickly ended the call before he could tell her he loved her over the phone. He already had a lot to make up for, and he didn't need to add that to the mix.

Cactus Grove seemed impossibly far away, but he hadn't been driving that long. He didn't see Lindsay in front of him, though the road had straightened. A few minutes later, he slowed, put on his blinker, and made the turn, and he still didn't see her truck.

He went up the hill to where they'd sat and watched the sunset, and there she was. The truck, the woman standing near the hood, everything Keith wanted. He could barely get his truck there fast enough and in park before he flew from the driver's seat.

"Linds." He jogged to her, wrapping her in his arms as she embraced him back. He threaded his fingers through her hair and held her so close, so close, so close. He breathed in the scent of her, something he'd completely forgotten already. "I missed you," he whispered. "I'm so sorry I abandoned you. I love you."

She wept into his chest, but on his last statement, she yanked back. "You love me?"

He nodded, not liking the dangerous edge in her eyes. She swatted at his chest, and he fell back, completely unprepared for this reaction. "You don't get to say it first," she said. "I yelled at my daddy tonight. I told him he better have proof for me in the morning that he's serious about finding an apartment, a condo, or a house so he can move out." Her shoulders lifted and fell in rapid breaths, pure desperate panic. "Because *I'm* in love with *you*, Keith Whettstein. I was driving over to Blackhorse to tell you."

A smile exploded across his face. "That's great, sweetheart." He held up both hands in defense. "I mean, not the yelling at your daddy part, but everything else."

"You said it first."

"So you're mad I told you I loved you?"

Lindsay softened, and Keith kept on grinning. "No," she mumbled, her gaze dropping to the ground. She scuffed her boots along the loose dirt and gravel there, and Keith found her to be the most amazing woman in the world.

He laughed as he hauled her back into his arms. "I love you," he said right out loud. "I was being stupid by not trying to be at your side while you dealt with your daddy, but I thought that's what you wanted."

"It was," she said. "Until it wasn't. Until I realized that I don't have to do this alone."

"I don't want you to."

"I was trying to protect you," she said. "Daddy is so mean. He says the cruelest things."

"Yeah, your uncle Jack told me."

Lindsay pulled away again and wiped her eyes. "You talked to Uncle Jack?"

"Just tonight." Keith tried to tame the smile on his face, but it was impossible. He did get it to fade a little, at least he thought so. He couldn't see his own face, though, so he wasn't sure. "You've been havin' secret meetings with him."

Lindsay blinked and opened her mouth. "He—"

"You've been trying to find a way for us to have a future, possibly at Blackhorse Bay." Keith ducked his head, losing sight of her for only a moment. Then he looked at her again. Tears filled her eyes.

"Keith—"

He took a step closer to her and covered her lips with his index finger. "I want that future with you. I can see us together, Lindsay, and it's amazing. We have kids and this cute little house, and if you want to keep Twilight Fields, I will do whatever I have to so you can. I'll work two jobs. I'll work three. I just want to come home to you at night. Every night."

She started to cry again, and Keith wrapped her in his arms. "I'm hoping these are happy tears and not sad ones."

"Yes," she said, practically choking on the word. "I thought I was going to have to explain everything. Beg you to take me back. Promise that I'd get help with my daddy. All of it."

Keith ran his hands up and down her back, the loneliness that had been festering inside him finally bleeding away. "I mean, I still think you should get help to deal with your daddy."

"I will." She stepped back and wiped her face with the hem of her shirt. She looked straight at him and said, "I'm in love with you. I was going to say I would do anything to have you back, and yes, I was hoping to tell you about Blackhorse as a way to entice you to take another chance on me."

"Baby, I don't need to be enticed."

Lindsay laced her fingers through his, her chin dropping as she looked at where they touched. "Okay, then."

"Okay." Keith stepped closer, and she looked up at him. "I don't think I'll be okay until I kiss you, though."

"Is that so?"

"That's so." Keith did kiss her then, and that simple gesture sealed all of the broken and tilted pieces inside him. Anything that had been confusing or jumbled melted into one smooth surface, one easily navigable plane. He could do anything, they could live anywhere, he and Lindsay would survive any storm...as long as they were together.

Now, he just needed to figure out how to get on her daddy's good side, because it sure seemed like John Hollowell would be staying in town for good. And if Keith wanted to be with Lindsay—and he did—he'd need to win over her daddy.

CHAPTER
Forty

LINDSAY PULLED the trigger on the lighter, and the flame burst out the end of the tube. She lit the wick on the two-shaped candle, and then the eight, and then she nodded to Keith. He'd been blocking the view of Britt's birthday cake, but now, he turned.

His voice led out the beginning of the song, and Lindsay turned carefully so as to not let the movement of the air extinguish the candles. She wore a grin that felt huge and pretty on her face, and she joined her voice to the rest of Keith's family as they sang Happy Birthday to Britt.

The young woman clapped her hands a couple of times as her eyes landed on the cake, and she said, "Lindsay, it's so gorgeous!" over the sound of the singing.

Lindsay had worked for two days on this birthday cake, and she would never do anything less for Britt. The young woman loved dogs and horses, and this cake had both. Lindsay had been working at Pony Power and the Hammond Family Farm all summer, and she'd crafted a scene from it for Britt.

A big barn, though it wasn't a replica. A couple of horses she'd sculpted out of modeling chocolate, and a golden retriever who sat by the fence that ran behind the barn and horses. It felt like she'd sliced through the farm and opened up the scene, and it was quaint and quiet and perfect. If she'd have been able to, Lindsay would've put a big blue sky above the cake, but she'd have to imagine it.

"...happy birthday to you!" Everyone really hung on that last note as Lindsay slid the cake onto the table in front of Britt. Lars, who beamed almost as brightly as his wife, handed her a knife, as Britt wanted to cut and serve her own birthday cake.

"I love this," Britt said, her blue eyes sparkling. "Thank you so much, Lindsay."

She sat next to Keith, and he smiled at her and put his arm around her. "I really enjoyed making it."

In her own kitchen. Without her daddy there. He'd ironed out all the conditions and stipulations to work for his brother, and he had a cabin at Blackhorse Bay. For now. Uncle Jack said he had to be out by the end of October, and that gave him a little less than two months. Turned out, Daddy responded well to deadlines, and Lindsay had found some of her freedom—along with her sanity—again.

Her new therapist helped with that too, and she gladly accepted her slice of chocolate cake with double-chocolate frosting. Britt loved all things chocolate, and Lindsay hoped she wouldn't get too many boxes of the chocolate hazelnut candies that Lindsay had learned she loved from other dinners like this one.

She truly felt like part of the Whettstein family, but Keith had not made any moves to ask her to actually become part of that family. They'd been back together for just over a month. School had started again for his sisters. Harvest season was in full swing, depending on which crop and which field and which farm Lindsay drove by.

He'd ask her to marry him when he was ready. He'd signed a new contract with Uncle Jack and Blackhorse Bay, and that included some options to buy into part of the farm. Lindsay had agreed to start looking at houses that didn't have forty acres of fields and several outbuildings to take care of, but the thought of not having her horses and chickens didn't bring her much peace.

She'd been offered a position at Blackhorse Bay too, as Uncle Jack's niece. She'd also been offered a full-time position at Pony Power. She wanted both jobs, though each farm operated on complete opposite ends of the spectrum. She hadn't accepted anything yet, because she still had Twilight Fields, and she was not wearing a diamond.

Once everyone had cake, Keith's dad looked at him. "Are you two coming to help Gray and Elise load the truck in the morning?" He watched them for a moment, something sharp and knowing in his eye.

Lindsay looked at Keith, sure his father had just told him something she wanted to know. But Keith gave nothing away. "Yeah," he said without looking at her. "Planning on it."

"I can't believe they're moving," Britt said with a measure of sadness in her voice. "I'm going to miss Elise so much." She looked across the table to Lindsay. "She taught me to braid my own hair."

"And yet, you still made me do it," Gloria said fondly. She smiled at Britt, and Lindsay felt such love between them.

"The farm won't be the same without them," Matt said. "But

Hunt's still there. And Deacon. Heck, Tucker lives and works there too."

"Jane's only one town over," Keith said. "Mike's here. There are still plenty of Hammond's to go around."

"Oh," Lindsay said. "I heard a rumor the other day." She slid a bite of chocolate cake off her fork and into her mouth. She ate it quickly while everyone stared at her. "About a Hammond."

"Rumor? Or gossip?" Gloria asked.

"I think they're the same thing," Matt said dryly.

Lindsay smiled at him all the same. "Well, when I was out at Gerty's, helping them fix up the back of that barn so she can get all of her horses inside this winter, Opal told me she's not going back to California. She's bought a house here."

"Oh, that." Gloria waved her hand. "Yes, that's true. That's fact." She looked over to her husband. "It's in the same neighborhood—or close to it—where Elise had her first house when she moved here."

"I think I heard that too," Matt said.

"Yeah," Gloria said as she elbowed him. "From me. A couple of days ago. I told you that on the way home on like, Tuesday."

Keith started to laugh as his daddy protested. Lindsay simply basked in the good energy of this family, and then Lars got to his feet. "All right, Roxy. Let's bring in the presents."

"Presents!" Alma yelled, and she went to help her sister and Lars get them for Britt. Lindsay snuggled in closer to Keith while they left the room, and Gloria's eyes landed pointedly on her this time.

"What about you two?" she asked. "Am I shopping for another sparkly dress soon? For a wedding?"

Keith looked at Lindsay, and Lindsay looked at Keith. "That's up to him," she said. "He knows what I want."

"Oh-ho, boy," Matt said with a chuckle, all eyes on Keith now.

"I have a plan," he said. "A *secret* plan."

"When might this secret plan take place?" Lindsay asked.

"You'll know when it happens," Keith said coolly. He glanced over to his parents. "Lindsay wants a spring wedding, so yeah. If it's going to take you eight months to find a dress, Momma, you should probably start looking now."

"What colors will you do?" Britt asked. "I love a good pink dress." She looked so hopeful, and Keith laughed as he shook his head.

Warmth filled Lindsay from head to toe, and she noticed how smiley and accepting Keith's parents were. Britt too. Gloria even reached across the table and squeezed Lindsay's hand. "I'm so excited for you two."

"All right," Lars said before anything else could be exchanged. "Britt, baby, it's time for presents."

Keith picked up empty plates of cake, half-eaten cake, and the plastic utensils while Lindsay grabbed the cake and moved it out of the way for the pile of presents getting deposited on the table.

A few steps away, in the kitchen, Keith threw away the plates and came to stand next to her. "You do still want a spring wedding, right?" He spoke in a low voice, his mouth almost at her ear. She nodded, and he said, "Okay," before moving back to the table for his sister's gift unwrapping.

Lindsay took a deep breath and held it for a count of four, just the way her therapist had taught her. That helped her focus on the numbers instead of whatever currently worried her. And she wasn't worried anyway.

She loved Keith, and she wanted to marry him. He just needed to ask her.

CHAPTER
Forty~One

GRAY STOOD in the kitchen of the generational house, his mouth set into a thin, straight line. Hunter had grounded him from helping with anything that weighed more than a watermelon—those were his exact instructions. "If it weighs more than a watermelon, Daddy, you don't touch it."

And Hunt could be very strict when he wanted to be.

Elise flitted around the house, writing last-minute on some of the boxes that weren't quite packed yet. Cords for the TV, their collection of CDs and DVDs, which Gray knew people didn't even use anymore. But he did. He had, at least.

Hunter and Molly had packed almost everything they owned over the past couple of months while Gray and Elise settled into their new house in Coral Canyon. But they'd been here for a couple of weeks now, and they needed food, clothes, dishes, and entertainment, just like everyone else.

"To the right," Hunter said, his voice strained. "We are not gonna clear this corner, Deac."

"I heard you," his youngest son growled.

Gray simply watched as his three sons, plus Cord and Mission, tried to get the couch through the front door. Truth be told, Gray could buy anything he wanted for the house in Coral Canyon.

And he had. He and Elise had been living there for two months, after all. But he wanted this couch. It had belonged to his father, and his grandfather before him. It had been a fixture in the generational house, and Gray hadn't wanted to leave it here.

The generational house was for the aging-out generation—right now, him and Elise. They'd been living here for almost two years now, and Gray enjoyed it. The mountains out his front door, the sun rising over the roof behind him, and the farm.

Ah, his farm. He'd lived here his entire life, and he honestly had no idea how to get behind the wheel of a truck and drive away. But today, that was exactly what he and Elise would do. She'd wanted to move back to Coral Canyon for a few years now, and it was time. It was right.

But that didn't mean it was going to be easy.

The boys got the couch out, and Gray looked at the living room. The generational house wasn't big by any means. It had been built close to the farmhouse and was meant for two people. One bedroom. One bath. A big kitchen, dining, and living room. A deck off the side, which wrapped around to the expansive front porch.

The house in Coral Canyon had three times this space. It wasn't space Gray missed. It was tradition.

You lived here, he told himself. And now, the generational house was going to a younger generation instead of an older one. Once all the cowboys who'd come to help Gray and Elise empty the house of their belongings finished, they'd be moving Deacon into this house.

Hunter owned the farm right now. Matthew Whettstein ran it. Deacon would have it next, and Gray had no idea who the foreman would be when Matt retired. The man wasn't that much younger than Gray, and he suspected Matt would be done here in the next couple-few years.

Gray had already consulted with Hunt on it, and the idea was to make Deacon the foreman. Then he'd know the ins and outs of this place—as if he didn't already—before he took it over and actually owned it.

But Gray didn't have to worry about any of that. He gathered his wife close and took the black marker from her. "We've got it all," he said.

"Yeah." She didn't sound sad, but she didn't sound happy either. They'd both laid in bed last night, awake and silent, unable to sleep because of what today was. What it truly meant.

"Those boxes," Hunt said. "Deac, grab that hat rack. I know Daddy made that when he was in high school."

Gray watched the hat rack go out the front door. Item by item, the house emptied, and he stood there and watched it. In Coral Canyon, his brothers and their kids stood ready to help him and Elise unpack the truck, and Gray's emotions flowed up his throat, burned in his nose, and pricked his eyes with tears.

Hunt faced him, and Gray failed in his quest to stay dry-eyed. Tears ran down his face, and his son rushed at him. "Daddy," he said. "There is always a place for you here."

"I know," Gray said into his son's shoulder. "I know that. It's just—I didn't think it would be this hard."

Out of his five brothers, Gray had stayed. He'd stayed down here in Ivory Peaks for thirty years, while the rest of them had made their homes, built their lives, and enjoyed each other's company.

Thirty years.

He could cry if he wanted to.

"Momma." Hunter pulled Elise into his arms too, and the three of them stood there while the last few things were taken out.

"These bags?" Tarr asked.

Hunt said, "Put 'em in the pick-up, please, Tarr. They're their overnight bags."

"Yes, sir."

Gray pulled away and wiped his face. "It's good. I'm good."

Elise's hand slipped into his, and Gray faced the open doorway. God had given them a perfect autumn day to move, and he moved out onto the porch. The sky above looked like the Lord had taken a brush filled with watery, white paint and swished it through the blue. The clouds feathered into the atmosphere in swirls and slashes, and Gray would never see a sky like this in Wyoming.

The very idea of that was ridiculous, of course. Coral Canyon and Wyoming had a beautiful sky too.

Elise leaned into him on one side, then Hunter on the other. Molly came up the steps, and she called, "Kids! Come say goodbye to Grandma and Grandpa."

Grandpa.

Gray couldn't believe he was leaving his grandchildren here.

Hunter's four children came closer, the littlest one—Clay—running to catch up. He turned and took them all into his arms. "You be so good for your momma," he whispered to Ryder. "You work hard for your daddy."

"Yes, sir," Ryder said. Charlotte and Lisa cried as Gray held them, and he kissed them on the forehead before releasing them to Elise. He picked up Clay, though he weighed more than a watermelon, and squeezed the little boy.

"Grandpa loves you so much," he said.

"Love you too, Grampa!" The moment Clay regained his feet, he ran back down the steps and out into the grass.

Jane cried openly as she moved up the steps and into her mother's arms. A fresh wave of emotion overcame Gray at the sight of Cord Behr. He pulled the man into his chest and held him tightly. "I have always thought of you as my son," he said fiercely. "Okay, Cord? You're mine."

Cord held him tightly too, and the cowboy didn't say much. What he did, he meant, and it took a great deal from him, Gray knew. He'd dressed down the man, and he'd stood there and taken it, hardly a defense or explanation given. He'd built him back up, and Cord would only say, "Thank you, sir," or "I'm tryin', sir."

Now, he put his mouth right at Gray's ear, and he said, "I love you, Gray. Thank you for seeing me and believing in me when no one else did." He stepped back, his tears burning brightly in his eyes. Gray didn't think he'd shed them though, because Cord hadn't even cried on his wedding day.

He held Gray's face in his hands and said, "Even me. You loved me and believed in me when even I didn't. I don't know how to repay that."

"You don't need to."

Cord nodded, drew in a breath, and dropped his hands. He and Jane switched places, and Gray once again found himself with tears dripping down his face. "We will come the moment you need us," he whispered.

"I know you will." Jane hugged him tight and then let go.

Tucker stepped into Gray and held him, saying, "Thanks for always providing this safe space for me, Daddy."

"You come home anytime you want," he said. "I mean it now."

"I can't get Tarr to leave," Tuck joked as he stepped back. He swiped at his eyes quickly. "He loves it here, and I have to say, I know why."

"It's you, Daddy," Deacon said quietly. "You're why everyone loves it here." He hugged Gray too, and oh, Gray couldn't leave his boys here. Not single as they were, especially Deacon. He didn't worry so much about Tuck, who'd lived on his own for years, traveling, dealing with strange places and people seemingly every other day.

Not only that, he had his best friend here with him. They lived together and worked here together.

Deac had no one. He'd always been a bit of a lone wolf, but Gray's father heart broke as his youngest whispered, "I love you, Daddy. Thank you for building this farm into what it is."

"Oh, Matt did that," Gray whispered back.

Deac smiled as he stepped away. "Maybe, but it's always been your vision."

"And Molly." Gray wiped his eyes. "They've brought the spirit of love, acceptance, growth, and family to this farm. I just facilitated it."

Molly wiped her eyes too, and she folded herself into Hunter's chest. Gray loved his daughter-in-law so much; she'd been by Hunt's side for nearly two decades now, and she never complained, always showed up on time, and led her family with a matronly spirit that only a woman could.

"Okay, okay," Mission said. "Why are we all crying? This is an amazing day." He grinned as he stepped into Gray's chest.

"Love you, brother. Thank you for putting up with me for so long."

"You're a good cowboy," Gray said. "It's been my pleasure."

Just when he thought he'd made it through all the good-byes, he went down the few steps to the yard, turned toward the truck, and saw the Whettsteins.

Matt looked away instantly, his hand coming up to his eyes, but Gloria, Keith, and Britt all looked right at Gray. Roxanne and Alma had grown up on this farm, and Gray could remember the days they'd been born.

Oh, how he loved the human memory. It could hold so much, simultaneously, and his heart expanded with more love than he thought possible.

Britt stepped away from her husband and into Elise's arms. "Oh, shh," Elise soothed. "You're okay, sweetie. It's all okay."

"I don't know who's going to teach me how to sew," Britt said.

Gray hugged Keith, holding on tightly for a moment. "I had no idea how hard it would be to leave," he said. "How did you do it?"

"I don't rightly know." Keith sniffled and stepped back. "It sure was hard, and it's not even my farm."

"It'll always be your farm," Gray said, switching his eyes to Matt, and then Gloria, and then Boone, and his wife Cosette. The four of them practically ran the farm and Pony Power by themselves.

"I don't know why the Good Lord blessed me with the Whettstein brothers," Gray said, his voice lodged way down in his chest, making him sound more baritone than tenor. "But I'm so glad and grateful He did." He opened his arms to both Boone and Matt, and though they were both strapping, wide-shoul-dered cowboys, they fit together in his arms.

"I know it wasn't easy for either of you to come here," he said.

"This place has been my sanctuary for twenty-five years," Matt murmured. "Thank you for sharing it with me."

Boone and Cosette still lived in a cabin on the other side of the family barn. They'd been raising their two children here. "It was exactly the new start I needed," Boone said. "It's home for me now."

"As it should be," Gray said, realizing how many people felt like this farm was a place of refuge, a calm in a stormy life, a home.

"Gloria." He hugged her, not sure what else to say. She alone had brought Pony Power to life. She brightened every person's day she came in contact with, including his, and Gray said, "I'll miss you."

"We'll miss you too," she said.

He made it through everyone first, and he headed for the driver's side of his truck. He and Elise were towing a horse trailer behind them, with three horses. Hunter was driving the big moving truck with Deacon, and they'd bring up the rear.

"Oh, boy," Gray said when he rounded the corner of the trailer and saw Mike and Gerty standing there with Travis Thatcher and his wife, Poppy. "What is that?"

"It's a treat for the road," Gerty said. "Opal made them. They're sandwich cookies."

"So don't choke on them, Uncle Gray," Opal said as she emerged from somewhere on his left. "I already called my daddy, and he's got his nose pressed to the window, watching for you." She grinned and hugged him.

She took the treats from Gerty and put them in the truck while Gray hugged Mike and Gerty good-bye. They took their chubby baby and faded away, leaving Travis and Poppy.

"You taught me how to be the man I am," Travis said, and no greater compliment could've been given to Gray. Travis pulled him into his chest and held him tight. "You're saving Steele, too, by the way."

"That's Matt," Gray said, though he knew of the boy's troubles. Steele was Poppy's son and Travis's step-son, and Gray had seen ranching and farming and all the hard work and responsibility that came with it save more than one man who'd lost his way. "He's a good man. He'll come around."

"I hope so." Travis pulled back and let Poppy squeeze Gray good-bye.

Finally, with all of that done, he climbed into the truck. Only a moment later, Elise joined him, and she pulled her seatbelt across her body, her eyes wet and her nose running.

She opened the glove box and pulled out a little packet of tissues. After peeling one out, she wiped her face and looked at him. "All right," she said. "Are we ready?"

Gray didn't know how he'd ever be ready to leave this farm. But he said, "Yes," and started the truck, put it in gear, and eased forward. When the clapping and cheering started, he rolled down all the windows in the king-cab truck so he could hear it.

Happiness and joy filled the shouts, filled the sun-filled sky, filled his soul. He waved one hand out his window while Elise used both of hers. It wasn't a total good-bye.

It was a *good-bye-for-now*.

It was an *I-love-you*.

It was *we're-all-family-here-and-we-all-belong*.

CHAPTER
Forty-Two

"ALL RIGHT," Keith said. "That's it." He moved the last box from the front of the bed of the truck to the back, where Derrick could reach it. He'd had enough of moving, thank you very much.

First, Gray and Elise had vacated the generational house on the farm. Then, Deacon had moved into it. Then, another cowgirl had joined the ranks there, and somehow, though he didn't work for the Hammonds anymore, he'd been roped into helping her move in.

That cabin hadn't had two beds or two dressers, and he'd found himself setting it all up for the new hire, the same as he would've had he still worked there. He knew it was because his momma had called and said his daddy was getting too old to do those types of things.

Plus, everyone had been neck-deep in the harvest, and helping each other was just what cowboys did. It was the cowboy way.

He'd mown field after field of alfalfa. He'd turned under his green compost for next year. They were in the thick of planting their winter wheat, and he'd planned to do twice as many fields this year, due to the robust and thriving crops that had come from the cover crop planting earlier this year.

Then, he'd gone to Lindsay's hobby farm and done the same for her. She'd never planted a winter crop before, and Keith had spent a few days testing her soil and making a plan for her. After all, they wouldn't be married before spring.

"Or at all, if you don't get your act together," he muttered to himself.

He did have a plan for the perfect proposal, but he needed the cooperation of Mother Nature. And so far, she'd been giving him perfect autumnal evenings, with sunshine and still skies for days.

He climbed down out of the back of her daddy's truck, because it was John they'd helped move today. He'd found a small house in town, about five miles from his brother, and everyone seemed to be getting along.

Jack claimed that was because of the iron-clad contracts he'd put in place, and Keith didn't doubt him. He had no idea how he'd ever afford to buy into Blackhorse Bay, because he and Lindsay would need a pretty big chunk of money to do so.

Still, his raise had gone into effect, and he'd used a little of his savings and the money from his new salary to buy Lindsay a diamond ring.

He closed the tailgate on the truck and headed for the house. Lindsay was inside, directing people who still had boxes in their hands, and then she exhaled heavily and turned toward him. "Is that really all of it?"

"Yes, ma'am," he drawled. He pulled her close and kept his hands on her lower back. "Just me and you tonight, right?"

"If I don't pass out on the couch by seven, then yes."

Keith grinned at her, because while she was used to working hard, this was that plus a lot of emotional experiences.

"You're coming over this weekend, too, right?" She peered up at him, her long, auburn hair falling down and brushing the backs of his hands. "It's supposed to storm next week, and I want to make sure everything is ready for winter."

"Yes." Keith's heartbeat boomed at him strangely, and he thanked God above for the forthcoming storm. If it really would pour rain, then Keith could get his proposal done. Passed off.

Across the room, John yelled something about being careful with a teapot that looked to be about a hundred years old.

"Let's go for a walk," he said, eyeing Derrick and John in the kitchen. "They've got things here." He took Lindsay's hand and led her out of the house. Across the street sat a fallow field, where the last of the wildflowers grew before autumn finally claimed them and winter arrived.

Lindsay sighed as she ran her hand along the tops of them, brushing by them as they strolled along. "Keith, I think I want to sell Twilight Fields."

They'd been talking about where they'd live for months now. "Yeah?"

"Yeah." She drew in a breath. "We can live here in Boulder too. There are places with gardens and pastures. I wouldn't have to sell all the horses."

"You don't have to sell any of them," he reminded her gently. "They can live at Blackhorse Bay." He glanced over to her to find her nodding.

"No big pig, though," she said.

"I'm sure we can arrange that."

"I want the chickens."

"As do I."

"There are places here like that," she said. "That aren't forty acres, with planting and spraying and harvesting."

"Sounds like someone's been looking at real estate listings." He bumped her with his hip, his smile matching hers.

"Maybe," she said, but her smile said yes all the way.

His phone rang, and he dropped her hand to get it out of his pocket. She continued on along the fence, and Keith watched her go in her pretty black flowery dress. Lindsay had a lot on her mind lately, and Keith felt nothing but love for her as she paced away from him.

Then he focused on his phone and swiped to answer his daddy's call. "Hey," he said, turning back to John's house. "We're done here and on the way soon."

"Momma just told me it's supposed to storm next week," Daddy said. "Am I making a drive out to Twilight Fields in a rainstorm?"

Keith grinned and twisted to look over his shoulder, just to make sure Lindsay had gone far enough away. "Yes," he murmured. "It'll take you two minutes."

"I'll be there," Daddy said. A moment went by, and Keith allowed the powerful bond between him and his father to fill that silence. "See you soon."

"Yeah," Keith said around the lump in his throat. "See you soon."

———

THE STORM KEITH had been counting on finally arrived. Thankfully, they were only two days into November, and Lindsay had a ton of Halloween candy at her house. That didn't really matter, because Keith had planned everything right down to making sure they had a ton of food—good food, too. Something they both liked, and he dashed through the first inklings of the rainstorm behind Lindsay.

"Phew." She pulled off her hat inside and shook it. "We barely made it." She grinned at him. "You better get back to Blackhorse." She tossed her hat on top of the dryer and turned to go into the kitchen.

"No," he said, following her. "I brought my last coupon, and you can't turn me away. I brought those pizzas." He turned the corner after her. "In fact, I don't even think I should have to turn in that coupon, because you did not make dinner for me."

Lindsay spun and put one hand on her hip. Keith couldn't help grinning at her. "Excuse me, cowboy?" She gave him the goosebumps with that fiery look in those pretty eyes. "I am baking the pizzas. You merely picked them up."

"Fine," he said good-naturedly. "But I want the whole experience. There's nothing better than a good movie, hot chocolate, and caramel corn during a storm."

She worried her bottom lip between her teeth for a moment, then moved to turn on the oven. "I just don't want you to be unsafe."

"I'll be fine," he said as the pounding of the rain intensified. "It's only supposed to be bad for a few minutes."

Lindsay did indeed bake the pizzas. They ate, and Keith let her pick the movie, though it was his coupon. He sighed as he laid down on her couch, his cowboy boots kicked off and the woman of his dreams easing into his arms.

"You're going to fall asleep," she said.

"Maybe," he admitted. "But it's okay. It's only six-thirty." It just felt later, because it had started getting dark so early, and tonight's storm had worsened that.

She started the movie, and while Keith was tired, there was no way he'd be able to fall asleep.

Because he had a diamond ring in his pocket and a proposal to make. Now, he just needed time to keep ticking....

CHAPTER
Forty~Three

WHEN THE RAIN beat against the roof, Keith sighed. "I should go," he said. He hadn't fallen asleep, and only about thirty minutes of the movie had gone by.

Lindsay didn't want him to go, but she agreed. "Yeah," she said. "You should. And you need to call me when you get back to the cabin, so I know you made it. That highway past Boulder is dark."

"I will." He got to his feet and drew her close. He kissed her in that slow, sweet, cowboy way he had, and oh, Lindsay really didn't want him to go then. She toyed with the buttons on his shirt, finally smoothing them down as she pulled away.

"You best go, cowboy."

"Yeah." He moved away from her then, shrugged into his leather jacket, stuffed his feet into his boots and his cowboy hat on his head and faced the door. "Here goes nothin'."

He left quickly, pulling the door closed behind him. She stood in her warm living room, a bit of guilt tugging through her that she got to stay safe, dry, and warm, and he had to drive forty-five minutes home in the torrential rain.

She picked up their hot chocolate mugs and took them into the kitchen. He'd left all the pizza too, and Lindsay sighed at the enormity of the leftovers. She could call her Ranch Sisters program director in the morning and see who could come for a leftover lunch.

She'd only put a few slices into a zipper bag when she heard the front door open and slam closed again. Fear spiked in her, and she looked that way, frozen to the spot in her kitchen.

"It's me," Keith called. "Stupid truck won't start."

Lindsay hurried around the corner now, just in time to catch Keith pulling off his cowboy hat and shaking water everywhere. Their eyes met, and the fire inside Lindsay roared to life. "Your truck won't start?"

"It's getting old," he said. "I knew it needed some mainte-nance, but I haven't had time." He shrugged out of his sopping wet jacket. "Let me get this in the utility room, so I'm not drip-ping all over your carpet."

He eased by her, not a smile in sight, and Lindsay spun to watch him walk through her house. He couldn't stay here.

Could he?

She took a breath to calm her nerves. "Well, we have power," she called, rooted to the spot, her hands going round and round one another. "So you can have the guest bedroom."

"Okay," he called back. "I promise I won't get up in the middle of the night and build a fire to freeze you out of the bedroom."

She heard him slam the dryer, and she couldn't believe he was putting his leather jacket in there again. She'd ruined the last one by doing that.

Lindsay took a step toward the laundry room, then stopped. Keith was a grown man, and he could do what he wanted.

His footsteps approached, but he wasn't wearing his boots anymore. She knew, though she couldn't see him, because they didn't make the tell-tale clunking sounds on her hard floor.

Then, Keith came around the corner, and he wasn't wearing anything he'd been dressed in only two minutes ago.

He wore a poncho.

Not the one she'd provided for him days before Christmas, but a different one. This one had a blue and white striped pattern, but his long legs stuck out the bottom of it all the same.

He lifted something, and Lindsay sucked in a breath at the glinting of a diamond.

"Lindsay," he said as he dropped to both knees. The poncho covered him better then. "Our romance started with a storm sort of like this one. I was stuck here with you, and I started to fall in love with you from the moment I laid eyes on you."

He smiled up at her, that diamond sitting prettily between them, pinched between his thumb and forefinger. He swallowed, and his nerves made him so humble and so stinking amazing.

"I love you," he said. "I will do my best to take care of you until the day I die. I want you to be happy, and I will do whatever I can to help with that."

Lindsay pressed both hands to her thundering heart, the question she'd been waiting months for surely about to come.

"Will you marry me?"

"Yes," whooshed out of her mouth. She started to laugh, and yes, she heard the trace of hysteria in it. She landed on her knees too, took the ring from him, and then held his face in her hands. "Yes, I'll marry you."

She kissed him, and he kissed her back, and nothing in her life had been so perfect as this proposal.

Until he took the ring back from her and slid it on her finger. She gazed at it, then him, and he said, "Do you like my new poncho?"

She burst into giggles, and Keith laughed with her. Yes, she liked his new poncho. She liked everything about him, and she got to her feet and helped him to his. "Come help me make up the guest bed. I don't think I did it after the Ranch Sisters sleep-over last week."

"Yes, ma'am," he murmured, and oh, how Lindsay loved him.

———

THE NEXT MORNING, Lindsay woke to the scent of bacon hanging in the air. A stream of panic moved through her, because she couldn't have overslept that much. In fact, she couldn't believe she'd slept as well as she had.

She and Keith had gone back to lying on the couch, where Keith indeed fell asleep before she put him to bed in the newly made-up guest room. She'd never lost power and his clothes weren't soaking wet, so their night together last night wasn't quite the same as the first night they'd spent together.

Lindsay always got up early, and she reached for her phone. Sure enough, it wasn't even seven yet. She got out of bed and pulled a sweatshirt over her pajama top. In the kitchen, she found Keith awake and moving around, frying eggs and pouring coffee.

"Aren't you a busy beaver this morning?" she asked from the doorway.

"Hey, gorgeous." He grinned at her and came over to kiss her. "Sorry, I have to get back to Blackhorse early today."

"Is Derrick coming to help with the truck?"

Keith shot her a look and then ducked his head as he turned back to the stove. "No."

"No?" Lindsay took the coffee cup he handed her and peered into it. "This has cream in it." She lifted her eyes to his. "I'm out of cream."

"I brought some," he said evasively.

Everything started to click in Lindsay's head. "You brought some? Or you went to the store this morning?" She looked at the crisp slices of bacon as he took the plate to the table. "Because I didn't have bacon either."

Keith turned toward her, that delicious smile curving his lips. "I brought it." He dug into his pocket and pulled out his car keys. "Why don't you go start my truck for me?"

Lindsay stared at him, the coffee mug in her hand feeling about ten pounds too heavy all of a sudden. "Start your truck?"

"I have to eat and run," he said. "It'll warm up while we scarf down some food." He crossed the room to her and pressed the keys into her palm. "Please?"

"All right," Lindsay said, still a bit groggy and not quite sure what was happening. Some of the pieces had clicked together, but not all of them, and she couldn't see the whole picture yet. "He brought bacon?" she asked herself as she stuck her feet in a pair of Crocs she kept by the front door and went outside.

A shiver ran through her at the chill in the air, but it hadn't snowed. The rain hadn't stopped until recently either, as everything seemed bogged down in water.

His truck wasn't locked, and Lindsay got behind the wheel

easily. She stuck the key in the ignition and twisted, fully expecting the truck to sit there dormant, silent.

It roared right to life.

She blinked, and her phone rang. "He lied," she whispered, a new kind of cold moving through her.

Keith's name also sat on the screen of her phone, and she swiped on the call. "This thing started right up."

"Check the passenger seat."

She looked over, now noticing the huge bouquet of yellow tulips there. How she'd missed them previously, she had no idea. They had streaks of pink moving through them, just like that sunsetty sky she'd told him about.

"My daddy dropped those off last night," he said. "About the time he took the spark plug out of my truck so I couldn't get home."

"I—what?" Lindsay reached over and felt the feathery, leathery petals on one tulip.

Keith opened the door of the truck, and she gasped as she looked that way. "He brought it back this morning. He had to do it, because I begged him to, and I needed a way to be here with you, just in case you tried to come start the truck for me."

Lindsay looked up to him, her handsome cowboy fiancé, in his sexy leather jacket and that big cowboy hat. "You wanted to stay here with me." The pieces started falling then, and Lindsay didn't need to gather them up and fit them together.

"It was part of the plan," he murmured. "And I don't have to get back to Blackhorse today at all. Jack gave me the day off." He licked his lips and reached across her to cut the engine. "So come back inside, and let's have our first breakfast as an engaged couple."

Keith smiled and smiled as Lindsay got out of the truck. He

let her go by him, and then he reached back inside for the vase of tulips. The numbness and shock had worn off by the time she entered her house, and she turned back to him the moment he'd closed the door and sealed out the cold.

"You staged all of that."

"Yes, ma'am," he said. "Just like God put me on this farm, during that snowstorm. He staged that, and I just wanted the proposal to be something amazing."

"It was," she murmured. "You are." She took the tulips from him and set them on the end table where she liked to store so many things. "I love you so much, Keith Whettstein."

"Good," he said. "Because I love you too." He kissed her, and now that she knew the lengths he'd gone to stay with her last night, to give her the perfect proposal, Lindsay loved him even more.

"I can't wait to marry you," she whispered.

"And I know where to get the perfect flowers now," he whispered back, just before he kissed her again.

————

I'm in love with this love story! I hope you are too. If so, please leave a review for Keith and Lindsay.

And now…

I give to you…

The power to choose the next book in the Ivory Peaks series!
Did you notice how I set up two couples for you?

Opal and Tag...
Or Tucker and Bobbie Jo?

Who should get their romance next? YOU GET TO VOTE! And when you make your choice, I will send you the sneak peek chapters for THAT COUPLE!

Ahhhh!

GO VOTE BY SCANNING THE QR CODE BELOW:

The next book will be called HIS EIGHTH RIDE, and the title and cover will work for both couples. You can preorder it exclusively on my Online Book Shop. I have both mini-blurbs there, for both Opal and Tag, or Tucker and Bobbie Jo.

I can't wait to see who YOU pick!

His First Love (Book 1): She broke up with him a decade ago. He's back in town after finishing a degree at MIT, ready to start his job at the family company. Can Hunter and Molly find their way through their pasts to build a future together?

USA TODAY BESTSELLING AUTHOR

LIZ ISAACSON

his Second Chance

His Second Chance (Book 2): They broke up over twenty years ago. She's lost everything when she shows up at the farm in Ivory Peaks where he works. Can Matt and Gloria heal from their pasts to find a future happily-ever-after with each other?

His Third Try (Book 3): He moved to Ivory Peaks with his daughter to start over after a devastating break-up. She's never had a meaningful relationship with a man, especially a cowboy. Can Boone and Cosette help each other heal enough to build a happily-ever-after...and a family?

His Fourth Date (Book 4): Their relationship has been nothing but loose goats, a leaking roof, and her complete humiliation after he pays her mortgage so she won't lose her farm. Travis wants to go back in time and start over with Poppy, but he doesn't know how. Can a small town speed-dating event get their second chance off on the right foot?

His Fifth Kiss (Book 5): They once had a few summers together. Now, Michael Hammond is back in town after a devastating injury overseas. He's looking to reset and recover...not to fall in love. But with Gertrude Whettstein also back at the farm, can Gerty and Mike make their second chance romance into a happily-ever-after?

His Sixth Sweetheart (Book 6): She's had a crush on him for decades. He's finally in a place where he feels ready to date the boss's daughter. Can Cord and Jane take their relationship to the next level without getting burned?

His Seventh Stop (Book 7): He's a seasoned cowboy on a delivery mission. She's a resilient hobby farm owner braving the winter storm. Can Keith and Lindsay forge a bond in the heart of a tempest and find love in the calm that follows?

His Eighth Ride (Book 8): You get to vote on who this book is about! Scan this QR code with your phone to go vote on whether Opal & Tag or Tucker & Bobbie Jo should go next!

Her Cowboy Billionaire Birthday Wish (Book 1): All the maid at Whiskey Mountain Lodge wants for her birthday is a handsome cowboy billionaire. And Colton can make that wish come true—if only he hadn't escaped to Coral Canyon after being left at the altar...

Her Cowboy Billionaire Butler (Book 2): She broke up with him to date another man...who broke her heart. He's a former CEO with nothing to do who can't get her out of his head. Can Wes and Bree find a way toward happily-ever-after at Whiskey Mountain Lodge?

Her Cowboy Billionaire Best Friend's Brother (Book 3): She's best friends with the single dad cowboy's brother and has watched two friends find love with the sexy new cowboys in town. When Gray Hammond comes to Whiskey Mountain Lodge with his son, will Elise finally get her own happily-ever-after with one of the Hammond brothers?

Her Cowboy Billionaire Beast (Book 4): A cowboy billionaire beast, his new manager, and the Christmas traditions that soften his heart and bring them together.

Her Cowboy Billionaire Bad Boy (Book 5): A cowboy billionaire cop who's a stickler for rules, the woman he pulls over when he's not even on duty, and the personal mandates he has to break to keep her in his life...

Books in the Christmas in Coral Canyon Romance series

Her Cowboy Billionaire Best Friend (Book 1): Graham Whittaker returns to Coral Canyon a few days after Christmas—after the death of his father. He takes over the energy company his dad built from the ground up and buys a high-end lodge to live in—only a mile from the home of his once-best friend, Laney McAllister. They were best friends once, but Laney's always entertained feelings for him, and spending so much time with him while they make Christmas memories puts her heart in danger of getting broken again…

Her Cowboy Billionaire Boss (Book 2): Since the death of his wife a few years ago, Eli Whittaker has been running from one job to another, unable to find somewhere for him and his son to settle. Meg Palmer is Stockton's nanny, and she comes with her boss, Eli, to the lodge, her long-time crush on the man no different in Wyoming than it was on the beach. When she confesses her feelings for him and gets nothing in return, she's crushed, embarrassed, and unsure if she can stay in Coral Canyon for Christmas. Then Eli starts to show some feelings for her too...

Her Cowboy Billionaire Boyfriend (Book 3): Andrew Whittaker is the public face for the Whittaker Brothers' family energy company, and with his older brother's robot about to be announced, he needs a press secretary to help him get everything ready and tour the state to make the announcements. When he's hit by a protest sign being carried by the company's biggest opponent, Rebecca Collings, he learns with a few clicks that she has the background they need. He offers her the job of press secretary when she thought she was going to be arrested, and not only because the spark between them in so hot Andrew can't see straight.

Can Becca and Andrew work together and keep their relationship a secret? Or will hearts break in this classic romance retelling reminiscent of *Two Weeks Notice*?

Her Cowboy Billionaire Bodyguard (Book 4): Beau Whittaker has watched his brothers find love one by one, but every attempt he's made has ended in disaster. Lily Everett has been in the spotlight since childhood and has half a dozen platinum records with her two sisters. She's taking a break from the brutal music industry and hiding out in Wyoming while her ex-husband continues to cause trouble for her. When she hears of Beau Whittaker and what he offers his clients, she wants to meet him. Beau is instantly attracted to Lily, but he tried a relationship with his last client that left a scar that still hasn't healed...

Can Lily use the spirit of Christmas to discover what matters most? Will Beau open his heart to the possibility of love with someone so different from him?

Her Cowboy Billionaire Bull Rider (Book 5): Todd Christopherson has just retired from the professional rodeo circuit and returned to his hometown of Coral Canyon. Problem is, he's got no family there anymore, no land, and no job. Not that he needs a job--he's got plenty of money from his illustrious career riding bulls.

Then Todd gets thrown during a routine horseback ride up the canyon, and his only support as he recovers physically is the beautiful Violet Everett. She's no nurse, but she does the best she can for the handsome cowboy. **Will she lose her heart to the billionaire bull rider? Can Todd trust that God led him to Coral Canyon...and Vi?**

Her Cowboy Billionaire Bachelor (Book 6): Rose Everett isn't sure what to do with her life now that her country music career is on hold. After all, with both of her sisters in Coral Canyon, and one about to have a baby, they're not making albums anymore.

Liam Murphy has been working for Doctors Without Borders, but he's back in the US now, and looking to start a new clinic in Coral Canyon, where he spent his summers.

When Rose wins a date with Liam in a bachelor auction, their relationship blooms and grows quickly. **Can Liam and Rose find a solution to their problems that doesn't involve one of them leaving Coral Canyon with a broken heart?**

Her Cowboy Billionaire Blind Date (Book 7): Her sons want her to be happy, but she's too old to be set up on a blind date...isn't she?

Amanda Whittaker has been looking for a second chance at love since the death of her husband several years ago. Finley Barber is a cowboy in every sense of the word. Born and raised on a racehorse farm in Kentucky, he's since moved to Dog Valley and started his own breeding stable for champion horses. He hasn't dated in years, and everything about Amanda makes him nervous.

Will Amanda take the leap of faith required to be with Finn? Or will he become just another boyfriend who doesn't make the cut?

Her Cowboy Billionaire Best Man (Book 8): When Celia Abbott-Armstrong runs into a gorgeous cowboy at her best friend's wedding, she decides she's ready to start dating again.

But the cowboy is Zach Zuckerman, and the Zuckermans and Abbotts have been at war for generations.

Can Zach and Celia find a way to reconcile their family's differences so they can have a future together?

Tex (Book 1): He's back in town after a successful country music career. She owns a bordering farm to the family land he wants to buy...and she outbids him at the auction. Can Tex and Abigail rekindle their old flame, or will the issue of land ownership come between them?

Otis (Book 2): He's finished with his last album and looking for a soft place to fall after a devastating break-up. She runs the small town bookshop in Coral Canyon and needs a new boyfriend to get her old one out of her life for good. Can Georgia convince Otis to take another shot at real love when their first kiss was fake?

Morris (Book 3): Morris Young is just settling into his new life as the manager of Country Quad when he attends a wedding. He sees his ex-wife there—apparently Leighann is back in Coral Canyon —along with a little boy who can't be more or less than five years old... Could he be Morris's? And why is his heart hoping for that, and for a reconciliation with the woman who left him because he traveled too much?

Trace (Book 4): He's been accused of only dating celebrities. She's a simple line dance instructor in small town Coral Canyon, with a soft spot for kids...and cowboys. Trace could use some dance lessons to go along with his love lessons... Can he and Everly fall in love with the beat, or will she dance her way right out of his arms?

Blaze (Book 5): He's dark as night, a single dad, and a retired bull riding champion. With all his money, his rugged good looks, and his ability to say all the right things, Faith has no chance against Blaze Young's charms. But she's his complete opposite, and she just doesn't see how they can be together...

...so she ends things with him.

Gabe (Book 6): He's a father's rights advocate lawyer with a sweet little girl. She's fighting for her own daughter. Can Gabe and Hilde find happily-ever-after when they're at such odds with one another?

Jem (Book 7): He's still healing from his vices, and Jem has dedicated everything he has to his two kids. At least he's not mourning his divorce anymore, and in fact, he might be ready to move on. She's his former best friend, and once he breaks his wrist, his nurse. Can Sunny somehow rope this cowboy's heart?

Luke (Book 8): He swore off women when his ex told him he might not be their daughter's father. But a paternity test confirmed he is, and Luke Young has dedicated his life to his little girl and his brothers' band. There hasn't been time for a girlfriend anyway. He's tried here and there, and the women in small-town Coral Canyon are certainly interested in him.

But he's been thinking about his massage therapist for a while now. Can he ask Sterling out when all they've ever been is professional? Oh, and there's the fact that she's seen practically every inch of his body... Awkward, right?

Bryce (Book 9): Bryce Young has been broken and drifting for years. After giving up his son for adoption, he left Coral Canyon and hasn't returned...until now.

CHRISTMAS AT SHILOH RIDGE RANCH

The
MECHANICS
of Mistletoe

USA Today Bestselling Author
LIZ ISAACSON

The Mechanics of Mistletoe (Book 1): Bear Glover can be a grizzly or a teddy, and he's always thought he'd be just fine working his generational family ranch and going back to the ancient homestead alone. But his crush on Samantha Benton won't go away. She's a genius with a wrench on Bear's tractors...and his heart. Can he tame his wild side and get the girl, or will he be left brokenhearted this Christmas season?

The Horsepower of the Holiday (Book 2): Ranger Glover has worked at Shiloh Ridge Ranch his entire life. The cowboys do everything from horseback there, but when he goes to town to trade in some trucks, somehow Oakley Hatch persuades him to take some ATVs back to the ranch. (Bear is NOT happy.)

She's a former race car driver who's got Ranger all revved up...

Can he remember who he is and get Oakley to slow down enough to fall in love, or will there simply be too much horsepower in the holiday this year for a real relationship?

The Construction of Cheer (Book 3): Bishop Glover is the youngest brother, and he usually keeps his head down and gets the job done. When Montana Martin shows up at Shiloh Ridge Ranch looking for work, he finds himself inventing construction projects that need doing just to keep her coming around. (Again, Bear is NOT happy.) She wants to build her own construction firm, but she ends up carving a place for herself inside Bishop's heart. Can he convince her *he's* all she needs this Christmas season, or will her cheer rest solely on the success of her business?

The Secret of Santa (Book 4): He's a fun-loving cowboy with a heart of gold. She's the woman who keeps putting him on hold. Can Ace and Holly Ann make a relationship work this Christmas?

USA Today Bestselling Author
LIZ ISAACSON

The Gift of Gingerbread (Book 5): She's the only daughter in the Glover family. He's got a secret that drove him out of town years ago. Can Arizona and Duke find common ground and their happily-ever-after this Christmas?

The Harmony of Holly (Book 6): He's as prickly as his name, but the new woman in town has caught his eye. Can Cactus shelve his temper and shed his cowboy hermit skin fast enough to make a relationship with Willa work?

The Chemistry of Christmas (Book 7): He's the black sheep of the family, and she's a chemist who understands formulas, not emotions. Can Preacher and Charlie take their quirks and turn them into a strong relationship this Christmas?

The Delivery of Decor (Book 8): When he falls, he falls hard and deep. She literally drives away from every relationship she's ever had. Can Ward somehow get Dot to stay this Christmas?

The Blessing of Babies (Book 9): Don't miss out on a single moment of the Glover family saga in this bridge story linking Ward and Judge's love stories!

The Glovers love God, country, dogs, horses, and family. Not necessarily in that order. ;)

Many of them are married now, with babies on the way, and there are lessons to be learned, forgiveness to be had and given, and new names coming to the family tree in southern Three Rivers!

The Networking of the Nativity (Book 10): He's had a crush on her for years. She doesn't want to date until her daughter is out of the house. Will June take a change on Judge when the success of his Christmas light display depends on her networking abilities?

The Wrangling of the Wreath

of the Wreath

USA Today Bestselling Author

LIZ ISAACSON

The Wrangling of the Wreath (Book 11): He's been so busy trying to find Miss Right. She's been right in front of him the whole time. This Christmas, can Mister and Libby take their relationship out of the best friend zone?

The Hope of Her Heart (Book 12): She's the only Glover without a significant other. He's been searching for someone who can love him *and* his daughter. Can Etta and August make a meaningful connection this Christmas?

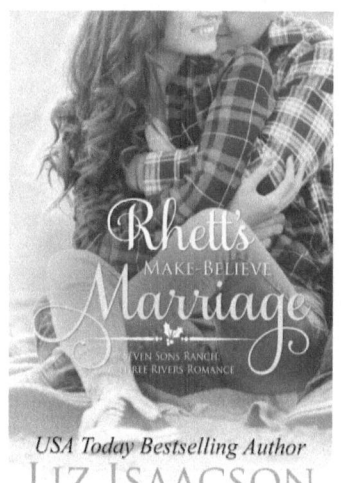

USA Today Bestselling Author
LIZ ISAACSON

Rhett's Make-Believe Marriage (Book 1): She needs a husband to be credible as a matchmaker. He wants to help a neighbor. Will their fake marriage take them out of the friend zone?

USA Today Bestselling Author
LIZ ISAACSON

Tripp's Trivial Tie (Book 2): She needs a husband to keep her son. He's wanted to take their relationship to the next level, but she's always pushing him away. Will their trivial tie take them all the way to happily-ever-after?

USA Today Bestselling Author
LIZ ISAACSON

Liam's Invented I-Do (Book 3): She's desperate to save her ranch. He wants to help her any way he can. Will their invented I-Do open doors that have previously been closed and lead to a happily-ever-after for both of them?

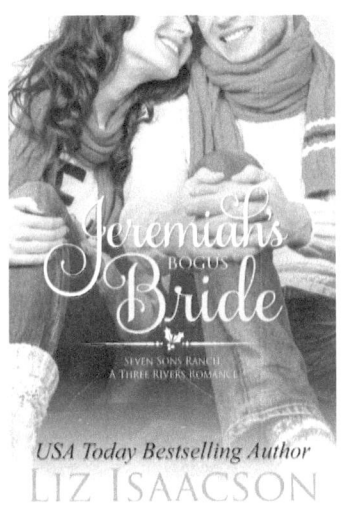

Jeremiah's Bogus Bride (Book 4): He wants to prove to his brothers that he's not broken. She just wants him. Will a fake marriage heal him or push her further away?

USA Today Bestselling Author
LIZ ISAACSON

Wyatt's Pretend Pledge (Book 5):
To get her inheritance, she needs a husband. He's wanted to fly with her for ages. Can their pretend pledge turn into something real?

USA Today Bestselling Author
LIZ ISAACSON

Skyler's Wanna-Be Wife (Book 6): She needs a new last name to stay in school. He's willing to help a fellow student. Can this wanna-be wife show the playboy that some things should be taken seriously?

Micah's Mock Matrimony (Book 7): They were just actors auditioning for a play. The marriage was just for the audition – until a clerical error results in a legal marriage. Can these two ex-lovers negotiate this new ground between them and achieve new roles in each other's lives?

About Liz

Liz Isaacson writes inspirational romance, usually set in Texas, or Wyoming, or anywhere else horses and cowboys exist. She lives in Utah, where she writes full-time, takes her two dogs to the park everyday, and eats a lot of veggies while writing. Find her on her website, along with all of her pen names, at feelgood-fictionbooks.com.

www.ingramcontent.com/pod-product-compliance
Lightning Source LLC
Chambersburg PA
CBHW020002120726
47903CB00004B/1097